Novice Threads

Book 1
The Silver Sampler Series

Nancy Jardine

Ocelot Press

This first novel of the Silver Sampler Series is dedicated to my sister Margaret.

Chapter One

"Will ye tell us again whit happened to ma grandfather?" Jessie asked.

Margaret Law knew her best friend Jessie was pestering Mistress Morison, but there was always a great need to get things straight in her head. She didn't really know why, but it seemed important to always remember everything and she was annoyed with herself that she'd forgotten this bit of Jessie's grandfather's story.

Jessie's grandmother's name was Janet but Margaret would never ever dare call the old woman that. She was Mistress Morison, an old lady who always scared Margaret near to death. And though Jessie was the one who had just asked the question, Margaret felt Mistress Morison's amber stare swivel around to fall upon her. It was so intense it made her squirm enough to take a wriggly step back, loosening the arm-bond that held her tight to Jessie.

"You're both going tae be the death o' me. Always prying. I've telt you before. I took your grandey his usual noon piece and left him tae eat it. I was no sooner back here in the house when young Johnnie came batterin' at that very door."

Margaret watched as Mistress Morison's bony finger swivelled round to point at it. She listened as Jessie asked another question.

"Is that why the door is all broken-up and flaky?"

1

Mistress Morison began to grin when Jessie persisted.

"Did Johnnie hit it wi' that huge pick he uses when he works at the gravel pit?"

Mistress Morison's chuckle was very loud. "Well, lass, a pick surely would make plenty o' holes but that's no' the reason it's a mess. That door there is that auld it's barely hanging on its hinges, and the wood's that rotten it's a wonder the wee speuggies cannae fly between the gaps."

Margaret's imagination flared. If tiny sparrows could fly right through the door cracks, she wondered what else could fly in? Distracted for a lovely moment, she had to pull back her concentration on Mistress Morison's words.

"Your grandey fell dead right there in the brewhouse, into a pile of dragcuddy keich. Dropped flat on his face, he did, his jaw still fu' o' his piece. God called him wi' no' a by yir leave."

Margaret had hoped Mistress Morison's story might have changed a wee bit. Now she remembered and it was exactly the same. It was really hard to conjure up an image of the man lying on the ground, face-down in a steaming pile of horse dung. She didn't know much yet, but surely that was the wrong way to face if God had summoned Jessie's grandfather? Weren't dead people supposed to go up the way to heaven?

Or was it, she feared, that Jessie's grandfather had been a really wicked man and that's why he was facing down towards that other place?

HELL.

She hardly dared think about the word never mind ever whisper it. She had been told that was where bad people go. What could Jessie's grandfather have done to make God so angry?

"Now, don't just stand there. Out wi the baith o' ye! I've all my washin' work still tae do."

Mistress Morison made shooing gestures at them, both hands waving them towards the door.

2

Margaret backed away even further when Mistress Morison's shaky finger pointed right at Jessie's face.

"An' you, young Jessie Morison, you have still tae pick up that basting work for me from Miss Reid's, though only the Lord kens when I'll ever get time tae do it, what wi' the other work I've lined up for the day. Go get it and nae lingerin'!"

Once again, Margaret felt the full force of Mistress Morison's glare turn on her, the old woman not yet done with her haranguing. The stare held a weird 'almost smirk' that Margaret couldn't quite understand.

"At least Miss Reid gives me some work, unlike the other highfalutin draper's wife that I could mention wha' trades here in the town of Milnathort."

Hearing the word draper made Margaret flinch and set her to feeling cold, even though the sun was blazing in the sky. Mistress Morison meant her mother. Her father's draper shop was bigger than Miss Reid's, since Miss Reid only sold goods for women. And there weren't any other drapers in Milnathort.

When she'd been playing in the street, outside their shop, she'd heard some customers call Mother a snobbish bitch because she'd married into a shop-keeping family and thought herself better than them. Grandfather Law had been a tailor with a draper's shop in the city of Perth, but he was dead. It was her Uncle James who ran that shop now.

"Not that yin, lass," Mistress Morison chided when Jessie slipped past her. "Ye best take the bigger basket that's over in the corner. An' I'm expecting Mistress Reid tae fill it."

Margaret stood stock still waiting for Mistress Morison to make more comments about her mother and father when the old woman's attention returned her way, because that's what Jessie's granny usually did. Though she'd not be able to answer because Father almost never mentioned his brother James. In fact, her father hardly ever talked at all, except when he was serving customers in the shop. Mother was always complaining '*He'd not spend the time of day with her*' but that was just silly because they were together all day, behind the counter or filling shelves.

Her head bursting with thinking, Margaret remained staring at Mistress Morison.

Auntie Jeannie had once said that Mother had not let the handsome new draper rest a single minute when he'd arrived to take over the shop in Milnathort. Jeannie had said that her sister Peggy had hated working at the mill so much that she'd do anything to avoid working there. Her mother Peggy – according to Auntie Jeannie – had been relentless and so determined to marry him that the stupid, glaikit man had eventually given in.

Margaret wasn't sure what relentless meant but she did know that her Auntie Jeannie didn't like Father very much, and she wasn't really that sure if Jeannie liked her mother, either.

"On yir way. The both o' ye. Get oot o' here so that I can get on wi' things!"

Margaret knew when Jessie's granny had had enough of them.

When that door was opened, and the big spikey besom was in Mistress Morison's gnarled, lumpy knuckles there was never any hanging about. Though always aimed at Jessie, she'd felt the jaggy spikes of the brush against the backs of her legs, and the wooden handle on her backside as well.

Stepping backwards from the now closing door, Margaret only just saved herself from tumbling onto the dirty gravel, slick with the recent rainfall and other disgusting stinky stuff that was regularly thrown out of the doors of the last cottages on that part of South Street. Up where she lived, near Milnathort Market Cross, the shopkeepers would never dare to throw a filthy mess out the front and onto the street.

It was at each shop's back door where that sort of thing happened.

'Out of sight,' her mother often chimed, *'out of mind!'*

Whirling herself around Margaret heard Jessie's huge sigh alongside, one that seemed to grumble up from the battered leather hob-nailed boots that were far too big. Jessie was winding the long bits of rough twine around her ankles yet one more time, in an attempt to make the too-wide boots stay on her feet. Jessie's footwear and clothes always looked clean enough but it was a shame that they never ever fitted properly, unlike the things that Margaret wore.

Margaret looked down at her feet. Her black leather boots had started off quite shiny that morning, even though it was days since their last polishing. Now the scuffs at the toes were getting harder to mask, even though her mother made her rub in the smelly boot-blacking into the leather. It was a messy job that she hated to do but according to her mother it was never too early to learn what it would take to be clean and tidy. The best thing about the boots was that they never pinched her toes. She knew now to sit very still when Mister Porter, the Boot Maker, held a cold metal last against her bare foot to measure it, to be sure he was about to make the right size.

If the bootmaker didn't make a good job of them, Margaret knew her father – William Law – would take Mister Porter to task. Father was always quiet when he made complaints but the other shopkeepers made scowling faces and then they sometimes used bad words. Even though their shops were only separated by Mister Thomson the Baker, her father and Mister Porter weren't friends. But then she didn't know anybody that her father would call a proper friend, in the way that she and Jessie were the best of friends.

The Lord, her father repeated almost every day, hadn't put the people in the town of Milnathort for life to be easy. But then again, her father's words were often the same as her mother's. The difference being it was generally Father who was doing the repeating. Mother was always the first to gripe about things.

Margaret whirled around and stared at Jessie's door as though seeing the old woman within. Mistress Morison was good at complaining, but she also had lots of good-mood days when she teased and cajoled Jessie into endless laughing fits. The old woman would catch Jessie and give her big hugs and smacking kisses to her cheeks smiling at her all the while. Margaret was surprised when the old woman did that because taking time out to giggle about something would mean that Mistress Morison would have to work harder to catch up with the endless tasks.

When Margaret thought about her mother, she always called her Peggy and that's what she was going to do now. Peggy always had a sour face. Margaret couldn't think of the last time she had seen Peggy smile about anything. And Peggy never hugged or kissed her. She couldn't ever remember her mother showing her any kind of cuddly loving. Any mother's touch was always practical, as when Peggy ushered her out of the door, to go out to play.

Margaret whiffed a bundle of air out of her lips making a lovely purring noise. It seemed the Lord made life hard for almost everybody in Milnathort. She looked up at the sky.

Except maybe the Free Kirk minister. He had an easy life, according to Mistress Morison, *'Idling in and out o' folks houses, and in some a whole lot more for an awfy lot longer than others'*.

Margaret didn't know what that meant, but sure enough every Monday and Tuesday she'd seen the Free Church minister walking up and down the five main streets in Milnathort. The Reverend Duncan knocked on doors and often stepped inside the ones belonging to the folk that attended his kirk on a Sunday. She went there and that's why she knew who he was.

"Are you winding them again?" she asked Jessie, not sure if her friend couldn't tie the laces properly, or if it was a reason to delay going to fetch the sewing from Miss Reid.

Having distracted herself, she drew her gaze from Jessie's feet and stared at the shenanigans going on just up the street. There was always some boy chasing after another, knocking lumps out of the one who was caught. There was shouting and bawling, and right now a boy was howling for his mammy to come to the door and help him.

Margaret huffed out another sigh. Why couldn't boys just stop and do a bit of thinking before they bloodied their knuckles? She and Jessie didn't always agree about things, but they never ever hit each other.

"I'm ready, but I'm fair burstin'," Jessie declared, her azure eyes twinkling full of mischief. "I need to go round the back or I might wet masel' before I pass those daft lads up there."

"You'd better not let your granny see that you're still here."

Margaret stared now at the grubby mess in the cart-ruts on the street, working hard to recall what she had been thinking about before all the distractions.

Oh, aye! It was about the Reverend Duncan being her minister.

Without fail, she dragged her feet to the Free Kirk twice every Sunday. It never mattered if they arrived really early, or just right on time, she was always urged to sit down in the pew nearest the entry door, squashed in between Peggy on one side and Father on the other. When asked to stand during the service, she could never see anything but the backs of the folks who were in the pew directly ahead of hers. Margaret wondered what it must be like to sit near the minister? What was his face like while he droned on? His words were called a sermon, but it was hard not to want to have a wee doze when it got really boring. She was sure the urge to nap wouldn't be there if she understood his words.

But only some of them made any sense.

The thought of falling fast asleep in the kirk made her grin.

"Whit's made that smirk?" Jessie asked when she returned and linked arms with her, before stepping them into motion.

Margaret's lips widened further. "I just remembered something from when I was just a wee thing."

"Oh, aye," Jessie nudged her elbow, her own laugh ringing across the street. "You're such a big thing now, aren't ye? You that's no' even five yet."

"I asked Father if the Reverend Duncan slept in the pulpit every night."

Jessie stopped dead and stared at her. "Whit made ye ask that?"

Margaret grinned. "I sometimes want to fall asleep when he's rambling on."

Jessie yanked her forward again. "That's natural. Same for me in the auld Parish Kirk." She felt Jessie nudge at her arm, a big guffaw breaking free. "When they let me in, that is."

Jessie had already told her that rich people paid a subscription for their pews in the auld kirk and that the other worshippers who didn't pay couldn't sit in those seats. But, when the ordinary pews got full and more adults needed a seat, the children had to wait outside regardless of the weather.

Jessie's breath now puffed at her ear; they were that closely snuggled together.

"So, whit was your da's answer?"

Margaret was now the one to halt their progress. "Father laughed so hard. And you know that he almost never laughs."

"Aye, so you telt me." Jessie's wide eyes were prompting her to continue.

"Well, after a big bit of belly-laughing, Father said '*It would be a terrible bad thing for all the gossipy Milnathort womenfolk if the golden-boy Reverend Duncan only wakened up for Sunday services, and wasn't around the rest of the week.*'"

Jessie gaped, her eyebrows quirking up. "That's awfy silly!"

"I know. But it made me giggle nearly as much as Father did."

"Whit did it have to do wi' the local chinwags?"

"I still haven't worked that out."

As they sauntered on a few paces, they talked about Jessie's minister from the auld Parish Church up Ba' Hill. He also wandered about Milnathort on a Monday and Tuesday, though it took him much longer to totter around the five streets.

"Why don't they pick another day o' the week to chap on doors?" Jessie asked.

"I don't know, but your minister is too scary an old man to ask." Margaret sighed and hugged Jessie's arm harder, nudging her face right into Jessie's cheek.

Jessie giggled. "My meenister is ancient and wheezy but he's no' that bad. Yours is no' an auld man, but I dinnae like him. He's no' kind and he's far too smirky-smiley."

That was so true! It made Margaret immediately feel sad because the Reverend Duncan's smile always disappeared when he caught sight of her and Jessie together. And that didn't happen when she was on her own. What made him displeased with Jessie just wasn't fair, because Jessie was the best friend in the whole world that anybody could ever have. She felt Jessie's arm slide away from her own.

"I better get that bastin' work from Miss Reid. You get on to Lethangie like we planned. I'll catch you up."

Chapter Two

Margaret watched Jessie set into a run up the road to where most of the shops were, Jessie hollering out to children playing at their doors as she sped past them. The street was rarely empty in rain, hail, shine, even snow, and there was generally someone to play with, if she wanted company, which Margaret usually didn't, except for Jessie.

She supposed she liked Jessie best because Jessie was so friendly with everybody. And Jessie didn't have any brothers or sisters either. That was quite unusual in Milnathort.

When she wasn't with Jessie, she just wanted to walk around on her own and practise all the new words that had recently crammed into her head.

"Do ye want to play ropes wi' me, Magrit?"

Margaret definitely didn't. She scowled at the girl, hating when somebody pronounced her name that way. It was so common, according to her mother Peggy, who insisted she was always called her full and proper name of Margaret.

She preferred to keep to herself the very confusing fact that her grandmother was really called Margaret, yet her every-day name was Maggie. And her mother's proper name was Margaret as well, though Mother was always called Peggy. Handing down the same first name in a family was such a stupid thing to do! There were so many lovely names to choose from that would make you feel more special not just borrowing a name.

She stared at the girl who had just asked her to play. Daft Lizzie's proper name was Elizabeth. As was the girl's mother, and probably her granny was called Elizabeth as well.

"I'm far too busy, Lizzie."

When the words came out, she knew they sounded prim but she didn't care.

Squashing down the urge to chortle at her funny-sounding rhyming words, Margaret shook her head again.

Lizzie stayed in the cottage on the other side of the road from Jessie, and was squatting on her doorstep attempting to get the tangles out of her worn-out ancient rope. Along with Jessie, Margaret had tried to unravel the frayed rope the day before but had eventually given up, though she had been extremely reluctant to abandon the task. It was only because it had got very late and Peggy would have been angry that she wasn't home for her tea. Margaret really hated it when she couldn't finish a complicated task.

"Busy doin' what, Magrit?" Daft Lizzie asked.

The girl squinted up at Margaret, shoving a handful of wispy, lank, near-orange coloured hair back behind her ear to see better.

Lizzie was already well over five years old – months older than she was, but not as old as Jessie who was going to be six just before Christmas. But Lizzie was really stupid. She could never say the name Margaret properly. And Lizzie couldn't even turn a rope when playing at skipping ropes.

"I'm going to Lethangie," she fired back at Lizzie, "on an important errand for my mother."

The words sounded businesslike to Margaret, but Daft Lizzie just stared as though she was talking gibberish. It was only a tiny lie, but she was sure Lizzie wouldn't notice the heat she felt warming her cheeks as she turned towards the Queich Bridge, the place that marked the south end of Milnathort on the main post road that continued on down to the town of Kinross.

As soon as she had crossed the rickety old bridge across the Queich Water, she stopped and sat down on the grassy verge. Would she really be brave enough to go as far as Lethangie? It wasn't a long walk but she'd never gone all that way on her own, though she and Jessie had ventured there together plenty of times.

The biggest problem was that there was more than one way to get to Lethangie.

Jessie had said she'd catch up with her, but once she got down the road a bit would Jessie think she had gone along the track to the Gravel Pit? Or would Jessie know that she would continue along past the Turnpike Lodge and then head to Lethangie that way?

Turnpike was a strange word. She'd been told that a long time ago her grandey, Peggy's father, had had to pay coins to get past the milestone at the turnpike, if he was going to the market at Kinross with his horse and cart. Margaret couldn't imagine anyone needing to pay to go past a stone in the road. A horrible thought came to her. Did people have to pay just to walk from Milnathort to Kinross?

There were so many things she had still to learn. But one thing she was sure of was that Daft Lizzie would feel so proud of herself if she told Jessie that Margaret had gone down towards the Queich Water. Lizzie was that nosey.

After one enormous breath, so deep that her nose rose up into air, Margaret decided that Jessie would expect her to have gone past the Lodge.

Picking up her pace, she sprinted a bit further along the road till she ran out of breath, and then ambled her way along in the cosy-warm sunshine. Lifting her chin skywards, she closed her eyes to appreciate the heat at her cheeks, a smile sneaking across her face. Her mother had grumbled earlier on that needing to be in the shop all day meant Margaret could get the benefit from the lovely summer day, but that her mother would not be able to. That was just before Peggy had shooed her out of the back door, to make her get out from under her feet.

'Under her feet.' That was another silly saying.

She looked down at her boots as they hit the embedded gravel of the roadway. That was the only thing that could get under her feet – not a person.

As she approached the house named Turnpike Lodge disgruntled mutters made her ears perk up and her eyes pop when the door creaked fully open, though she pretended not to hear anything. That was always a better thing to do while she bypassed Mister Young, the very turnpike-man who had pocketed so many of her grandey's pennies. She slowed her steps and watched the old man slap down his rickety three-legged stool alongside his doorstep. And then, using the cottage wall as a prop, he gingerly lowered himself onto it before he nodded her a hello.

His name never failed to make Margaret smile. She thought he must be over a hundred years old because his face was so crinkly, yet he was still called Mister Young. That was another silly name to be given as a baby because everybody knew that you didn't stay young forever. She waited patiently. A wee smile was hard to squelch at the side of her mouth. A family in Milnathort was named Auld and that was even worse because everybody knew auld meant old. What must it be like for Eddie Auld to say that was his name, and him only five?

A big sigh slipped free as Mister Young eventually stopped his coughing and spitting-out of disgusting phlegm. There were so many things that she had to wait for before she could get on with the next thing!

"How's yir ma today?"

Margaret held back from answering immediately, knowing by now that the stinky old man would rattle on. He was smelly because of the tobacco that he smoked in his big long pipe but also something that meant he needed the chamber pot.

"And how's yir auntie? Is she still the risin' star up at that woollen mill?" After the tiniest pause to gather his breath again, the old man added, "And is that granny o' yours in her usual fine fettle? Ha! That woman's got a tongue on her that could strip the bark off a pine tree in a blink!"

She expected the hearty chortles that followed his comments, and liked that Mister Young always laughed at his own jokes. He was a nosey auld tyke according to her granny, but she had been taught to respect her elders and he was definitely the oldest elder she knew of. As well as her mother, Mister Young always asked after her Aunt Jeannie and her granny – who lived together in a cottage that was up the street from her own house – but Margaret had no idea what the mill her aunt worked in had to do with rising stars.

She'd heard Reverend Duncan mention special rising stars at Christmas time in the kirk, but much as she'd sometimes sneaked up to her window after dark, Margaret had never ever seen a star going from the bottom of the sky to the top.

Old people were sometimes peculiar, and it wasn't just Mister Young and her granny who used strange phrases.

"My granny's fine. It's her baking day, so she's very busy."

Margaret chose not to answer about the stars. However, she decided to do the 'in for a penny, in for a pound thing' by embellishing her earlier fib just a little bit more.

"I'm on my way to Lethangie, on an errand for my granny."

"Oh, aye! And whit would that be?"

She gulped, her mind spinning. Her cheeks went all warm. It was hard to make things up on the spot. "I'm

14

just to go and check if…the brambles up there are ready for picking."

"Och, aye!" Mister Young's lips smacked together. "It's many a year since I tasted your granny's blackberry pies but she wis always the best up there in the row at baking them. You mind an' tell me on yir way home if those berries are ready."

Giving him a wee nod and a hint of a smile, Margaret carried on, taking the path that ran to the left, off the main road and led along past the big fields. She didn't mind Mister Young, though she could never go to her granny's house and mention that she'd spent time with him.

Granny Maggie never tolerated any talk about men in her house – except if it was to tear a strip off them.

After a while Margaret halted. To reach the old well, and further along where the huge Stannin' Stanes stuck right up out of the ground, she had to go up the narrow path between the fields. There was usually just one row of bushes separating the farm fields around Lethangie, according to Auntie Jeannie, but at this particular bit there were two high hedge rows sprinkled with trees that nearly reached the sun. Auntie Jeannie had said it was because the well was sacred and the great muckle stones were very special. They were so ancient people told scary stories about them. Auntie Jeannie, annoyingly, couldn't tell her any of the stories though she really wanted to know.

Margaret looked all around but there was nobody anywhere in sight. She pushed her hand against her middle. The little fluttery wobbles in her tummy didn't mean she was scared to go near the stones and the well. It was just that, at this time of the summer, the bushes were so full and jaggy, and it always seemed darker and creepier as she tiptoed further into the rutted lane. Over and over in her head she told herself to not be a feartie because the bramble bushes were right at the far end, and she had to keep on walking to reach them. She had to at

15

least check on the brambles for her granny, even if she didn't pick any.

Margaret stopped dead in the middle of the lane. Telling Mister Young that had been a big fib.

"Oh, buggration!"

Her eyes darted up to the sky when Mister Young's bad words flew out of her mouth.

"Oh, no!" One palm flew up to cover her mouth, and her next words slid through her open fingers. "I don't have a basket to collect any brambles."

Mister Young would know she had told a lie! Would he tell her granny? If he did, she'd be in such trouble with her parents. The tummy flutters got much worse, so awful she felt she'd maybe need to squat by the hedge. Instead, she turned and flew back down the lane, right back to the beginning. She bent over almost double while she got her breath back, surprised with herself at how quickly she'd managed it.

Undecided for a moment about what to do next, the raucous bellowing of the young cows nearby reminded her of the regular angry arguments between her auntie and her granny. They happened nearly every week now and got louder and louder. During the last one, Granny Maggie had shouted, *'You need to earn a lot more pennies at that mill, Jeannie, because everything costs such a lot of money. Keeping you fed and clothed is damned near impossible.'*

Feeling a lot braver now, Margaret grinned at the nearest cow.

"Don't you dare tell anybody but Granny Maggie used that bad word. Though I don't think it should be bad because it's easy to remember, and you can say it with your teeth clenched."

After looking around she practised it with increasing vehemence. "Damn. Damn. Damn!"

Granny Maggie had also shouted *'it was well past time Jeannie found a man who would appreciate her snivelling, scowling face. That she'd wasted her best years hankering after a lost cause and that Jeannie needed to find a man who wouldn't leave her jilted, like before'.*

While the hollering was going on, Margaret had cowered at the end of her granny's bed. She had covered her ears tightly when Jeannie yelled back that Granny Maggie was telling big fat fibs, because her Paul had called her pretty all the time. Her granny had then screeched that '*a pretty face meant nothing to a man like Paul, especially if it was dark*'.

Margaret still hadn't worked out the meaning of that, but she didn't dare ask anybody because she'd get a split lip. Or she'd get a warmed lug, and she liked her ears the way they were and not burning hot like a coal fire.

She perched her elbows on the middle rail of the wide wooden gate and balanced her chin on her cupped palms before peering through the gap. She sighed and puffed out some lovely warm air through her mouth. The cows would hear her, but she knew they'd not be shouting back.

"Do you know that Granny Maggie really hates that trollop along at your Lethangie farm?"

One of the cows came closer to stare at her so she addressed her words in its direction.

"You'll know the farmer's daughter better than me. The one that's named Sarah?"

The cow sputtered and shook its head to ward off a swarm of flies.

"Aye! Granny Maggie says that jezebel lifted her skirts for Paul and made him marry Sarah instead of Paul marrying my Auntie Jeannie. But I don't understand that. How come the jezebel Sarah's skirts are that different from my Auntie Jeannie's? Enough to make him change his mind about who to marry?"

The cow came closer but Margaret wasn't afraid of it. She knew it was just curious, like she was.

Chapter Three

"Do you know that you belong to that farmer along at Lethangie?" Margaret said.

The cow stared back, its harrumphs and stinky smelly spits an answer of sorts.

"I dinnae belong to the farmer. Whatever gave you that idea?"

Jessie's voice at Margaret's ear gave her a start, so much so that Margaret bumped her chin on the gate rail.

"Oh, you gave me such a fright, Jessie!" Wriggling her hand up, Margaret rubbed her chin. "I was just telling the cow about what Granny Maggie was saying last week."

Margaret felt Jessie nudge her along a bit as she squeezed her way in between the fence railings. A huge grin was splitting Jessie's cheeky face.

"Your Granny Maggie has a lot to say about…well, just about everybody."

"She does, doesn't she!" Margaret said, her turn to giggle. "I was telling the cow about my Auntie Jeannie and her problems. Granny Maggie says that man Paul – the one that used to court Auntie Jeannie – only married that strumpet Sarah up at Lethangie so he could get a job at the farm. She also said…"

Once more Margaret halted to look around her, to be sure that nobody else was around. She whispered into Jessie's ear. "Granny Maggie said, '*That lazy bugger, Paul, has much better prospects up at Lethangie, and that he's got an eye to whit's maist important for his pocket.*'"

Jessie appeared fascinated with her conversation, her eyes sparkling and mouth agape, so Margaret continued with her story.

"I'm never supposed to be hearing everything my granny says, especially when she's muttering over her washing board, but I just wish she'd speak the words I'm learning from my mother because they're the proper ones to say."

Jessie cuddled in even closer. "Ma granny calls your mother a snob because of the way your mother speaks, but I dinnae think ma granny hates her."

Margaret wasn't sure about that. Grannies were that strange.

"Granny Maggie moans all the time that my grandey dumped two useless females on her, and that God claimed her two useful sons in bairnhood, sons that would have given her an easier old age."

Margaret felt Jessie's hand pull her back and away from the gate rail when the cow's long tail began to swoosh and swish at the clouds of flies that hovered around.

"How can your granny know that her sons would have been better at working than your mother and your auntie?" Jessie asked.

"I don't know." Margaret looked heavenward. The sky was now marred by fluffy white clouds, the solid blue cover of earlier having disappeared without her even noticing.

"Granny Maggie says God claimed my grandey too soon, yet she also sometimes thanks God because she said that four bairns in five years of marriage was mair than enough."

Since neither God nor Jessie answered right away, Margaret stepped back and sat down at the beginning of the rough track, on a bit where the stone-studded earth was nicely dried-up. Jessie followed and plopped down beside her.

"I don't know how many children fit into one of those new-fangled train carriages that my father reads about in his newspaper," Margaret said. "Do you know, Jessie?"

The look Jessie gave her was comical, as if Margaret had suddenly grown horns.

"I dinnae ken but whit's that got to do wi' your Auntie Jeannie?" Jessie asked.

"Granny Maggie says that if God hadn't called my grandey to him before he was thirty, she reckons she would have easily filled one of those carriages. My grandey she said, *'would rut aroon' her skirts all day long if she gave him the leeway, and she wonders how the kitchen table still has four good legs'."*

Margaret lifted her chin even higher. "Jessie? Am I ever going to understand what my granny murmurs to herself when she thinks I'm not listening?"

"Ah dinnae understand ma granny either." Jessie now sounded just as reflective as she felt.

Margaret idly picked up some loose stones and tossed them about in her fingers. Although they were mostly grey-coloured, they were quite pretty with lots of twinkly bits.

"Look at these, Jessie." She held out her stones. "Granny Maggie would say that the most sparkly stone there was my mother, Peggy, and that the rounded plainer one was my Auntie Jeannie."

"Why would she say that? Your Auntie Jeannie is quite pretty!" Jessie cried.

"I think she's pretty, as well." Margaret nodded her head. "Granny Maggie's words were…" Margaret stopped for a moment to recall them then she tried to make it seem like it was her granny speaking.

'Peggy's an even bigger disappointment and more stupid than Jeannie because she picked the wrong kind of horse to back for a husband. A few pokes with Peggy have put William right off women. That man's learned too late that what he covets is quite different.'

20

"I don't understand those words either, but that's what Granny Maggie was muttering."

The fluffy clouds above moved very slowly as Margaret stared at them, She pinged away the rest of the stones in her hand without looking at where they were going.

"Did your Granny Maggie say anything else that did make sense?" Jessie asked, that thoughtful look on her face that Margaret had seen before when she turned to look at her friend.

Margaret thought for another moment. "I only remember that she thinks my mother's '*made a poor bed in her haste and will just have to lump it for the rest of her life.*'"

Jessie sniggered. "Ah don't like lumps in ma mattress, either, but if ah say anything about them ma granny will make me sleep on the floor."

Inhaling deeply, Margaret closed her eyes and tried to work out what smells were the strongest around her.

"Can you smell the grass?" Margaret asked, changing the subject.

"Aye," Jessie answered. "That's because it rained early this morning."

Margaret detected a flowery smell as well. "And I can smell that yellow stuff that's all over the place."

Jessie wriggled right next to her, tickling her under her armpit. "That's because it's really smelly. It's nearly as bad as a stinking pile of horse keich."

Margaret laughed as hard as Jessie and then stared at her best friend when another memory popped into her head.

"Granny Maggie doesn't like the Free Kirk minister."

Jessie huffed and plopped down on the grassy bank. "I dinnae like him either. And, for sure, he disnae like me."

"Granny Maggie doesn't know what God was thinking of when he sent that two-faced Free Kirk

Reverend Duncan to Milnathort. Granny said: '*Handsome is as handsome does but that's an awfy big joke in Milnathort because there's a puir wee bairn doon near the Queich Bridge that's the result of that meenister's being too freenly wi' wan o' his parishioners.*'

Jessie sat up quickly. "Who was your granny meaning?"

"I don't know. She never said a name." Margaret got to her feet and waited for Jessie to do the same before she linked their arms together and set them both into walking up the lane. "Do you know something? If you were my real sister, I'd be the happiest lassie that lived in Milnathort."

Margaret stared up at the next tree she came to, the twinkling sunlight dappling through the leaves and warming her cheeks. She blinked her eyes a lot because it was too hard to gawp at the pretty green rippling foliage. A big lump came to her throat and her lips wobbled, but she worked hard to convince herself that the tears she tried to stop falling were because of the sun. It wasn't that God was ignoring her, and didn't like her. Or because she didn't have a real sister.

She used the back of her hand to scrub away the wet at her cheeks and attempted a smile.

"I've asked God to make you my real sister but he never talks to me. Not here, nor when I'm in the Free Kirk on a Sunday, either."

Sunday.

Margaret's chin dropped. "Aw, buggration!"

Slapping her palm across her mouth, she whirled all around once more to see if anyone – apart from Jessie – could have heard her. She knew that was a really, really bad word and it was the second time she'd used it, but she had a feeling it was old Mister Young's favourite one. Removing her palm gingerly, another smirk beamed across her cheeks.

"Honestly, Jessie. That just popped out when I remembered tomorrow is Sunday."

Jessie's arm had slipped free and she was doubled up with mirth.

"I hate a bath!" Margaret stamped her foot onto the hard-packed soil.

"How come?" Jessie was still guffawing.

"Last Saturday, that muckle wooden tub – the one that Father fetches from the shed outside – wobbled and landed on Father's big toe when he was setting it by our kitchen range."

She recalled scurrying well-out of her father's reach. "Father griped so loudly. *'That blasted old tub.'* he shouted, but he wasn't really annoyed when it happened. It was only after my mother snarled at him that the anger came."

Margaret found she couldn't prevent fat tears from dripping down her cheeks. "Mother was so nasty. She told him that it was the only appendage that he had that worked."

Margaret felt Jessie squeeze her hand in sympathy, the cuddle a reassuring one.

"I don't think they like each other very much. Father's teeth gritted so loudly before he hissed back *'Don't you say another word!'*"

Jessie's touch continued to soothe. "Then what happened?"

"I don't know what appendages means, but Father never said another thing. He stomped off outside with the empty bucket to fetch more cold water from the well by the Market Cross. Mother scratched my neck when she stripped off my clothes so quickly. I don't think she even noticed she had a raggedy nail because she was fuming so much."

Margaret paused for a moment still reflecting.

"And when Mother fetched the enamelled tin jug from the shelf near the door, dipped it into the water and dumped it over my head, I didn't even squirm. I was too scared to hardly breathe. I usually wriggle around when Mother plasters on that horrible smelly soap to wash my hair. She rubs and rubs till she thinks it's clean enough then dumps more water from the jug to rinse it." Margaret pulled her plaits forward to show Jessie her reddish-brown long hair. "That soap stings like a swarm of bees if I've got any scrapes, but I don't yelp too much because my mother has threatened to keep me in the house. Not getting out to play, or to come and talk to you, would be a horrible thing."

"Why must you have a bath every Saturday?"

Margaret was surprised by Jessie's question, staring to see if Jessie was just kidding. "Everybody has to be clean for the kirk on Sunday."

Margaret watched Jessie's head shake, a doubtful expression on her pretty face.

"No, they don't." Jessie sounded so sure.

"Father says everybody must be clean in the sight of God," Margaret said. "That's why we wear our best clothes, as well."

Jessie's smile made her change from making a scowling face to a grin.

"Only those with other clothes can do that!" Jessie nudged her elbow. "Anyway. Jesus and God are supposed to love everybody."

Margaret squeezed Jessie's arm in sympathy. "I thought you told me that your mother Ruth has three or four new dresses every year? How come you don't even have one new frock?"

Jessie sidled away from Margaret, her expression looking a bit shirty.

"Ma mither is the most beautiful woman in Milnathort. She always needs to look her best."

Chapter Four

October 1844

"Come back down here, Margaret!"

Her mother's command had Margaret clumping her way down the narrow stairs from her room. It wasn't a tone used often, but she knew not to dither when she did hear it.

"Sit on the stool." Her father sounded much as he normally did so she gave him a tentative smile. "We've got something to tell you."

Father and mother weren't scowling, so she wondered why she'd been summoned. She didn't remember doing anything that day that might have got her into trouble. It was Sunday. She hadn't been allowed outside to play but she hadn't broken anything in the house. She'd been quiet all day long. When the last Sunday reading from the big family bible was over, as was normal, she had been sent upstairs to get her nightgown on and ready herself for bed. Being called back down to the kitchen was strange.

"Do you know which church we attended this morning, and earlier this evening?"

Her father's question was just as odd.

She looked from one to the other of her parents. Neither of them smiled, nor looked angry, but just waited for her answer.

"The Muckle Kirk." Her response was hesitant because the question was puzzling. "Well, I know its proper name is the Free Kirk, but everybody calls it the

Muckle." She took a breath and then carried on since they were still waiting. "We don't go to the old Parish Kirk."

Margaret quite liked wandering up the Ba' Hill brae to the old Parish Kirk, the one that had the gravestones dotted all around it. Granny Maggie said it had been ages since her mother and father went to the Parish Kirk, though she wasn't sure why. But Granny Maggie still went there. And, when she thought about it, so did Jessie's granny.

"Just tell her, William, and be done with it."

Margaret made sure to keep looking at her father, avoiding Peggy's growing irritation. She had heard plenty of words from her granny, many of them not good ones, about the folks in Milnathort that were as changeable as the weather about their church allegiance. Whatever that might mean. It was a nice word to say, so she had made sure to remember it. Granny Maggie thought her parents were wrong to be thinking of changing their tune even more, and should steer clear of the big rift that was coming.

Margaret thought a big rift meant somebody had too much wind that came out of their mouth. At least that's what the word meant according to Mistress Morison.

Did it mean that in some church that she hadn't been to, yet, the whole congregation all belched at the same time? That thought made her stifle a grin. Would God be impressed, or would he be frowning down on them? And how did they manage to all belch while changing the tune-words that they were chanting? She knew she was good at singing because plenty of people had told her so, but she'd only learned three different song tunes in the Free Kirk, and sometimes they weren't really songs. They were more of a chant where everyone in the congregation repeated a few words at a time after the man who stood near the minister. He was called the precentor, the first singing person. She didn't much like him because he sometimes changed the words! She hated when the precentor did that because it was very confusing when the words weren't what she thought they were going to be.

Once she'd learned something new, she wanted it to always stay the same!

"Listen carefully now, Margaret." Her father's tone pulled back her straying attention.

She nodded, though didn't dare utter a sound.

"Last Easter time, a few Milnathort people began to attend worship at a different place – not the Muckle Free Kirk, nor the Parish Church. The new one is called the United Presbyterian Church, and they've started to meet on a Sunday evening in the big old disused shed down by Cockamey."

Margaret stared at her father. That was definitely a new thing to learn. But why did her father mention it to her?

Though she didn't look, the huff and rustling alongside meant that her mother had picked up the sewing basket that was always filled with shop orders, Peggy already fed up with how long it was taking her father to tell her whatever it was that was important enough to drag her downstairs.

"A lot of people, your mother and I included, have decided to leave the Muckle Kirk to become United Presbyterian worshippers. It will take a long time and a lot of money to build a brand new United Presbyterian church building here in Milnathort, but a collection is already being raised for it. Your mother and I will be giving any spare money we have to help it get built as quickly as possible."

Margaret thought that sounded like the kind of thing her parents might want to do, since they often complained about things that happened at the Free Kirk, things that they didn't approve of. But why did her father need to tell her about it? She didn't have any money of her own to give to anybody. Her head felt so full of questions.

"The collection of money will also be used for building a new school that the United Presbyterian Church will open."

A new school? That fairly perked up her attention!

She looked at her father first and then her mother. Father now had a strange smirk creasing his cheeks, though Peggy's face was frosty as usual.

"Now listen very carefully. Though we'd prefer to be sending you to a brand new United Presbyterian school, it'll probably be years before there's enough money collected to have a schoolroom built."

Margaret's lips wobbled. It was hard to keep paying her father the attention he was demanding from her when disappointment washed all over her. She didn't want to wait so long to go to school. She forced her eyelids to shut and open lots of times to stop tears from spilling out. But that just made her eyes sting and she didn't know what was worse.

"However, since you don't have any brothers and sisters…" Her mother's splutter made her father pause, his tone harshening just a little when he continued. "Before we send our savings to the new church fund, we will set aside the few pennies a quarter that's needed to send you to the Subscription School that's already here in Milnathort." Father's volume raised a little. "But if you don't work hard there, you won't be allowed to stay. Do you understand that?"

"You must be on your best behaviour. All the time!" Peggy always got the last word in.

Margaret watched as Peggy deliberately set aside the needle that had just been threaded. She then felt her mother's piercing walnut stare land upon her before Peggy grasped her fingers: not tightly enough to make her squeal, but enough to be uncomfortable.

"Do you understand? There will be no going off wandering around Milnathort any more, just when you feel like it. Those days are now behind you."

"I'm going to the proper school? Not the Dame School?" Margaret hardly knew how to contain the excitement that rippled through her, her mother's firm fist keeping her on the seat that she wanted to fly up from and do a dance around the room. "Will it be tomorrow? Will I start school tomorrow?"

"Look at me! And stop fidgeting." Her mother griped, rattling her like a bunch of keys. "I hope you realise the sacrifices I'm making, Margaret."

Somehow, her mother always managed to dampen her enthusiasm.

"There are a multitude of things that you need to learn to do around this house, to help me, but your father – in his infinite wisdom – has decided that you'll go to the Subscription School instead."

Margaret forced herself to be still.

"It would cost less to send you to the Dame School for Girls, but I can easily teach you all the sewing and cooking skills that you'd learn there," Peggy stated.

Margaret stared as her mother's attention shifted to her father, the sourness not leaving Peggy's tone, though the words were still all for her.

"Your father has declared that since he has no son to read the bible to us on a Sunday, you're going to have to do it instead. It's against my better judgement, as we'll have to save on something else to send you to school."

Margaret stopped listening to her mother's haranguing. She could hardly believe it. Above all things she desperately wanted was to be able to read the words in the Lord's Book. Getting a bit above herself, she bobbed her clenched forefinger against her bottom lip. "And will I learn to write as well?"

Peggy's reply was as scathing as she'd ever heard. "Write? What would you be doing wanting to write as well as read?"

"So that I can help father in the shop? Maybe write down the names of the people who order things that he has to get from Kinross, or somewhere else?" Her words tapered off at the sight of Peggy's sarcastic expression.

Her father just grunted, one of his quiet little noises that barely made any sound at all. "Well, that would be very helpful, Margaret, but do you know that only a few of the children who learn to read, also learn to write properly?"

She could only stare at him. How could that be? "But…you and mother can read. And you can both write, and count as well." Her head hurt with confusion.

Her mother scoffed, but it wasn't a pleasant one. "Some girls might learn to write their own name on a piece of paper, Margaret, but that's about all they learn at school."

She couldn't believe it. She'd seen her mother write things down in the shop. In the big order books. Or was it only her father who did the writing? Now she couldn't remember, because they mostly shooed her out from under their feet when they were busy in the shop.

Her father's tone was serious enough to draw back her attention. "We'd have to find more money every quarter for you to attend the full writing class. But we don't need to think about that, yet. Learning to write would only be done a long time after you begin to read."

"But what if I'm really quick? I already have a lot of words in my head."

"Well, we'll have to see about that," her father said. "I wouldn't be paying good money if I thought you were stupid, Margaret."

She looked at Peggy, who had gone back to her endless sewing of shifts for customers.

"But I've seen you write in the big order books downstairs, Mother. And you count out the change for customers right into their palms. How did you learn to do that?"

It was rare to see her mother's expression lose the disdain in any way when looking at her father, but this time she did. No smile, but just enough to make her lips curl up a tiny bit.

"I went to school just long enough to read reasonably well. Your father is the one who taught me to count properly, and to record orders in the big ledgers when he's busy with a customer."

Margaret was fascinated. "Father is a teacher? I didn't know that."

Her father spluttered. "I'm definitely not that, Margaret, but your mother and I have had plenty of evening time to spare over the years. That's when I helped her learn to write better, and to count."

A deep sniff was the only sound her mother made, her head down and seemingly concentrating on her stitches. "I did what was needed since I had nothing else to occupy my time. Till after you were – eventually – born and I was looking after you. And now, it seems, I'll have plenty of evening time again in the future, since you're never going to have any brothers or sisters."

The pointed stare that followed between her mother and father was now a bit frightening.

"Let it rest, Peggy. The Good Lord has spoken and has shown me where my future lies."

"Your future!" Peggy was incensed. "And what about my life?"

Margaret looked at the way her father gripped his newspaper as though he'd strangle it.

"I don't need to remind you that you pursued me, Peggy, not the other way around. Being single wasn't a problem for me."

She knew from the tone that her father didn't expect any responses, even before he mouthed some more words, his chin raised to the ceiling and not looking at anyone. "God has decided that my path in life is not to beget a brood of children."

"So, I am to be thankful to God that you have tolerated my nearness just enough to produce one child?"

Her father's sombre grey gaze returned to Margaret after Peggy's acrimonious comment.

"Off you go to bed now, Margaret," he said. "We'll discuss this again in the morning."

Margaret felt it was as if he'd just realised that she was still in the room.

Feeling very confused, she trotted upstairs and crawled into bed, though she was too excited to fall asleep. Questions rattled around inside her head.

What about Jessie? Would she be starting school as well? Her euphoria dampened and a shiver racked her body. Who would pay for Jessie to go to school? Jessie didn't have a father. If Mistress Morison and Ruth couldn't pay for decent boots for Jessie, how were they going to pay for school? If Jessie wasn't up at the school on Stirling Road with her every day, who would Jessie find to play with?

Most of the boys and girls that lived down near Jessie had recently been out harvesting in the fields. When the time for crop gathering came, there was never anybody to play with for weeks because the children in Milnathort spent all day long at the farms earning a few pennies.

Oh, no!

Margaret buried herself under her blanket. Apart from the oldest pupils who often continued to be schooled during the summer, was the school going to be empty if it was still harvesting time, because the parents relied on the money that the children brought back from the farmer's wife?

She hadn't been paying enough attention because she couldn't answer her own questions. She couldn't remember if the farmers were still looking for field labourers.

Who would she play with if the school was empty?

Chapter Five

The following day, Margaret skipped away from her mother who stood at the front door of their draper's shop. She sped past the Market Cross and along Stirling Street where she skidded to a stop. There she joined the small queue of girls who lined up at the side door of the Subscription School. Smoothing her dress down at her thighs, she knew she looked a lot cleaner and better-clad than many of the other children standing near her, even though the material of her frock had been well-worn by Peggy and then re-fashioned to fit her. She glanced across at the shabby sleeve cuffs alongside her – the boys' line being a much longer one than the girls' – but then wished she hadn't.

It made her raise her chin, almost to the point where her neck was creaking to avoid the sight of the boy opposite, and the smell of him which had suddenly hit her nostrils. Maybe Peggy was right after all about the Saturday night scrub; it did make her feel more important, more respectable, than some of the other children.

She knew that particular boy from playing in the street down at Jessie's house. Samuel the Sniveller was a terrible stinker. Holding her breath, she dared another peek. On second thoughts, though raggedy-edged, the shirt actually did look as though his mother might have tried to wash it. It looked a lot less grubby than usual, but his trousers were as muckin and clarted as ever she'd seen them. The reek from the smelly wool wafted everywhere

– like he'd wet his breeks and she didn't even want to think of what else!

She yanked her gaze back towards the double wooden doors up ahead, breathed in little short puffs through her mouth, and willed the school to begin. For once, it seemed that God must be able to understand her pleas because one of the doors swung open.

Margaret was taken aback when Reverend Duncan walked out, followed by a tall thin man dressed in black that she had never seen before.

Her insides jumped and her tummy fluttered. What was Reverend Duncan doing at the school? Surely, he wasn't going to be her teacher?

A young woman, and then a young man, filed out to stand behind them, but they were familiar people to Margret because she'd seen them around the streets of Milnathort.

The minister began to speak in the big loud voice he used inside the Muckle Free Kirk. "This is Mister Anderson."

Margaret looked at the schoolmaster. Mister Anderson looked annoyed, his nostrils flaring. She watched his wishy-washy blue eyes dart to the side, a big frown appearing when the minister rattled on. She wondered if Mister Anderson didn't like Reverend Duncan? Though maybe the schoolmaster scowled all the time?

She might have to get used to that, and she wasn't sure how that would feel.

Reverend Duncan was using the big bellow that she was sometimes frightened of, his head swivelling from line to line where he seemed to be staring longer at the smallest children in the lines, like he had just done when his gaze picked her out.

Margaret couldn't be sure, but it seemed his glower had lingered on her and then darted up and down the girls' line as though seeking someone.

Oh! It looked as though Reverend Duncan wasn't fretting now because there was the tiniest twitch at the side of his mouth.

"Mister Anderson has come here all the way from Glasgow to replace Mister Black, who has just last week been sent to a different school. You will all pay very good attention and heed Mister Anderson well. Especially those of you who are the new pupils. Since you are having the privilege of being taught here, I expect you all to be reading the Lord's Book to me very soon."

Margaret could barely breathe. She was so excited she felt her knees knocking together and decided not to be scared of the minister's very solemn voice. Reading the Lord's Book would be very fine, but reading a storybook from the little Lending Library in Milnathort was also what she was desperate to do!

In her exhilaration, she realised that she'd missed hearing the name of the young man who stood behind the minister and the schoolmaster.

She breathed normally again when Reverend Duncan's voice quietened down a little.

"Now, I have my own work to do so I will leave you to your studies."

Margaret didn't watch the minister stepping away towards the street because Mister Anderson began to bark out instructions.

"Now that Reverend Duncan has departed, we can eventually make some progress."

The nasty tone she was sure definitely meant Mister Anderson didn't like the minister.

"Master Forfair."

Margaret watched the solemn-gazed young man take a step forward to come alongside the schoolmaster.

"Miss Patterson."

The young woman did the same on the opposite side.

"My assistants will also be instructing you, and you will pay them as much heed as you will do to me." Mister

35

Anderson's tone was fierce enough to make her tummy-flutters start up all over again.

She repeated the name Patterson in her head, so that she'd not forget. The big girl's first name was Agnes. She lived a few doors down from her grandmother and Agnes sometimes worked in the Post Office that was near her father's shop. Containing her huge grin was so close to impossible because she also knew that Agnes was only seventeen and she was already a teacher!

"You will state your name clearly when I stop beside you in the line." Mister Anderson's voice was probably now even louder than the minister's had been.

Margaret stood up straighter when the schoolmaster stepped forward to the beginning of the boys' line and stared at the first person there.

"Good morning!" Mister Anderson's greeting was abrupt, not angry-sounding but Margaret thought it very firm.

"N…Neil…White."

Neil sounded terrified, because his words stuttered out in a timid voice. When the schoolmaster glared at him, she watched the boy's shoulders give a little tremor.

"You will each return my greeting as in 'Good Morning, Mister Anderson' and then, after a tiny pause, you will state your name clearly so that I may know who you are! You will address me similarly anytime you find yourself in front of me, though you will change the greeting to an appropriate 'Good Afternoon', depending on the time of day."

Panic flared, because Margaret had already forgotten what she was supposed to do. However, by the time it came to her own turn, she had heard the new schoolmaster's name so often she doubted she'd ever forget it.

"If you have had any schooling before, and can already read some words of the bible, raise your hand."

Most of the children obeyed his instruction.

Mister Anderson then proceeded to rattle out a number of names from a piece of paper he had extracted from the pocket of his black coat. The children he called out, who looked to be the oldest pupils, were ordered to follow him into the building, the remainder of the boys bid to follow Master Forfair's instructions and the girls Miss Patterson's.

Chapter Six

It was Margaret's turn to go into the school! The excitement began to build again so much she was fit to burst.

"Come to the front of the line if this is your first day at school!" Miss Patterson's voice was different to how Margaret remembered it when the young woman was at the sorting desk in the Post Office.

Shuffling out of her present place, she shunted forward to the front.

"If you are a new girl, you will walk in behind me and then wait for further instructions. Those I know from last session will seat yourselves as you were placed before the end of last term."

Miss Paterson's words were barely finished before Margaret watched the assistant teacher turn on her heel to stride into the schoolroom.

Margaret took in the scene as she stepped into the room, unable to stop a big smile from breaking free. The boys were already seated on the floor, in rows, over at the opposite end of the room from the entry door and were facing the back wall with Master Forfair standing in front of them.

Mister Anderson was sitting at a wide table that held a few books and a stack of slates. He was facing the smallest group of older children who were already settled at long desks in the middle part of the room. Most of the group were boys, but it was cheering to see a few older girls there.

Margaret was trying to work out why Mister Anderson's group of children faced a different way from the big group of boys who were seated on the floor, but her attention was drawn back to the instructions being issued by Miss Patterson.

In barely a blink, she found herself settled into place cross-legged on the floor alongside the other new girls in the front row.

She sneaked a peek behind her, wanting to know what was happening all around the room, but was disappointed that she could hardly see anything at all except the knees and bodies of the girls behind her.

"You will pay attention to me and will face me at all times!" Miss Patterson's tone was firm though not loud as she sat down behind a small table that looked a bit wobbly when she leaned on it.

Margaret sat fascinated, as still as a stone, when Miss Patterson drew forward a great big book that looked all shiny and new from a pile on the table. After carefully opening it, Miss Patterson turned it around and showed it to the girls in her front row, the one ones who were the new pupils.

"This is the register for Class Three. Your class. Your name will be entered and every time you attend class it will be noted down. That also means that if you do not turn up to school when you are expected, Mister Anderson will want a very good excuse as to why not." Miss Patterson then looked almost as solemn as the schoolmaster had been earlier. "Your names will be entered alphabetically into this book, later on today. What does the word alphabetical mean?"

Margaret squirmed on her bottom, desperate to make a guess but was too scared to try in case she was wrong. She couldn't see if anyone behind her on the floor had a hand up but there was definitely nobody alongside trying to answer. Surely the girls at the back knew the word? Was it that they were also too scared to answer?

Miss Patterson's head moved from side to side as her green-eyed gaze seemed to take in the girls in the front row. "Not a single one of you?"

Emboldened, Margaret raised her hand, just up as far as her ear, but it was enough for the teacher to point to her.

"And what do you think it means?"

"My father told me I will have to learn twenty-six letters of the alphabet." Margaret faltered a little under the stern gaze of Miss Patterson and couldn't help the hesitation from creeping in. "Your word sounded a bit like alphabet."

Miss Patterson's green gaze was still so solemn Margaret wasn't sure if she should have stayed silent.

"There are indeed twenty-six letters in the alphabet and you will eventually learn them all. Alphabetical means written in the order in which a letter occurs in the alphabet. Later today, your names will be listed in this book according to the beginning letter of your surname. Therefore, it is important that I hear your name correctly and record it properly now."

Miss Patterson lifted a pen, dipped it into the open ink pot on her desk, tapped off some excess and then pointed to the first girl in Margaret's row. After asking the girl her name, Miss Patterson began to write. Then followed the girl's age: her birth day, month, and year. Last came the request for where the girl lived.

Margaret barely breathed till it came her turn to answer after Miss Patterson pointed to her. Not all of the new girls could tell Miss Patterson their proper birthday information, and some were very vague about where they lived, but it was thrilling that she could do it all without any hesitation. Her father and mother had instructed her at breakfast on those details.

A huge thrill made Margaret shiver. Her name was down on a register.

Well, not the proper register. Not yet. But it would be.

Her thoughts drifted for a moment while Miss Patterson checked the attendance of the girls sitting behind her, those who had attended her class the previous session.

Margaret remembered her father pointing to some letters in the big family bible that was dutifully taken down from its shelf every Sunday. When had that been…? She felt a smile widening when the recall came to her, but she quickly suppressed it.

One Sunday afternoon, well before summertime, the big bible had sat on the kitchen table for a lot longer than usual, her father lovingly smoothing down the black leather on the outside before choosing yet another passage. He had read at least two more readings than usual.

She recalled pestering him to teach her to read the parable he had just read out to her and her mother. It had been so exciting when he had gathered her closer to him, because he never ever did that, and then he had put his finger on a letter at the top of the page.

'That's the letter J for Jesus.' She remembered him saying, and then he had gone on to point out some more letters.

Her smile dipped at the next memory because it wasn't such a good one. Father had gone too fast for her to remember any of the letters the following day, except for that big special letter J for Jesus. But, since she wasn't allowed to touch the bible by herself, she couldn't even practise finding it again.

There had never been any more lessons from her father, but it would be different now.

She was at school.

Miss Patterson's voice drew back her attention.

"Those of you who are new girls are seated in Row Six."

Margaret looked alongside her, now having an idea of who else was a new girl.

Her teacher continued speaking. "You will soon learn that if you are eventually moved to Row One, then you are heeding your lessons very well."

Margaret gulped. She would have to try very hard if Row One meant good and Row Six meant bad. Row One was so many lines behind her!

Looking left out of the side of her eye, to the girl who sat at the end of the row, wasn't so easy but she didn't want to stare. The girl was much older than she was and was what Jessie's grandmother would call '*filthy, dirty maukit*'. It looked as though the girl's nose and cheeks had been wiped but not much else. The smell coming from that side of the row, though not as bad as Stinky Samuel, wasn't very nice.

Right that moment the girl's forefinger was scratching behind her right ear, her head not far from Margaret's own. Margaret sidled as far away as she could without bumping into her neighbour on the other side. Peggy had warned her plenty of times to keep a good distance if she noticed anybody scratching that hard. Beasties had got into her hair before and she didn't want them there again.

She decided there and then that she was never, ever, going to be filthy and scratchy! No matter what she had to do to avoid it.

"I'm going to read you a story about someone important who was a very great teacher. I'll be asking you questions afterwards, so be sure that you all listen really well. If you know what the answer is to a question you will not say it, or shout it out, but you will raise your hand. You will wait patiently to see if you are chosen to answer."

Margaret's smirk sneaked out again as she listened enrapt, appreciating Miss Patterson's nice voice. She loved retelling a story to herself after she'd heard one, even if she didn't remember all the correct words. She often spent a Sunday night in bed before going to sleep trying to remember what the minister had been talking about earlier that day, though it was usually easier to remember the ones her father read in the afternoon.

Miss Patterson's story was the one about Jesus and the multitudes. It wasn't Margaret's favourite. There were too many words she still didn't understand – like multitudes. She dreaded being asked what it meant, though she really hoped Miss Patterson would explain it to her.

When the teacher asked the first question, Margaret shoved her hand up. It was hard to contain her disappointment when she wasn't chosen for that first one, and not for the next few either because the questions that followed on seemed much harder to answer.

When Miss Patterson asked if Jesus went in amongst all of the people of Galilee with a big family bible in his hand, she noticed she was the only one to put her hand up, even tentatively as hers was.

When requested to speak she said, "Jesus only talked to people for them to learn his stories, he never had to read the stories to them." She hesitated because Miss Patterson looked as if her answer wasn't good enough. "My father says he doesn't even know if Jesus could read properly, since it isn't mentioned more than a time or two in his big bible, but…"

"Go on." Miss Patterson's prompt came quickly but it was hard to tell if her teacher was now angry with her answer.

"Father thinks Jesus was able to read some of the books in the big temple but my father couldn't remember where to find the correct answer for me." She found it difficult to continue and in panic looked behind her, over each shoulder in turn. All the girls close by were staring at her, though her teacher's nod seemed to want her to finish. "Mother got cross since it was time for me to go to bed and, well… I still don't know."

The breath seemed to all swish out of her, her last words said so quickly she wished she'd not started

43

talking at all because there were some titters and giggles being suppressed alongside her.

"Well, Margaret, your father maybe needs to read his bible more often so that he does know which page to look at." Miss Patterson clearly wasn't amused since Margaret felt her teacher's gaze hover over her before moving to those who had made the noises. "Some of you in this class will eventually learn to read adequately enough and may very well find the answers to my questions, though others are far more likely to fail to learn the skills of reading through lack of serious effort and dedication."

Margaret gulped, and shut her eyelids to suppress the tears that wanted to fall. She wanted so much to learn to read well.

"Everyone in the schoolroom stand up!" The command came from Mister Anderson.

Unfurling her legs, Margaret rose to her feet.

"All turn and face me!"

Miss Patterson made beckoning motions with her arms, Margaret realising she was supposed to turn all the way around, so that it was easier to face the headmaster.

There was a great shuffling of feet and turning as the rows of boys all whirled around.

"Come along! Quickly now," Mister Anderson urged, "or we'll have no time to learn this new hymn."

The sound of the stern voice was muffled by whispered groans, mainly coming from the boys.

Though it was hard to see over all the people in front of her, Margaret watched Mister Anderson beckoning Miss Patterson forward to stand alongside him at his desk. She watched him gesture at something in front of him, after which Miss Patterson nodded, though said nothing.

"Stand up straight. Miss Patterson and I will sing the whole of the first verse. You will listen. You will not sing just now, even if you think you have heard this hymn before."

Mister Anderson tapped three times with his knuckles on his desk after which the two of them launched into a tune that Margaret thought she might have heard before.

"Now repeat after me…"

Line by line, Mister Anderson said the words and she did her best to repeat them. There was never any time to draw breath and not much to decide if she was saying them correctly before the next line began. When everybody was singing along, it made it easier if she couldn't remember the next word – she just joined in when she could. She was confident that, after weeks of practising the hymn, she'd know it all.

By the time they had worked through the third verse Margaret felt very fluttery inside, and felt her face redden because she had already forgotten what the first one was. Her fear was short-lived, thankfully, when the schoolmaster declared they had done enough for the day and they would do more tomorrow. She heaved a sigh of relief because all of this learning was a big challenge. Lots of the words were difficult and worse than that most of them didn't make any sense at all.

Someday, she vowed, she'd know absolutely every single word in the world!

Chapter Seven

June 1845

"How's your mother, Jessie?"

Margaret's question came out in bits as she pushed faster and faster with her leg muscles to make the twine swing go higher. The rope that hung from a tree down near the rickety Queich Bridge wasn't up to much now that it was even shorter than before, the fraying having unravelled most of the twine. It was a much bigger effort now to jump up and grasp the rope above the big fat knot and then clutch it between her legs.

Jessie was waiting her turn, kicking a stone around her feet. "Better enough to be back at the mill this week."

Margaret could tell that didn't mean Jessie's mother, Ruth, had actually recovered from the bouts of coughing that had been plaguing her. You had to be almost dead before you took a day off work; she knew that from her Auntie Jeannie who worked at the same mill but in a different area. According to Auntie Jeannie, Ruth had an easy job being a Fine Drawer. Whereas her auntie was a Whitener, her hands worn away with handling the bleach used in the Whitening Fields.

As Margaret swung back and forth, prolonging her turn, she thought of those strange words. A Fine Drawer had absolutely nothing to do with drawing pictures. Ruth was supposed to be the best Fine Drawer in the mill, since her mending of tears in the newly-produced bales of cloth really couldn't be seen at all. That took really good stitching, according to Peggy, who often complained that she herself shouldn't have to sew so much in the evenings to complete alterations to orders made in their shop.

"Is your mother able to help with any of the tacking of new corsets that Miss Reid sends to your granny? The stuff you collect in the big basket?"

"Why would ma mither help with that?"

Miss Reid sold what Father would call 'made-to-measure' women's underclothing, cut-to-size to be sure the garments would fit properly. That thought made her laugh. She couldn't imagine dumpy Mistress Morison squeezing into her mother's corset, since Peggy was tall and thin.

Jessie sounded a bit huffy, so Margaret's next question was hesitant. "Well, nearly everybody in Milnathort works at something in the evening, after their day's work at the mill, I mean."

"Ma mither says she needs her evening time to be free. So that she can walk and get fresh air, and things like that."

Again, Jessie was snippily defensive so Margaret changed the subject.

"My mother gets out her big sewing basket every evening. I hate it when she does that because I've got to sew for ages and ages. Peggy taught me how to thread a needle and now I've got to practise different kinds of stitches on waste pieces of cloth every single night, for a long time before I'm sent to bed. Peggy insists it's important that I can make neat little rows of stitches on a piece of cotton or linen."

"Well, I do a lot of sewing, too!"

Margaret realised she was going to have to work really hard to not fall out with her best friend, but it was unfair that nearly everybody except Ruth worked after tea-time.

"Peggy growls and pulls away the fabric when my finger bleeds, if I prick it with the needle. That sometimes happens because she's made me use a really tiny wee needle now, especially on the fine lawn cloth."

Below her, Jessie kicked at a stone. "Aye! That happens to me a lot, as well."

"I'm supposed to be able to properly hem a whole man's handkerchief. They're this big." Margaret exhaled loudly and almost fell off when she demonstrated with her hands held wide. Once she grasped the rope again, she had to swing her legs harder to make it twirl. "A woman's handkerchief is so much shorter to sew all the way around the edge!"

Jessie looked up at her. "Jist you wait till you hae to do the basting stitches on a corset. That's nae easy!"

"I wish Peggy could afford to pay somebody else but she says I have to earn my keep. I'd rather spend all my spare time practising my new words so that I can get on to reading proper big books."

"Ha! Reading books will nae put cooked food on yir table."

Margaret was puzzled. "What do you mean, Jessie?"

Jessie stared at her. "Can you cook anything, yet?"

Margaret snorted. "Me? Peggy would never trust me to make anything."

Jessie's smile was beginning to look more like a preen. "Granny's taught me how to chop vegetables and make soup. And I can get the tatties ready to boil, as well."

"Does Ruth never help with that, either? Is it just you and your granny that do everything else?"

Jessie was the one who now looked perplexed. "Whit dae ye mean?"

"Well, sweeping your cottage for a start. I sometimes help Father sweep his office at the back of the shop."

Margaret was now bragging since it only took about three swipes to clean that tiny space.

"Ma mither sometimes helps wi that kind of stuff, if it's raining at night and she can't go out. She sometimes helps with the sewing but she never cooks or bakes. That's my granny's job."

Jessie was always telling her that Sunday was the best day of the week because her mother didn't work up at the mill, and always seemed to be a lot happier because Sunday was a church day.

Margaret had a feeling that it wasn't because Ruth was a lot more religious than her own mother and father. Jessie had mentioned plenty of times that she loved watching her mother getting dressed in her best clothes and doing her golden hair up in a fancy style, unlike the simple wound-braid that Ruth wore to work.

It only made Margaret a tiny bit jealous when Jessie, her granny, and Ruth all trooped up to the Parish Church. Margaret thought Ruth must be very keen to be good for God, since she primped herself so well.

"Has her cough gone away?" she idly asked while she made the rope spin around like a wooden top.

"Whit dae ye think?" Jessie didn't sound, or look, too happy when Margaret was able to catch a glimpse. "Mill workers always hae a cough."

That was true enough. Margaret's Auntie Jeannie often had a bit of a bark. At those times Jeannie's throat always sounded hoarse and sore, even when Jeannie said it wasn't. Auntie Jeannie didn't actually work out in the fields like a farmer, though the huge open-ended shed where she worked was called the Whitening Fields. Jeannie mostly bemoaned the fact that her hands were red raw with handling the 'bloody bleaches' used to whiten the cloth bales. Margaret knew never to call them 'bloody' but it was what her auntie always called them. It was such a shame because she thought that the word bloody went very well with bleaches.

Even though she could now read quite a lot of words, there were so many still to be learned and then savoured! It hadn't taken long for her to be moved into Row Five, even though she was younger than some of the girls who had started on that same October day that she had. A trickle more girls had joined the class after the turn of the New Year, but Jessie hadn't been one of them. There was still no money to pay for her to join the class.

That wasn't fair at all, because Margaret's father was now paying more every quarter so that she could attend the Beginners Writing class. Those writing lessons came after the main class was over and the bulk of the children had been sent home for the day. So far, she'd only had six writing lessons, but she was pleased beyond pleased that she never had a problem with practising the words she knew.

During the past winter-into-springtime, she and Jessie had snatched a little time together on a Saturday afternoon. That was the best they could do, and that was only after they'd both finished the chores they'd been set at home. Now that it was early summer it was a bit better because the sun lingered for longer.

"Git off!"

Jessie's prompt made Margaret pay her friend some attention.

"It's my turn and unlike you ah' hivnae got the hale day tae play."

Margaret dropped down to her feet and handed Jessie the bunch of frayed fibres she'd been clutching.

Jessie's chores list was even more huge since Mistress Morison had fallen down in the late February snowfall and had crippled herself so badly that she could barely hobble around now. Jessie was still collecting and delivering all the work for Miss Reid's shop, but now she was trundling back and forth with the laundry, as well.

"Do you have to collect laundry for your granny?" Margaret asked.

"No' the day! Some people have complained aboot the quality o' the cleaning."

When Margaret looked up, she thought that Jessie looked really sad.

"I'm strong, Margaret, but jist nae as strong at thumpin' the stained sheets against the washboards the way ma granny used to manage."

Margaret thought it might be a good thing that Jessie had less of the laundry to help with. She'd often looked at Jessie's chapped hands and thanked the lord that she didn't need to do all of the rough work that her friend had to.

She decided that hemming handkerchiefs every night wasn't so bad, after all.

"Have you time for me to show you some of my new letters and words, Jessie?" she asked.

Margaret's attempt to change the subject from dreary drudgery worked because Jessie jumped off the rope grinning like a mad person.

Margaret felt Jessie's grab at her elbow before she was towed along the riverbank, out of sight of anybody on South Street. Jessie was desperate to learn to read as well as she could, but Jessie guarded it as their secret, not to be known by anybody else – not even Mistress Morison, or Ruth.

And certainly, never nosey Daft Lizzie.

Jessie picked up a stick and used the soles of her boots to flatten off the dirt on the pathway, boots that eventually fitted her feet. Margaret grinned when Jessie drew a couple of the letters that they had practised the previous Saturday. They were a bit wobbly but recognisable as a capital J and a small letter 'e'

Margaret found a stick of her own and carefully drew a letter 's'. "After you learn this one, you only need to learn a small letter 'i' and then we can practise your complete name."

Jessie's grin was so close to her own as they hunkered down, shoulder to shoulder, and practised writing the new letters. They rubbed them out and drew them over and over.

"Jessie! Where are you?"

51

Margaret felt Jessie's disappointment all the way to her boots when her friend clutched her hand and stood up.

"That's Mistress Stewart frae next door shouting oan me. Ah hiv tae go. Mibbe ma granny has hurt hersel' again."

Margaret nodded as she rose and gave Jessie a big hug. "We'll write your whole name next time."

When they got back to Jessie's doorstep, she could see that it wasn't Mistress Morison that had a problem. They were just in time to see a very limp Ruth being supported into the house, her hacking cough bending her double and halting her progress. Mistress Morison assisted on one side and one of the foremen up at the mill supported Ruth's arm on the other side.

"Ah'll leave her in yir able hauns, Mistress Morison," the man said backing out into the street. "That's the third time this week that she's collapsed beside the loom. We cannae hiv that happen again since it's no' just her whose work is interruptit when she's pulled awa' to the side. Her replacement has already taken over. Somebody will be doon next week wi' what Ruth's owed."

Margaret looked at Jessie's white face when Mistress Morison didn't hold back her words.

"Oh, aye? Ruth's cried the best Fine Drawer in the mill when she's fine and healthy, but as soon as the dust that's in her lungs bothers her, there's nae job for her ony mair." Mistress Morison took Ruth by the shoulders, ushering her inside, but turned back to the foreman. "Ye a' should be ashamed o' whit goes on at that mill!"

The man shuffled away, his chin down and the cap in his hand being wrung out better than the finest washerwoman could twist with both fists.

Ruth's coughing kept her just inside the doorstep for a bit longer before she could speak. Margaret squeezed Jessie's hand in comfort, the best she could think of to help her friend since Ruth was so distressed.

"I cannae lose ma job," Ruth wailed, allowing Mistress Morison to drag her all the way inside. "How will I ever get new Sunday clothes if I dinnae hae a job?"

"Fancy clothes?" Mistress Morison's wails were nearly as loud but Margaret could see they were pure anger and not like Ruth's anguish. "Yir half dead oan yir feet and all you can think aboot is the way you might look at the kirk on a Sunday! And it's nae really even that! It's how ye might look to a' the toons folk o' Milnathort as ye swan yir way up there! All ye think aboot is drawin' the attention o' a married man who has nae business straying from his wife. Wha kens whit else that sanctimonious rascal does, an' him up at that Muckle kirk, railing aboot everybody's misdeeds. This has tae stop, Ruth. Ye ken fine well that smoothed-tongued man will be ablow your skirts anytime ye let him but he will nivver acknowledge a bastard."

Margaret felt Jessie's flinch at her granny's words. Then, Mistress Morison's next words were even worse. They set tremors all over Jessie that rippled through to Margaret in the fingers she was still clutching.

"Dinnae tell me that this illness o' yours is more than just your hacking cough. If you're wi' bairn again, I'll no be keeping you in this house. Bearing a bastard by that lecher once was bad enough, but to bear two wid be weel-beyond redemption!"

As though Mistress Morison had just realised where she was and what she'd just bellowed, her copper-pan glare descended upon Margaret. The old woman held on to Ruth but kicked back with her foot to shut the door, keeping Margaret and Jessie outside.

Margaret pulled Jessie back from the doorstep, their hands still clutched together. She tried hard to console Jessie who looked as if she was going to hurl up her insides right there on the street. "I don't understand all of those words but you're not to be upset. Your granny is so angry she probably doesn't know what she's saying."

Big fat tears dripped from Jessie's miserable blue eyes. "Aye, she does. She kens exactly whit she's saying, Margaret. My granny's called me a bastard before, when she thought I wisnae listenin', an' I do ken whit that word means."

Margaret wasn't completely sure of what it meant but held her tongue. Jessie was upset enough.

Chapter Eight

September 1847

Margaret skipped her way down South Street in the hope that Jessie would already be outside and down at the Queich Bridge. It had been weeks since they'd been able to play together, poor Jessie having to do even more work at home since Ruth was really poorly now. The cough that had plagued Ruth for years had got a lot worse. Ruth had never been able to go back to the mill as a Fine Drawer. The mill wouldn't employ her in any capacity, not even for sweeping the floor.

For a few months, Ruth had been doing some sewing work when she could get it, but it wasn't for Miss Reid. It was just poorly-paid mending that other women couldn't find time to do. Worst of all, Jessie had said that her mother had stopped going outside the house in the evenings and was now like a shadow moping around all the time.

"She nivver gets oot her bed noo, except to go tae the necessary," Jessie had said the last time they'd seen each other. "She mends a bit, here and there, propped up oan pillows. But she maistly falls asleep."

That meant that Jessie had to lie on the floor to sleep on a couple of old blankets because there was only room for her granny at the edge of the bed, since Ruth took up most of the space.

Margaret didn't think that sounded very comfortable. Or fair.

July had been cold and all-the-time rainy, August not much better. That wasn't fair either, because school had stopped at the end of May for the younger children and Margaret was bored. When it rained and she couldn't get out to play, Peggy made her do even more sewing. It was so repetitive that the only thing that stopped her from falling asleep was the needle stabbing into her fingers.

It wasn't the actual rain that kept Margaret from playing outside, it was more that Peggy got so cross when she returned home soaked. It was worse for Jessie if her clothes got wet because Jessie didn't have a Sunday dress to change into dry clothes.

As soon as she got closer to Jessie's house, Margaret knew that something was going on. Jessie was sitting outside on her doorstep and looked as if she'd been crying for days on end, her hair all mussed up like a haystack.

Margaret didn't say anything at first. She just sat next to Jessie and took her hand into her own, giving it a very gentle squeeze. Jessie didn't even look at her. Big tears leaked out of her eyes and slid down to drip off her chin, her gaze focused straight ahead at the cottage on the other side of the road, but since Margaret could see nothing happening over there, she didn't think that Jessie was seeing anything at all. After a tiny while she couldn't keep quiet.

"Is your ma very bad?" She kept her voice to a whisper.

Eventually, Jessie's anguished blue gaze turned towards her. "Ruth's gone."

Margaret didn't know what to say. She had a feeling that the 'gone' wasn't to Kinross, or any other place that she knew of. Her fears were confirmed when Jessie hiccupped, her eyes overflowing with distress.

"I dinnae think she's gone tae heaven." Big sobs now racked poor Jessie's body. Margaret snuggled in even closer and put her arm around Jessie's shoulder.

"Why would she not go there?" She wasn't sure how to console.

"Ma granny told Ruth last night tae prepare hersel'. Because she'd never repented properly, heaven wisnae where she'd eventually be bidin'"

Margaret felt her mouth gape open. Hell was for terrible people. Ruth had seemed a bit selfish, but surely, she wasn't that bad?

"I've been telt to sit outside but I've no tae move frae the step. There's a wifie wha' bides up the street called Mistress Byers. She's a freen o' ma granny and she's in there jist noo. Granny says that she's the best at the laying-out duties in Milnathort, whitiver that means. They're getting ma mither into her best Sunday dress, though I dinnae ken how they're doing that, because she cannae move or talk ony mair."

Margaret thought about that. "Your mother always liked to wear her best clothes when she went to your Parish Kirk on a Sunday. And you said she always did her hair all fancy. Maybe it's because she's not managed to go there for a while, and…" she hesitated before continuing, not sure about her words, "…because she'll not be going again."

Jessie's expression was so sad. "Ma granny said she disnae wint to ever clap eyes on that Muckle Kirk meenister ever again." Big gulps interrupted Jessie's words. "Granny says that since he kens fine well who made Ruth quicken, and then sicken and fade away, it's well-past time he stepped up and showed some responsibility."

"What does that mean?"

Jessie's handgrip tightened and made her wince, but she held on.

"All ah' ken is that it's definitely got somethin' tae dae wi' me."

"How come?" Margaret asked, still not sure what else to say. She broke the hand contact then inched her arm

57

across Jessie's shoulders before pulling her closer into a gentle hug.

Jessie gulped at her neck. "I dinnae ken, but Granny says he has to do more than he has up till now."

Margaret felt the sadness leak out of Jessie's eyes, the drips making them both shiver.

"Reverend Duncan never ever even looks at me if I see him in the street, so why would he wint tae dae more for me?"

When the door behind them started to open, Margaret jumped to her feet, somehow knowing that it wasn't the place for her to be any more.

"You come with me now, Jessie," Mistress Byers said once she was outside. "We'll have a wee bite to eat up at my house."

"Am I not to stay wi' ma granny?"

Jessie was so confused that Margaret felt it inside herself, but didn't know how to make it all seem better.

Mistress Byers took Jessie by the elbow. "You'll come back later and help yir granny, as usual. But the Parish meenister is due to visit soon, so I'll get you looking a bit more like yersel'."

Margaret wasn't sure about that. You could tell Jessie had been crying but she looked just the same to her. She walked alongside her best friend, keeping their hands clasped tight together till they reached Mistress Byers' door.

October 1847

A few weeks later, Margaret woke up earlier than usual, not even needing her mother to shake her shoulders like she normally did to rouse her. School was restarting and she couldn't wait.

A new room had gradually taken shape during the summer months, built onto the back of the big schoolroom. The local Milnathort gossips had a field day about it. Some enthusiastically claimed that the Subscription School was so successful that it was bursting at the seams and needed to expand, the new room meaning that the pupils didn't need to all crush into the one area. Others grumbled outside her father's shop door that if the Subscription School could afford to build a new room, then the parents were paying too much money in fees for their children, and that one big room had been sufficient for years and years. A small cohort of gossips went further down that line and blamed the newest schoolmaster, Mister Anderson. They declared if his complaints had instigated the new building programme, then he must be unfit at keeping control of his pupils, if he needed more space for teaching.

Margaret had occasionally nipped along the Stirling Road during her summer weeks of leisure. It was so exciting to see the progress being made with the new room. And by the time the roof slates were in place, she desperately hoped that she would end up being schooled in it, because it had sometimes been difficult to hear Miss Patterson over the noise of the big class of boys.

Having gobbled down her breakfast porridge and her milk, she sprinted along Stirling Road, arriving far too early for the start of school. The area was deserted, and with an excitement hard to contain, she skipped around the outside of the big room to admire the new extension.

Class Three girls should form a line here.

The sign on the newly-varnished door confirmed her desperate hopes. Marking her place at the front of the queue, she awaited the appearance of the other girls who had been in her class the previous session. Some of them grinned like she did and were excited by the new development, but loads of them bemoaned the fact that they wouldn't be able to play away the days any more, as they had done during the holidays. She would miss that freedom too, to play at will, but it was no substitute for being back to learning.

The line gradually grew longer, Margaret sneaking looks over her shoulder from her position at the front. She could hardly credit it when she noticed Jessie coming around the corner to join the end of the queue of girls. Desperately wanting to know what Jessie was doing vied with losing her first-in-the-queue position. She stepped a tiny bit to the side and opted for a holler over the noise of the other girls' chatter.

"Why are you in the queue, Jessie?"

She watched Jessie slide to the side and cup her hands around her mouth, a big grin fit to split her face in two.

"Ah'm starting school today!"

Margaret could barely stop jumping up and down on the spot. She had no idea how Jessie's grandmother had managed to scrape up enough money to pay for Jessie's lessons, but only cared that her almost-sister was going to be at school. She turned to face front just as Miss Patterson stepped out.

"Silence!" The command was powerful, loud enough for all of the girls to obey immediately. "New girls come and stand here. The rest of you, file inside and seat yourself as you were last session."

The routine for enrolment, Margaret found, was no different from when she had first started school. This time the registration was accomplished swiftly, because there were no distractions from Master Forfair's class, or from Mister Anderson's.

They were soon ready for lessons to begin in the brand new room, and Margaret found she couldn't wipe the enormous grin from splitting her cheeks as she looked around. There were rows and rows of long table tops attached to bench seating which could seat two or three pupils. Each block of desks was separated by a space for the teacher to walk up and down, like the aisle between the pews in a church.

Margaret was beyond excited because she had hoped to be writing at a proper desk more often, instead of writing with a slate pen onto a slate balanced on her knee. The previous year, in Mister Anderson's area, she'd had to wait till some other pupil's writing work was finished before she could sit down to properly practise writing her own words.

Now there was a surface for each girl to place their slate upon!

Miss Patterson's new table, that didn't wobble, sat up higher on a wooden platform at the front of the room. Margaret grinned again. She could see her teacher so much better than in the previous schoolroom.

The lessons eventually began, Margaret stifling her impatience at having to go over lots of things she knew already. However, she acknowledged more than a little smugly that few of the girls remembered as well as she did, if the concentration on their faces was anything to go by.

It seemed a long while before Miss Patterson asked questions of her newest pupils. Too much pride was a bad thing, but Margaret couldn't help being gratified by Jessie's answers when questioned about how much she knew of the alphabet and about numbers to ten. Margaret thought that Miss Patterson looked impressed as she made some notes in the big comments book that always sat near her elbow. Margaret now knew that it was a record of each pupil's progress that her teacher could consult when necessary.

"How did your granny manage to find the money for your school lessons?" Margaret asked at the end of the day, heading away from the new schoolroom with Jessie's arm tucked in under her own.

"Ah dinnae ken," Jessie replied, nudging her with her shoulder and her smirk wide. "Ah'm nae bothered about who's handed over the money, so long as it wisnae just for today."

Margaret sniggered. "That's not how school fees work. Somebody has to pay the money for a whole quarter-year in one go. I never see how much my father pays, but he's the one who sends what's due to Mister Anderson."

"Oh!" Jessie stopped their progress and stared at her. "So, somebody is going directly tae the schoolmaister wi' the money for me?"

"I suppose so." Margaret just thought of something. "Are you only getting basic lessons? You have to pay more for extra writing and arithmetic classes beyond the elementary levels."

She could see Jessie's disappointment, her friend's mouth puckering.

"But ah want tae learn tae write as well as read, like you." Jessie was near to crying. "How will ah ken what's being paid for me?"

"When Miss Paterson tells us class has ended, most people file out and go home. On some days of the week, I stay on in the classroom for additional writing and counting lessons. Though not today, since this was the first day of the session."

Jessie brightened up a tiny bit. "So, if Miss Paterson asks me to bide in the classroom, ah'll ken that the person is paying for extra writing and counting, as well as reading?"

Taking Jessie's arm again, Margaret walked them further away from the schoolroom. "I think so. But I had to learn to read a lot for weeks and weeks before my writing and proper counting lessons began."

Jessie looked stunned. "But you could count to twenty when you were only five!"

Margaret nodded back, "Yes, because my father taught me. But the basic counting lessons that you'll get along with reading isn't proper arithmetic where you write down the sums."

"Then ah'm going tae be doubly good wi' ma reading lessons so that ah can get the same writing and counting as you've had."

"Is your granny able to do more of her basting and sewing work, now that she doesn't need to be tending to your mother?" she asked Jessie.

As soon as the words were spoken Margaret wished she could claw them back, for Jessie's face fell again, a little wobble appearing at her friend's bottom lip.

"I mean now that your granny's got more time in the day?" Her garbled apology seemed to help, Jessie turning to face her but still keeping their arms linked.

"Ma granny's no' doing any o' Miss Reid's sewing work now because her knuckles are so gnarled. She can only keep a needle in her fingers for a few stitches before she drops' it." Jessie moved on again.

"Ouch! That sounds really sore." Margaret's chest hurt, a strange feeling, when she thought about how much pain there must be in Mistress Morison's fingers because they were so bent and red raw all the time. "But if your granny isn't sewing for Miss Reid, and doing no laundry either, where is her money coming from?"

"Ah dinnae ken and when I've asked about it, she just tells me it's high time some money came our way and that I've no to poke ma nose into other folk's responsibilities." Jessie nudged her shoulder again. "It's the strangest thing. Since my mother died, Granny seems to manage on the little we get from my work for Miss Reid. Ah'm still basting the corsets together with the big stitches, but I'm also cutting out the cotton chemises. Granny showed me how to cut wi' her sharpest scissors."

"Well, that's very good," Margaret declared, quite astounded that her friend seemed to be what her father would call a breadwinner at so young an age. "What will happen, though, if you're now at school every day? How will you manage everything?"

Jessie's smile was twisted. "I suppose I'll have tae sew even faster when I get home, till it's too dark for me to see properly. We can only afford to use a candle for a wee while each evening when it darkens at dusk."

Pulling Jessie into a faster skip, Margaret determined not to send her best friend further down into the dumps. She headed down towards the Queich Bridge after bypassing Jessie's door, desperate to spend just a few more minutes together.

"I could tell that Miss Patterson was really impressed with what you know already," she said, to bolster Jessie's confidence. "I don't think it'll be long till you're also learning to write."

Jessie's giggles set up a flurry of birds from the banks of the Queich Water.

"She was surprised, wasn't she, that I ken all the alphabet letters that she asked about! I think she expected me to say I kent nothing at all."

Margaret grinned at Jessie. "I wonder how long it'll take before she realises that you're my best friend and that I'm the one whose been teaching you?"

"Well, dinnae you dare teach me anything that isne correct! I'll…" Jessie seemed at a loss for words and so full of laughter she could hardly speak. "Ah'll stop being your best friend if you teach me bad spellin'!"

Margaret guffawed and pointed down to the far side of the Queich Bridge.

"Have I shown you how to spell *'Buggration'* like old turnpike Mister Young is always muttering?"

They collapsed down on the banking, still giggling and staring up at the cloudless sky till they both gained their breath again.

"Oh, Margaret," Jessie giggled as she reached for her hand. "Ah'm that glad your ma best friend."

Margaret squeezed back and snuggled right in close, so tight they were like one person. "Forever, Jessie. Near-sisters forever!"

Chapter Nine

October 1849

The October after her tenth birthday, Margaret was so
excited about moving up into Mister Anderson's class,
because she felt more than ready to cope with lessons in
the big classroom. What made her sad, though, as she
stood in her new line, was that Jessie wasn't moving up
with her. Though Jessie had made really excellent
progress with her reading, the mysterious payments to
Mister Anderson didn't include any extra writing or
counting. And, as far as Margaret knew, no amount of
continued prodding on Jessie's part provided any
information from Mistress Morison about who was
paying the money.

They had long since worked out that Jessie's basting
money from Miss Reid was paying for their meagre food
bills, but not the rent of the cottage. It seemed likely that
the person paying for Jessie's reading was also paying
rent directly to the factor, because Jessie had told her that
the bad-tempered rent collector no longer rapped on
Mistress Morison's door every week demanding rent
payment.

Anything extra that Jessie knew, beyond the basic
schoolroom writing and counting under Miss Patterson's
guidance, had come from Margaret herself.
Unfortunately, their out-of-school time was always so
limited that Margaret had only been able to pass on a little
of the rudiments of arithmetic to her friend. Regrettably,

winter time was rarely good weather for them using the towpath to write upon. The broken slate that she had acquired, with the precious pieces of chalk her father had given her from the shop, was too small for Jessie to practise proper sentences on, or for forming long column sums.

Jessie was still not allowed in Margaret's house, though Mistress Morison never forbade her from entering their cottage. However, since Jessie still kept their extra lessons a secret from Mistress Morison, they had to work elsewhere. Jessie had never explained why she wouldn't relent, but Margaret had a feeling that Jessie's granny would think it was too uppity a thing to do and a waste of good light. If Jessie was at home, there was only time for her house cleaning chores, for cooking their meals which she was doing all the time, or for her evening sewing tasks. Mistress Morison, according to Jessie, spent a lot of her time now just sitting on her chair near the fire because walking around was so difficult for her.

As the winter progressed, the bitter cold winds that whistled regularly around Milnathort tended to drive them each to their own homes at the end of their school day.

Margaret often trudged home to the shop bemoaning that life just wasn't fair, and God definitely wasn't being just to her beloved almost-sister. She grumbled about the fact that she had to do more of the general housework for Peggy, a little of the cooking, and even more boring stitching of an evening. She'd progressed to helping with more complicated hemming and embroidery on women's underclothing, but it was still very repetitive. And, though Peggy was always impatient with her instructions, Margaret was now able to knit very simple woollen scarves and mittens which her mother deemed good enough quality to add to the stock they sold in the shop.

On Saturdays, after her extra morning-counting-classes were over, Margaret helped her father with tidying his shop, or cleaning his small stockroom. She loved to help him, especially when he had few customers to tend to because he asked her lots of questions which whiled away the time. Sometimes it was money sums to do in her head before giving him her answer. On other occasions, it was how to spell difficult words. Even better was when he asked her to summarise stories from the bible, ones he had read to her on a Sunday. Mister Anderson had taught her that summarising meant thinking about which important bits were needed to re-tell the story using the smallest number of words, so she didn't mind when her father had to talk to a customer because it gave her time to compose her answers.

One huge regret about working in the shop was that her father mostly seemed such a sad man, and she could never work out why. Her parents had come to some kind of truce, though, because their arguments were much less common. Actually, when she really thought about it, they only spoke to each other when they had to, and any conversation could be termed polite and little more.

Time to spend with Jessie, on Saturday or otherwise, only happened on a very rare occasion for a very short duration.

December 1849

"Margaret!"

Margaret was surprised to hear Jessie call her when she exited the door of her classroom. It was perishing, the leaden skies promising snow before dusk. She wondered what Jessie was doing waiting for her, since her friend had finished her own class much earlier. There were only two days left before New Year, a day when there was no school, even though it wasn't a Sunday.

"You look frozen." Margaret skipped her way to the end of the path where Jessie huddled near the gate, out of the ferocious wind. Her friend's face was pinched with cold, but she was guessing it could only be a very big reason that would make Jessie wait for her on such a day. "I didn't see you in your line this morning. Is anything wrong?"

"This time it's Granny."

"Oh, no!"

Margaret pulled her best friend into an enveloping hug. She tucked Jessie's face into her neck and patted her back through the thickness of her woollen shawl. What could she say to console? She was much better than she used to be at being tactful, according to Peggy, but for Jessie to lose her grandmother, as well as her mother, was just not fair. God, yet again, was not playing fair at all!

"Is it the cholera?" she asked over Jessie's slightly-shaking head. She didn't know much about it, but people were talking about lots of Edinburgh folk dying of it.

"Ah dinnae think sae," Jessie gulped. "I think she was just auld, though I heard that lots of folk up at the mill have come down wi' dysentery this week."

Margaret had heard her mother and father mention that just the day before. They'd told her to steer clear of the children of mill workers who were in her class.

Jessie sniffled, "Ah hope ma granny goes tae heaven."

Margaret gave Jessie another squeeze and more gentle back pats. "Of course, she will."

"Maybe nae right away." Jessie's big fat tears dripped onto her shawl. "Granny sometimes said awful things about some folk but she wisnae that bad." Jessie lifted her chin and stared at her. Her watery gaze was anguished. "Really, she wisnae."

"Of course, she wasn't." Margaret realised she was repeating herself then something dreadful occurred to her. "Who's going to look after you now?"

Although it seemed like a reasonable question, she knew that for months it had been Jessie who had actually been looking after her bedridden granny, but she was fairly sure that Jessie wouldn't be allowed to stay in the

68

cottage on her own. However, asking Peggy to look after Jessie would be like talking to a stone wall because her mother's attitude to Jessie's so-called-tainted background had never changed one iota.

She felt Jessie slide out from her grip before her arm was looped through her friend's. Setting off with firm strides, Jessie dragged her along towards the Market Cross.

"Mistress Byers says ah'm going tae be bidin' wi' her till things get sorted. I dinnae ken what exactly that means, but she telt me that a new family will be moving intae our cottage after Ne'erday."

"What? How can that happen so soon? That's only two days away." Margaret's mind whirred. "When did your granny die?"

"She wouldn't wake up this morn. Ah shook and shook her shoulders but nothing happened. Ah ran up to get Mistress Byers, but she said it was nae use and that Granny was well-gone."

Margaret tried to console Jessie by clasping her close. "But how can Mistress Byers know about your house already?"

"The factor got wind immediately about Granny and came round before noon. He said that Granny canny lie in the cottage for ever, an' that he needs the cottage to make money. That started a big fight wi' Mistress Byers. She shooed him out of the house, but he was still yellin' and bawlin' at her, even after she slammed the door on him. He shouted Granny has to be out the house and be buried right away in the kirkyard. But Mistress Byers says Granny had no money put past for a funeral. I dinnae ken what's going tae happen."

Dead bodies were sometimes put in a common grave, just at the edge of the old graveyard in Milnathort, if there was no money for a special plot with a name on a piece of wood, or a gravestone. The boys at school tormented the girls all the time, telling them that the dead from the common graves wandered around the town at night since the shared grave-pits were always being opened to dump in another body.

That would be a horrible thing for Mistress Morison if she was just thrown in there. Squashing down the ghastly thoughts, Margaret almost repeated herself. "But the New Year is almost here. Can she be put in the earth just now? Especially since I heard tell it's going to snow."

She didn't know the answers and neither did Jessie, but she remembered that Jessie's mother Ruth was buried very quickly.

Margaret kept her tones soft. "Can your granny not go in beside your mother?"

"Ah dinnae think sae." Jessie sobbed her heart out. "Granny took me tae the graveyard a few times after my mother died, but we always just said a few prayers on the bit o' grass near the gate. We didnae go tae a special part, and ah dinnae think my mother's name is written on anything."

They reached the town square. Margaret grasped both of Jessie's hands and squeezed them gently, trying to give her the best support that she could think of. "Come with me into the shop while I tell my mother."

Jessie's lips pursed. "Ah cannae. Ah have tae go back tae Mistress Byers' house then we're going down to collect ma things. She only let me out her house for a wee while so that ah could tell you what's happened."

Margaret knew that Jessie had few things to call her own and that there would be precious little to trek up to Mistress Byers' house.

"I'll come and see you at Mistress Byers' house tomorrow."

Jessie's hug was a barely-there one before Margaret watched her best friend turn away to run down South Street. She hovered between being distressed by the situation and proud of her friend. Jessie had been so determined not to cry too much.

Though she told her parents of Mistress Morison's death as soon as she got into the shop, the gossip had already reached them.

"It's not the best situation for young Jessie," her mother stated, briefly interrupting her counting up one of the columns of her big account ledger, "but there's nothing we can do, Margaret. It's being dealt with by Mistress Byers and that's all you need to know."

"But what will happen to Jessie after her granny's funeral?"

"Well, how should I know?" Peggy sounded exasperated. "It's not our business. We let you remain friends with Jessie because it meant so much to you, but from now on you need to find another friend who comes from a more respectable background."

Margaret knew not to continue with the conversation. She knew how much her mother set store on appearances, and Jessie had never fitted into her mother's idea of well-brought-up people.

Her mother was such a snob.

Margaret vowed she would never become as stuck-up, or as heartless, as her mother.

Chapter Ten

February 1850

"There's a letter for you on the table," Peggy stated, not looking up from her sewing after Margaret opened the door to the kitchen on her return from school.

"For me?" Margaret was stunned. She'd never had a letter before. "Are you sure?"

Peggy looked up briefly, her expression a bit bemused. "Well, the handwriting is very poor but it looks like your name."

She popped her shawl on the hook near the door, a much easier task now that she had grown quite tall, and hurried to pick up the correspondence.

The letter definitely had her name on it, and below that it said Mister Law's Draper Shop, Milnathort.

"Who can it be from?" she asked, but the question really wasn't to her mother, it was more that she was wondering out loud.

"I can guess, but it's for you to find out."

Peggy's answer was a bit whimsical, which Margaret thought wasn't usually her mother's nature at all.

She stared at the folded paper for a bit longer, her stomach making some very funny gurgles. She was far too excited to open the seal since the only person who might write to her was Jessie, but how could it be from Jessie when her best friend had hardly managed to practise any writing beyond her own name?

She hesitated even more.

She wasn't sure she could bear the disappointment of it not being from Jessie.

It had been such a lonely time earlier that year, after Jessie had been spirited away from Milnathort just mere days after Mistress Morison's funeral on the second day of January. Margaret had not even been given the chance to bid her best friend goodbye.

The distressing memory of her father asking her to sit down at the kitchen table was one Margaret had unsuccessfully tried to suppress for weeks.

"Mistress Byers came to speak to me today, Margaret," her father had said, his tone sombre though his expression was one of sympathy. "She told me that Reverend Duncan of the Free Church has organised a place for Jessie to work, since she's now an orphan and can't stay by herself."

She'd asked him where Jessie was.

"All I know from Mistress Byers," he'd said, "is that she's no longer in Milnathort."

The days after that had been horrible. The town gossips claimed Jessie had been sent off to all sorts of places. The biggest rumour was that she was in a nasty orphanage near Perth that sounded more like a prison. Other rumours had Jessie in a workhouse down in Dunfermline. Another story was that she'd been indentured to a farmer on the far side of Kinross as a dairy servant.

"What are you waiting for?" her mother urged, making her think of the present and not the recent past. "You'll never know who is writing to you, if you don't open it. Use the little sharp knife over there to break the wax and get on with it."

Taking a deep breath, Margaret steeled herself for the unknown. Picking up the blade she slid it beneath the wax seal and gingerly unfolded the paper. Excitement blossomed when she looked at the bottom of the writing to find the sender.

"It is from Jessie!"

Peggy snipped off the thread, the hemming of the garment finished. "I thought it might be. What does she say?"

There were many crossings out and marks on the paper where Jessie had rewritten words.

"Jessie writes…" Her reading was hesitant since there was no punctuation.

'dear Margaret I am scullery maid in Edinburgh and am well your best friend Jessie.'

She grinned while trying to decipher it. It was brutally short, but it at least told her Jessie was alive and living in Edinburgh. And there was an address at the bottom to reply to. Not in the correct place, but she wasn't fussed about the mistake.

The thought of writing back to Jessie and asking her friend questions to answer was so thrilling it had her jumping up and down on the spot.

"Would father post a reply letter for me?"

Her mother stashed away her sewing basket at the side of her chair and got up to prepare their evening meal.

"Calm down, Margaret, and think of the poor old floorboards."

Margaret planted her feet firmly on the rug, though her mother's words weren't censorious.

"I don't see why not," Peggy said. "So long as you don't expect him to pay the postage for one every week."

Margaret didn't know what to do next. She was torn between re-reading Jessie's letter and the mechanics of sending her own, her dancing around the kitchen table an indicator of her enthusiasm.

"I'll set the table, tonight," Peggy sighed. "You'll probably make a muck of it. Go through and ask your father for a sheet of paper."

Margaret could tell the moan was faked since her mother wasn't her usual exasperated self. Hugging the letter to her chest, she skipped out of the room.

Though, not quickly enough to miss her mother's last words.

"You'll get extra sewing tonight, since you're not doing your other domestic chores, my girl."

Patiently waiting till her father finished with a customer, her gaze wandered along the goods lining the shop shelves. Would Jessie have to wear a special apron, she wondered? Or a mobcap for her kitchen job like the ones in the glass-fronted cabinets? Peggy supplied uniforms to a number of the bigger houses in and around Milnathort – all made of serviceable materials for the drab dresses, the starched white aprons, and the headwear. Margaret's fingers itched to draw what a uniform might look like on Jessie, but since she'd never had any drawing lessons, her people all looked like twigs off a dead tree.

She wasted no time in creating a letter the minute she got the paper from her father; his permission having been given to write it in the little office that was used for the shop accounts. The desk sloped a bit, but she took her time thinking through her reply, ensuring no mistakes had to be crossed out. It was all written in her best handwriting. Having sanded the ink, she paused till it was fully dry before she turned the paper over.

As instructed, she waited till her father was not serving anyone.

"I've finished my letter, father. Can you help me with the rest?"

She'd never sent a letter before. She guessed what might come next, but didn't want to waste the piece of paper by sealing it wrongly.

"Well, now," William declared, after a quick read. "This is very nicely written, Margaret. Now you need to write Jessie's address in the correct place before the folds are finished." He broke off speaking to indicate how the folding was done and where he expected her to write the address in the middle of the reverse side. "Your writing needs to be small and neat because you must leave a clear space up here." Again, he stopped to point to the corner of the address space. "The postmaster must frank it there."

Margaret had been taught how to do a pretend letter on her slate at school, but it seemed so different actually doing a genuine one.

Having written Jessie's name, she copied the Edinburgh address from Jessie's letter. She beamed as she watched William carefully flatten the folded edges. He warmed up the end of his stick of wax with a lit taper and allowed some drips to carefully fall onto the top of the fold.

"Hand me the seal, please, Margaret," he instructed. "Use it to press gently on the wax. Not too hard, or it'll spread too thin and will break when it dries."

Excitement flared then she exhaled the breath she realised she'd been holding for quite a while. Her first ever letter was done.

"Now leave it there for me to post." Her father then waved her off to do her sewing chores, though not before he chimed, "Your handwriting is so perfect now. Maybe it'll be time soon for you to learn to do some of the shop correspondence!"

Skipping back to the kitchen, Margaret was thrilled with everything around her. She engrossed herself in her needlework and though it was as repetitive as it was every evening, she didn't find it too boring.

May 1850

It was only a few months later when William strolled through to the kitchen, brandishing a letter in the air.

Margaret looked up from her hemming work. Her father looked slightly amused, and that was so unlike his normal sad face.

"Aren't you a lucky girl?" he declared.

76

"Me?" She watched as her father's hand slowly reached towards her, offering the letter to her.

"Jessie?" Almost throwing her never-ending sewing on the floor, she grasped it from him and broke the seal. Unfolding the paper, her fingers were shaking, excitement taking over as she read it out.

'Dear Margaret. I help cook get meals made. I have own bed and two hot meals minus bed and board three pounds is mine at year's end. Your best friend Jessie'.

Margaret took time to re-read it in her head but was still confused. Returning her father's smile was odd, since he was clearly amused by the short missive. "What does she mean three pounds is hers?"

Her mother joined in the laughter, too, after Margaret had held out the letter for Peggy to read herself.

"I think Jessie means that she's to be paid three pounds a year but the cost of bed and board will be deducted from that. Bed and board generally mean the amount that an employer will charge live-in servants for the bed space given to them, and for the meals provided for them."

"How much would that be for a whole year?" she asked, taking back the valuable paper.

"I don't know." Peggy's shoulders rose, the gesture an unanswered question. "If Jessie has been given a bed of her own it will probably mean she is charged more money than if she has to share with another servant. I've heard of many live-in scullery maids around Milnathort who have to 'top and tail' sharing a bed with a number of other female servants. It sounds like Jessie must be in a well-to-do house in Edinburgh."

"If she has her own bed, does that mean she'll have her own room like I do?"

Peggy's answer was cynical. "I doubt that, but you'll need to wait for more information to know. You'd best get on with a new letter and ask all those questions, even if she can't answer you yet."

Margaret nodded absently as she re-read Jessie's few lines. She felt the gentle nudge at her elbow.

"Did you notice there are no less than four full stops in the letter?" Peggy's smirk indicated possible approval.

"Yes." Margaret grinned back. "Though I'll say it first. She has a lot of rubbing out, but the handwriting is a tiny little bit more legible."

As she clattered along the corridor to get a piece of paper from the office, she thought about Jessie's situation. Sharing a sleeping space with another person was such a strange idea to contemplate. Margaret had always had her own small bedroom upstairs, and there being only two rooms in the upstairs living quarters above the shop, her parents occupied the bigger room with the double bed. Of course, Jessie had been used to sharing the one and only bed with her mother and her granny, when both had been alive and living in their cottage.

Counting up the meals she had every day, Margaret wondered if Jessie would be starving if she only got two meals. Peggy always put porridge on the table for her with a cup of milk, to break her fast every morning. Later there was their main meal at mid-day when her father closed the shop for a half-hour. After the shop was closed up for the day and the preparation was done for the following day, they usually had a cup of tea with some bread and butter, sometimes toasted if the bread was old, or if she was really lucky a scone with home-made jam would be popped onto her plate.

Her life was so much better when compared to Jessie's. The sewing she did in the evenings for her mother didn't earn her a single penny but her parents were paying for her to remain at school, and her clothes and boots were always good quality. Staying at school was so important because she now knew that becoming a teacher, and sharing her learning, was what she wanted to do when she was older.

A terrible thought slammed into her. Was Jessie allowed to go to school if she was a scullery maid? Her friend hadn't had all that much time at the Subscription School in Milnathort. Lots of other fears flooded her as she walked into the rear of the shop. She must ask Jessie if she was going to school.

It was so important that Jessie still got the chance to learn. Perhaps not as much as Margaret was being allowed, but being good at reading and writing was so necessary to improve your future.

Chapter 11

September 1850

"What do you need help with, Father?" Margaret asked on her return from assisting Granny Maggie to bake a batch of fruit pies, the apple harvest having been plentiful as had the plums in the little strip of garden behind her granny's house.

"I'm not sure you'll be so keen in a minute, lass." Her father's expression was a little bit whimsical and lit up his unusually bright grey eyes. It was a sight to see replacing the usual serious and sombre. "However, you can help me tidy some shelves later on."

She had been expecting to spend the rest of the day doing shop chores, since it was still September and her new school session was not due to restart before mid-October. She'd attended a smattering of classes during July and August, though most of Mister Anderson's summer teaching time was being spent with his most senior pupils who were learning Latin and Greek.

The smile she sent her father's way was a puzzled one.

"I'm not sure I understand you."

William leant closer, still teasing her with a whisper. "You have another letter."

She flew along the passage and opened the kitchen door so quickly it startled her mother who was placing a pot of soup to heat on the range.

"I've another letter from Jessie?"

"That you have. It's here on the table."

Snatching it into her eager fingers, Margaret first savoured the writing on the front.

"Look, at how carefully she's written my name," she cried.

Her mother glanced at the letter. "She's still making mistakes, though. Our shop name has been written twice."

Margaret was undaunted. "I couldn't have written an address if I had never had writing lessons from Mister Anderson. Would you have had the courage to try if you were in Jessie's shoes?"

To her relief, Peggy didn't take offence. "No, I suppose not. Your father needed me to compose and address our shop correspondence so I learned quickly to produce a good standard."

Opening the seal, Margaret wandered around the room as she read.

"Jessie's handwriting is much less scratchy, this time. I can read it more easily."

"That's good," Peggy said. "I wonder how she's managing to practise?"

Margaret agreed that was a very good question. It looked as though someone might be helping Jessie.

"Oh, my!" she declared, her tone making her mother lay down her sharp knife.

"What's wrong?"

"Not wrong exactly. Jessie says the family she's been sent to are related to the minister of the Free Kirk here in Milnathort."

"That's interesting," Peggy declared, something odd lighting up her expression.

"I think Jessie means that it's the Reverend Leslie Duncan's brother, a man named Stewart, that she's working for?" She handed the letter over to Peggy to help her understand it.

"Yes, that seems to be what she's writing. And that it's a very big house." Peggy looked as puzzled as

81

Margaret felt. "Now, I wonder why Jessie was sent there?"

Her grin was an excited one. "Isn't she lucky to have got the work there?"

Peggy lifted the bread knife to slice a fresh loaf for their mid-day meal. "Well, until Jessie is able to tell you more, you'll just have to assume that she's found her feet."

"What?" She questioned the now doubtful look on her mother's face.

"Jessie doesn't yet say if there are a lot of servants. If it's a very big house then I hope she's one of many servants, and not being expected to do too much on her own."

"Oh!" Margaret hadn't thought of that, just imagining that it must be fun to work in the big city of Edinburgh. She'd been thinking that it was a privilege for Jessie to work there, in the same way that it had been a privilege for Jessie to get some basic schooling in Milnathort paid for by her mystery benefactor – though now she wasn't so sure. It was a pity to be so undecided, because having a benefactor had sounded special.

"Have you ever heard of the Reverend Duncan organising anything like this for other girls in Milnathort?" she asked Peggy.

Her mother shook her head. "Not until now, but who knows what that man's likely to do?"

"What do you mean?" Margaret was puzzled.

"Never you mind. There's always gossip enough in Milnathort, and I for one will not be adding to it. You just be careful who you tell about Jessie's good fortune."

Margaret realised her mother had grown quite serious, though she was happy to keep her knowledge of Jessie's plight a secret. Apart from herself, Jessie hadn't made other proper friends in Milnathort.

"And if Mistress Byers asks if you've heard anything from Jessie, you just tell her that all you know is that she arrived safely and is working. Nothing about where her job is. Mind my words! Since your father moved us all to the United Presbyterian Church, I never hear anything about the Free Kirk anyway, and that's how I want it to stay!"

Margaret knew there was never a time to share any of her memories of Mistress Morison's gripes. She could almost hear the old woman mouthing the words *'That Free Kirk Reverend ought to have known better. The man should have left Ruth's skirts well alone. That one mistake was bad enough but more were unforgiveable.'* Margaret couldn't stop those memories from surfacing every now and then, but she'd vowed to keep them secret forever.

Now that she was older, she'd a better inkling of what Mistress Morison's grumbles might have meant. Men chasing skirts she now knew often led to surprise babies being born, but exactly how they were produced was for her to learn another day.

It was confusing. Many of her conclusions were very disheartening.

The Reverend Duncan was supposed to be a pious religious leader, like the other ministers in Milnathort. Was it because he knew who had been messing about under Ruth's skirts, and that was why he had sent Jessie to his brother's home in Edinburgh?

Questions swirled around her head, and some of her thoughts were even more terrifying. Could Jessie's unknown father be a friend of the Reverend Duncan? Was that what Peggy's veiled comment was all about?

Much worse, if the minister was concerned, why did he not keep Jessie at his own house in Milnathort?

There were plenty of children in the town who were brought up by their auntie and uncle instead of their real mother and father. Or sometimes, it was the grandparents who brought them up, if the mother wasn't married, like Ruth hadn't been. Or even some unrelated people.

There were so many possibilities taking flight around Margaret's head.

Why did Jessie have to be an orphan servant? It was so unfair of God to allow such a thing. Jessie was the kindest person ever.

When Margaret returned from running errands for her father the following day, Betty Campbell – her mother's friend who lived near the Free Church – was whispering over the counter.

"Did you hear that Reverend Duncan is now awful friendly with that new female parishioner? The widow-woman who moved in recently to one of the cottages near the brewery."

Her mother's face was tight-lipped and a bit stoney-looking, as though she wanted nothing to do with hearing gossip.

Margaret prayed that Peggy would always keep Jessie's secrets.

Unfortunately, her mother shooed her away to the kitchen so she only just managed to catch Mistress Campbell's next words.

"It's a downright shame, it is, because Mistress Duncan – the minister's wife – is such a kind and helpful woman."

She turned round to find her mother staying tight-lipped but her head was nodding.

Mistress Campbell continued with, "Mistress Duncan always seems to be a wee bit downtrodden and sad, likely because the Good Lord hasn't sent her any children. Knowing what that man's smarm is like, I'd hazard a guess that it's not for want of them trying for years! Some men who think they're the Lord's gift to women just can't keep themselves tucked away."

Trying to do what with Mistress Duncan Margaret didn't know. And she'd yet to work out how it could have anything to do with him being over-friendly with some new woman in Milnathort.

Before heading for the kitchen, she looked back to hear her mother's reply. No words came out, but Peggy looked absolutely stricken. She had no idea what her mother's expression was all about but as soon as Peggy came back to herself, her mouth pursed in that sneering way that was too familiar.

As she opened the door into the kitchen, Margaret shook her head. Someday she'd properly understand adult conversations and how much truth there was in them. Peggy had told her to steer clear of gossips, but wasn't her mother gossiping just now with Mistress Campbell?

Giving people your trust was such a strange thing. She vowed she'd master it someday when she was older.

Chapter Twelve

December 1850

A few months later, after they'd finished their tea, her father popped back through to the shop. Not a usual event at that time of night, though not completely unheard-of either.

On his return he handed Margaret a letter.

"Sorry. I forgot to bring you this earlier. I'm sure you'll not be wanting to wait for it till tomorrow? It feels like more than one sheet of paper."

She forgave his lapse, excited to open yet another missive, and especially a long one.

"Oh, listen to this," she urged her parents, after she had quickly skimmed down what was actually the longest letter, so far, from Jessie. "The reason that I can read Jessie's letters better each time is that she's attending a Sessional School not far from the house, and is getting lessons in reading, basic counting, and writing." She grinned, thinking how excited Jessie would be. "Two days a week, when she can be freed from her chores, but not on a Saturday or Sunday."

Her mother nodded her approval. "You did wonder about that."

"I did! And that's better than the basic reading she got in Milnathort." She was so pleased to learn that Jessie was eventually getting proper writing lessons. She continued to read on. "She doesn't mention what a Sessional School is.

She paused to check if her parents' expression indicated they knew what it meant, but they looked as blank as she felt.

Peggy's shoulders rose in question. "Maybe it's similar to the Subscription School here in Milnathort?"

Margaret thought for a moment. If that was the case, she wondered who was paying for Jessie's lessons? At her mother's prompt she read on.

"Jessie says there are hundreds of children attending her school every day, but she only has to walk along a few streets to get to the Royal Circus in the New Town." She stopped and re-read. "Royal Circus?"

One of William's rare chuckles echoed around the kitchen. "There are a few streets in the Edinburgh New Town that are built around a half-circle with a communal garden right in the centre, a space that all the residents can use. The Royal Circus is one of those."

"How come I didn't know that?" she asked her father.

Again, her father's tight smile was a welcome sight. "You just don't read my newspapers well enough, young lady!"

Margaret accepted his mild chastisement. Sometimes she did skip bits of his newspapers because she found the information boring, and preferred to read books borrowed from Milnathort Lending Library during her leisure time.

"Does she tell you anything else about living there?" Peggy prompted.

Margaret scanned her letter for the place she had stopped reading.

"Yes. She's writing about the family! There are five Duncan children. The second-oldest is David. He's the one who has been helping Jessie to write the letters, especially this long one because he saw her struggling one day and helped her."

"Does she write about how old this boy David is?" her father asked.

87

"He's twelve. The same as Jessie. He goes to the Royal High School at Calton Hill. This also seems to be near where their house is, but not the way she goes to school. She says I'll like him because his nose is always in a book."

"Hmm," Peggy sniffed. "She might be right about that."

Margaret continued with her reading out loud. "The eldest child is called Robert. He's almost fifteen, but he's at school in…" She passed the letter to her mother to see if Peggy could work out the word.

"St. Andrews?" Peggy guessed.

"Yes," Margaret said, taking back the paper. "That's probably what she means. He's only home three or four times a year."

She looked across at where her father was sitting. "Why is he home so few times?"

Her father's expression indicated he was impressed. "Well, he could be at a boarding school where he has to stay most of the time, or if he's a very bright boy he might already be attending the university at St. Andrews and living in the accommodation provided for the students."

"Really?" She was very taken with both ideas, imagining that spending all day and all night at a school would be marvellous. She read on a bit more. "Ah, Jessie doesn't think much of snobby Victoria, who is nine, because she never speaks to servants unless she absolutely has to, and then only to order them about."

"I hope that lass isn't horrible to Jessie," William declared.

Turning to her father, Margaret was surprised by his support of her friend, for he never normally showed much interest in Jessie.

"That would be downright nasty of her if she does!" she declared, defending Jessie as well.

"What of the other two children? Does she say anything else?" Peggy inquired.

"Yes, Rachel is closer to five than four. Jessie likes her because she's friendly." The next bit made her grin even more at her mother. "And there's another girl, a spoiled little brat who is only two, called Elspeth. Jessie declares she's a handful."

"Oh, my, and she's actually written that?" Peggy's amusement startled Margaret.

Her father's lips twitched. "If the lad, David, is helping Jessie with her letter writing, then I'm guessing he must think the same of his sisters since he knows what's on that letter?"

"Oh, aye." Margaret smirked. "He must do."

She was quite taken aback when her father changed the subject. "Has Jessie said which church they all attend?"

"No, that hasn't been mentioned yet." She looked at her father. "Why would that be important?"

"Your mother…" He stopped to look across the fireside at her mother. "She just mentioned that they probably attend the Free Kirk, since that's the Reverend Leslie Duncan's church."

Margaret didn't see how it mattered but she said, "I'll ask in my next letter."

"You do, that." William's words were muffled into the rippling of his newspaper, the discussion of Jessie's letter now over.

May 1851

The month of May's cold and dreich weather reflected the sombre mood of her mother when Margaret breezed into the kitchen, her latest letter to Jessie in her hand.

"So, you're eventually here. Help me dish up our dinner."

Peggy was harassed as she stirred the heavy iron soup pot that sat on the range, the smell coming from it so delicious that Margaret's stomach was gurgling.

Saturdays at the shop were always busy enough to make her mother cross, though the furrows at Peggy's forehead seemed even more pronounced than usual.

"I have to fetch your father or he'll never stop to eat anything."

The shop only closed for a half hour at midday, so timing was crucial.

Margaret popped her letter onto the table and reached for the cutlery Peggy had just removed from the drawer in the wooden cabinet that sat next to the cooking range, the top of which served as a preparation board.

She deftly set the spoons down in their usual three places on the pristine white cotton cloth that covered the table, and laid the bread knife in the centre next to the bread board. Just one step took her to the shelving on the side wall. She collected their soup bowls, set them down next to Peggy, and then finished laying the table with their tea cups and saucers.

"I'll fetch him," Margaret said after she cut three slices from the loaf that she'd taken from the wooden bread bin that sat in the shade near the sink. "I need to take my letter to Jessie to the office."

She wrote at the small dressing table in her bedroom, but usually sealed her missive down in the shop with her father's red wax and metal seal. There were no fancy wax colours for Jessie's letters, though some ladies used pretty shades of blue and yellow wax. She'd seen them at the Post Office and determined that some future day her own letters would be more colourfully closed with a proper seal of her own. Her father's seal was adorned simply with his initials, WL, but she hankered for one with her initials and a pretty embossed pattern as well.

She reread the page she'd just written one last time, out loud, as she made her way along the short hallway to the shop. It had been quite a difficult letter to write, because it brought back memories that had faded over the time since she'd actually seen Jessie.

Dear Jessie,

I'm sorry I missed sending you a letter last month, but a lot of things have been happening here, of late. This time it's my family who are still grieving the loss of my Granny Maggie. She died four weeks ago. The only good thing about it, I think, is that my granny's heart suddenly gave up. It was over very quickly, in fact only a matter of hours after she collapsed outside in her garden. My Auntie Jeannie says she was so glad that my granny didn't suffer for years, not like your granny did with her creaky joints and gnarled fingers.

Then, only a little over three weeks after we buried Granny Maggie in the graveyard of the Parish Church up Ba' Hill, there was another family gathering in the same place, though as you know there are very few of the Wylie family left in Milnathort to celebrate anything. It was quite a subdued wedding with no frills, but I'm so very delighted for my Auntie Jeannie.

Everything has eventually worked out well, but at first the whole situation reminded me of when your granny died. Granny Maggie's factor was at the door immediately he heard of her death and gave my Auntie Jeannie an ultimatum. She could stay on in the cottage but he was putting the rent up! I think you can imagine how angry Jeannie was. She called him all sorts of names I can't possibly write in this letter, but the egg was on the factor's face when she told him she'd be moving out as soon as she could, and he knew what he could do with his cottage. As you know, Jeannie doesn't earn enough at the mill. My granny only managed to feed them both out of the money she earned from selling the vegetables and fruit from her garden, and from her cleaning work up at the big house outside Milnathort.

At first my mother was angry that Jeannie had been so rash, and that she only had a few days to clear out the cottage. Granny Maggie was buried as soon as it could be arranged, which was almost as quick as when your granny was buried, though I wasn't allowed at the graveside. Then the following day my parents, and the two Wylie cousins who still live in Milnathort, rallied around and between them helped move the belongings Jeannie wanted to keep. It is just as well we have a good shed outside the back of the shop since Jeannie kept all the furniture, and bits and bobs, that my granny owned. I had to share my bedroom with Jeannie for a couple of weeks while the marriage bans were read. It was a squeeze in my narrow bed but we managed without falling out.

Margaret fast-read the rest, happy with that last bit of jocularity, and hopeful that Jessie would understand it. The flow of the remainder of the letter, she was happy with, too. She was sure that Jessie would be sad hearing about the death in the family but would be pleased to learn that her Auntie Jeannie's admirer from Perth, the one who'd been courting her for over a year, had suggested their marriage be brought forward to as soon as they possibly could arrange it. Jessie already knew from a previous letter that he'd proposed to Jeannie and that she'd accepted.

Margaret particularly liked how she'd written:

Auntie Jeannie loves him so much and I think Calum is just as besotted with her. I'm already missing her badly, since she's now living with Calum in a house in Perth, but we can go to visit some Sunday, since it's not too far away. I think my parents will arrange something, so long as it's after our morning church service.

"Margaret!" Her mother's cross voice intruded down the corridor. "The broth is on the table!"

She giggled. A good thing to have already learned. Some priorities just couldn't wait!

Chapter Thirteen

A reply from Jessie came the following week, the quickest return of any of their correspondence so far.

'Dear Margaret,

I am sorry to hear about your granny but I'm sure that heaven had a place all ready for her...'

Margaret read quickly, finding Jessie's handwriting was better, as was her spelling. She must be practising a lot in her spare time, though the question was when that might be?

'I'm doing a very good job now. All that training from my granny in sewing, cleaning, and cooking is very handy. Though cook does most of the cooking and Kate does most of the cleaning...'

Margaret's opinion was that her friend seemed to be doing just about everything now at the Duncan house and yet was still paid almost nothing, certainly not enough to do very much on the rare time off that Jessie seemed to be granted.

Jessie had written that Edinburgh was such a wonderful city and there were plenty of places to walk to from the Duncan house since it was almost right in the centre of the city. It had made her more than a tiny bit jealous when Jessie had regaled her with mentions of going to the parks nearby, and that seeing Edinburgh

Castle and the old town streets were such a special treat on her half-day off, every fourth Sunday. Margaret had only ever seen some pictures of Edinburgh in one of Mister Anderson's books.

A trip back to Milnathort was out of the question for Jessie because of the time it would take for a return journey, regardless of whether she saved up the money for the fare.

"Oh, that's awful!" Margaret gasped.

"What's she writing now?" Peggy queried.

Margaret was amazed that Peggy was now keen to know what was in the letters Jessie sent.

"The middle girl, Rachel, fell down a set of stairs in Edinburgh's Old Town."

Peggy did a couple of small stitches to tie off her thread before putting down her needle. "Does Jessie say if Rachel is badly hurt?"

Margaret read more of the letter. "Yes, poor Rachel's legs aren't working. Jessie says something's damaged her back and the doctor doesn't think she'll ever walk again. And she's got a broken arm and wrist." She looked up at Peggy. "You wouldn't think falling down some stairs would cause so serious an injury."

"Oh, that's very distressing. It isn't going to be easy for the rest of the family. Having someone so dependent on help will take its toll on the rest of them, especially Mistress Duncan."

Margaret watched her mother go over to the range to poke at the coals, stirring up some heat before popping her kettle into place having checked there was sufficient water in it.

"Is it going to affect Jessie in any way?" Peggy asked.

She read down to the end of the letter; her breaths even more pronounced. "Oh, no! Yes. It is. She's not going to the school any more. She says that she's now needed to help look after Rachel in addition to her scullery duties." She looked at Peggy before speaking further. "I don't know how Jessie can look after a girl of five who is bedridden. What would she need to do?"

Peggy removed plates from the shelf on the kitchen wall, her brown-eyed expression reflective.

"Maybe Jessie will have to help with washing the girl's nightclothes, if they need changed more often, depending on how Rachel manages to use a chamber pot? Or perhaps Jessie might brush Rachel's hair which could get very tuggy if she's in bed, or reclining all the time? Maybe even feeding her and then wiping her face will be necessary?"

Margaret looked at her mother who for once really did look as though she was sorry for what her friend was having to bear.

"It really will depend on what the girl is able to do for herself," Peggy stated. "But let's not worry about Jessie till she tells you more. Jessie is resilient and will manage whatever they ask of her. You know your friend well enough for that to be true."

Margaret was astonished to receive another letter from Jessie that arrived almost on the heel of the previous one. A gap of two weeks between correspondence wasn't usual.

"What's Jessie's latest news?" Peggy was straight in with the question as soon as Margaret had broken the seal.

Margaret scanned the letter before answering, pleased that her mother's interest was genuine now.

"Jessie's confirming that Rachel really is bedridden, that the girl stays in her bedroom except when they carry her to a daybed in the parlour."

Margaret looked to Peggy for an explanation.

"Instead of having a chair with two arms, a daybed has a much longer seat for lying stretched out. They usually have one rounded end which is like a pillow to rest the head on."

Margaret's nod accepted the information. Having a daybed in the parlour sounded so different from most houses she visited, though she did know a few people in Milnathort who had a small parlour. Theirs were generally only used on a Sunday for family worship, or on rare special occasions.

She returned to the letter, reading it out. "Jessie is having to feed Rachel, since only one of the girl's arms works properly and she can't hold a bowl, or a plate. Oh, the poor little thing…" She stopped momentarily, the mere thought of the girl's plight upsetting her. At her mother's silent prompt, she resumed reading. "Jessie says Rachel's now able to sit propped up on pillows, which means she doesn't choke so often on her food as when she was flat in her bed."

"That'll be easier for Jessie to manage as well." Peggy's positive expression encouraged her to continue.

Further down the letter she gulped. "Oh, listen to this. Jessie says the family are looking for someone else to help Rachel. It's not to help with her physical care, but they're looking to employ someone who will carry on with Rachel's schooling. They want to continue with teaching her to read. It seems she's not learned much yet, since she only started school at the beginning of this year. According to Jessie, the parents don't want to pay the fees of an expensive governess since Rachel can't manage all the things that a governess would teach. But they're willing to spend some money for someone to do basic reading, and maybe later on with writing tasks."

"I wonder what they would pay for that? It's not the job of a hired domestic like Jessie, so the wage should reflect that."

Margaret was stunned. Her mother's question sounded serious. Why would she want to know such a thing? She read down to the end of the letter.

"Jessie doesn't say anything about how much money. She adds that she wonders if they would consider me."

Peggy's harrumph drew back her attention to her mother's speculative expression. "Write back to Jessie and ask her if she can find out what the conditions would be. They'd have to make sure the person was given bed and board."

"Why?" Margaret stared at Peggy. "Why that if the person was only teaching Rachel to read?"

Her mother's no-nonsense voice cut across the kitchen as she collected the cutlery and set it down on the table. "If the assistant they hire isn't an adult, then they'd have to make sure the girl either lived near their house to attend on a daily basis, or they'd need to offer bed and board as part of the job."

Margaret absorbed the information, thinking her way through it. "Are you suggesting that if they only want to pay a very low wage to the youngest person who could do the job, then a lived-in position would be most likely? Wouldn't that be an expensive option as they'd have to feed the person?"

Peggy's sneer indicated her attitude. "Feeding a young person not much more than scraps, and fitting yet another truckle bed into a room that already houses downstairs staff, is probably much cheaper than paying for the services of a governess, which is what they really should be doing. A governess would insist on a separate room of her own, I should imagine. She wouldn't sleep down beside the rest of the servants."

"Why don't they consider Jessie for the job? She can read. She's already sharing a room with the housemaid, and her board's part of her annual wages."

Peggy's sardonic laugh rippled around the room. "Jessie can read, but she's not nearly up to your standards, Margaret. And her writing still needs to be worked on. Just look at that bit of paper! Jessie's penmanship, in places, is like a hen scratching around for dropped seeds. Your handwriting, on thc other hand, is exceptionally good."

Margaret felt her jaw dropping. Her mother had never offered this sort of praise before.

Peggy fussed a bit with wiping down plates that were already clean before setting them down on the little shelf near the range. "Now, this hearty stew can wait a bit longer before I serve it. Write back immediately and tell Jessie you're interested to know more."

She could hardly believe what her mother was telling her. "Don't we need to talk to Father before I make inquiries about something like this?"

"He'll know soon enough."

With a grumbling stomach, the smell of the delicious beef sparking it into action, she sped back upstairs.

The conversation that night wasn't something Margaret had anticipated. She'd read about revelations in the bible but the revelations from her parents were truly shocking. So much so she felt physically sick.

"Are you saying, Father, that I won't…that I wouldn't…be continuing at school after my birthday in September?"

The concept of her carrying on at school for another year had never recently been discussed. Milnathort girls tended to leave after achieving the basic standards in reading, and sometimes in writing, but she had long-since moved on to achieving the highest standards of certificates awarded at Subscription Schools. She was expecting to be given the certificates due for her current standards on the last day of the school term, which was three days hence.

Training to become a pupil-teacher would be the next step that she'd be working towards. For that, she would have to take lessons in more subject areas, including Mathematics, and possibly Latin and Greek, the concept of which excited her beyond anything, though she knew she was more than capable. It wouldn't be easy but she was quick to learn new things.

"Margaret, I hoped never to have this conversation with you since I know how much you have loved being at school. We appreciate that you want to become a pupil-teacher and had thought you'd be moving towards that next session." Her father sounded so regretful, his expression the saddest she'd probably ever seen. "But that can't happen, now. Things aren't going well in the shop. They haven't been for a long time. Since old Miss Reid sold her business, the new owner is taking more and more of our custom away from us. You already know that they're now catering for both female and male undergarments, like we do, but they're also offering a full-tailoring service as well. Their goods are sold at lower prices than I can set, so more people are buying from them."

Margaret wasn't sure what to say into the dead silence that followed. Her mother sat tight-lipped.

The best she could come up with was, "How is it possible for them to make virtually the same goods as you do, Father, yet sell them cheaper?"

"It's all about more hands doing the jobs!" Margaret felt it was inevitable that Peggy's silence wouldn't last, but she couldn't help but notice her mother's ire was directed at her father, rather than her. "It's because they have plenty of offspring who are already skilled at tailoring, and in doing all the other sewing tasks."

Her father got up to pace around the kitchen, small as it was. "We are not going over this ground again, Peggy."

Margaret watched him glare at her mother.

"We both agreed years ago that Margaret would take advantage of her schooling, so that she wouldn't need to sew her fingers to the bone!"

Her mother harrumphed, "Yes. I know full-well that it's all fine and good for me to work myself to death but not your precious Margaret."

Margaret sat in silence. Her mother was often sharp with her when her studies got in the way of her

99

compulsory evening sewing tasks and household chores, but she hadn't realised it rankled so much.

Being an only child was unusual, yet siblings had never come along to fill up their house. Peggy regularly railed about that, though Margaret was sure that her mother didn't actually want more children to look after. Peggy had mentioned that fact many times when the local gossip was about huge families who ended up being unable to feed their vast broods. Peggy's grouse was about having to do all the housework herself since they couldn't afford a skivvy.

Margaret gulped, the air in the kitchen now thick with so much tension. She looked towards her father who stood rigid in silence, staring out of the window that looked onto the bare back yard.

"Father? Were you planning for me to be working with you in the shop, after school finishes next week?" She was addressing his back before she turned to her mother, who in turn gazed into the dying embers in the range, avoiding her gaze. "Or, were you going to be giving me more sewing work, Mother?"

The scoff that came her way was predictable. And so very hurtful. "What work? Have you been listening to your father, Margaret? We have very few orders in the books and they will not need more than one pair of hands to fulfil them. My hands, and my skills."

Margaret looked away, unable to confront her mother's acrimonious gaze any further. Sometimes she didn't like her mother very much; she disliked Peggy's cold attitude to almost everything, but right that very moment her feelings bordered on hating the woman who had given birth to her.

If not allowed to train to become a pupil-teacher, Margaret had expected that she would just learn to do more to help around the shop. Taking over the ordering and bookkeeping was something she just thought she'd be doing some day.

And maybe even eventually take over the whole business from her father.

Everything was now just a fanciful notion.

It was so difficult to think. And the decision wasn't going to be hers, even though it was her future. How could they be so cruel to her?

She vowed never to let anyone down in the way they were letting her down right now.

Her father began to speak again, still solemn, though not sharp-toned like he had been with his wife. "Your mother has told me of Jessie's letter. This type of position is not something that will come up very often, and would rarely be offered to someone of your background and limited experience."

She knew how true that was. Milnathort girls mostly ended up working at the local mills, or were indentured as a servant in a big house, or at a local farm. Only a few worked for their parents, if there was a family business of some sort.

William turned away from the window and went to sit down on his usual chair at the range. He pinned her with a serious gaze. "With money being so scarce, I was going to find you a placement next week, after your last day at school, hopefully somewhere that you could use your sewing skills."

Her mother's sarcastic words spat, "Oh, so now her sewing might be important! Skills, I'll remind you, that I have taught her. God forbid that she becomes a kitchen skivvy for someone else!"

"That's enough, Peggy." William was angry again. "Margaret will never end up working as a scullery maid, if I have any say in the matter!"

Chapter Fourteen

June 1851

A mere two weeks later, and a few return-letters sent between Milnathort and Edinburgh, Margaret wakened up to a pinkish pre-dawn glow creeping through the gap between her curtains and the windowsill, the material having become a shade too short with frequent washing. Rising so early was not a usual thing for her, but after shrugging a shawl over her nightdress, she padded over to the window, knowing that sleep would now be far too elusive.

She watched the earliest slivers of light gradually banishing all of the darkness around Milnathort Town Square, though it wasn't actually square-shaped at all having five roads lead off it. Almost nothing moved out there, so she sat back down on the edge of her bed, a numbness filling her. As the loud clock down in the kitchen dragged on to chime five o'clock and then six, her thoughts were engulfing. New fears and old memories seemed to vie for spaces too small in her head while she idly stared, barely noting the early morning traffic increasing below.

Knowing her parents would now be stirring, she rose and lifted the chipped pitcher that lay on her bedside table. She let the cold water flow into the big china bowl she had inherited from her granny's house. After a good thorough scrub with her washcloth, she donned her new dress that reached all the way down below her ankles.

The length of the dress was a signal of maturity that she didn't yet feel she deserved, but Peggy had decided that the possible job in Edinburgh merited a mature young lady rather than a girl. Having wound her thick auburn hair into a curled braid at her nape, and satisfied with her appearance, she went down to the kitchen for her breakfast.

Promptly at eight o'clock, Margaret alternated between pure excitement and sheer terror as she faced her parents on the front doorstep of the shop, though it was still early for shop trading.

The carter was due to arrive, once he had finished loading up at the mill.

"Well, lass." Her mother's voice was the determined sound she was well used to before Margaret felt herself drawn into a low-hugged squeeze, Peggy's arms around her forearms, the first embrace she had received in a very long time from her mother. "Remember what I've told you. You mind your manners and don't entertain strangers in the street who try on the charm, or who might take advantage of you."

She gripped her mother tight, her words almost lost in Peggy's shawl that closely wrapped against the unseasonably biting, morning nip. The last days had been like tip-toeing over eggshells, the air so thick in the house with almost no one talking to anyone else, but now that the time to leave really had come she wasn't sure she was ready. "I'll not forget all your warnings."

"My turn," her father said, sliding her out of her mother's grasp and into his own loose attempt at shoulder-patting when the clip-clop of the horses could be heard turning the long four-wheeled cart on the cobbles. The jingle of the harness was harsh as she stared, mutely, up at William Law.

"Mister Gordon will get you all the way to Burntisland. Mind you don't wander away from when you need to get off the cart. After he's unloaded his shipment, he'll make sure you get safely on to the passenger ferry."

Her father's hands sliding down to cradle her own made her feel even worse. She was not used to him touching her in any manner. Before he set her a little way away, she thought his eyes looked strained and as though he was confused over what he should be feeling or doing.

She couldn't help staring when he took a big gulp before he spoke.

"You'll be right fine, lass. That brain of yours is a keen one, and I know you'll always use it well. Write to me as soon as you can?"

Margaret swiped away her tears. "You can be sure I will, Father."

The horses completed the turn around the square and stopped right beside them on the driver's command, the stench of horse droppings immediately permeating the street around her.

"Come on, young lady, get up here and don't keep me waiting!" Mister Gordon urged, bringing an end to the farewell with her parents.

As though an afterthought, her father's expression was intent. Even fervent. "You make sure to attend church regularly. I know Jessie wrote that the Duncans attend the Episcopalian Kirk, and not the Free Kirk like the Reverend Duncan here, but you find yourself a United Presbyterian. There are plenty of them in Edinburgh."

"I will, Father," she said as she climbed up and settled beside the carter on the high bench seat.

Her father tucked her cloth bag under the canvas covering of the cart, just behind her seat. There was only time for William to give her knee a last reassuring pat before the horses lurched into motion to head round the corner and down South Street towards Kinross.

Looking back over her shoulder, it was only a few moments before her parents disappeared from her sight, their cries of goodbye and encouraging waving fading into blurred movements. Her fingers frantically clutched the wooden edge while she willed herself not to cry out at the unexpected swaying.

"You ever been on a horse n' cart ride afore, lass?" Mister Gordon drew her attention to him.

She wiped away more tears, willing them to be the last. "Not really," she gulped. "I don't think going to Kinross market would count?"

The carter's guffaw made her feel a little better. "Nay, lass. A long ride would mean a good bit more than four miles."

A good while later she was grateful for Mister Gordon's innocuous chatter. He seemed to be trying to banish her insecurity, if only a little, and was achieving it. Her previous contact with the man had solely been to give him parcels from the shop to take to various markets, or to receive others from him to add to the stock in the draper's shop. He wasn't a complete stranger, but she'd not known of his tendency to humour.

"You can have a wee nap, if you like, since it'll be a while before we reach the ferry at Burntisland. This is a heavy load I'm carting today and we'll not arrive much before mid-day."

Margaret stared at the carter. She'd studied the route to Edinburgh and had asked enough questions about how long each step of the journey would take.

"I'll not let you slide off, lass, but just don't you startle my horses with your snoring." Mister Gordon's smirking was infectious.

"I don't snore!" She grinned back, though she didn't have a clue if she snored, or not. "Anyhow, I'm far too excited to sleep."

She'd never been as far south before. The northern shores of the Firth of Forth were only places heard of, and crossing by ferry was an experience she'd yet to savour. Actually, being in a boat of any kind was going to be a first time for her.

To her great relief the day warmed up into a fine one, albeit a bit breezy around her cheeks when Mister Gordon maintained a steady clop along the main road that traversed the flat fields of Fife, after the hills near Loch Leven had been skirted around. The satin bow under her chin kept her new bonnet neatly in place safely enough.

She'd not expected the lovely new hat, or the cosy woollen cloak, that Peggy had acquired for her. Like her new dress, they were both of a much more mature style than she'd worn before, womanly rather than girlish, and they boosted her confidence. Growing up was not something she'd thought much of before. It was going to happen sometime but this journey, and her immediate future, had already started.

She didn't know how to be mature, yet she suddenly didn't feel a young girl any more either. Eleven years and seven months was far too young to think of herself as being grown up. Body changes had to happen first, but like the fledgling birds she viewed as they passed by the busy hedgerows, she had to become responsible for herself, whether she wanted to, or not. Jessie had already experienced a huge change of circumstances and so could she!

Excitement rippled.

What she was embarking on was going to be so different from what she was used to!

Her mother's extensive warnings took some thinking about as the time passed, field after field of flax and root vegetables colouring the landscape. Peggy had said she must use good judgement when meeting new people: that a pretty girl like she was had to take care not to get too close to any philandering wandering hands. Thinking of Peggy's words made her cheeks hot, so she took care to face away from Mister Gordon who was old enough to be a grandfather.

Her mother had never openly called her pretty before, not even when fussing over her Sunday best outfits.

Peggy had then confused her by saying she should be wary of the Reverend Leslie Duncan's brother; in case they were moulded from the same block. That made no sense, but it wasn't the time to ask further.

"That building you can see over there is the Old Inn at Cowdenbeath," Mister Gordon stated, breaking the silence as they clopped on southwards.

Her mother's phrase would take a bit of unravelling, but she set it aside for another day and listened to the carter.

"Now why would that place yonder be one you should know about?"

Mister Gordon was teasing her, but she had no answer. "I'm sure you're going to tell me."

"Well, lass. That old coaching inn is quite famous now because Queen Victoria deigned to stop there some years back, on her first ever visit to Scotland."

"Really?" She had read many things about the sovereign, though not that.

"Aye, indeed. On her way to her castle at Balmoral, she was." Mister Gordon's eyebrows rose in appreciation of his knowledge.

"I'll be sure not to forget that," she answered, and went on to relate some things about Queen Victoria and her love of Balmoral up in Aberdeenshire. The schoolmaster, Mister Anderson, had been at pains plenty of times to tell his pupils all he knew of the royal family.

As the horses clopped onwards, Mister Gordon pointed out places that he thought were interesting. He couldn't tell her everything about the history, nevertheless, he knew quite a lot about the present around them as the sun moved overhead across the sky.

"Are all those carts and waggons crossing on the ferry?"

It was astounding how busy the quayside was when they arrived at Burntisland close to noon, people scuttling around everywhere, making a tremendous racket. She imagined the long queues and constant movements of goods would mean an extensive halt to the good progress they'd made so far. The main road south to Burntisland had been in fine condition, according to the carter, since they'd not had much rain during the previous weeks.

"Nay, lass." Mister Gordon's answer was short as he manoeuvred his horses behind one particular line of carts. "All these carts around us will be emptied quickly and the contents loaded onto one of those big train waggons over there. And when I get my return load of raw materials settled, I'll be turning around to go back to the mill at Milnathort. These carts around me will likely be doing something similar, with the carters heading back to the yards they work from."

Margaret willed her panic to subside. She knew Mister Gordon would not be crossing the River Forth, but how was she going to cope by herself? The din around her was daunting.

"Do I have to get down now, Mister Gordon?" She tried really hard not to sound fearful but it was so difficult.

"Nay, lass, not yet. Once I get my goods offloaded, I'll see you over to the passenger ferry myself. I can't leave my load unattended in this queue. Don't you worry now. You'll be going over on a smaller boat than that great smoky, smelly train-ferry that's just arriving at the quay."

She felt the tiniest of reassuring pats on her gloved fingers.

"I'll try to find some nice kind lady who will see you right when you arrive on the far side."

Mister Gordon's voice got brisk again, jolting her out of her nervous dread.

"Now, while you're up high enough to see easily around you, watch the movement of those goods on the small carts in that line over there," he declared, pointing to a different queue from the one they'd joined.

Margaret concentrated on the place he was pointing to. The men who were working in the area were removing packages from carts and setting them down in organised stacks.

"Those goods don't linger there for long, lass. Do you see the next crews coming to pick them up almost immediately?"

"Yes," Margaret answered. "They're loading them into those big metal-wheeled waggons that are sitting on the rails alongside them."

She watched the men collect the wrapped-up bales, noting that they didn't dump them in the same waggons.

"So, although those piles look a bit messy when they're unloaded from the carts, they're actually arranged to go to particular destinations?" It was a wild guess. She expected to be completely wrong since she'd never read about the processes before.

"Aye, that's it. More or less correct. Those dockworkers you can hear bawling and shouting – at the biggest docks they name them stevedores – they're learning which piles to put them in, depending on which market they're going to."

She studied Mister Gordon's expression. "Does the same thing happen on the other side?"

The carter laughed. "I don't think so, lass, because they're already organised on this side. But how would I know? I only ever stop here."

"Oh." Margaret was sure from his grin that her naïve question hadn't offended him.

"Those full rail waggons are offloaded from the ferry on the far side of the Firth of Forth, at Granton, and then they're hitched to an engine which hauls the rail waggons to Edinburgh."

"Is it only goods waggons that go by train to Edinburgh?"

Another guffaw almost deafened her, Mister Gordon inching his horse forward as their queue diminished.

They had almost reached its beginning. "If you've got the money, I'm told, you can travel by train all the way into the middle of Edinburgh."

Margaret knew she wasn't doing that. The coins that were tucked away in the cloth bag in her pocket were for a ride on the public coach.

She'd never ridden a public coach before! What if she got on the wrong one?

Could that happen?

She didn't even know if there was more than one coach leaving Granton.

The next minutes passed in a blur, then it was time for Mister Gordon's cart to be unloaded. A swarm of grasping arms reached in behind Margaret for the wrapped bales from the mill. Fascinated by the speed the men worked at, she realised she was staring when some overly dramatic winks and lewd banter guffawed around her. She whipped her gaze away, a horrifying heat flooding her cheeks. Was this what her mother had warned her against? Peggy had told her that pretty girls always attracted wayward men like moths to a flame, and that she should never encourage them.

When the cart was completely emptied, a single click from Mister Gordon had his horses turning away and clopping over to another area. Once manoeuvred into an empty space, the carter turned to her.

"It's time, lass. Off you get."

Swallowing down her anxiety, looking all around to make sure the rude men were busy elsewhere, she grabbed her bag and followed him to another much less busy quayside. As they walked, the noise and bustle behind them diminished, making it a bit easier for Margaret to breathe normally as they got closer to the lapping waters of the Firth of Forth.

A much smaller queue had gathered near a short ramp that led down to the shingle where some rowing boats were tied up. She'd seen similar boats on Loch Leven, but they weren't big enough to be the ferry she'd be crossing on. She'd read that the passenger ferry could hold quite a lot of people. She assessed the waiting queue and reckoned she'd soon be across the Firth.

"Look there, Margaret." Mister Gordon nudged her elbow. "The passenger ferry is coming in now."

While she steeled herself to embrace the next new adventure, Mister Gordon waited no time before drumming up a conversation with a woman just ahead of her in the queue.

"The lass here needs to get on a coach to central Edinburgh. One that will drop her near St. Andrew Square. Are you able to help her, mistress?"

Margaret felt an assessing stare before a smile bracketed the woman's face.

"I can certainly do that, so long as she has her own fare for both the ferry, and for the Edinburgh coach."

Margaret dared to answer the woman, who looked about the same age as her mother. "I have the money to pay, mistress. My father asked around for the costs and that's exactly what he's given me."

"A wise father, indeed," the woman said before she turned to address Mister Gordon. "I take it you're not her father?"

The carter's laugh startled a few people around them. "Nay, I shuttle cartloads back and forth from the Milnathort Mill. But this young lady, Margaret Law, the daughter of one of our local drapers, is going to Edinburgh to help tutor a poorly, bedridden young lassie."

"You can call me Mistress Martin."

Margaret couldn't be sure, but she guessed either the carter's explanation, or her own neat and tidy appearance, impressed the woman sufficiently for the smile to seem a genuine one.

Her farewell of Mister Gordon wasn't as emotional as with her parents, but her thanks were heartfelt.

"Now, all that talk of me asking you to mind what was going on with the stevedores wasn't just so you'd learn new things about what men do, lass. It was meant to make you always be aware of your surroundings. Don't ever let anything untoward surprise you!"

The ferry ride on the small sailing boat was a whole new experience. Bobbing about on the Firth of Forth was vastly different from being on land, but Margaret managed to keep herself upright on the bench seating, glad the crossing took only a short time. Being able to see the receding coast of Fife and the approaching Lothian one was an experience to tuck away to savour later. Light cloud cover made the sky grey, the wind seeming much stronger than on land. She couldn't explain it, even to herself, but it seemed such a pivotal moment in her life.

She was going south to a new future, but would she ever go back north again?

"I cross over a few times every year to visit my family in Dunfermline." Mistress Martin's voice was whipped away by the cross winds. "Sometimes the weather is really poor and the crossing is very unpleasant, though today is not so bad. Not bad at all. You get used to the rocking and rolling."

Margaret's hands gripped tight to the bench she was sitting on, her bag of extra clothing nestled between her feet which she kept planted as steady as she could. Nodding back, she was too scared to lift a hand to wipe away the occasional salty spit thrown up from the waves. She wasn't sure if she wanted to know what a bad crossing was like, but there was no reason to disbelieve anything her companion said as the woman described the scenery and where the ferry was aiming for.

Margaret gaped around her, after having disembarked on the shore at Granton, her balance still a bit unsteady as she tottered away up the shingle following those passengers in front of her. Once again, there was a lot more noise and bustle along from where the passenger ferry beached, but thankfully only a few coaches sat nearby. Taking a deep breath, she prepared herself for yet another stage in her whole new adventure. She was well-used to seeing the mail coaches as they thundered down South Street towards Kinross having picked up passengers in Milnathort, but she'd never ever ridden in any kind of coach. She followed Mistress Martin as the woman headed towards a particular coach in the huddle of conveyances lined up near the quayside. It wasn't the newest-looking one, but it didn't look as though ready to collapse into firewood either.

"Can you set this young lady down on Princes Street, near St. Andrew Square?" Mistress Martin called up to the driver.

"That I can, mistress. You, too? Although it'll be a bit of a squash. It's already near full inside."

Mistress Martin's laugh was quite amused. "Nay, not such a posh destination for me. My coach will set me down near Tollcross!"

Margaret couldn't help but show her dismay as she stared at the woman alongside. "You aren't getting on the same one as me?"

Mistress Martin's head shook, her smile wide.

"This coach here will go along to the central streets of Edinburgh where you need to go, lass. Mine heads off in a different direction from yours once we get near the city. But don't you worry. The coachman will make sure to let you off at the correct spot."

Margaret gulped. What if he forgot she was inside?

Mistress Martin seemed to sense her distress. "Will you show the driver the money your father gave you for your coach fare, lass?"

Having fumbled out the last few coins in her cloth purse, Margaret held them flat.

The coachman looked down at her hand. "Aye, that'll get you an inside seat, but as you can see, I'm already almost full. Though, if you want to settle up here beside me on the outside, you'll save yourself a penny or two. It won't be that comfortable, but you'll not be squashed, either."

"Oh, thank you. I'd rather be outside, please." Margaret was less bothered about saving some pennies right at that moment. She was more concerned that the man wouldn't forget about her, and being inside with loads of people she didn't know was a terror she'd rather experience another day.

Thinking briefly about her mother's ominous warnings about judging the character of men that she encountered, she reckoned the coach driver would be far too busy handling the reins of his horses to be bothering her!

Becoming responsible for herself was a terrifying experience. She'd no option but to suppress the panic that gripped her insides and made her skin tingle all over. The shivers that were besetting her were not flooding her in a nice way, and they had nothing to do with the fact that the sky was darkening. She needed to replace the fear with something more like a thirst for adventure. Whatever that was? She'd only read about such in stories.

Was this another life stage still to be learned?

To embrace the future with adventure?

Chapter Fifteen

"Look at you!"

Jessie's cry came after opening the door that Margaret had rapped tentatively at with shaking, damp knuckles.

She hovered at the bottom of the set of stairs that led down from Albany Street to the basement level of the Duncan house in the New Town area of Edinburgh. Her cloth bag was clutched so tightly she feared her fingers wouldn't ever straighten out again. Her mother's dire warnings ringing in her head, she had dreaded it being snatched by some opportunistic thief as she had walked away from the coach to find her destination.

"Oh, Jessie, I'm really pleased that it was you who opened the door. I was scared I wouldn't find the correct house." Her sigh of relief was squashed by the huge hug she was enveloped in, Jessie not taking any account of the fact that she was like a drowned rat. "I'm dripping wet. You'll get soaked."

"I don't care." Jessie grinned, "Wet or dry, it's wonderful to see you again!"

Jessie's last letter had been quite explicit that she should not go to the main door from the street – making it clear that entrance was only for family and friends of Mister and Mistress Duncan. She, instead, was to open the gate in the railings and take the short flight of stairs that led down to the dunny door, the servant entrance. Jessie had written that she should wait patiently for someone to answer since the kitchen was often empty, the cook only there around meal times.

Jessie had not grown as tall as Margaret was, but was more than capable of giving a welcome cuddle.

"It's so good to see you, too," Margaret said.

They each relinquished the embrace and stepped back to regard each other.

Jessie's smile had never changed though her cheeks had broadened out a bit, with pretty pink tinges to skin that was flawless. Margaret was delighted to find that her best friend hadn't been starved since they'd last met. Small amounts of hair that were sneaking out from under Jessie's cap had darkened from pale-yellow to a very bonny golden shade. It was difficult to remember what Jessie's mother Ruth had been like, apart from her being a beautiful woman with probably the same colour of hair as Jessie now had, but her memories were of Ruth having arresting deep-brown eyes. The eyes that were currently smiling back at her were a stunning warm blue that Margaret definitely remembered.

"What are we doing still staring at each other? Come in, come in," Jessie urged, her laughter ringing out. "I need to take you straight up to Mistress Duncan, but we'll get your wet cloak off first and hang it up."

Margaret looked around as she stepped inside, Jessie quickly closing the door behind her to keep out the vicious windy draughts. On both sides of the corridor there were wide wooden battens set high up on the wall below a long shelf, most of the brass hooks on them currently filled with various outdoor clothes. The ones nearest the outside door were draped with coats and shawls of poorer quality. Those hanging further along the corridor were clearly not the outdoor clothes of servants.

Undoing the tape at her neck, she handed over the dark green woollen cloak that her mother had acquired for her. It wasn't new, and had a few good mends in it, but Peggy had declared it was long enough to do her for a few more years of growth. It had been really appreciated during the last hour of her travel, when

116

lowering clouds darkened the skies and rain had pelted down as soon as they'd reached the outskirts of the city. By the time the coach driver had set her down at St. Andrew Square, she was absolutely soaking-drookit from being seated on the driver's bench.

Jessie moved a couple of garments to free a space nearest the door where she deftly hung up Margaret's sopping cloak that now reeked of wet wool. Underneath, there were coir doormats to absorb the drips and wet footwear.

"Give those wet boots of yours a good wipe on that mat there, or both Kate and the Mistress will have your hide. And mine, too. Leave your dripping bag there, as well." Jessie laughed, a wagging finger pointing to the mat to be used.

Jessie then led the way along the dim, wood-panelled corridor that had numerous doors leading from it. "We'll just find you a cloth first, to wipe the drips from your chin before you go up the stairs."

The room Jessie led her into was clearly the kitchen – a room that was a good size but which was chock-full of kitchen equipment. Having accepted the cloth that Jessie whisked free from a chair-back, Margaret used it to dry her face and hands.

"Later on, you can tell me of your adventures while getting here but, right now, Mistress Duncan is expecting you."

That was puzzling. "How can she know I've arrived?" Margaret shook out the piece of material and draped it on the same chair that it had come from.

"I saw you from the upstairs parlour window." Jessie urged her into the downstairs corridor. "I knew it was you when you lifted back your hood to peer at the house number. You haven't changed much from the beauty who was my best friend in Milnathort, apart from you now being as tall as a bean pole! Mistress Duncan told me to fetch you after she heard my excited gasp."

Margaret followed Jessie up two flights of wooden stairs and along a short passageway, the walls of which had dark wood-panelling from floor level to a dado rail set at her chest level.

Above the dado rail, her gaze was snared by a fascinating pale yellow, flowery wallpaper which brightened the whole corridor. At one of the closed doors, her friend halted and rapped twice with the knuckles of her right hand.

Jessie whispered, "Tap twice, just twice, for entry to a room and then wait. When you are inside, only say yes or no in answer to a question. The Mistress is quite abrupt with the staff."

"Enter!"

It was surprising when Jessie's upturned palm indicated Margaret should wait where she was. Jessie opened the door and stood no more than a step inside the room.

"What is it, Jessie?"

Jessie's voice was clear, if detached. "Margaret Law is here."

"That will be all, Jessie. Get back down to your kitchen duties."

Margaret heard no mention of a thank you from the woman. Jessie whirled around, flashed her a silly grin since her back was to the woman within, then stepped aside so that Margaret could enter the room. There were fearful flutters at the bottom of her stomach when the door closed behind her friend, suddenly terrified of what her future might bring.

"Come over here! Stand beside me, girl, so that I can see what Jessie has recommended."

Margaret assumed the person speaking so imperiously had to be Mistress Duncan, since there were no other adults present. She did as bid, trying not to gawp at the colourful elegance of the large room. Her boots made a crisp clopping over the highly-polished floorboard edge before she stepped across an expensive colourful rug that protected the central space.

The woman, seated in a striking button-backed armchair near one of the tall windows, continued in the same abrupt tone. "Jessie speaks highly of you, although I know full-well that it has been a long time since she has set eyes on you."

The slight pause made Margaret sure that it was a prompt for her to say something, though the woman's expression held a strong note of disdain. Talking about her friendship with Jessie didn't seem appropriate.

"Good afternoon, Mistress Duncan." When silence continued, she ventured a little more, though her smile was restrained. "I'm very pleased to be here."

Mistress Duncan ignored her comment and looked down at the girl who reclined on the daybed that lay next to her. "This is my daughter, Rachel."

Not even a hint of fondness bracketed the woman's expression.

Margaret smiled down at the young girl whose stunningly blue eyes flared with interest though the girl's general appearance was pale. "Good afternoon, Rachel."

"Good afternoon." The tentative reply was barely a whisper.

"You will have time to get acquainted with Rachel soon," Mistress Duncan declared as she rose up to her feet, her hands pushing against the light beige upholstered chair arms. "But for the moment, you will follow me."

Though desperate to absorb more of the fascinating room, Margaret watched the woman choose a book from a bookcase under the window before striding towards the door. Having sent Rachel another smile, Margaret traipsed after Mistress Duncan out of the parlour, across the passage and into a room which had to be their dining room. A highly-polished walnut table dominated the central space with what, at first glance, looked to be a dozen chairs set around it. Waist-high walnut sideboards lay along two sides of the moss-green papered walls, the surfaces of the furniture dotted with pieces of floral china that looked too large to be encased below. An ornate cast-iron fireplace took up most of the far wall, the tiling surrounding the chimney breast of a shade and pattern which matched the wallcoverings.

Margaret stood attentively, just inside the open door, while Mistress Duncan seated herself at the nearest chair and set the book down on the table. After peering over Margaret's shoulder, the woman's frosty face became even more hostile when Mistress Duncan realised that the parlour door was fully open.

"Close the door!" The tone brooked no alternatives.

Doing as bid, Margaret then turned back to her interrogator.

"I know that Jessie has been writing to you, so I am sure that she will have explained some of Rachel's situation. I have seen your letters which means I know that you write reasonably well, and your penmanship passes muster."

Margaret was almost shocked into making a reply. Her letters were for Jessie to read, not for anyone else!

The dreadful woman droned on. "You should know now that it is my husband who is the one who has decided that Rachel needs to continue her education. I fail to see why, since the doctors we have consulted give no indications that she can ever lead a normal life. But since he insists, I therefore have particular requirements for the person filling this post."

Margaret wasn't sure what Mistress Duncan could mean. The woman was so cold and calculating when speaking of her own daughter. However, she hoped her expression didn't show any of her uncertainties.

"You already know that the successful candidate will continue with Rachel's education. She had barely started her schooling when this disaster descended upon us. I would teach her the basics myself, but I have her little sister Elspeth to look after every day."

Margaret bent her head slightly in acknowledgement, her gaze fixed on the woman whom she had hoped would be her employer, though now she wasn't so sure she could work for such an unfeeling woman. She also wondered where little Elspeth was, because the child was not in the parlour.

Mistress Duncan continued; her fern-green eyes brittle. "Since Rachel tires very easily, her lessons across in the parlour will need to be much shorter than in a normal school classroom. I have absolutely no intention of paying for a tutor to be idle in between those teaching times. As such, I will expect other household tasks to be undertaken during Rachel's naps. Is that understood by you?"

Margaret bit down a huge wave of disappointment. Had she come all the way to Edinburgh to do the kind of skivvy job that her father had sought to prevent her from doing? Though, what alternative did she have but to agree to the conditions? The travel to get to Edinburgh had been long, and she had no intention of going back to Milnathort to work in a mill.

"I understand," she answered in as steady a voice as she could manage, banishing the crushing apprehension.

"Good. See that you do. Also know that you are here on a trial basis for one month. During this period, you will not be paid but you will be provided with a bed and two cooked meals per day. Our cook, Mistress Abernethy, does not have a live-in position but she feeds our staff when she is on duty in the kitchen preparing the family meals three times a day. If, at the end of the month, you prove to be suitable – and naturally if Rachel enjoys her lessons with you – we will then discuss an annual remuneration."

What could she answer? Jessie had been unable to share any of these conditions in her letter, but staying in

Milnathort was likely to be much worse. Margaret wasn't sure right that moment if Mistress Duncan was hoping, or even expecting, that Rachel would dislike her and the tutoring.

Her mind whirled. It seemed that time was standing still as she stared at the callous woman who expected an answer from her. And yet, as Jessie had cautioned, she couldn't be too effusive in response to this awful person.

The lease for the shop in Milnathort was due to change hands within the month, it being in a lucrative location, but her father would make very little profit from selling off his remaining stock to the new draper. William and Peggy were looking for a house to rent, but housing in Milnathort was in short supply.

A conversation from the previous evening flashed through her mind.

'Your father contacted your uncle when he realised our situation was so bad," her mother had said. *"James' reply came this morning. There might be an opening for your father to return to do tailoring for him.'*

Her father's elder brother lived in the town of Perth, but she'd barely seen Uncle James during the years of her growing up. Contact was infrequent – a brief New Year greeting, or information of some distant relative having died. A letter had come the previous year when James' wife had died giving birth to their fourth child. The baby had also been poorly and had slipped into death within days of its mother. William had gone off to the funeral, leaving Peggy to run the shop on her own.

On her mother's side, there were a few Wylie relatives in Milnathort, but none of them could offer any of them a bed. Banishing her panicked thoughts, Margaret prayed that her reply would sound positive, and wasn't displaying her inner fears.

"Thank you, Mistress Duncan."

"My husband and I have talked about how you should be named in the household. Were you a proper governess there would be no issue over you being called Miss Law. You are not a governess, and as you are still so young, you will be addressed by your first name, similar to Jessie and our housemaid, Kate. However, Mistress Abernethy, our cook, is always referred to by her title. Is that clear?"

"Yes, Mistress Duncan."

Margaret was definitely sure that she wasn't going to like her employer very much. She felt the displeasure on Mistress Duncan's face right down to her boots. She had only been in the woman's company for a few minutes, yet it seemed her new employer wasn't pleased about anything. And seemingly not herself.

Reeling from the way the interview was being conducted, she watched the woman thrust the book in her direction.

"I need to judge your competence in reading. Pick a page, any page, and begin."

Margaret accepted the book, hoping her shaking fingers weren't visible. Choosing a page at random she began at the first full paragraph. She had read no more than the rest of the page when the woman's voice intruded.

"That will be sufficient. I have heard enough. Give me the book." Mistress Duncan's hand waved at Margaret in an irritated fashion.

Now feeling nauseated by the awful interlude, Margaret handed it back.

"Since you have arrived so late this afternoon, your official tutoring duties will not begin till eight a.m. tomorrow. However, after Cook feeds you this evening, you will report to me in the ground-floor drawing room for a household task."

Margaret watched Mistress Duncan rise from the chair, not sure what to do next since the information given so far was pretty scant. Nevertheless, she found that her potential employer was not finished. The woman fussed around, somewhat nervously, with the lace shawl that covered her shoulders, though Mistress Duncan's nose was imperiously stuck up in the air

"Since Rachel's accident, and her need for a peaceful location, I am mostly to be found in the drawing room during the day with Elspeth and her other siblings. And, of course, with Mister Duncan when he is home of an evening."

Margaret noted the emphasis the woman placed on Rachel's need for a peaceful place to spend her day but couldn't warm to the brittle way it was explained. It sounded as though the woman was deliberately segregating the poor little girl from the rest of the family.

"Now, go and find Jessie in the kitchen. Tell her I will stay with Rachel till she comes up with my daughter's food. Jessie will introduce you to Cook, who should be there by now. You will help Cook in any way you can, And later, when Kate is free, she will show you where you will sleep."

"Yes, Mistress Duncan."

As an afterthought Mistress Duncan added, "I take it that you have brought at least one change of clothes with you to Edinburgh?"

"Yes, Mistress Duncan. Jessie asked me to leave my bag near the dunny door since it's soaking wet." She thought that was the name that Jessie had used; her prospective employer's approving nod sufficient before the woman waved a dismissal with the flick of a finger.

Turning away from the dining room, Margaret felt dazed, which had nothing to do with the light-headedness she was experiencing due to lack of food. The oats her mother had prepared for her, and the small piece of bread and chunk of cheese she'd been given for a mid-day snack in Burntisland, were a distant memory.

She wondered what constituted *'staying with Rachel'*. The woman had bid her close the door of the dining room to cut off all possible conversation, during which time the poor wee thing on the daybed was all alone..

Chapter Sixteen

The first evening in Edinburgh was exhilarating but also so strange. Used to being in a house with only her mother and father, Margaret was now in a household of many people. Jessie had said that she was well-familiar with hearing footsteps along corridors and on stairs, but it was all too new for Margaret. Neither was she used to being in a house with so many rooms, only a few of which she was allowed to enter with permission.

She had spent a short time getting to know Rachel during the early evening, while the Duncan parents were having dinner, though as instructed by Mistress Duncan no actual tutoring had been started. She had found Rachel to be delightfully shy with her answers, but she was sure that was just the newness of the situation. There was a hopeful twinkle in the girl's expression when she had explained about her background schooling in Milnathort and that becoming a teacher had been her ambition till recent events had changed that plan.

One of the few unprompted responses from Rachel had been heartrending, though she was sure it hadn't been the little girl's intent.

"Will you do the proper training to become a teacher when you're no longer tutoring me?"

"Who knows what the future will bring?" Margaret had smiled a difficult smile, for the innocent question was laced with potentially darker tones. "Perhaps I will love tutoring you so much I will never ever want to stop doing the job."

Rachel, it seemed, had no idea that a permanent tutoring future depended on the whim of Mistress Duncan.

Much later that first evening, with Jessie as her only companion in the kitchen and with the rare treat of a bedtime drink of warm milk sprinkled with nutmeg cradled in her hand, she broached a tentative subject. Her words were almost a whisper in case someone entered and heard her.

"Mistress Duncan seems a bit uncaring of her invalid daughter."

She looked intently at Jessie's expression to gauge whether she was being too judgemental too quickly. Her own mother, Peggy, had never been a warm person to her, but surely an accident to a young child should make a mother even more caring afterwards?

"Does Mistress Duncan deliberately keep little Elspeth and the other siblings away from Rachel all day long?"

"Ah!" Jessie's tones were also hushed, her gaze sliding upwards in reflection. A huge sigh escaped followed by a rapid eye-blinking. "The Mistress can be a difficult woman to understand."

Margaret waited patiently till Jessie's focus returned to her, though when it did, she almost regretted her question. Jessie's expression was bleak. The hurt of a wounded creature was fleeting, but she caught it.

After a brief, pain-repressed inhaled smirk, Jessie's customary expression returned. Margaret thought her friend still seemed a mite philosophical, yet was back to the positive nature she had experience of.

"When I first came here, the Mistress barely spoke to me, and when she deigned to, she wouldn't look me directly in the eye. At first, I thought she truly disliked me. But then I realised it's more that she's just very abrasive with a lot of people, though she's particularly uncomfortable when anywhere near me."

Margaret felt her own eyes stretch at the information. "But you get on well with everybody!"

Jessie grinned above the rim of her cup, but then her humour slipped as though remembering the subject of their conversation.

"I can't be sure, Margaret. It's just a hunch, but I think the Mistress bears a tremendous guilt over the condition that Rachel's in now."

Margaret was intrigued. It seemed gossipy to probe, but knowing as much as possible about the situation would help her to tutor Rachel.

"Why would that be?"

Jessie set down her empty cup. "The Mistress was with Rachel when the accident happened up near Edinburgh Castle. Mistress Duncan says she was distracted by someone she knew calling her name from across the street, and wasn't watching Rachel carefully enough when the disaster occurred."

"I don't think you ever wrote in your letters exactly what did happen."

"They were passing the top of a particularly steep staircase that flanks the side of the castle wall and leads right down to Johnstone Terrace." Jessie stopped as though it was difficult to even talk, her bottom lip trembling.

Margaret squeezed her friend's fingers in sympathy. "Go on."

"Rachel, being a curious child, was on the top step looking down when the Mistress bawled at her to move away from the edge, and to come over to where she was talking the time of day with the friend. Rachel was startled, since her mother didn't normally shout so angrily, and it made her overbalance. She tumbled down and down, bumping off lots of the steps to land more than half way down. Old Edinburgh has many flights of steep stairs but those ones are probably the steepest."

"Oh, that was awful."

Margaret hardly knew what else to say, yet it still didn't explain everything. "I can imagine why Mistress Duncan would feel guilty, though why keep Elspeth and Rachel apart so much? I don't really understand that."

Jessie shook her head, a degree of frustration marring her usually cheery features. "Elspeth is a spoiled, very active little brat who demands her mother's attention all the time. The Mistress dotes on her youngest child, even though Elspeth clearly has her running ragged. Unfortunately, Helen Duncan can't seem to manage to cope with both Rachel and Elspeth at the same time. Hence the upstairs downstairs situations. I actually think, sometimes, it is better for Elspeth to give Rachel some peace and quiet."

Margaret thought carefully before asking her next question. "But if Mistress Duncan is down in the Drawing Room with Elspeth, who has been looking after Rachel most of the time?"

"Who do you think?" Jessie's laugh was cynical. "And don't dare suggest it might be the high-and-mighty eldest daughter, Victoria."

"But how can you do your kitchen jobs and also look after Rachel? I thought you meant in your letter that you had to break off from skivvying to help with Rachel's feeding and cleaning?"

The look Jessie gave her was priceless.

"So, you've also had to keep the poor little thing amused when she's not napping?"

Jessie shrugged, now looking resigned. Though, perhaps 'accepting' was a better term.

Margaret nodded a few times, her lips pursing. "Let me guess. When Rachel naps you have to catch up with what you've not yet managed to do in the scullery, and in the kitchen?"

The next laugh from Jessie was more of the bitter kind. "Why do you think the Mistress agreed so quickly to you coming here?"

She hazarded a guess. "Mistress Abernethy has been complaining?"

A series of nods was followed by, "Yes. Exactly. Also, the fact that the Mistress has no idea of how to entertain her invalid daughter. She can barely tolerate my presence, but her speaking to Rachel and finding things for them to do together is impossible. She has no idea what to say to her own sick child."

Something suddenly occurred to Margaret. "Where does Kate fit in with all this? Could she not have been looking after Rachel sometimes?"

Again, Jessie's laugh was a snort.

"Kate has a huge amount of work to do. She does all the house cleaning and most of the laundry."

Margaret watched Jessie gather up the cups to take them to the scullery, and noted the sadness in her friend's gaze.

"There's been quite a bit more of that since Rachel's accident."

Having mentioned Mistress Duncan's stipulations to Jessie already, she was beginning to wonder what exactly she had come to do at the Duncan house.

"Do either you, or Kate, ever have time off during the day?"

Jessie answered from the scullery doorway. "Supposedly, yes, we are due an hour off. Sometimes in the afternoon we can snatch it, if we avoid being anywhere near the drawing room."

While waiting for Jessie to return Margaret pondered that.

"Do you mean Kate is sometimes roped in to look after Elspeth?"

On her return, Jessie's manner was brisk. "It's time for bed."

"Not yet. Tell me more." Margaret made sure her expression meant she was serious about learning what she needed to know.

Jessie huffed and folded her arms over her now developing bosom. "Sometimes Victoria helps entertain the little madam, or even David when he emerges from his bedroom. That's when David isn't studying this or that, and Victoria isn't doing her piano lessons. The piano used to be up in the parlour, but that was the first change to that room after Rachel's accident. And what a palaver it was to get it moved downstairs!"

Margaret was puzzled. "Why could the piano not be played up in the parlour?"

Jessie's expression was comical and very entertaining when she mimicked Victoria's whiny voice, Margaret having only barely been introduced to the eldest Duncan sister during the early evening. *Mama! I can't possibly do my piano exercises with Rachel in the room. I'd be constantly looking over my shoulder to see if she's being disturbed by me and not sleeping!*

Margaret pursed her lips. "Do they expect Rachel to be asleep all day long?"

Jessie nodded. "Something like that. Silent. Out of sight out of mind. Let's just say, the Mistress lets me deal with Rachel up in the parlour, but an extreme crisis has to have occurred if she summons me to look after her precious Elspeth down in the drawing room."

As requested, Margaret had attended Mistress Duncan in the drawing room after she had eaten a meal. The ground-floor drawing room was highly impressive with huge leafy plants dotted here and there around the space. The parlour, she now realised, was directly above.

An after-thought seemed to occur to Jessie as she ushered Margaret out of the kitchen and towards the bedroom she'd been given. "The Mistress used to be found up in the parlour a lot of the time during the day before Rachel's accident, the drawing room being only used for entertaining visitors."

"I see," Margaret answered, though she wasn't entirely sure since she didn't know how anyone would

130

want to visit the awful woman who was her prospective employer.

"The Mistress now has no bolt-hole to escape to when Elspeth gets a bit overmuch. And, as you can imagine, that's not going down well with the Mistress' nerves, which are a terrible bother, I'll have you know! Though to be fair, it's Cook and Kate who have to listen to the whines, since she steers well clear of me."

Jessie's mood suddenly brightened. Keeping her tones low, she mimicked her employer. *"My nerves! You have no idea how much I am suffering!"*

Margaret couldn't help her giggles.

Jessie's sudden hug was unexpected but so welcome. "Sleep well. I'll see you in the morning!"

There was a lot to think about before Margaret fell asleep that first night.

Though in a strange environment, with many new things to learn about the Duncan household, the following days passed quickly.

Margaret settled into the role she was to play. True to her word, when she wasn't getting to know her little charge and establishing their teaching schedules, Mistress Duncan found plenty of other tasks to occupy the remainder of her day. Many were sewing or mending tasks, though also general help if Kate needed it for cleaning the parlour, or the other public rooms, when Rachel was napping on her daybed. Thankfully, Margaret had not yet been tasked with looking after Elspeth, though she admitted a curiosity about the youngest child, whom she could often hear from above. Elspeth was definitely not a quiet child when at play.

She found the evenings were nothing like as boring as the repetitive sewing and knitting tasks had been back in Milnathort, though there was rarely time for leisure after Rachel was in her bedroom and ready for sleep, routinely around eight o'clock in the evening.

The bed she'd been given in the downstairs servants' area, she soon learned, was in what had once been a storeroom near the back door but it had been cleared out for her use. She settled in to it, finding it not so much different in size from her own small bedroom above the shop in Milnathort.

It lacked the dressing table and stool that she'd used for writing letters to Jessie, and it only had a tiny window high up on the wall that allowed some light in from the basement-level passageway that led to back yard at the rear of the property, but she determined to get accustomed to that in time. Apart from the bed, which wasn't as comfortable as her own had been in Milnathort, the only other furniture was a basic wooden washstand near the door. It had one drawer below the surface and an old, chipped, floral-bedecked china basin and ewer on top. A rack to one side of the washstand had her one and only towel draped over it. The mirror that sat propped up behind the china bowl was so old there wasn't much silvering left on it, and she needed to bend a lot to see her face in it, but it was better than nothing at all. The chamber pot under her bed was ancient, but was neither worse nor better than what she was used to.

After a couple of weeks had passed, Margaret was in the kitchen having a welcome afternoon break when Jessie breezed in.

"I've got wonderful news!"

Margaret thought her friend looked like the proverbial cat that had licked the cream. "And…?" she prompted unable to resist returning Jessie's smiles.

"I'm so happy!" Jessie was almost beside herself with glee.

She couldn't help her staring. "What…?"

"Close your eyes and keep them closed till I tell you to open them!" Jessie ordered.

Bemused, Margaret did as bid.

She then felt Jessie grab hold of her hand before she was dragged from the kitchen, coming to a halt a few steps later. The sound of a door being opened with a flourish came to her ears.

"Now you can look!"

Inside what she realised was her own room, an extra truckle bed had been squeezed in.

"As from now, I'm officially sharing this room with you!"

Almost as excited as Jessie about the new development, Margaret couldn't help but think of what the changes would mean.

"Will Kate be upset that you're no longer going to be sharing with her?"

Jessie's mirth was spilling over.

"Not at all. Kate's delighted to have her own room after having to share for so long, with me and with the scullery maid before I came here. Kate turned eighteen months ago, and is quite taken with the idea of being alone, or perhaps, not so very alone sometimes!"

The fluttering eyelash movements that followed were blatant. It took Margaret a moment to process it. Surely, Jessie couldn't mean that Kate would entertain people in her room?

Could Jessie possibly mean Tom the coachman? Who was clearly very taken with Kate?

Keeping her naughty thoughts to herself, Margaret didn't actually think Kate was brave enough to invite Tom, or any other man, to her room. Even if the visit was entirely innocent, it would be such a huge scandal.

Something disturbing occurred to her. "Did the Mistress move you out because she's employing another housemaid?"

Jessie plonked herself down onto the newly-placed bed. "Ha! That will be the day! She's nearly had an apoplexy already, knowing she has to pay you, if she makes your job permanent."

Jessie's laughter was so infectious that Margret followed suit, flopping down onto her own bed.

That night, before they went to sleep, catching up with their lives during the previous few years was more thorough than they had managed during the past weeks.

Although Margaret's daily routine with Rachel was mostly becoming established during those first weeks, her duties becoming clearer, there were a few incidents that intrigued, yet disturbed, her more than others. There was one occasion, in particular, that she had no idea what to do about when she recalled the conversation.

She'd been sent to the dining room to polish the silverware, since guests – colleagues of Mister Duncan – were expected for dinner the following evening. Kate was busy with laundering the table linens so Margaret had been tasked with the polishing job, a repetitive one though not arduous. As she rubbed and rubbed the cloth over one of the heavy silver knives, she was thinking about what she'd write in a letter to her parents, to update them on her situation. She'd sent a brief note after her arrival, but at that point she really had little more to add than she'd arrived safely. Now she had lots to relate.

She'd turned her head away, avoiding the stink of the bicarbonate cleaning paste that Kate had given her, a much different mix from the one her mother used. Peggy's paste had almost no smell, but this one must have had something like vinegar, or much worse, added to it, and she had no desire to really know what had turned it so pungent.

The murmuring that she'd been hearing coming from the parlour had grown in intensity. Rachel had been settled in her bedroom some time before, so the conversation wasn't revolving around her.

"Helen! You know I agreed to find housing and employment for the girl, years ago, for my brother's sake, but what you ask of me now cannot be done. Do not ever raise this matter again, for it is impossible to acknowledge the situation without his permission, and I do not have it."

Mistress Duncan's reply had indicated her extreme level of anxiety, more than was usual. During the last couple of weeks, Margaret had already worked out that was quite a lot. Jessie might have mocked the Mistress' nerves when she'd first arrived at Albany Street, but she'd come to realise that Helen Duncan definitely did have what her mother Peggy would term a nervous, fidgety disposition.

"The girl's parentage is becoming more and more evident as each day dawns, Stewart. Her features do not lie. Why cannot your brother see that!"

"My brother rarely sets foot in Edinburgh, as you well know. How would he see it?"

"Then make him come here more frequently. Or tell him to do something about her himself! She cannot remain in her present ignominious position."

Margaret had thought Mistress Duncan's volume would mean even passers-by in the street below would hear her furious words.

"My integrity will not allow me to abandon the girl, but I also cannot do more to acknowledge her. Why can you not appreciate that?"

Margaret had gulped. Mister Duncan had been so angry and that wasn't how she normally found him on his daily, if very brief, visit to the parlour to see Rachel. Regardless of his antagonism, it had seemed that Mistress Duncan was unable to let the conversation go.

"Well, it's always been clear that your brother has never had a single shred of integrity. And don't tell me that his standing in his own community prevents him from doing more for the girl. You've protected your feckless brother far too many times, Stewart. It should not be our responsibility. I can hardly bear to look upon the girl knowing her true circumstances."

"If this is about the money that he pays for her keep, which you say is a paltry sum, Helen, then I am in a position now to add a little more each month."

Margaret hadn't dared to move a muscle, since she'd suspected that Mistress Duncan had stomped to the open parlour door, clearly not expecting any of the servants to be on that floor.

"Why can't you understand that this is nothing to do with the 'hush' money he is paying! Keeping this secret makes us just as culpable as he is, and I cannot bear to live the lie."

The slamming of the parlour door, and the determined clip of Mistress Duncan's feet along to her bedroom, had ended the explosive conversation. Margaret had only begun to breathe again after she'd heard Mister Duncan leave the parlour and make his way downstairs.

She'd wondered who on earth they could be talking about. Since her arrival in Albany Street, she'd learned that the Reverend Leslie Duncan of Milnathort wasn't her employer's only brother, so Leslie might not be the man they were referring to.

Unbidden, her mother's dire warnings of not trusting men with smooth tongues had come to mind. Peggy had never met Mister Stewart Duncan, but she'd always shown little respect for the Reverend Leslie Duncan. Could a third brother be similar in nature to the Reverend Duncan?

Chapter Seventeen

July 1851

A few evenings short of the trial period, Jessie staggered into their room and dramatically plopped down onto her narrow cot, her feet still firmly on the floor though her body was prostrate. A huge sigh escaped.

"Oh, what a day!"

Margaret set down her book on the floor. "You need to be allowed to rest more than you are. You're exhausted, Jessie. They work you far too hard."

Jessie's worn-out laugh trilled out. "Honestly, I'm not really that tired. If my feet didn't hurt so much, it would be fine."

The boots were relatively new, and fitted her quite well compared to those she had worn when she was little, but Jessie rarely got to sit down. Carefully undoing the laces of both boots, Margaret slid them from her friend's feet and laid them aside.

"What were you needed for this time?"

"Don't sound so peeved, my friend, but thanks for removing them. I'd probably have slumped over onto my nose untying my laces."

How Jessie could always find humour in her situations was difficult to believe.

"Rachel's bedding got wet again." Jessie's eyes momentarily closed, a satisfied expression replacing the wincing one she'd been wearing on entry to the room. "Not her fault."

It just wasn't fair that Mistress Duncan used Jessie as a skivvy. "That woman needs to employ a live-in nurse! The girl's needs are all-day-long ones."

There was no need to name who she spoke of. Mistress Duncan only got worse in Margaret's opinion as she learned more of the family circumstances.

"Don't you say a thing, Margaret!" Jessie struggled her way onto the bedcover, her legs now straight out. "You need to be careful, or your job won't become a permanent one. You know how much she's still testing you."

"Well, it just isn't right what they expect you to do!"

She hotly defended her best friend, her feelings of injustice heightened by another conversation she'd recently overheard, though as before she'd not intended to eavesdrop. Words spoken clarified some of the earlier volatile conversation between the Duncan parents. Margaret now had a better idea of the person they were referring to, but the concept of what she had heard was so horrendous that she couldn't divulge anything till she was absolutely sure of all of the facts.

"I don't mind helping when Rachel needs cleaned, or turned in bed." Jessie's gaze pleaded, so Margaret retreated backwards to sit on her own cot, though they maintained eye contact. "Mistress Duncan is looking more and more for my help because she knows I'm competent at doing the necessaries. I had to do a lot of wiping, and changing of cloth pads and bed-linen, to help my granny before she died."

Margaret didn't know what to say so remained silent. Jessie looked as though she wanted to talk, remembering some of the bad times back in Milnathort, situations she herself had never had to help with since her parents were always fine and healthy.

"It's actually easier with Rachel, because she's much smaller than my granny was and less of a rickle of sensitive bones." Jessie adjusted her body even more comfortably and folded her arms behind her head on the low pillow. "Another thing is that although Rachel gets some awful bed sores, her skin being younger and softer means it doesn't weep and scab so much as Granny's did. It was really distressing when that happened. I felt so helpless."

"You were always the opposite, Jessie," Margaret confirmed quite vehemently. "You're the best person I know at helping people, but some folk need to show you more appreciation for what you do."

Jessie's weary voice drifted over. "Mistress Duncan is less awful to me when we're tending to Rachel."

"Really?" Margaret could hardly credit that. The woman was so snippy with everyone.

Except, when she pondered it, Mistress Duncan was always more circumspect when she came up to the parlour for some reason or other. Her words in front of Rachel were delivered in a different tone from when it was just the two of them.

The hygiene rituals were aspects of Rachel's care that Margaret had no experience of. She wasn't there to nurse, but then neither was Jessie supposed to be doing the tending that she did. Something occurred to her that she'd not yet considered.

"What happens if Rachel needs to be changed during the night? Did they send for you before I came here?"

Jessie half-sat-up on her elbows. "No. The Mistress does the overnight changing herself, if it's needed. Didn't you know that?"

Margaret shook her head, her shoulders rising accordingly.

"That's one reason why the Mistress is so short with everybody. She rarely gets caught up on her sleep, even though she swapped bedrooms with Robert."

"I'm not sure I understand."

"The ground-floor bedroom is the largest in the house, normally called the master bedroom. That's where Mister and Mistress Duncan slept before Rachel's accident, and as the elder son, Robert had the largest bedroom on the first floor."

"Ah! They did the swap to be nearer to Rachel, to tend to her when necessary. Now I understand." Margaret didn't know whether to feel ashamed or not, since her thoughts on Mistress Duncan were so poor.

Jessie's laugh tinkled. "Though, don't get me wrong. Even before Rachel's accident the Mistress was always crabby with her staff!"

"So, she doesn't just pick on you?" It was really important to know that answer.

"What?" Jessie's guffaw echoed around the room. "You think she only targets me? You've clearly not been here long enough."

Jessie rose to collect a book from the small pile that lay stacked on the floor between the beds. There was no table, but that hadn't stopped them from gathering a collection of materials to help with Jessie's reading and writing.

Since it was still the month of July, the daylight hadn't quite faded. Though the room was always dim, they didn't yet need an expensive candle to continue with some lessons started earlier that week.

After a short time listening to Jessie read, Margaret's declaration was heartfelt. "You really don't need me anymore, Jessie, for your reading. Though I do love to listen to you. Even when you've had a heavy day, your expressive delivery still manages to keep me... entertained."

"Entertained!" Jessie pretended to throw the book at her. "I would say I keep you awake. It's you who taught me to be animated."

After some giggling, Jessie's tone sobered a little. "I still need your help with my writing, though." She placed the book on the floor and lifted up a large slate and slate nib. After getting into a better position for doing the writing on her lap, she declared, "Give me some dictation."

"Dear Mistress Duncan…" Margaret loved inventing cheeky letters, though they were always erased as quickly as possible after correction, a benefit of using a slate. The problem with a slate, however, was still the limited space on it, but using the slate nib took up much less space than a piece of chalk would have done.

"Stop! You can't possibly say that." Jessie's giggling pleaded just into the second sentence. "As well as spelling practice this is supposed to help with my penmanship. I can't possibly write neatly when laughter shakes my hand so much."

Margaret grinned. "My actual letter of acceptance of a permanent position will be suitably concise, and exactly as subservient as Mistress Duncan will expect and approve of."

"Oh, Margaret," Jessie's trills ceased. "I haven't had so much fun for ages. I missed those grey-blue eyes of yours so much when I was first brought here. Sharing this room with you now is the best thing that has happened to me in years. You're my best friend ever."

Margaret seriously hoped that Jessie would have many even better times, though she agreed that it was much better fun being together than being the sole occupant of a bedroom.

"Well, even if Mistress Duncan pays you a pittance, you're getting free education from me."

Fending off the pillow attack with her forearms, Margaret collected it up and sent it back over the small space.

Jessie wasn't quite done. "If I don't get writing help from you, then David will help if I ask him."

Ah! The elusive David. In the more-than-three weeks she'd been in the household, she'd seen David face-to face precisely four times., and his rear only a few more.

"Does he always skulk around the house?"

141

Jessie sat up, adjusting the retrieved pillow against the wall for better comfort. "Not at all. David doesn't skulk. He's just shy."

"How is it that I've rarely seen him? He doesn't speak if he comes into the parlour and finds me with Rachel. He just mumbles something that resembles '*I'll come back later, Rachel.*' Does he dislike me?"

Jessie shook her head. "He's probably not even there to see Rachel. More likely that he's collecting a book. His nose is always in a book."

"Mmm." Realising the night darkness was setting in, Margaret rose from her cot and collected her nightdress from a peg on the door. Beginning to undo the buttons at the front of her dress, she was careful with her words. "Do you like David?"

Jessie stared at her before also rising to whip the nightdress off her own peg. "I like him as well as anyone else around here." Her white apron untied, it was shaken vigorously and held up to the remaining light to check it for stains. "Though, actually, when you make me think about it, I do like him better than some others in this house."

Margaret was finding the conversation so difficult. Guilt was eating at her, because she wasn't quite ready to divulge what was potentially a huge, disturbing secret.

"What was he like when he helped you write your letters to me?"

"Ah, that was quite awkward." Jessie removed her dark-grey dress, giving it a good shake before she routinely scrutinised it for any marks.

Margaret assumed that Jessie decided she was satisfied with it, since she watched Jessie hanging it on her peg.

"The first time I was at the kitchen table, after Mistress Abernethy had gone home for the day. The breakfast things for the following day left little room on the surface, but I'd made a little space to work at. I was staring at the almost empty sheet of paper, the ink pot and pen alongside it that I'd removed from Mistress Abernethy's shelf, when David walked in to get a cup of milk for little Elspeth who was being fussy about going to sleep. In my haste to stand up, I almost spilled the ink."

Working her way around Jessie, Margaret removed her hairbrush from the drawer of the wooden utility washstand that sat alongside the door. She sat back down on her bed, and undid her braids before brushing her waist-length, wavy, auburn tresses.

"When David noticed I'd only written *'Dear Margaret'* he asked if I was stuck over what to write. I told him I knew exactly what I wanted to write, but not how to write the words. Suffice to say, he collected the milk for his sister, delivered it and came back down to help me."

"That was very nice of him,"

"It was." Jessie, having stripped to her underclothes, poured some water from the chipped porcelain ewer that had been nestling inside the equally chipped basin which now provided washing water for both of them. In between wipes of her washcloth, she continued the conversation. "He gets embarrassed very easily, but he's kind and patient and nearly as good a teacher as you are."

"A fine recommendation."

"Anyhow, he said to let him know when I wanted more help with a next letter to you." Having completed her personal wash, Jessie picked up her birch twig from the side of the bowl and proceeded to scrape it around her teeth. "That was before they sent me to the Sessional School." When she'd finished her spitting out into the bowl, Jessie dumped the washing water into the ancient metal pail that now sat under the washstand, and rinsed the bowl with a trickle of fresh water.

"And did you ask?" Margaret thought she knew the answer as she rewound her hair into one thick braid, but clarification was good.

"Of course," Jessie grinned through the neck of her nightdress as she pulled it on. "Accepting help from him to write a letter quickly meant I had more time to do what I wanted, which was to continue to read the book he had given me."

She mulled over Jessie's answer. "It wasn't that you wanted to spend some time in his company because you like him a lot?"

Jessie's expression made her giggle.

"What? Are you asking me if I'm attracted to him?" Plopping down onto her own bed, Jessie's hairbrush was at the ready.

"I suppose I am." Margaret began to make her own night-time ablutions since the washstand was free, pouring some fresh water from the ewer into the empty basin.

Jessie snickered. "He's nice enough, Margaret, but not that nice. He just happens to be much more approachable than his snooty big brother Robert. I'm sure my taste will run to something other than either of the Duncan brothers when I go looking for a man."

Margaret raised her eyebrows encouragingly but stayed silent as she wiped herself down. Jessie was now what might be called a young woman, her monthly courses already having begun, much earlier than many girls of her age. It was hard not to wonder if her best friend was going through the other body changes Peggy had mentioned the night before she had left Milnathort.

Her mother had been so agitated about having the conversation that only afterwards did she realise that Peggy hadn't given her any proper details. Save that she had commented that body changes during the entry into womanhood also meant a different way of thinking about young men.

'You must avoid making the mistakes that I made,' Peggy had warned. *'Don't ever trust the feelings that might creep into your heart that make you think a man is*

144

the future husband for you, because those feelings will most likely be false!'

She remembered staring at Peggy, who seemed to be talking to her, yet was not talking to her at all, the wringing of her mother's fingers a fixation of her downbent focus.

'Don't ever rush into marriage, Margaret!' Peggy's agitation had increased even further, her tones low and menacing to a growl. *'And don't believe that all marriages are ones that the Good Lord approves of, no matter how pious and devout that people seem.'*

Peggy had then paced around so much that Margaret had felt dizzy, yet was frozen in her seat.

'Some men...' Her mother's voice was breaking before Peggy had made a hasty retreat out of the kitchen, her words lingering behind her. *'...make useless, impotent husbands.'*

Margaret mentally shook herself. Peggy's little talk before she had left Milnathort had left her with too many unanswered questions, though she had ensured she'd found out the meaning of impotent which left her with an abundance of curiosity. She clawed back her attention to what Jessie was currently saying.

Jessie's eyes crinkled, her expression rueful. "I'd like to say Robert is pleasant, but it would be a downright lie. Robert is a snob, just like his mother." Jessie aped Mistress Duncan's voice. She was so expert at mimicking her employer. *'One only speaks to one's servants to give them orders.'*

The smile on Margaret's face dipped quickly. "When you were sent away from Milnathort, after your granny died, did you know what was going to happen to you? Were you scared?"

"Scared?" Jessie scoffed. "I was terrified. I was put on a cart like you, though it wasn't Mister Gordon's. I didn't know the carter that the Reverend Duncan took me to."

Margaret warred between curiosity and shock.

"The Free Kirk minister put you on the cart?"

"Yes, he did. The man who could never look at me without a scowl on his face, put me on the brewery dray." Jessie's grin was peculiar, her derision evident.

"What did the Reverend Duncan tell you was about to happen?"

"The minister told me that, as an orphan, I couldn't stay in Milnathort. He said that he'd arranged for me to go to work in Edinburgh for a lady that he'd heard was looking for a kitchen skivvy. The Reverend Duncan then gave the carter the coins for my ferry fare and told me to look out for someone who would be there to pick me up at the other side of the Firth of Forth."

"That was it?" Margaret's horror was even more acute.

Jessie was staring at the ceiling, her expression tight. "I got off the ferry and just stood at the side of the ramp that led up off the shingle."

She not only heard Jessie's huge exhalation; it was so palpable that she felt it ripple down her own bones.

"I was so alone, even though there was a noisy bustle all around me." After a slight pause Jessie turned her head and smiled at her, a less painful smile. "I heard my name being shouted a couple of times, and it was the best thing of the whole day."

Margaret's voice was a squeak. "Who came to meet you?"

"It was Tom." Jessie grinned. "He was just new in the job and was so excited that he'd been ordered to collect me."

Margaret had met Tom, the young man who was the Duncan family coachman. "So, Mistress Duncan sent her carriage to collect you in style?"

Jessie's guffaws nearly made her fall off her bed. "Not at all. Tom was driving the shoogly goods-cart. His exhilaration was about travelling so far out of Edinburgh and that he could give the horse a good run for a change."

"It must still have been scary, though, to come here knowing none of the family."

A big sigh came her way from Jessie. A reflective one. "Did I tell you that I'd been here for nearly nine months before the Reverend Duncan visited?"

"No! You never mentioned that in any of your letters. Though I do remember you wrote in one letter that he was related to your employers." Margaret was immediately alert. "What happened when he visited?"

"What do you mean, happened?" Jessie yawned and crawled under her blanket. "I know that he stayed for two days, because Kate told me about that, but I never caught a single glimpse of him."

"Did he not even ask to see you?" She wanted to probe, though also didn't want to upset Jessie in any way. "To find out for himself if you were well and happy enough?"

Jessie's sniggers were muffled since she was pulling her bedclothes up over her chin and was snuggling down into a more comfortable position. "Why would he even think about that? I'm just the orphan from Milnathort!"

There was no answer that would be honest. Margaret still didn't know for sure.

She didn't even know if what was in her head and heart needed to be kept a secret, or not.

Lying in bed before sleep claimed her, she mulled over the odd situation of Jessie in the Duncan household. Her best friend didn't seem to be bothered about how she had ended up in Edinburgh with the Duncans. Jessie just seemed glad to have a job and a roof over her head.

Another thing that Margaret suddenly realised was that over the last few years the bulk of Jessie's broad Milnathort accent had been polished away.

Time spent in Edinburgh had definitely been life-changing for Jessie! Would she find that too?

***

Two days later, Margaret was working on a new alphabet letter with Rachel when Kate entered the parlour.

"The mistress wants you down in the drawing room. I'll keep Rachel company till you return."

Kate's expression was sympathetic though also encouraging when Margaret slid past her at the open door. The whisper at Margaret's cheek wasn't meant for Rachel's ears. "Chin up. The Mistress isn't in a good mood but neither is it a bad one."

Margaret felt a good deal of trepidation when she knocked on the drawing room door.

"Enter!"

The relief that Margaret felt on hearing Mister Duncan's voice was a balm to her confidence.

"Good afternoon, Margaret. Come closer," her employer urged.

On seeing the frosty expression on Mistress Duncan's face, Margaret's confidence fluctuated.

"We have called you here to discuss your position." Mistress Duncan's tone was at her most lofty.

Mister Duncan intervened, having turned to face his wife. "Thank you, Helen. I will deal with this."

Margaret gulped, though she pretended to be unaware of the tension she sensed between the two adults as she waited for Mister Duncan's gaze to return her way.

"Rachel tells me she has enjoyed you teaching her very much." Mister Duncan's tone was kindly. "I, too, have been quite satisfied on entering the parlour for my daily visit. Rachel has been so actively attentive to whatever you have set her that, sometimes, she hasn't even noticed my presence immediately."

Margaret felt sufficiently confident to allow her solemn expression to relax a little on noticing his sincere smile.

"That is quite a change, which you possibly have not realised. Before your arrival, Rachel was finding it very difficult to settle to anything suggested to her. Her gaze

148

was always towards the door, seeking someone to distract her from her situation."

There was a slight hesitation before Margaret answered, since Mistress Duncan still looked so disapproving.

"It's been my pleasure to help Rachel learn the basics. She's quick to learn what we've managed so far, considering her circumstances don't make any learning easy."

It was inevitable that Mistress Duncan would spoil the tone of the conversation. "I have found Rachel to be quite exhausted when I have visited in the afternoons. I think she needs far more rest than you have been allowing her this past month."

"Does Rachel have an afternoon nap, Margaret?" Mister Duncan's tone was firm.

"Yes, sir, she does." Margaret made sure her answer was candid. "Rachel tires after her light luncheon, and is even more so after the personal cleansing routine which follows it. We've found that the best time for Rachel to have a reviving rest is just after those processes are completed. Though, if I feel she's tiring at any time during the day, we take a break and do something different. An activity that still claims her attention, but is less onerous."

Mister Duncan resumed. "Thank you, Margaret. I am perfectly content with what you have done during your trial month, and will expect you to continue with the same manner of care that you have exhibited so far. It's far too early to see any real progress yet in Rachel's reading development, but I think it will not be too unreasonable to agree that we will do another education appraisal in three months' time."

Margaret felt fluttery inside. Was Mister Duncan saying that he liked her work but that he was only prepared to hire her for three months instead of the usual one year of employment?

"Are you satisfied with the results of the household tasks Margaret has been assigned, when not teaching our daughter?" The question Mister Duncan put to his wife was so firm that Margaret wondered about their general relationship. Or, perhaps it was how the Duncan parents always were when negotiating with their employees?

The pursed lips and haughty stare on Mistress Duncan's face was unmistakable, though the words spoken were insipid. "She has conducted any task I've set her well enough; I suppose. But you know my feelings on this. I do not think it is necessary to spend money on anyone to teach Rachel to read and write."

Mister Duncan rose from his chair and indicated that Margaret should go to the door. After he opened it and ushered Margaret over the threshold and into the corridor, his words were much more generous when she felt his full attention on her.

"Providing you are willing to continue doing household tasks when Rachel naps, or when my wife and Rachel's siblings go in for their afternoon visit, then I am satisfied about making the post a permanent one."

Margaret managed a nod and a brief thank you.

"Now, we shall speak of the wage I am prepared to offer you, which you should find is appropriate for your age and lack of experience in tutoring."

After Mister Duncan nominated the annual salary that he was offering, and the other conditions of her employment, Margaret gratefully accepted. The money was a bit more than what Jessie had said she was earning, but the official time off during the week was definitely more generous than Jessie was contracted to.

That night when she described the interview to Jessie, Margaret acknowledged how relieved she'd been that it hadn't been Mistress Helen Duncan who had conducted it.

Jessie gurgled, "I would have loved to see the Mistress face. Be prepared, Margaret, to spend years here before you will see a change of opinion. That woman clings like a limpet to judgements she's made, and rarely softens or changes her mind."

Margaret easily believed her friend. Jessie had a lot more experience of Mistress Duncan's crabby attitude.

Jessie's reaction to Margaret telling her about the daily time-off allowance was expected. Jessie almost rolled off her bed, her mirth so great.

"Ha, ha!" Jessie's giggling was so infectious. "In addition to the half-day off on every-fourth-Sunday, you're expecting to have two hours off every day? And you finish duties after Rachel is in bed?"

Margaret laughed, too. She'd learned how difficult it was for Helen Duncan's staff to take their daily allocation of time off.

Maybe it was time that she set some kind of precedent? Margaret didn't think of herself as militant in any way or form, but there was a first time for everything!

Education and learning were precious, though so was time to savour any newly-acquired knowledge.

Chapter Eighteen

May 1852

"This letter is for you, Margaret," Kate declared after entering the parlour.

The housemaid walked across the rug to where Margaret was sitting alongside Rachel and handed her the missive.

A frisson of apprehension trickled down Margaret's spine, though she suppressed it because the only people who had written to her were her father and her Aunt Jeannie.

"Thank you, Kate."

"What's this you are working very hard at, Rachel?" Kate asked.

As Margaret broke the wax seal, she was delighted to see her charge's bright answering smile. "We're making alphabet capital letters beautiful."

"You are indeed. Would that be a capital letter R for Rachel that you are designing?"

Rachel's answer was filled with enthusiasm. "It is. I'm practising my writing skills, but I can also use them to design my special silver-threaded embroidery sampler."

Margaret moved away a little to read the letter, grateful for the way Kate continued to distract Rachel.

The short letter was from her father, but thankfully indicated some good news.

"Is everything well, Margaret?" Rachel asked.

She hadn't realised her gasp of surprise had been so loud.

"Yes. It's good news. My parents are hoping to come to visit me, but they wonder if they can arrange it for a Saturday."

"They don't want to come on a Sunday? The Mistress might be more likely to agree to give you more than your usual time off on a Sunday afternoon."

Kate's comment was a reasonable one, but wasn't what her father would be comfortable with.

"My father wouldn't want to miss his church observances. And travelling so far on a Sunday would be a bad thing on the Lord's Day."

"You must go and explain to Mama. Go now, Margaret. I know what I need to do to finish this lesson."

Rachel was much more enthusiastic than she was about a trip downstairs.

Kate winked, though it was unseen by Rachel. "I'm happy to remain up here for a little while. As Rachel says, best go now and get the permission."

Traipsing down the stairs, Margaret braced herself to beard the lion in its very noisy den. She had no idea what Elspeth was doing but it was an extremely noisy game. Fisting her fingers to rap twice, she wondered if they'd even hear her inside.

It was extremely rare for her to be in the drawing room, but she had gained the status of Jessie and Kate in that if she needed to enter a room for some reason she did so after knocking, if no 'enter' had been called.

She hovered just inside the opened door and looked for the Mistress, ignoring the fact that Elspeth was lying flat down on her back, drumming her heels on the wooden floor. Mistress Duncan was seated near the tall windows, staring out as though deaf to everything that was going on around her.

Margaret decided the only way to gain attention was to make sufficient noise herself.

Clapping her hands in rhythm to Elspeth's beating feet, she approached the unruly child and ensured her voice was loud enough, the beaming smile on her face a very forced one.

"That's a fine military beat, Elspeth. Do you have any words to go with your marching music?"

Her statement was so unexpected it produced exactly the effect she wanted. Elspeth scrambled up from the floor and stared at her. Completely silently.

Margaret stepped past the toddler towards the Mistress, who also stared but with an entirely different sort of expression on her face. She couldn't tell if there was any gratitude in it that she had put paid to a tantrum, or if there was a tinge of guilt, or even embarrassment. Mistress Duncan's eyes were almost glassy as though seeing things in a fog.

"I've just received a letter from my father, and wondered if now was a good time to speak to you? Kate is upstairs with Rachel."

No words passed the Mistress' lips but the imperious nod was sufficient for Margaret to continue. She explained the contents of the letter.

"Why are they unable to come on what would be your monthly Sunday afternoon off?" The tone of the question wasn't encouraging.

"My father is very devout. My parents attend morning and evening church services, with Sunday afternoon bible readings."

"I cannot possibly give permission without speaking to Mister Duncan first. Sunday is your afternoon off as per our employment agreement with you."

Margaret gave no indication of her feelings on the dismissal but she had at least asked. Having nodded a thank you of sorts, she turned back towards the door.

"I know your family are not Episcopalian, as we are, but I cannot remember what sect your parents are members of."

Margaret turned back, suppressing a small smile. The word 'sect' did not nearly cover the rapidly-growing denomination.

"They attend the United Presbyterian Church."

"Ah, yes. So, they do." Mistress Duncan's indifferent gaze returned to looking out the window.

The very next day, Mister Duncan paid his regular evening visit to the parlour. After greeting his daughter, and spending sufficient time to find out what they were currently working on, Margaret found herself the focus of his attention.

"My wife mentioned that your father has a request of us?"

Since he didn't look in any way displeased, she repeated the communication.

"I take it that your parents cannot come on a weekday since they are at work?"

It seemed very personal, but her parents' situation had never been discussed with her employers.

"Yes. My father is employed as a senior tailor in my uncle's draper's shop in Perth, and my mother is my uncle's housekeeper. My aunt died a couple of years ago, so my mother also looks after my three cousins, all much younger than I am. My parents are very occupied during the week, but my uncle will give them time off on a Saturday to come to Edinburgh."

She tried to make it seem good reasons for their request, but it was always very difficult to interpret Mister Duncan's expression.

"Haven't you seen them during the time that you've spent here tutoring Rachel? It's been almost a year since you came."

"No, I haven't spoken to them since I left Milnathort to come here." At times she had missed them, but when she'd left Milnathort she'd had no expectations of seeing them soon.

"Write to your father and say that you can swap your next free Sunday afternoon at the end of June, to the Saturday before. Do you expect them to arrive by train from Perth?"

"I imagine so, sir. That would be the quickest way."

"Find out which train they will arrive on and their planned departure. You may organise your free time to suit their duration in Edinburgh, even if it straddles from mid-morning to mid-afternoon and is more than your usual time off."

"That's very kind of you, sir. Thank you." Margaret was unable to suppress her delight.

Mister Duncan's parlour visit held a surprise for Margaret on the last Friday of June.

"I believe it's tomorrow that your parents are coming to Edinburgh?" he asked.

"Yes, it is, sir."

She experienced a sudden rush of disappointment. Was her employer going to cancel her time off at such a late date?

"My wife and I will not be at home tomorrow afternoon, so cannot meet your parents, but there is no reason why you cannot invite them to see where you work."

She'd hardly been able to give proper thanks before he went on to quiz Rachel about her latest lessons.

The following day, at just short of one o'clock in the afternoon, Margaret stood waiting in some trepidation, the connecting train from Glasgow having just arrived at the platform. Searching the sea of people who surged from the open carriage doors, under a fog of steam and desperate-sounding hissing from the overpoweringly reeking engine, she eventually located William and Peggy. Waving like fury, she couldn't help her fluctuating feelings. She hadn't anticipated that she'd be so nervous in addition to being eager to see them again.

In some ways she had dreaded meeting them again under such different circumstances than when they lived in Milnathort, but those worries were suppressed by an appreciation that they had taken the time and trouble to come all the way to Edinburgh to see her. Excitement won out, her smiles beaming across her cheeks.

Her father reached her first and took hold of her outstretched hands, her mother arriving behind him a second or two later. Awkward hugs then enfolded her, her father's, then her mother's, both looking quite overwhelmed.

"Margaret! You've grown into an elegant young lady," William declared.

Peggy's small smile was so rare, but very welcome.

"Yes. You are so stylishly dressed. I can see that your sewing skills are coming in useful."

Margaret rushed in with her explanations, so excited to see them both looking hale and hearty, her mother looking particularly rosy-cheeked. "Jessie helps me make my clothes, and I help her."

"Of, course. I should have known you'd both still be thick as thieves." Her father looked a tiny bit amused.

"But surely this isn't your everyday work dress?" Peggy asked.

Margaret was proud of her new Easter outfit that she and Jessie had created, aware of the newest fashion trends out on the streets of Edinburgh.

"Not nearly!" she answered, aware that not smirking was impossible. "I saved up my wages to buy the materials and trimmings for this. By helping each other, Jessie and I managed to make new outfits at Easter time."

An approving smile from Peggy was surprising. "Do you have a uniform dress provided by Mistress Duncan?"

"I don't, though the other servants do wear a uniform."

Peggy's smile dipped. "Does your employer expects you to pay for your own clothes for your workdays?"

"Not quite. My annual salary includes an amount for me to wear a simple, dark-coloured dress." She rushed in since she could see plenty more questions coming from Peggy. "I've made two work dresses from my allowance. Making them myself has meant I could afford to buy much nicer material than if I bought them ready made, or by a seamstress."

Peggy harrumphed. "I'm sure that has worked out very well for you, Margaret, but I still think that your employer is paying you far too little for the work you are doing."

She was fairly sure it was true but she wasn't ready to change her employment. And the thought of going back to stay with her parents didn't appeal at all.

"That's very nice of Jessie to help you, though she always was a hard worker, and a kind girl."

Margaret was delighted to hear that Peggy's words about Jessie were complimentary, yet she wondered at the change of heart from her childhood when Jessie's background was never good enough. Perhaps people did change as they got older?

Maybe it was yet another lesson worth learning about? She vowed to try to keep an open mind about personal situations in the future.

As she led her parents out of the busy station near the North Bridge, she was almost tripping over her words trying to describe their surroundings. When they got to an empty space where they could stop and talk, she rushed in. "I made a list of places that you might want to see in Edinburgh, but Mister Duncan surprised me yesterday afternoon with an invitation for you."

She watched an uncomfortable expression settle across her father's face, but kept going. Though happy that she loved her tutoring job, her father had also written of his disapproval that the Duncans had not given her a sufficient salary when the post had been made permanent the previous July. It had gladdened her that he'd only mentioned his censure just the once, and then had let the matter rest. She hoped he wasn't going to raise the matter again.

"The Master and Mistress are out visiting friends today, and cannot meet you, but he has told me I can take you to the house in Albany Street for a light meal down in the kitchen, knowing that you've already had quite a long journey to get here."

William looked quite stunned, but it was Peggy who answered. "Well, we didn't expect anything like that."

For once, she watched her mother look to William for his opinion.

"That would be very nice, Margaret. If you think it won't disturb the rest of the staff routine." One of William's understated small smiles appeared. "Will we be able to see the infamous Jessie?"

His levity made her grin.

"Yes, but only briefly. Most of the family are out visiting this afternoon, though not Rachel. She's never invited to anything like that, so Jessie is spending the day with her, instead of me."

Having been given the option of going a-wandering first around Edinburgh, or visiting Albany Street, Peggy declared that some food might make her stomach feel less queasy. The train ride had been the first her parents had ever made, and Peggy declared it was quite an unsettling experience.

Margaret sighed and then chortled. "I don't know when I'll ever get the opportunity to be on a train but I look forward to being jostled about. It can't be worse than the ferry across to Granton!"

While she led them to Albany Street via St. Andrew Square, she asked them lots of questions about their journey.

"Yes, I knew you'd have to make a change from the Scottish Central Railway to get on to the Edinburgh Glasgow line. Was there a long wait?"

"Not at all."

William's enthusiastic description of the trains and the stations took them all the way to the gate on Albany Street, down to the basement door and into the servant corridor, his animation quite unlike how he'd been when she was younger. It was obvious that her father was quite taken with railway travel in general, even though he mentioned that the expense of it meant he'd not be travelling very often.

"This is the room I share with Jessie."

Margaret opened the door to let them have a peek inside while she hung up their coats on pegs near the outside door. She then led them into the empty kitchen and bade them take a seat while she checked the kettle was filled before setting it over the coals, to boil water.

"Mistress Abernethy, the cook, fed the family an early luncheon since they were going out visiting this afternoon."

She explained that Cook didn't have to be back till closer to when she served the evening meal, some of which they could smell slow-cooking in the oven, giving off a delicious meaty aroma.

Kate appeared just after they had finished the bread, cheese, and most of the succulent seed cake that Mistress Abernethy had laid ready for them.

"Oh, you lovely people. You've left me a little piece."

Kate's beaming smile was an introduction in itself. She popped down the dishes that Margaret knew to be from Rachel's mid-day meal and picked up the last bit of cake.

"Oh, I am so sorry," Peggy rushed in with her regrets. "I wouldn't have had two pieces."

Kate explained she was just teasing them and put her parents at ease.

"I'll just pop these in the scullery for you." Kate pointed to the now empty plates and cups her parents had used. "Rachel won't be having her afternoon nap just yet,

160

at least not before I go back up to take Jessie's place and give her a break. This would be a good time to go up, if you'd like to see them."

Margaret didn't quite know how she was feeling as she led her parents up the two flights of stairs, explaining the layout of the house as they went. There was a definite pride that she was working in a house of some distinction, in a situation that none of them had dreamed of many months ago when William and Peggy had had to make the decision to close down their draper shop. But there was something else that made her feel odd. She supposed it was an acknowledgement that she had grown apart from them and was now an almost mature young woman managing on her own, or as close as one could be in a position that was barely a notch up from household service.

She did the usual of two raps on the parlour door and then walked in, her parents trailing in behind her.

"Oh, please come in!" Rachel was so excited that a touch of pink blossomed across her wan cheeks. "I've been so wanting to meet you."

While she made the almost unnecessary introductions, Margaret carefully watched her mother's expressions. As she dreaded, yet expected, Peggy had made an audible gasp when she'd viewed the two blonde, similarly blue-eyed females, their heads close together reading a book. Though, on seeing them enter, Jessie had immediately risen to stand at the side of the daybed.

William made a short bow. "It's very nice to meet you, Rachel. Margaret has told us a lot about you in the letters she has sent me."

Rachel's response pleased Margaret, that impish streak that was mostly hidden coming to the fore.

"Oh, I hope she's not told you about all the naughty things I do, and about the terrible tricks that I play on her?"

That made them all smile, even Peggy.

Jessie was first to respond, bending forward towards the little girl. "Well, now I feel really left out, young lady. After all the things I do for you. Why don't I get some of this treatment?"

Margaret had never felt so good in her parents' company when she saw them responding to Jessie's humorous chiding.

William replied, giving Rachel her proper title.

"I don't believe a word of that, Miss Duncan. How could you possibly play tricks on these two young ladies?"

"Ah, you've caught me out." Rachel grinned. "It wasn't really me telling lies, you know."

"No," Margaret agreed, ruffling Rachel's braids affectionately. "You know by now that I would never encourage such behaviour."

Her father turned to Jessie. "You are looking very well, Jessie. And so grown-up since I last saw you."

His compliment made Jessie guffaw. "Well, I'm very glad you can see that they don't starve me here in the Duncan house!"

Margaret detected a slight strain in Jessie's expressive eyes, though she was sure her parents didn't notice anything.

Rachel was innocently curious. "What do you mean, Jessie?"

"It's just a little joke that Jessie is now playing to entertain my parents," Margaret quipped, to deflect any continuation of the conversation that might follow.

They didn't stay long up in the parlour, but Margaret found great delight in Rachel's enthusiastic admiration regarding her tutoring.

She was heartened that her mother and father seemed genuinely reassured about what her job entailed, and was grateful they were circumspect about her earnings.

"Rachel is a delightful little girl," William praised as they made their way back down to the basement. "You are clearly doing a very good teaching job, Margaret. And Jessie is nearly as pretty as I remembered."

"Nearly?" she queried.

"She's now a very attractive young woman, well-grown, and no longer a little girl."

William's glance towards Peggy was fleeting, which Margaret thought seemed a trifle embarrassed, as though he didn't know what to say next.

After receiving her coat from William, Peggy shrugged her way into the sleeves and eventually managed to button it down the front. Margaret was surprised that her mother was wearing an ill-fitting coat, though it was of a very nice material and didn't look particularly worn. She wondered if her parents' finances were really constrained.

Peggy put paid to the awkward pause with her more usual forthright attitude. "It may just be me, but don't you think that Rachel and Jessie are quite alike?"

She nodded. "Yes. They are."

"Like two peas in a pod." Peggy stated while drawing on her gloves. Even though it was summer weather gloves were still a fashion necessity.

William cleared his throat but sliced straight to the heart of the issue. "Does the Reverend Duncan often visit?"

"No. Jessie says his visits are rare, and he's not been here at all since I started to tutor Rachel."

Peggy was like a dog with a particularly juicy bone. "Does Jessie feel he should visit more regularly?"

Margaret hardly knew what to answer. The questions were quite intrusive and far too intuitive. "Jessie's very happy for him to stay away. He wasn't kind to her in Milnathort. And on his one and only visit since she came to work here, he didn't inquire about her at all, or attempt to speak to her."

"Does Jessie never seem to wonder why she was sent to work here?"

Peggy's question was too near the bone, but Margaret would not be drawn into speaking of something she still had no proof of. "Jessie prefers not to speak of the Reverend Duncan. She likes her job here and is grateful that she has a bed to sleep in at night. She told me she's even happier since I came, because any free time we spend together continues our friendship from back in Milnathort."

Peggy harrumphed. "More like these Duncans are just happy to pay her a skivvy's wage."

Margaret didn't want to lie to her parents, yet had to say something. "Why Jessie was brought here is a matter for the Duncans. They have increased her wages, recently, though. Not by much, but better than she had before."

William held open the basement door, ending the conversation. "Now, Margaret. What do you think we should see in Edinburgh, given the time we have left?"

Chapter Nineteen

"I thought you'd maybe like to see the United Presbyterian Church that's on South College Street?"

William's smile showed his approval. "Is it a long walk from here?"

"I've never timed it taking the long way round, but I think perhaps an hour? Though there are so many beautiful buildings in Edinburgh that it's very easy to lose track gawping at them."

Peggy reached the top of the basement stairs a step or so behind them. Not quite out of puff, but Margaret wondered if the extra weight her mother now seemed to be carrying wasn't so kind to her.

"Is The United Presbyterian the church you go to on a Sunday?" William's question about her worship was expected at some point, and Margaret had rehearsed her answer so many times.

She explained that the Duncan family went to the Sunday morning service at the Episcopalian Church of Saint John the Evangelist which was located at the west end of Princes Street.

"I'll point St. John out to you when we do a big loop along Princes Street and round the back of the castle to the Grassmarket. Mistress Duncan's only stipulation is that the servants attend worship at least once on a Sunday. She doesn't mind which church, or sect, and doesn't force us all to attend their Episcopalian services."

She told them that Kate, and Tom the coachman, went to a local Baptist meeting hall on a Sunday evening, since the servants couldn't all be out of the house at the same time on a Sunday.

"Then are you saying that you and Jessie attend church together?" Peggy was more curious than Margaret had expected.

"No. Jessie goes to the Church of Scotland service that's an hour earlier than the Episcopalian one, three Sundays in a row."

There was an awkward pause. She faced down her father's almost scowl.

"Then where do you go?"

"I observe Sunday worship with Rachel, up in the parlour, since she can't attend church with her parents. I choose a passage to read from the bible, just like you used to do on Sunday afternoons, Father, and Rachel and I talk about it afterwards. I've taught her some hymns, even if our singing leaves a little to be desired."

Peggy frowned as well. "Can't Rachel be taken to church in their carriage?"

Margaret didn't really have a proper answer, save that it was unthinkable that Mistress Duncan would take her daughter outside, even to a church service.

Her father was almost apoplectic. "I suppose they think that Rachel can't do all the ups and downs from their pews during their service that's much more like an Anglican ritual than ours is."

William seemed displeased that she wasn't getting to see the inside of a church herself.

"Oh, I do go to church on every fourth Sunday, Father. Jessie stays with Rachel while I'm out.." She smiled to take away the sting. "I actually have two services that day, since I go back and do the one for Rachel and myself."

She felt the need to lighten the conversation. "On that fourth Sunday, Jessie and I also have a half-day off, so the afternoon is always looked forward to. We have such fun together exploring Edinburgh."

What she didn't mention was that she attended the Episcopalian service, in order to give Rachel some semblance of what happened when her parents attended a service. She didn't think that the Duncans knew that she always walked well in their wake, and sat in the back pews a good distance away from where they tended to sit. She also didn't divulge to William that she derived a strange comfort from attending the Episcopalian church, though she had no idea why because it was very different to what she had been used to in Milnathort.

William turned to her as they waited for a horse and carriage to pass by at the junction of St David Street and Princes Street. "I suppose we have ruined that pleasure for you this month? I don't imagine you'll be having today and tomorrow off?"

Margaret smirked. "Not likely. But I will be going to church."

"Do you and Jessie only have that one afternoon off?"

It was such an unexpected question Margaret stared at Peggy while she worked out her answer. "It's usual in domestic service to just have that time off. We're no different from most households who employ downstairs staff."

"That's true," Peggy agreed, "but I really should have asked if you get any other time off."

"Oh, yes, I see what you mean." Margaret nodded. "We all get a one-hour break during the day, but it's not at a set time, and sometimes not even a complete hour at a time."

"That doesn't sound organised at all, or even very useful." Peggy was typically quite snippy.

Margaret sought to reassure her mother. "Jessie usually manages to take some time off time around mid-morning, and Kate sometimes before the children's meal in the evening."

"What about you, Margaret?" William's expression was back to sober.

"Well," she said. "I have time off after Rachel is in bed, after I finish my evening task for the Mistress, which sometimes doesn't take very long."

She explained what that might entail, then added more.

"The Mistress also comes up to the parlour to be with Rachel for a while every day."

"I hope she doesn't interfere with your lesson times?" Peggy sounded quite censorious.

Margaret quite liked that Peggy sounded like she was defending her.

"Sometimes the Mistress does come during a lesson, but since Rachel needs to have irregular breaks to bolster her energy levels, we stop when she needs a breather rather than at set times."

Peggy's tone was still sharp when she continued. "I hope Mistress Duncan doesn't think you're lazy at doing your job."

Margaret chuckled. "Actually, I did have to convince her a few times during my trial month that Rachel really needed a different activity, but that doesn't happen now. Mistress Duncan accepts if we stop, there's a good reason for it. The Master, too."

"You said your Mistress visits Rachel every day?" William asked.

Margaret almost prevaricated, but realised her parents were genuinely trying to assure themselves that she wasn't being too exploited.

"The Mistress always pops up at some point, though rarely stays for long. Lately, the most usual time has been just before the other children are home from school. When they arrive to speak to Rachel, I generally get some time to myself."

She didn't specify that the other children were only with Rachel for a short time during their daily duty call, before they followed their mother back down to the drawing room.

It was much later when they were traipsing up and down the High Street, having stopped at Parliament Square to admire the impressive architecture of the Kirk of St. Giles, that Margaret remembered to ask if her mother met up regularly with Aunt Jeannie, since they were both now living in Perth.

William interrupted the conversation before it even properly started. He was quite knowledgeable about the restoration of the ancient building of St. Giles, a few decades previously, by an architect named William Burn. Margaret was glad she knew a little about the aspects of the church that had been renovated. Walking all around the perimeter of the building William noticed an open door, his curiosity about viewing the inside too much to repress.

Peggy whispered once they were inside the huge building, restarting the conversation about Jeannie. "I've actually only seen Jeannie once since we moved to Perth. She's living on the far side of the town from us."

Peggy looked around the nave, though not before some sort of tension tweaked her lips.

"Jeannie's very happy with her choices."

"Is she working at a mill in Perth?" Margaret asked, also keeping her voice low.

Her mother's focus returned to her. "She hadn't been able to get a mill to take her on when I saw her, but she was doing some cleaning for the leather-works place where her husband has a job."

"Her husband earns enough that she doesn't need to work." William's unexpected comment was more akin to those her mother used to make.

Margaret didn't think she was supposed to have heard the sniff from her mother, but she had. Peggy's face had gone back to the rigid disapproval that she had been used to in Milnathort.

It was usual for most working-class women to work whether they were married or not, if money was needed.

Sometimes even after the bairns arrived a woman would supplement the man's wages.

The conversation about Jeannie had petered out so Margaret trailed around after William who was torn between admiring the opulence of the structure and being derogatory about the decadence of it being so copiously embellished. When they had looked their fill and had stepped back outside, William's opinion was that a church never needed to be so ostentatious. That was as Margaret had expected, though she was surprised that her father had even shown the inclination to see the inside, knowing that it had been of Roman Catholic origins before the Reformation and the Great Disruption of the churches.

Maybe people do change as they get older, she thought, yet again.

During their walk up towards the castle esplanade, a little slower than Margaret would have expected since Peggy was a little out of puff, she asked about Uncle James and how things were going for them.

"You've written a little about you now doing just tailoring, Father," she asked carefully, aware that it might be a sensitive subject. "But do you miss being at the shop counter?"

The tiniest of gleams lightened William's expression. "Not at all. I much prefer being in the back room making suits for your uncle's customers. He has built up a fine following for his workmanship, and I have none of the extra hassle of balancing the books of an evening. I now have plenty of free time to indulge in my own pastimes."

She ignored her mother's sideways glance and pursed lips. Her parents had never done anything together out of the shop hours when she was growing up.

"I'm glad to hear you are liking it so well in Perth, Father."

She turned to Peggy. They'd reached the flat esplanade outside Edinburgh Castle where a good

170

smattering of people wandered around, admiring the fortified castle walls and what they could see beyond them. Peggy regained her breath while they stood to take in the buildings behind the rampart, some of them huge rounded ones and others like square country keeps with many storeys.

"I've not really learned anything about Uncle James' house. What's it like?"

For the next little while Peggy was actually quite animated as she told Margaret about her three little cousins and gave a vibrant description of the house that was a pleasure to look after.

"Your uncle had only moved to the current house a short while before your aunt died. They needed a bigger one thinking there were going to be four children, and James had made enough money to merit moving into one with four bedrooms." Peggy went on to describe the house which wasn't nearly as grand as Albany Street but was quite substantial and was in a reputable area of Perth. "It also has two tiny attic bedrooms, so your father and I moving in hasn't meant a huge crush at all."

During Peggy's explanations, her father seemed to be totally absorbed by the fabulous Edinburgh architecture that was all around them.

By the time she'd waved her parents off on the first of their return trains, she was almost hoarse with explaining many of the buildings they'd passed on the way back down to the train station. They had clearly enjoyed her guided tour and had been delighted with her knowledge. She was proud that she and Jessie always made the most of the Sunday afternoon off that they had once a month, and had learned so much.

One concern she'd had, though it seemed minor, was that her mother had needed to slow their pace on occasion. When they'd returned to the railway platform, she'd been almost sure that her mother had wanted to say something but Peggy had hesitated too long, they were being urged to board the carriages, and then there was no more time for anything apart from a swift goodbye.

It was thought-provoking to hear about William's life in Perth, though in his usual reticent way she'd had to tease out the finer details from her father. She'd had a fear that William would feel resentment that he was now working for his brother, and that he'd feel a failure, but that didn't seem to be the case. Even in such a short time, William seemed far more outgoing than he'd been in Milnathort, having talked of joining a couple of local societies. One of these met on a Wednesday evening and the other on a Saturday night.

On the other hand, her mother's update explained a little of why Peggy seemed a happier person. Not being required to work in Margaret's uncle's shop made all the difference to how Peggy spent her days. Hearing the details of her three young cousins was very strange, since they had just been names with no personalities. She still couldn't quite envisage them, but Peggy had given enough details to bring them alive.

Margaret decided it was a very good thing that Peggy was less condescending and abrasive than she used to be, and William's more relaxed demeanour was perhaps because Peggy was happier and it relieved him in some way. Each of them had talked to her more than she ever remembered before.

However, there was clearly no connection to each other. There were no shared smiles between her parents, and certainly no loving gestures – just two people seemingly happier in their own selves in their new situations.

Still, their reserve was perplexing. She decided there and then that the man she married would know of, and see, her love all the time. Every single second of the day!

Lowering her hand from her last wave to her parents as they disappeared inside the carriage, a rush of sadness engulfed her. She could hardly explain it, but she somehow felt she had already outgrown them. Their visit had clarified that although she would always be their daughter, and she would like to see them in the future, they were not the ones who had gained her everlasting love though nurturing bonds.

Jessie was the only one who held that accolade.

Turning away from the receding cloud of engulfing pungent smoke from the panting railway engine, her thoughts tumbled over one another. Being free of her father's rigid religious dogma was probably the greatest benefit of living out of their environment. Though she did attend church irregularly, as dictated by Mistress Duncan, she pondered the question of whether she would go at all if it was not required by her employers.

As she neared Albany Street she chortled, startling a passerby who looked at her strangely. The answer was probably not. Freedom from rigid routines beckoned, and she felt well along that road.

All in all, she was pleased her parents had made the effort to come, even if never repeated.

Chapter Twenty

1853 October

"Are you ready to start, Rachel?"

Margaret gathered up the slate and nib from the table under the parlour window where the writing and reading materials were stored and waited for the girl to answer.

It wasn't difficult to bring forth a smile, because the day was a beautiful one and her planned work shouldn't be in any way arduous. Though there was a necessary repetition to every day, and nothing particularly ever happened to upset the routine, Margaret appreciated that what she was doing was infinitely better than the monotonous and exhausting work which would have been her daily fare, if she'd been employed in a mill. She was aware that apart from spending free time with only Jessie, which was always a treat, she had no life outside of Albany Street. Yet she spent little time deliberating about whether any kind of skivvy or sewing job would have provided her much opportunity to meet new people, either.

Margaret loved her days helping Rachel with her education. though it was sometimes difficult when the little girl got despondent about her inability to move around on her own.

During the year after her arrival to do the tutoring job, the Duncan parents had consulted a succession of doctors. These had resulted in various treatment and manipulation programmes, though nothing had given the girl back the use of her legs. However, the manipulation exercises had benefitted the lame arm she had been left with. The wrist and forearm bone breaks hadn't healed properly, leaving the limb permanently curved at the wrist, though after a programme of repeated exercises, Rachel's hand functions became less troublesome after she'd learned strategies which helped her grasp with her fingers when an object was held tight to her body.

"Please can we continue with our storytelling, Margaret?"

Rachel sounded so hopeful that she always hated to disappoint. "Aye, indeed we will, you young scamp, but later on. Long after we do lots more of your own reading and writing." Creating stories together orally was what perked the little girl up the most, but there was no tangible evidence for that activity to show to Helen Duncan.

Her charge was progressing at a good pace with her reading standards, and with her basic arithmetic, but Rachel was less interested in applying herself to improve her handwriting skills. Margaret had taught her the basics of neat handwriting but it wasn't of interest, and getting Rachel to do daily practice had become a chore. Of course, getting the girl propped into a suitably upright position on her daybed, with stacks of pillows, was part of the problem. When she slumped to the side, as inevitably happened, the angle for writing became too awkward, especially since Rachel could only use one side properly. Margaret had learned how to slide her pupil back into position, but had to be very cautious about not making the girl's elbow sores weep any more than they already did.

It was just as well that the poor little thing didn't seem to have the same skin sensations as was usual below the waist, though the general discomfort in Rachel's upper torso, and chafing at her elbows, were issues that Margaret knew the girl felt keenly.

175

Margaret hadn't yet worked out how to resolve the problem of Rachel's posture but was determined she'd not give up.

"We'll begin with Chapter Three." She handed Rachel the book they had been looking at the previous day, a well-written book on Scottish folk tales.

She allowed Rachel time to open the book, easy for most but more time-consuming for Rachel to select the proper page. She'd learned quickly that it did Rachel no favours to do too much for the girl.

Rachel's animated voice soon filled the parlour. The stories were excellent for immediately transporting the reader to another world, one that was less confining than the realities.

Only a few words had to be explained, so it was easy for Margaret to split her mind to thinking about other things.

Though she still disliked Mistress Duncan's continuing dismissive and sometimes terse attitude towards Rachel, and the almost palpable disdain of herself, Margaret was gratified that she had gradually been given a few freedoms within the household after her status had become permanent. The small bookcases that lay under the windows in the parlour held a varied selection of books which she was allowed to use for Rachel's instruction. And so far, no-one had ever challenged the fact that she took books down to the bedroom she shared with Jessie, to read them after her workday was over.

"I'm so pleased that Father now allows us to borrow books like this one from the Central Lending Library," Rachel said as she turned the page to the next short story in the book. "Aren't you?"

"I most definitely am," Margaret replied as she wiggled the end of one of Rachel's braids to tickle under the little girl's chin, a gesture that showed her increasing love for her pupil. Overt displays of a kiss to her cheek or her forehead would be stepping beyond her position as a non-family member, but there were little ways that she could let Rachel know that tutoring her was never a burden. "Your father is very indulgent."

It had been a delightful surprise when Mister Duncan had organised payments for her to borrow books suitable for Rachel's education from one of the local lending libraries. The selection meant she always had four new books to share with Rachel every week, fresh approaches to what might have been otherwise repetitive materials. She was able to extend Rachel's knowledge of geography, of history, of flora and fauna, and of the wider world in general, even if it was unlikely the poor little girl would ever experience anything much outside her house.

And, as a consequence, in choosing a wide selection to share with her charge, Margaret had also been furthering her own educational knowledge.

"Oh, look! This story says it's set in Edinburgh," Rachel declared, having read her way through the explanatory page for each separate folk tale. "I hope it's as good as the trows from their trowie knowes that we read about in Chapter One."

Margaret grinned at Rachel's excitement over the mischievous fairies they had been savouring in their current book. "I don't know many stories that are set in this very city but I doubt any Edinburgh creatures would be as scary as the trows are."

Another coveted aspect of Margaret popping out to the lending library once every week meant she had some freedom to learn about the city centre of Edinburgh. By timing her library visits with her official daily hour off duty, she was able to cover a greater distance. Though in all truth, she found it difficult to claim a full hour on most days, since it was taken when Rachel napped in the afternoon and not a specified time of day.

Her more predictable time off was her every-fourth-Sunday half-day that both she and Jessie had as part of

177

their working conditions. Those coveted afternoons were anticipated with great excitement and planned well in advance – come rain or come shine. With hardly any money between them they could never venture very far, or pay for much in the way of entertainment, but being together with no Duncan demands on them for a few hours was just heaven.

They would both have loved to visit buildings like the imposing National Institution which housed the Antiquarian Museum and a collection of fine classical statues, or the National Gallery of Painting – both of which had periods of Free entry – but, to their great frustration, those opening times were never on a Sunday. The best they could do was admire the grand architecture of those institutions when strolling around Princes Street, or wherever the buildings were located.

Getting to know the streets of Edinburgh meant Margaret had lots of little anecdotes to tell Rachel, which she always shared in light-hearted fashion to amuse her little pupil. She'd recall things about how ladies were dressed in the streets, their fashion sense much more up-to-date than what she herself was wearing. Or it might be her having seen a very fancy new parasol made from one of the new Paisley pattern designs. Or how some well-dressed young gentleman's top hat had blown off in the strong winds that seemed very prevalent in the wide Edinburgh streets.

What she kept to herself was the occasional sight of a uniformed soldier taking leave of his family, or sweetheart, before heading towards Leith to board a ship bound for a southern port. The long journey after that would be to sail for the Black Sea, via the Mediterranean Sea. Many of the soldiers were the equestrian Royal Scots Greys, or from battalions of mainly local men who were infantry and being popularly called the Royal Scots. Heading off to battle in the Crimean War was too depressing a topic for Rachel's young ears, though it was mentioned plenty of times in the Duncan servant quarters.

Mistress Abernethy's sharp tongue was too inclined to niggle at Tom, the coachman, if he had reason to enter her hallowed kitchen. Margaret thought the cook's pride in her own nephew, and in Tom's older brother was misplaced, both young men having gone to war with the Royal Scots. What Margaret had gleaned of the reasons for being at war with Russia didn't seem to justify the recent reports of heavy casualties on both sides. Choosing to sign up to the army was not for the faint-hearted, or for anyone who could envisage themselves being alive as an old man.

The heated words between the Duncan parents were sometimes too loud to ignore when Margaret was assisting Jessie to get Rachel ready for bed in the evening. The construction of the walls of the house in Albany Street was good, however they was not entirely soundproof. Mistress Duncan's whines about Robert being far too young to think of going to war were balanced by Mister Duncan's vehement outlining of the many even younger boys he'd read of who had already been killed in the conflict.

There was a sense of relief that Robert wasn't heading off to war but was to continue his studies at St. Andrews University. That wasn't because Margaret had any tender feelings for the eldest son, since he remained very stand-offish, but she sympathised with any family whose sons were setting off to the conflict in the Crimea.

Margaret peered over Rachel's shoulder to gauge how much might be left of the current story.

Bright-blue eager eyes swept up from the page before Rachel pleaded. "It's almost finished, Margaret."

There was always a need to keep Rachel's lessons short and snappy, to gain the best of the girl's attention span. Over the last year of tutoring, Margaret had learned how to pace and intersperse the lesson contents, though sometimes something really gripped the girl's focus, as was currently happening, and was to be encouraged.

A few pages later, and after a number of questions had been successfully answered, Margaret closed the book she had just been handed by Rachel and set it on a side table.

"Well done, young lady! Your reading is so much improved that we'll soon have you reading the big fat tomes over there in those wall cases."

She pointed to the hefty law book collections that belonged to Mister Duncan, who had recently become a Queen's Council. Margaret didn't really know exactly what that meant in terms of becoming a better lawyer, but it was an important step for Mistress Helen Duncan who liked the idea of more money being earned by her husband, and the increased social standing it brought.

"I don't think I'll ever want to read them!" Rachel's giggles filled the room. "I'll just leave those boring books to my brothers."

"Do you think they will want to become advocates like your father?" She didn't know Robert well-enough to make any judgement on his future since he was rarely home from St. Andrews.

"Robert says he wants to stay at university and study history for ever, but I don't think that's what Father plans for him."

Margaret could easily see that Robert's future wouldn't be decided by himself. If it wasn't Mister Duncan who would lay down the stipulations, then it would be his wife who had very definite ideas of what elevated one in society. Mistress Duncan was very much the snob that Margaret vowed never to become no matter how much money she had at her disposal.

Picking up two of the library books that she'd borrowed the previous morning, she settled down on her chair that was set near Rachel's right shoulder. There were no sides on the daybed, but through experience she'd found this the best side to share books which had illustrations.

Her pupil was soon laughing at the sound of the word penguin even more than the illustration of it. Margaret was painstakingly repeating the spelling of the creature's name when Mister Duncan unexpectedly walked into the parlour, home from his chambers much earlier than was usual.

"What amuses you so, Rachel?"

Rachel's face lit with surprise, it being a rare occurrence to see her father in the daytime during the week.

"We're investigating lots of weirdly strange animals, Father."

"Weirdly strange, indeed." Mister Duncan's impressive dark-blonde-tinged moustache twitched. "Which is the target of today's lesson?"

Margaret felt his gaze alight upon her, though Rachel dived straight in with the answer.

"It's a penguin. We've just started to investigate it so I don't know much about it, yet. Yesterday we looked at a leopard and not only can I remember lots about it, I can spell it, too!"

"Can you, now. I'd best stay long enough for a demonstration, then."

Margaret watched Rachel suppress disappointment that her father's unusual visit was going to be fleeting, but was proud when her charge began to hesitantly spell the animal's name. It wasn't correct, but made her father chortle.

"Oh, I remember now. It needs an 'a' near the end." Rachel rushed in with a second spelling, desperate to demonstrate her prowess. She then barely drew breath as she outlined all that she had learned the previous day about leopards.

"So, you think that this creature is really just a big spotted cat?" Mister Duncan's gaze teased. "Should I be fearful of meeting one at the Edinburgh Zoological Garden on East Claremont Street?"

That perked up Margaret's attention. She'd not yet heard of Edinburgh having a Zoological Garden.

Rachel looked endearingly confused. "They wander about in Africa, Father, but I don't think they do that here in Edinburgh gardens."

Margaret felt Mister Duncan's gaze alight on her, his expression still amused at his daughter's answer. "Do you think I will find one at the Edinburgh Zoological Garden?"

"I don't know, sir. I haven't ever heard of the place till now, but I'm sure the lending library will have some information on it." She held up the books in her hand. "I borrowed this guide of the Great Exhibition at Crystal Palace from the library. It has an engraving of the hall which demonstrated lots of furs, and those are the creatures we've decided to start with. And this other library book has information on creatures from all over the world."

"You're finding the library useful, then?"

"Oh, indeed, sir. Thank you. The selection on their shelves is very impressive." Margaret was glad of the chance to show her gratitude. She was rarely ever in conversation with Mister Duncan, who had already turned back towards Rachel.

"Does the guide have an illustration of the elephant and howdah that was in the Great Exhibition?"

"I'm not sure. We haven't looked at the whole book yet, Father. We chose the leopard yesterday so that I could try to draw one for myself."

"Are you giving Rachel drawing lessons?"

Margaret couldn't tell if there was censure in his voice, though she hoped not. She decided it would be best to be totally honest. "I think you could say that we are learning about how to draw together. My own drawing skills are quite rudimentary, though Rachel is showing excellent promise and will be very much the expert soon, since she has a natural talent for it."

Mister Duncan took the piece of paper that she fished out from the folder that lay under a little side table, the drawing amazingly having been executed without smudges.

There was an awkward moment, a deathly hush before Rachel broke the silence. "That's just my first try from yesterday."

Margaret felt her charge's agony as the girl's desire to please her father was so painfully strong.

Mister Duncan handed his daughter the charcoal drawing. "I think it is very well done, Rachel. It has an extremely good likeness to the one I saw at the Great Exhibition."

"Oh, thank you, Father." Rachel's little smile beamed, her animation a joy to see. "I had forgotten you went there with Mother!"

Margaret hadn't known that. She'd naturally heard about the Great Exhibition of 1851 in London but the Duncans were the first people she'd known to have visited. So many questions were on the tip of her tongue.

"Tell me about the leopard first, please?" Rachel's tone wasn't whiny, but Margaret could tell her little charge so desperately wanted more of her father's attention.

Mister Duncan's gaze strayed swiftly to the clock on the mantlepiece. "I have to be back in my chambers soon, I'm afraid. I'll tell you a little of it now, but remind me to tell you more before you go to bed this evening."

"Yes, I will."

Margaret listened as avidly as Rachel.

"The leopard was very nearly lost in amongst the creatures in the Room of Furs. If I say imagine a huge shape like this, can you do that?" Mister Duncan placed his thumbnails together and steepled his hands to show an empty triangle.

Rachel nodded, and nodded again, but didn't interrupt the flow of her father's explanation. As Margaret listened, she could see where Rachel's interest in oral stories came from. Mister Duncan, she thought, must be good at his job in court, because he was a natural storyteller.

"At the top of this shape called a triangle, up high in the room, was an ermine fur robe that would be worn by a king or a queen, mostly white but with dark lines here and there. Then, hanging over suitable frames, row after row beneath the ermine robe there was a wonderful selection of clothing made from all different animal pelts."

Mister Duncan had used his hands during his description to aid Rachel's imagining of the scene but then he stopped on seeing Rachel's unsure expression.

"Sometimes a fur coat or jacket can be made from the skin of just one animal, though more often, if the animal is a smaller one, it takes quite a few skins sewn together to make the coat fit a person."

Rachel's swift nods showed her better understanding.

Her father continued, "As each row of items got closer to the floor level, the items would have been less expensive to buy."

It was clear to Margaret that Rachel was probably seeing the room as well as she was from the excellent descriptions given.

"Were the bottom row furs for little children, because they took less fur to make them?" Rachel asked.

"That's a very well-put question, Rachel, but there's a tricky answer to it. The lowest tier of garments definitely held items for small children, though that row also contained small pieces like fur muffs, and collars to wear around the neck, or add to coats. However, there was one very expensive item right near the bottom row, slap bang in the middle which outshone everything else. Can you imagine what that was?"

There was no nodding this time from Rachel, and Margaret also hadn't a clue.

"It was a jewelled crown with a fur edging, just like Queen Victoria might wear to very important state events."

"Oh, that must have been wonderful to see, Father." The little girl was in awe, as was Margaret when he related that he and his wife had managed to squeeze through the crowds to get to the front and into a close enough position to appreciate the spectacular jewels embedded in the golden frame.

Rachel awkwardly clapped her hands, indicating her great delight, then, after the tiniest pause, her brows furrowed very slightly. "But you've said nothing at all about a leopard."

Mister Duncan's laugh rang clear. "You are correct. All around the bottom of this triangular display of furs were some of the animals the pelts might have come from. There was a fierce lion with huge bared teeth, and a leopard with its spots, and animals you will already have heard of like a wolf and a beaver." Mister Duncan's voice hushed as he stretched his head closer to Rachel's. "There was a little penguin and a beautiful gazelle. You should learn more about the gazelle in your next lesson. It's a magnificently elegant creature!"

Rachel's mouth opened wide. "But how could they make the animals stay still while all those crowds of people looked at everything?"

Again, her father's mirth was evident. "Well, the saddest thing of all was that none of the animals were alive. They were very cleverly made to look as though they were just standing still, so that the visitors could see what size the animal was, and appreciate its shape and colouring."

The chimes from the clock on the mantlepiece drew Mister Duncan's attention. "I really must go now, Rachel, but if you and Margaret can find engravings of

185

the penguin, and the gazelle, and even the elephant and howdah that was in a different room, I'll tell you more about them later."

Mister Duncan patted Rachel's shoulder. "But all this talk of weird and wonderful animals made me almost forget why I'm here this afternoon."

Chapter Twenty-One

October1853

The sudden tension at Rachel's shoulders was apparent to Margaret, but she wasn't sure if Mister Duncan would be so aware.

His short chuckle immediately dispelled any anxiety when he ruffled his daughter's hair. "From tomorrow you will not have to spend so long on this daybed, young lady."

Margaret hoped her gasp of surprise wasn't as obvious as Rachel's.

"There will be a delivery of a very special chair with wheels that can be used for getting you out in the fresh air, when the weather is not inclement." Mister Duncan sent a fond look Rachel's way. "What do you think of that?"

Rachel was almost beside herself, unable to prevent fat tears from falling to drip from her chin, but answering was something she was not quite able to do just yet, her little lips quivering and the sniffles pronounced through the smiles she was trying to form.

"I will take that as a yes that the idea has your favour." Rachel's nods earned her a small cuddle across her shoulders before Margaret's gaze met her employer's. "I did not intend to leave you in such disarray, daughter, but I'm sure Margaret can dry your happy tears."

She felt his gaze return to her. "Tom will be storing the wheelchair in the coach house, and will help when you are both ready to try it out." He turned towards the door but then looked back over his shoulder. "I am very pleased indeed that Rachel is enjoying her lessons with you, Miss Law. With your admirable teaching, she is making excellent progress."

Colour flared at Margaret's cheeks, though she managed to acknowledge the compliment with a brief nod and thank you.

A bit later on, as it approached time for Margaret to finish the lessons for the day – Rachel was far too excited to concentrate on anything at all – she belatedly realised Mister Duncan had called her Miss Law and not Margaret. She felt it was significant in that her employer no longer regarded her as someone to keep Rachel company and amused, but more of a proper tutor. The idea of being acknowledged as a proper teacher thrilled her.

She also reflected that she would love to have had a father who told stories like Mister Duncan had. It wasn't that her own father lacked imagination, he probably had as much as any man had, but the difference was, possibly, all in the life experiences that could come from having the money and freedom to visit interesting places. Perhaps that would have made her father happier, because in her heart she knew that there was little in his life to find happiness with. Certainly not her mother.

Margaret vowed to learn as much about the world as she could and actually see as many interesting things that she could manage. If that took finding the best possible job, earning her a whole lot more money, then she'd work towards that. And if such an ambition proved impossible, then knowledge coming second-hand from books would be better than none at all.

It was less than two months later when Mister Duncan paid an afternoon visit to Rachel, that he had Margaret speechless again.

"I'm hearing from Tom the coachman that you are thoroughly enjoying getting outside in the wheelchair even though we are approaching wintertime."

She watched the affectionate kiss her employer bestowed on Rachel's crown and the gentle pats to her shoulder before Mister Duncan kneeled down to his daughter's eye level.

"I do love it, Father! It's very comfortable and so lovely to see people outside. It's wonderful seeing the sky, the trees, the flowers, and the grass – just everything beyond the window! Margaret has managed to push me all the way to Princes Street Gardens, though not right to the very bottom."

"Has she indeed. She must be a very strong young lady."

Margaret felt his amused eyes descend upon her. "It's marvellous to be out in the fresh air with her," she said. "And we're even able to venture into the Central Lending Library."

Mister Duncan looked impressed, if a little bemused.

"Margaret pushes me just inside the door and settles me beside the librarian's desk. He chats to me while Margaret fetches new books – if he's not serving anyone else – and I can even get to choose the ones to bring home from the selection she shows me."

Mister Duncan's smile was appreciative. "Well, that definitely makes it all the easier for me to tell you why I'm here today."

Margaret had no idea what he might be referring to.

"Since your outside wheelchair is such a great success, I think we should try to get something similar for you to use here in the parlour and for getting you to and from your bedroom."

Rachel's bright blue eyes immediately filled with tears and flooded over, to run down and drip off her chin.

"What do you think, Miss Law? Rachel, I can see, is a bit overwhelmed and needs a moment to compose herself." Mister Duncan's words were far from censorious.

Margaret felt her pulse rate rise, since the prospect was so exhilarating. She had lately wondered if such a thing would be possible, but it hadn't been her place to suggest such an expense. Nevertheless, she was determined not to miss the opportunity to give her opinion of what would be best.

"The semi-recumbent basket chair is excellent for Rachel's comfort outside, sir, but I don't think that same design would be so good for her doing her lessons up here in the parlour."

Mister Duncan nodded, reflectively. "Then, what do you think would be best for your needs?"

She pointed to the pillow support that Rachel currently had on her daybed. "It's always tricky to keep Rachel upright. She tends to slip to the side and then can't right herself very easily."

Margaret smiled down at her charge. "You tell me I fuss too much with those pillows, don't you?"

Rachel grinned. "Yes, you do. But without Margaret constantly propping me up, Father, I'd not be able to do any of my drawing, or writing, or even my special silver sampler sewing."

Mister Duncan laughed. "You definitely don't want any little sharp needles poking at you, instead of the cloth you're working on."

Margaret felt his attention return to her.

"What kind of chair would be best?"

Clearing her throat, she delved in. "A highbacked armchair, well-padded all around with some form of shoulder and waist harnesses to keep her upright and in place, would be good. They'd need to be comfortable for her, though, and the shoulder restraints would need to leave her arms free to hold and manipulate things in her lap. Though how to add the wheels to that is something I can't work out how to do."

Mister Duncan grinned. "The designer of her outside chair did a fine job. I'm sure he could take advantage of the many new inventions the Crystal Palace Exhibition had on show to create what we need. I will confer with Doctor Oliver first over the health aspects for daily use, and then see what can be done. What about the height of it allowing her to be seated at a proper table for working on her lessons?"

Margaret couldn't contain her excitement. "Yes! Something like that would be marvellous. And would also be good for her meals."

When it arrived, only a few weeks later, the indoor wheelchair made such a difference. The parlour had some small adjustments made to accommodate the moving around of the wheelchair. A couple of the small occasional tables went into storage, and a more substantial rectangular table was set up near the window, at a height that was perfect to slip the wheelchair under with an extra seat for Margaret to sit alongside.

She and Jessie quickly got into a new routine of getting Rachel ready for the day. Then together they got her seated in the wheelchair without needing Tom's carrying assistance to the parlour, which had sometimes caused delays if he was not immediately free to help get her onto the daybed.

A later addition of the swivelled wooden lap tray was another wonderful benefit for Rachel. It was just the right depth for holding writing and sewing materials and was perfect for times when the big teaching table wasn't needed.

Margaret's only regret was that she'd not thought about such an item after her arrival to tutor the little girl.

Of course, back then, the Mistress would have summarily dismissed it out of hand as an unnecessary expense. Margaret was well aware – and had heard sufficient heated conversations between the Duncan parents to know for sure – that the chairs for both inside and outside use had caused no end of moaning on the Mistress' part, and had only arrived at the insistence of Mister Duncan.

It seemed that he had eventually accepted that Rachel was never going to walk again and needed all the help possible, whereas Mistress Duncan accepted the hopeless situation but didn't think it merited any extra expense.

Helen Duncan had become more and more disagreeable as the months had progressed during Margaret's employment. The woman's tetchy attitude caused by her 'poor nerves' was a thing to avoid when at all possible, and that was beginning to mean most of the time.

Though in some respects Margaret was thankful that the arrival of the wheelchairs seemed to signal a certain degree of independence for Rachel in her mother's mind's eye. The Mistress' visits up to the parlour became less frequent though, when they did happen, they were rarely times of pleasure for the little girl.

"I'm not at all sure of what I'm supposed to be seeing in this drawing." Helen Duncan was scathing during one of her visits as she held the paper at arm's length. "You tell me it is very cleverly executed, Margaret, but all I see are some flowers, some grass and the metal railings of one of the local gardens."

"Rachel did this charcoal drawing from her semi-recumbent position in her outside wheelchair. That's not the easiest angle to be at when drawing."

Helen Duncan harrumphed, and twitched even more with the edges of her lace shawl whilst ogling the mantlepiece clock.

"You might have explained that first, then." The woman's tone was unfairly snippy as she headed for the door. "I have some things to see to, Rachel. Be sure to make a better drawing for me to see next time."

It took Margaret some time to simmer down though she showed Rachel none of her feelings.

The poor girl had already sunk into a good degree of despondency.

Helen Duncan was impossible. Unstable of mind wasn't a nice thing to contemplate, but that was what Margaret was coming to think about her deranged, and spitefully cruel employer.

"Oh, Margaret, forgive me." Kate had already bid them goodnight but rushed back in to the kitchen where she and Jessie were lingering over a bedtime drink. "This arrived for you and I put it in my pocket. I'm sorry you didn't get it earlier."

"Thank you." Margaret reassured Kate. "Don't worry. The day has been so hectic, I'd probably not have managed to read it before now, anyway." She looked at the handwriting. "Oh! I think I'll get into bed first and then read it."

Kate snickered. "It's from an admirer, then?"

Margaret snorted in response. "No such luck. Unlike some females around here, I don't have a line of interested young men queuing up to get to know me. I'm still on that very high shelf."

Jessie lifted the cups, a fine smirk on her face. "Cue for me to wash these. Goodnight, Kate!"

Once she was under the covers, Margaret broke the seal of the letter.

"Oh, it has some wonderful news, Jessie," she spoke aloud, "but it's also confusing."

Jessie, surprisingly in bed before she was, was just getting engrossed in the book in her hands, her response vague. "Mmm. What's wrong with it? Is it from William?"

Jessie had long since started to use William and Peggy when referring to Margaret's parents.

"No. The letter's from my Auntie Jeannie."

That got Jessie's proper attention. "Has Jeannie written to you before?"

"Just the once. After she got married and moved to Perth, though it's her husband who does the actual writing."

"So, tell me the wonderful bit first."

"Jeannie says she's expecting her first baby, and it's due just before Christmas."

"Maybe it'll arrive on my birthday!" Jessie grinned. "That would be an easy date for you to remember."

Margaret nodded. "Maybe? But she goes on to write that at least she's had an easy pregnancy this year, unlike her sister's last autumn."

Jessie's squirmy lips and raised eyebrows were comical. "I always thought there was just your mother and then Jeannie?"

"There are only the two of them!"

Jessie whiffed out a large breath. "That must mean your mother was pregnant last year but they never told you a thing about it. That's odd. It might be a big gap between you and a new baby, but your mother isn't past childbearing? Is she?"

Margaret was stunned. She never normally thought of her mother's age.

"Peggy was thirty-five last year. She was only eighteen when she married William and he was twenty-six."

Jessie put down her book, saying sleep was beckoning. A huge sigh escaped after she snuggled under her covers.

"Parents are such odd people," Jessie mumbled. "My mother wasn't in her right mind for most of my life, and I have never known a father."

Margaret's breath hitched. She let the letter fall to the floor and tucked the covers up to her chin. She'd no idea how to respond to that last part, but Jessie's low tones drifted across the space.

"Well, not one who counts."

"Jessie?" Margaret turned towards her best friend.

"No. I absolutely refuse to talk about what you're going to say. Go to sleep, Margaret!"

Jessie wasn't angry with her, Margaret knew that, but didn't prod. There was no point when Jessie got irritated like this.

Margaret tossed and turned for what seemed like hours. Could her mother's weight gain, and inclination to be a little tired when they had visited Edinburgh the previous summer, have been because Peggy was already some months pregnant?

A number of questions that night repeated over and over before she finally fell asleep. Why did they not tell her? Was that why Peggy had never answered the letters she had sent? Did the baby die? It must have, and that was why Peggy did not talk about it.

William had never even hinted either, in any of his letters.

How could her parents leave her out of something so momentous? And if Peggy had been pregnant, why were they still so disconnected from each other?

Chapter Twenty-Two

December 1854

There was a general excitement in the Duncan household that wasn't normal. It was affecting everyone, including Margaret. Christmas Day was fast approaching, and all of the rooms were being thoroughly spruced up for the event. This was her third Christmas season in Edinburgh, but the novelty factor of how the Duncan family celebrated the occasion still generated an irrepressible excitement.

Christmas Day had been so different in Milnathort. Across Scotland, unless the twenty-fifth of December fell on a Sunday, it was just a normal working day. The only exception for her had been that she'd trundled along to whichever kirk her parents were attending on the evening of the twenty-fifth for a service, regardless of which day of the week it was.

The Duncan family celebrations of the birth of Jesus were a lot more festive, much more colourful, and involved the household staff in non-standard preparations.

A light knock at the parlour door had her looking across at Rachel. The household staff knocked then entered, so it was unlikely to be any of them.

Rachel's eyelids twitched expectantly. "Whoever can that be? It won't be Mother at this time of day. She'll be in one of her nervous fuddles."

Margaret put her charcoal drawing on the side table.

It would definitely not be the Mistress, who was, as Rachel suspected, lying down for her euphemistic afternoon rest. What was really disturbing was that even Rachel had obviously noticed Helen Duncan's tendency towards being unable to walk straight into the parlour. Helen was rarely steady on her feet these days, and was frequently confused over what she was trying to do. Then the woman got irrationally angry when she realised that she wasn't where she wanted to be, or doing what she thought she was doing. Helen's condition was worrying for the whole household, except for Mister Duncan, who often as not didn't return for dinner during the week any more, and who wasn't around to witness Helen's erratic daytime behaviour.

During the last few days, the Mistress had been more on-edge than ever, all of the staff bearing the brunt of a tongue-lashing for almost nothing. Relatives on Helen Duncan's side intended to visit on Christmas Day, some of whom Margaret had seen before. However, preparations were also being made for a couple who would be overnight guests during the festivities, and who were to be given Robert's ground-floor bedroom. The entertaining planned was on a scale that Margaret hadn't yet experienced, though Jessie had said that before Rachel's accident there had occasionally been overnight visitors who weren't relatives.

Before she'd taken two steps the door opened, and the doctor and his assistant, Bernard Jackson, strode in.

"Good afternoon, young lady! It's time for those exercises that you love to hate," the doctor said, his usual encouraging tones ringing across the room.

Doctor Oliver, the current family physician, always tried to make light of the fact that Rachel groaned and complained vehemently when it was time for the weekly session of arm and leg manipulation that was designed to avert muscle atrophy. Margaret sympathised greatly, since Rachel's general condition wasn't always the best.

Though the little girl ate the food put in front of her, and they managed to snatch a bit of fresh air whenever possible with the use of the outside wheelchair, Rachel tended towards coughs and sniffles, even when none of the rest of the household were bothered by a head cold.

Margaret remained at the door to hold it wide open for Bernard Jackson to wheel the invalid out of the parlour.

"Don't worry your pretty little head, Margaret, I won't scrape the varnish." Bernard's quip made the object of his conversation shudder.

"I've learned by now how this monstrosity of a wheeled chair is a tight fit for squeezing past the doorframe. Whoever designed it should learn to measure more accurately."

Margaret refrained from reminding the repulsive obsequious toad that it wasn't so much that the wheels themselves were a tight fit, it was the special lap tray that had been an addition to the original specification which widened the whole vehicle. But Bernard Jackson wasn't interested in the technicalities; he was scathing about any profession that wasn't a medical one.

She purposely did not meet the young man's gaze. Margaret wasn't in the least keen on the interest he seemed to be bestowing on her, if real interest it was? There was just something she couldn't quite stomach about the sycophantic preening of Bernard Jackson. His eyes were too closely set for her to feel he was genuine about anything. He had been accompanying Doctor Oliver on his visits to Rachel for the last couple of months, and was inclined to be over-friendly to Margaret during the time that the doctor was giving a progress report to Mistress Duncan down in the drawing room. Bernard's whispered comments to Margaret about her being a very beautiful young woman made her flesh creep.

It had only taken a couple of Bernard Jackson's appearances for her to determine that she would never

ever consult the man, if he eventually graduated as a fully-fledged doctor.

She hurried past the wheelchair and sped across the corridor to open Rachel's bedroom door, then ensured that Rachel's bedcovers were tight and flat before she positioned herself at the foot of the bed.

Bernard Jackson's fingertips were too keen to stray light touches to her lower back, or to her shoulders, or her arm, if she walked alongside him. From anyone else they might be coveted but not from him.

"Do the usual, if you please, Mister Jackson," Doctor Oliver instructed as he took up his position on the right-hand side of the bed.

Margaret knew by now to wait for her instructions. Mostly she was asked to remain, though do nothing but observe. However, she was occasionally excused from the room if Rachel was not overly fussing about her treatment.

Since Rachel was so slight, it was no hardship for Bernard Jackson to open the protective restraints and then lift Rachel free of the chair by himself, before he positioned her flat on the bed.

"You seem a little out of sorts, young miss." Doctor Oliver's tone was kindly. "Is there anything you'd like to tell me about how you are feeling?"

Rachel's head shook, though she said nothing, her eyes not straying from the doctor's face.

Margaret watched the man go through his usual medical checks before any manipulation would take place. She knew that the doctor's hand to her charge's wrist was to check the pulse rate.

"Mmm, that is a little irregular." The doctor cleared his throat before lifting Rachel's eyelids to observe the colour, after which he laid the back of his fingers to the girl's forehead. "Mmm…I thought you might be a little feverish, but that does not seem the case."

Margaret dared to add some information.

"Would it be because Rachel is very excited about the approach of Christmas, and the preparations we're all making?"

Doctor Oliver chuckled. "That might indeed be an explanation."

Margaret felt his gaze slide back to the little girl. "Then, I believe we had best get on with your exercises, young lady. Shall we allow Margaret to go and help elsewhere, or will you need her to stay, today?"

She was pleased to see the grin sliding free on Rachel's face.

"No, I won't fuss today, I promise. We need to make the parlour fit for our guests who may arrive very soon."

After a slight flick of Doctor Oliver's finger towards the door, Margaret carefully slid past Bernard Jackson and left them to the exercise programme.

On reaching the parlour, she found Kate attempting to haul out the large centre-of-the-floor carpet rug, having dragged the furniture aside and rolled up the rug like a sausage.

"Let me take the other end," she chided, "it's far too heavy for one person."

Kate chuckled. "I don't lift them down the stairs, I just slide them."

"Well, not today. Doctor Oliver won't need me for a little while, so I'm free to help."

While they slid the rug down two flights of stairs and hauled it along the corridor, Kate explained, "The doctor's visit means a good opportunity for me to get this large rug beaten. Cleaning this parlour rug is probably the most difficult."

Margaret understood what Kate meant. It wasn't a harder rug to actually clean, but the parlour was rarely empty so it took good timing to get it done every week.

Once they had lugged the rug outside and into the yard, Margaret was startled by the volume that Kate produced.

"Thomas Nisbet! Are you down there? Come and help us get this up over the rope."

Margaret looked down the space that was too bare to be called a back garden. In Milnathort, the land beyond her grandmother's kitchen door had been crammed with strips for growing vegetables, and the boundaries had been lined with fruit trees and other bushes. What faced her now was about the same length, but beyond the rope that was used to drape the wet clothes for drying, there were only a few straggly bushes and the rest was stubbly grass and wildflowers.

She watched the young coachman rise up from the bench outside the combined coach house and stable that lay at the far end of the yard, where he had been cleaning some horse tack.

"Kate Hyne!" Tom echoed her demand. "Have you ever heard of the word please?"

Margaret ignored the banter that followed on between Kate and Tom as he helped flip the rug up and over the clothes rope that was strung across the yard between tall fence posts. Though older than Kate by a couple of years, it was well-known in the kitchen that Tom wanted to make Kate his wife as soon as possible. She, on the other hand, was taking her time.

"Ha!" Kate chided without bite. "Do you know what? I'll give you a lovely thank you if you help me with the beating."

"Make it a kiss and I'm your man!" Tom grinned at Kate's blushes, as he accepted the wooden carpet beater and began to whack the dust free from the rug, a smoky cloud wafting in all directions. "Just as well I'm here then, and not off yet to collect Mister Duncan."

"Is he coming home early today?" Margaret hadn't known that information.

"Not till five o'clock, but that's a short day for him, as you well know." Tom stood back to admire his handiwork, interspersing that with admiring Kate as well.

201

Feeling she was one-too-many out in the yard and not needed, Margaret slipped back inside and hurried up to the parlour. She was curious, like any young woman probably would be, about what it must be like to be so well-admired by a beau, and to reciprocate that feeling. The bond that was already well-established between Kate and Tom was so visible, and so genuine in every joke or gesture between the two servants. So far, Margaret just hadn't met any young man who stirred her senses in the way that was so obvious between Kate and Tom. Would it ever happen to her?

Though not her usual job, once she reached the parlour, Margaret picked up the feather duster Kate had left out ready and set to cleaning the surfaces around her – the bookcases, the window ledges, the table tops and the mantlepiece. The ornate black cast-iron clock in front of her chimed three times as she whiffed the feathers around it, not daring to move it as it was incredibly heavy. She wondered what Mister Duncan's early return might mean. He wasn't generally home till after six on weekday evenings when he did come home for dinner, though often it was much later. Perhaps he was bringing the guests?

Having dusted all of the surfaces, she laid the duster back where she had found it and looked around. While the rug was still downstairs getting a good beating, it was the perfect time to sweep the floor. As expected, the broom and dustpan were waiting at the door.

A short while later, she glanced at the clock. The doctor would soon be finished with Rachel. That thought had her reaching for the two cloths and the beeswax furniture polish. She knew the order of working that Kate adhered to and followed it, removing the bits and bobs of ornaments from the occasional tables that dotted the room, setting them down on the floor. Opening the polish jar, she dipped in the rough cloth and began to rub hard in circular motions, to ensure the polish seeped into the wood. It was the kind of repetitive job she didn't mind undertaking, since her thoughts could drift. Replacing the rough cloth with the smooth one, she burnished the table tops to a lustrous sheen, the powerful smell of the beeswax and linseed oil at war with the scents from the pile of pine cones that lay in a box near her feet, ready to be used for decorations.

For no accountable reason Margaret thought of her mother, wondering what Peggy might be doing. As the housekeeper, would Peggy be sprucing up her uncle's house? She just couldn't imagine that.

Her uncle was a member of a Methodist church, which as far as she knew was more like an Anglican Church than the United Presbyterian that her father wrote about attending in Perth. Uncle James didn't sound as religious as her father, but she didn't think he would be doing up his house in Christmas fripperies similar to how they were decorating in Albany Street. She had a feeling that the good Methodists of Perth weren't so influenced by Victorian royal traditions quite so much as Edinburgh advocates.

Her parents' move to Perth now seemed such a long time ago.

She'd no idea how Peggy felt about them still living in Uncle James' house, since the quarterly letters that arrived for her were always written by William.

His missives were very short updates about his attendance at his various evening groups, but none of his letters told her anything about her mother.

Margaret had been aware of the lack of information about Peggy but had not been unduly concerned. She'd written a few letters directly to her mother, though had never quite known how to broach the subject of a miscarriage, or still-birth, having decided that must have been what had happened.

Peggy was perfectly capable of writing her own letters, so Margaret felt slighted that her mother never replied, yet leaving such a task to William was also very credible.

She'd no illusions that Peggy pined for her in any way at all, since William had occasionally mentioned early on during their stay in Perth that her mother was fully occupied in looking after her young cousins.

Whatever Peggy was doing, Margaret hoped her mother was getting some joy from it. It was well over a year since her parents had come to Edinburgh, but they had never indicated they'd come a second time. Her half-day off remained the same, so travelling to Perth wasn't an option for her, even if she saved up the fare, which she acknowledged she probably could if she was really inclined.

Exhaling loudly, she shook her head to banish her wayward thoughts, but made a pact with herself to send a New Year Greeting to her father and a separate one to her mother. It seemed like an unfruitful chore, but it was the respectable thing a daughter would do, and Peggy was such a stickler about being seen to be respectable. Margaret looked around for another task. Time was precious away from Rachel, and there was still much to do.

The grunts at the doorway heralded the return of Kate and the rug, ably assisted up the stairs by Tom who helped bring it inside.

"Thank you, kindly, sir."

Kate's quip and little bob were cheeky ones which Tom acknowledged with a pretend tug of his forelock. "Anything else you require of me?"

Kate's laugh rang out. "Aye, indeed. You can lift that brush and sweep the room for me. I'll just steady this rug roll till you're finished."

"No need, Tom." Margaret was quick to intervene. "It's already done."

She acknowledged Kate's head bob of thanks with a wide grin.

"Well then, Tom Nisbet. You can help set the furniture back in place so that Margaret and I don't knock our backs out."

Margaret drew her gaze away from the smouldering looks that passed between the other two occupants of the room as the heavy occasional tables and chairs were strategically replaced on top of the carpet. The obvious sizzling love between Kate and Tom was nothing like what Margaret imagined she would encounter with the likes of smarmy Bernard Jackson.

Her reverie of what kind of man she would want to pay her some attention was interrupted by the exit of Kate and Tom and the flurried arrival of Jessie.

"I can't possibly miss whatever is going on up here, can I?"

Jessie's grin was a mile wide as she deposited a deep dish filled with deliciously-scented items on top of the bookcase that sat under the middle window. "Mistress Abernethy says these are ready for wiring but to be really careful as they're extremely fragile. Not to mention the ridiculous expense which has our cook in flurry, since the price of the oranges and cloves have come out of her Christmas expenses."

Margaret snickered. "Where else would she expect it to come from?"

"Oh, you know Mistress Abernethy." Jessie folded her arms under her chest, pretending it was as generously rounded as the woman she mimicked, though in fact Jessie's chest was already well-developed for a young woman of her age. *'Shouldn't be out of my budget,'* Jessie griped, in the haughty way Cook often did when making a poor point. *'It's not as if we're going to eat them after they've been in a smoky room for days on end.'*

Margaret loved it when Jessie did her impersonations. Her friend had got even better at copying other people's voices and mannerisms.

Jessie sobered, back to practicality.

"What's needing done first? I only have a little while before I need to go back down again."

"Help me with this wreath?"

Jessie stepped forward and grasped the end of the red ribbon.

Rachel had painstakingly attached a varied selection of red-berried holly, ivy leaves, pine cones and little sprigs clipped from the conifer bushes that flanked the sides of the back yard, with only a little input from herself.

The mantlepiece wasn't so high that Margaret couldn't reach it. It was more that the weight of the wreath needed someone at the other end to help stretch the ribbon along the relatively narrow mantle top. Usually, there was only a matching pair of gold candlesticks in front of the huge gilt-edged mirror, and a clock in the middle, but she always had a fear that the immensely heavy mirror would one day tip free from its wall fastenings.

"That's lovely and just the perfect size," Jessie enthused when the garland was in place.

She nodded before turning towards the little tree that was set upon a table near the windows. "Yes. Rachel did a very good job with estimating how much ribbon we needed to purchase from the draper's shop, and she's attached the items really professionally."

Jessie scoffed. "Credit where credit is due, Margaret. It's much more to do with your teaching skills. I recall a dreadful decoration being put up the first Christmas I spent here. The twine used was far too short for the mantlepiece, and the greenery was haphazardly knotted on to it. If I had been the one to make it, I'd have been very disappointed."

Margaret was intrigued. "Who made it?"

Another of Jessie's laughs pealed around the room. "Mistress Duncan found the twine in the outside shed. It was Victoria who added the greenery."

Margaret carefully picked up a dried orange slice and inhaled. The combination of citrus fruit and cloves warmed her insides. "Oh, that smells so wonderful."

"Did you plan to add them to the mantle wreath?" Jessie's gaze was fixed in that direction.

She nodded. "That was our original intention, but the wreath is already quite full. What do you think?"

Jessie's contemplation was thorough. "I'd only add three or four slices, just to give an orange glow here and there, to enhance the red berries."

The full blast of Jessie's humour hit Margaret when her friend turned back. "Did you know that our Tom pinched that berried holly from three doors down?"

"No!" Margaret grinned, pointing to the pieces of wire she'd cut ready for the orange slices. "How did he dare do that? Mister Cruickshank is the crabbiest neighbour in the street. He never has a good word for anyone."

Jessie picked up a piece of wire and carefully threaded it through the firm edge of the orange slice. "Tom sneaked in after dark, having seen that old Cruickshank's bushes had more berries than ours."

Four of the orange slices were set into the fireplace garland, Jessie catching her up on the latest downstairs gossip. Chinwagging with anyone else was never a done thing but it didn't seem like idle chatter when it was Jessie who gave the latest news.

"I'll get Rachel to help lay out the rest of the orange slices around the tree when she's finished with her exercises."

"Ah, yes." Jessie scowled. "I had to open the door to that ghastly creep today, when I got back from the market, since Kate was elsewhere." Jessie's voice dropped to a whisper. "You stay clear of that man. There's something about that doctor's assistant that I just can't warm to."

Margaret heartily agreed, and didn't mind Jessie being like a mother hen.

"Me neither. I avoid being in close proximity to him."

Jessie groaned when she approached the mahogany grandfather clock that stood near the door, quite a bit taller than she was. "Oh, look at the time. I'll be lucky to get a cold cup of tea from Mistress Abernethy."

Margaret looked at Jessie. She didn't think her best friend was all that bothered since her grin was the kind that was irrepressible.

"What's got you into such a wonderful mood?" she asked.

Jessie stuck out her tongue, playfully, and not in the least ladylike. "Wouldn't you like to know?" Her wink was unmissable as she exited the room.

Margaret shouted at the disappearing back. "I'm guessing you met up with that mystery man from your church services?"

Jessie's head popped back in. "Don't you dare say a word, or Dragon Abernethy won't be asking me to do any more shopping for her."

Back to finalising the preparations, Margaret mused about Jessie's love life. There was definitely someone out there who had gained her best friend's attention, but Jessie just would not divulge a single thing about the young man. She had a sneaky feeling that Jessie now made more excuses to be outside the Duncan house than Margaret knew about. When she was upstairs with Rachel for hours on end, Margaret often had no idea what Jessie was supposedly doing downstairs.

Or wherever Jessie was.

A huge smile broke free. It was well-past time that Jessie had more to be truly happy about. The staff had just celebrated Jessie's birthday the previous day with a small cake and cup of tea provided by Mistress Abernethy in the kitchen. A birthday tea was a brief interlude during the working day, but the Duncan staff much appreciated the gesture because Margaret knew it didn't happen in all domestic work situations.

Jessie, now sixteen, was entering a phase of life that Margaret knew she herself just wasn't ready for. Though only nine months older than Margaret was, Jessie's life experiences seemed to have made Jessie mature earlier, both emotionally and physically.

It was an incredible thought that her best friend, her almost-sister, had a secret admirer – someone Margaret hoped to find out the identity of very soon. At present, it was a tantalising and entertaining secret that Jessie was hoarding, but Margaret knew her patience might not last. She wanted to know all that happened to her best friend, having shared everything for almost their whole lives.

What was Jessie doing now that she couldn't share with her?

Sudden heat flared at Margaret's cheeks when she contemplated Jessie doing things with her young man that might lead to complications. The kind of unwanted pregnancy problems that Kate had recently warned them about. Surely Jessie's friendship with her beau hadn't developed that far?

A more horrifying thought was that Jessie could leave the Duncan household and get married!

Indeed, she herself could even be married at fifteen! She didn't remember any Milnathort girl who had married that young, but under Scots law marriage for a girl over twelve was technically possible.

Would her thoughts on having a sweetheart, or even on marriage at the age of fifteen or sixteen, have been any different if she'd gone to work at the mill in Milnathort after leaving school? Would that have made her mature much faster than she felt she was doing? Margaret answered her own questions with a fairly resounding yes. Although her tutoring job had given her a degree of maturity and responsibility, she also acknowledged that her life in the Duncan household had sheltered her from many of the harsh realities of life for young women living in much poorer circumstances. Nothing much happened to her out of the daily norm to thrust her into any precarious situations. Yet, though her days may be humdrum and never truly exciting, she appreciated that she was living in a secure environment – if she ignored the now more frequent temperamental rages of Mistress Duncan.

Margaret just wished that she'd paid more attention to the young men who flattered Jessie when they were out together of a Sunday afternoon, idly strolling around the Edinburgh city streets. Could it have been one of those forward lads who whistled and whispered naughty things about what fun they'd have with Jessie?

Selfishly, Margaret also wondered why they didn't pay her more attention in the way they paid it to Jessie. Was it because her friend had beautiful blonde hair? Or was it just that Jessie's cheery nature was so easily appreciated by strangers?

If she herself became less serious, less shy around the opposite sex and more whimsical, would that attract the men? Young men very different to the repellent Bernard Jackson?

Oh, dear! Peggy would be horrified by her thoughts.

That made Margaret giggle so much!

Chapter Twenty-Three

Later, in the early evening, Margaret heard a commotion in the corridor before she set eyes on those involved in the noisy banter, the deep guffaws loud enough to halt her reading. The door to the parlour blasted open, and a figure with long legs propelled over to Rachel.

"It's good to see you, sister," Robert Duncan exclaimed before he knelt down to be at the girl's eye level. "How are you this Christmas Eve?"

Closing the book that she'd been sharing with Rachel, Margaret eased away to give the elder Duncan brother more space to greet his sibling. He'd not been home since the previous summer, but his greeting was always the same. Rachel received a quick shoulder hug, followed by a ruffling of her hair, before Robert stood up again.

She couldn't avoid noting that Robert was much taller than during his last visit. She herself had grown during the past year and at five feet eight was taller than many girls of her age, including Jessie who had stubbornly remained at five feet three, much to her friend's disgust. Margaret had often tried to console Jessie by saying that being smaller meant less cost in buying material for dresses. It might be amusing to say but it actually wasn't true.

She was gauging if Robert was now over six feet tall when an unknown voice intruded making her aware of the other person involved in the noisy teasing that she'd heard before the door opened.

"Do introduce me, Robert, to these lovely ladies."

Margaret turned back towards the doorway, her eyes widening on seeing the face that went with the voice. The young man who hesitated there bore a huge grin. However, it wasn't the obvious humour that gained her full attention. The attractive young man, who looked to be a shade older than Robert, she instinctively knew would be drawing the gaze of many young women.

"Come over here Francis and greet my sister."

Margaret felt herself staring as the visitor walked towards Rachel's wheelchair, and also bent down on one knee in similar fashion to Robert.

"Francis Douglas Scott at your service, young lady. I'm very pleased to meet you again, Rachel, even if you don't recall me from before. Robert has been telling me many things about your keen interests this past year, and especially about your love of drawing."

Francis didn't hug Rachel, or ruffle her hair, but he did lift the girl's thin fingers to bestow a brief kiss on them before he rose up to his full height, which was only a little shorter than that of Robert. The latter drew back Margaret's attention with his next words.

"Margaret Law is my sister's tutor. Meet Francis, one of my reprobate friends from St. Andrews."

Margaret watched in fascination as Francis' hand stretched out towards her own, the expectation for her to tender the back of her hand in response.

Confusion flooded Margaret. It had been her duty to ensure that Rachel knew how to hold her hand out for her fingers to be saluted in acknowledgement, if not actually touched by the person's lips, as Rachel had indeed done with Francis. However, a *baisemain* – she had recently learned the French word for such a formal greeting – was for her superiors, not for her.

Somewhat frozen, she felt her hand being lifted high enough for the young man, Francis, to briefly touch his lips to the skin of her fingers, leaving them tingling. His deep voice then caressed her strangled senses.

"It truly is a pleasure to eventually meet you, Miss Law. Robert has mentioned your work with his sister many times."

Rachel's light trill broke the stupor that Margaret had found herself in. "We just call her Margaret. She's never called Miss Law."

Francis turned back towards Rachel.

Margaret felt a blush rising and that was only from looking at his deep hazel eyes, the irises of which were acutely pronounced.

"Nevertheless, it would not be appropriate for me to call her Margaret. That would be far too familiar. I don't know her well enough for that, yet."

Robert's snort was deep and just short of derision. "Margaret understands her place well enough in this household."

An icy shower descended, pulling Margaret out of her thrall.

It was definitely time to be circumspect. She had never had an issue of how to behave in Robert's company. He had always maintained a degree of distance, that of employer and servant, even though it was his father who paid her wages. Robert was the brother who had inherited his mother's tendency towards snobbishness, unlike David who continued to bear a much friendlier disposition.

"Would you like some time alone with Rachel?" she asked.

Robert nodded in her direction after a quick look at the grandfather clock in the corner.

"Come back in fifteen minutes. That should be plenty of time since Francis and I have an appointment to go to in a half-hour."

She stepped to the door, Robert already quizzing his little sister about her recent activities.

"I made all of the festive decorations in the parlour, with Margaret's help. Are they not really fine?"

213

Rachel's excitement was worth Robert's somewhat abrupt dismissal of her.

Once out and into the corridor, Margaret's hesitation was not a normal occurrence. If dismissed from Rachel's presence, it was generally easy to assess what could purposefully be done in the interim before she returned to her charge. This time there was a tussle inside her head. She could use the fifteen minutes to help Jessie with something downstairs. Since the dining room was free, she could fetch her mending basket and continue with the repairs set her by Mistress Duncan. She even deliberated that she could spend the time in leisurely reading, a very rare luxury during the day.

The current dilemma was that she wanted desperately to eavesdrop, in the hope that she'd hear more of the delicious deep tones of Robert's intriguing friend. Had this tingly feeling only happened because she had been thinking about Jessie and her sweetheart earlier that afternoon?

A sudden clatter from downstairs had Margaret shaking her head, freeing her of her fanciful thoughts, and had her automatically heading for the staircase.

"What happened to make such a din?" she asked on reaching the kitchen door.

Jessie looked up from the mess she was clearing up, her smile full of humour. "Although her heart is engaged to Tom, it seems our Kate isn't impervious to a bit of flattery from a handsome young man! In her hurry to tell me of her encounter with the latest visitor at the front door, she managed to drop the soup tureen which, as you can see, still had some leftovers in it."

Margaret knew immediately who the visitor was likely to be.

"Why isn't Kate cleaning up the mess?" she asked.

Jessie straightened up, having put the sopping mop-up cloth into a large enamel bowl. "She's outside, howling her eyes out. No doubt haranguing poor Tom about the fact that the cost of a replacement tureen will have to come out of her wages."

Unfortunately, Margaret knew it might actually come to that, depending on whether Mistress Abernethy could jiggle the finances to buy a new matching tureen from her always-stretched kitchen budget.

"I'll clean that up for you. Robert has kindly dismissed me for the next fifteen minutes. You go back to whatever you were doing."

"Yes, I believe the lordly Master Duncan Senior deigns to grace us with his presence!" Jessie quipped before Margaret felt a grateful smile come her way. "I was scraping the carrots in the scullery. It's not currently my favourite job, since this year's crop hasn't stored well. It's difficult to have any carrot left at all after I peel away the rough, and there I was about to take my due time off."

Margaret spoke to Jessie's back as her friend moved across the kitchen. "I didn't realise Mistress Abernethy was storing vegetables."

Jessie turned back. "She isn't. These were the best available from the nearby market, so they're being used for tonight's meal. She's livid about the quality of vegetables for her Christmas menu tomorrow, and not just the state of the carrots. The harvests this year all over Scotland have been poor, due to all the rain we had in the early autumn. I recommend you don't mention anything about the food!"

Margaret was happy not to get into any such discussions. She ate what was provided and was thankful to receive it, even though most of what she and the household staff got wasn't what went onto the table for the Duncan family.

Sweeping up the broken crockery was the work of moments, but Margaret's thoughts lingered on the people up in the parlour.

Sliding the crockery remains from the dustpan into the box outside in the yard that was earmarked for such items, to possibly be used as pot fillers when replanting some of Mistress Duncan's impressive large houseplants that dominated the drawing room, she almost bumped into Jessie when she stepped back inside the kitchen. Her friend's expression was business-like, a finger pointing towards her for emphasis.

"And don't you go getting side-tracked either by a certain handsome face that happens to be upstairs just now."

Margaret chuckled as she side-stepped out of reach. "I didn't know you had met Robert's friend."

Jessie still looked chastising. "If he goes by the name of Francis and is a friend from St. Andrews, then yes, I have met him before. A few years ago, mind. But you definitely need to steer clear of him, Margaret. He might dally all day long with a domestic, but he will definitely never marry one."

"Who said I was looking for marriage? Like you seem to have with your mysterious friend, a dalliance or a fleeting romance with a handsome young gent might be…" Margaret grinned as she made her escape.

"Don't even think what I think you are thinking!"

"So, it's fine for you to traipse out every now and then, when you've time off, to meet up with your undisclosed young man, but it's not good for me to even talk to someone conveniently eligible?"

Jessie's finger wagged in her direction. "Just remember at this time of year I'm a whole year older and a lot wiser than you are!"

"Ha!" Margaret guffawed. "Wiser? That'll be the day, old lady!" She neatly fielded the dishcloth that sailed her way and tossed it back, the two of them chuckling like demented hens.

Jessie's warning echoed in Margaret's head as she trooped her way back upstairs. Perhaps, with any luck, the stunning-looking, slightly swarthy young man would have transformed into an ugly trow and slipped away to his trowie-knowe by the time she got there. She grinned as she recalled Rachel having loved reading about the mischievous fairy folk from the Shetland Isles in one of the books from the lending library.

"Margaret?"

Kate was preparing yet more drinks to take up to the drawing room, later that night.

"Could you take some towels up to the attic bedrooms? I meant to do it earlier but haven't had a breathing space. Robert and Francis used the ones that were in their rooms when they freshened up before their dinner this evening."

Margaret set aside the mending she'd been doing at the kitchen table. "Of, course I can help you, but why can't they use the same ones tonight?"

Kate's ice-blue eyes nearly popped out of her eye sockets. "I can see you've not had enough of the sharp end of Mistress Duncan's tongue, of late."

Jessie, unaccustomedly also sitting at the table, was polishing a huge heap of silver cutlery that had been washed after dinner. She chipped in with one of her mimics. '*My guests must have every convenience, Kate. They must never go away from Albany Street complaining of poor services.*'

Jessie grinned and returned to her own voice. "And that, my dear Margaret, includes fresh towels at least twice a day."

Margaret made a face, and not a particularly complimentary one, before she turned her attention to Kate. "How on earth does she expect you to launder multiple towels for everyone in December?"

Kate nodded her head towards the door, indicating she needed someone to open it for her. Her hands were fully occupied with a very heavily laden tray, the special after-dinner treats Mistress Abernethy had made dripping over the sides of the cake rack.

"The bedlinens are sent to the laundrywoman who lives near the market, but as you've suspected, I do the towels. You've clearly not been in the laundry room recently. That's where you'll get the stack of dry ones. It's the pile nearest the door. And while you're in there, can you check that there's enough coal dross on to keep the fire at a low ebb?"

Margaret held open the kitchen door for Kate, and then padded along to the room that had the dubious title of laundry. She'd not been there for months. Her household tasks never included the cleaning of clothes and, slightly to her shame, she acknowledged Kate always laundered her underclothes, the clean set re-appearing on her bedroom shelf a few days later.

An unmistakable reek of wet cotton and linen, which vied with an even worse stench of wet wool, hit her as soon as she opened the door to the extremely cluttered area. The two walls to her left and right were shelved from ceiling to floor, stacked with all manner of sheets, towels, table linens and folded underclothing. At the far end of the room there were two large sinks set together, a range of wooden buckets and metal pails beneath them. Paraphernalia for washing clothes, including a wooden-edged metal washboard, lay on a slatted wooden surface next to the left-hand sink. On the right hand side stood a cast iron mangle, with a large wooden bucket lying ready to catch the squeezed-out water when cloth was squashed between the rollers.

The small window, which sat high above the sinks, was presently obscured by condensation, from heat created in the tiny hearth that was fitted into the corner of the room. Tending to the fire needed to come first, but it was difficult to move into the room since the overhead clothing pulley was jammed full of drying linens, positioned to ensure the maximum hanging length that was possible. Drying the laundry quickly couldn't possibly be an easy job.

Kate was right about the fire. It did need some dross added to it, and though Margaret was careful when she added a shovelful of the gritty little bits of coal, she needed to clean her hands free of coal dust before she lifted the pile of towels for the attic bedrooms. Stepping back out into the basement corridor she felt quite flushed, and murmured sincere thanks to the corridor walls that she had avoided being employed in some household as a laundry maid.

The climb up three flights of stairs to the attic floor made her feel even more heated as she thought of who was sleeping up there during the festive period. When there was no response to her knock on the door of the first small room, she entered and looked around for a free surface to set down the clean towels. Whoever was staying in the room was not a tidy person at all. Popping her whole pile on the bedcover, she lifted up a used towel from the floor and placed it over her arm. After two clean towels had been set beside the basin and ewer on the dressing table, she lifted her now smaller pile and left the room.

She clenched her knuckles to knock on the next door but was startled when the door opened. Overbalancing into the empty space, she found herself tight in the clutches of Francis Douglas Scott, who took his time about removing his steadying palms from her shoulders, his mesmerising hazel eyes capturing her gaze. Feeling her cheeks heat even more than in the laundry room, she dropped her gaze, her embarrassment acute as she attempted to take a step backwards.

"If I had known you were going to come and visit me, I'd not have arranged to play cards with Robert, downstairs in the parlour, in five minutes time," he jested.

Raising her head at his playful tone, Margaret's breath hitched when his slow sensual smile captivated her, so close that she could see every single hair of his neatly-trimmed moustache.

"I'd much rather play a different sort of game with you, Miss Margaret Law."

Completely flustered at the flaring heat in his gaze, and annoyed with her lack of poise, she stuttered, "I brought clean towels."

"I can see that." His voice had dropped to a whisper.

Before she could attempt another word, his head dipped and his lips touched her own.

Startled for the second time in as many moments, her mouth opened. To say something, to protest at his presumption, she didn't quite know what she was intending, but she found she barely had the strength of a new-born kitten. Somewhat mortified, she closed her eyes yet allowed herself to marvel at what was happening.

She found herself entirely cradled by his arms; the towel pile crushed against her breasts as he deepened the kiss and drew her in towards him. His questing palms then caressed a pathway down her back to her buttocks where they splayed open and massaged through her numerous clothing layers. As the kisses deepened, so did the pressure of his touches.

The disturbance at his groin seemed to have a will of its own and made her gasp into his mouth. If anything, her reaction seemed to make Francis smile into their kisses.

She was naïve, for sure, but not completely unworldly. She and Jessie had had recent conversations with Kate, some of which had been utterly revealing. She knew what was likely happening to him, but having never been kissed before she was in thrall and had absolutely no idea of what to do. Only when she was gasping for air, did the amused man free her lips.

"Well, this is the best surprise of the day. I was not expecting this early Christmas gift."

Before she could reply, his smiling lips returned. This time she had an idea of how to respond and revelled in how he changed the angle of his kisses, his palms moving up to bracket her cheeks. When his tongue probed at her lips, she opened up and revelled in the experience, a delicious and tingling heat warming her even more than before. She was only barely aware that the towels she'd been clutching had been released from her grasp and were now trapped between them, her arms sneaking through to creep up to his shoulders.

After a few lingering moments, and more gentle caresses of his fingers at her lower back, she sensed Francis draw away.

Daring to open her eyes to look at him, she could see his humour was evident, his words a terrible tease when he set her well back from him. The towel pile drifted to the floor, but Francis seemed completely unaware of them. "You have no idea how much I would rather remain up here with you and continue with what we've started, but…alas, I am a mere guest here and must hasten down to my hosts."

Without another word, Francis released her. Flashing her a rueful grin and an upturn of his eyebrows, he tugged his waistcoat down and pulled the edges of his jacket forward so that he could fasten the buttons. After a final peck to her cheek, he stepped past to make his way downstairs, leaving Margaret staring at an empty space, her feet leaden. She couldn't even describe how her body felt, apart from moving from stunned to bereft.

She found herself skulking in the corridors as she moved around helping with household tasks during what was left of the long Christmas Eve, desperately wanting more than one repeat of the breath-stealing kisses.

On Christmas Day, Margaret wasn't expected to do any tutoring. She was to eat meals with Rachel in the parlour, and to help Jessie with personal care which would be conducted in the girl's bedroom – well out of sight of the guests and the family. Margaret hadn't actually been banished from the parlour, but the Mistress had told her she wouldn't be needed to join in any of the family games or pastimes, since there were plenty of people around to keep Rachel company.

Margaret had expected to catch glimpses of Francis, and perhaps have exchanges of words early on Christmas Day – when he and Robert moved around the house from drawing room to parlour, or to the dining room – but he was never alone anytime they did inhabit the same room, or corridor. She knew his gaze lingered on her perhaps a little longer than was sensible, as hers had remained on him, but those times were frustratingly momentary.

It didn't come as a surprise when she was told to keep Rachel company while the rest attended a church service on Christmas morning. Margaret told herself she wasn't disappointed, and she certainly was never disappointed with Rachel, but even just a little more of Francis' intoxicating presence would have been nice.

After lunch with Rachel in the parlour, she was sent to help elsewhere.

The rest of Christmas Day passed according to Mistress Duncan's plans. Margaret joined in with the limited festivities allowed to the staff down in the kitchen, after the family and guests had been served their multiple course dinner. Cook had prepared a special meal for the staff to eat together, although it was enjoyed long after their normal times and after Cook had gone home. Mistress Abernethy had left some sherry and a special ale for them which they consumed with slices of Cook's best heavy fruit cake. The company was amiable and Margaret really did appreciate the special effort the staff all made to make it an out-of-the-ordinary event, but she found it so difficult to suppress a yearning for a repeat session of kisses with Francis Douglas Scott.

Lying in bed that night, sleep still elusive, her fluctuating feelings made her wonder if she was wanton, especially when she recalled that Francis had been aroused. When she considered his physical reaction to her, it made her cheeks flare. Maybe she was of easy virtue, because she had certainly enjoyed the experience!

Had she been warned sufficiently by her mother, and by Jessie, about philanderers? Peggy had told her to steer clear of flatterers, but she hadn't told her that kisses from someone like Francis could be so enjoyable and would stir up such aching feelings. Would she have allowed him even more liberties if he hadn't stopped when he did? She honestly wasn't sure she'd have been able to do much resisting at all.

Till the arrival of Francis, she'd never been affected in an emotional or physical way by any young man, not by those in the street who whistled as she passed them, or who sent flattering comments her way. She sometimes generated interest in older men as well, but on those occasions which were entertaining, it was really an embarrassed pride in her appearance. Nothing else.

That was entirely different from the jittery flutters she was now feeling deep inside.

Margaret recalled asking Jessie years before, if Jessie harboured any strong feelings for David Duncan, and remembered Jessie's negative reply. Did she herself now harbour strong romantic feelings for Francis Douglas Scott? Even carnal? Thinking of such a word as carnal, a word that her mother would be horrified that she had even come across, far less knew its meaning, with its intimate associations, made blushes flare at her cheeks. It had been such a fleeting interaction with the mercurial Francis that she hadn't a clue. Yet she couldn't put it aside, or forget it happened.

The only thing she could truly be sure of was that she had liked the kisses, and his wandering caresses. She really had

Loitering around the corridors and not encountering him at all the next morning, before both he and Robert returned to St. Andrews, was so disappointing.

223

Chapter Twenty-Four

Easter 1855

"Did Mother remember to let Kate know that my little cousins will be sleeping in Victoria's room?"

Rachel's question was tinged with excitement. Having guests again, this time to celebrate Easter with the family, was a high spot in a run of repetitive days.

Margaret looked up from the embroidery frame that lay stretched across her knees, unable to prevent the tiny smirk that stretched her cheeks on hearing the words 'Victoria's room'. She had just unpicked a few poorly-made stitches that Rachel had been struggling to fix. Though in all fairness, the girl had become much better at applying herself to sewing tasks since Rachel had learned to create her own designs, rather than use a preset pattern. The one Margaret held was the special silver-threaded sampler.

Margaret wished that the pinkish hue at Rachel's cheeks was caused by anticipated excitement, akin to the enthusiasm Rachel had experienced the previous Christmas when expecting overnight visitors. Regrettably, Margaret feared it was caused by something entirely different. She dreaded that the flaring colour, faint though it was against Rachel's pale cheeks, indicated that Rachel's health was deteriorating rather than it being a sign of a robust constitution.

"I imagine your mother did, but I can check later, once we have finished for the day."

It was a discussion she would take up with Kate, and not Helen Duncan if she could avoid it. Any conversations of late with the Mistress had been fraught with misconceptions and difficult to understand. Margaret had found that she might be trying to tell Helen Duncan something about Rachel, but her employer seemed to be in a different conversation entirely. It was almost as though the woman was even in a different place, and not inhabiting the same house as everyone else.

She handed the embroidery sampler frame back to Rachel, who pouted, the earlier enthusiasm gone from her expression.

"Surely it's time for the sewing lesson time to be over, Margaret?"

"No, it's barely started, you young scamp." She ruffled the ends of Rachel's braids, tickling her under the chin to produce a tiny grin. "You can do the clock-watching just as well as I can."

Rachel pouted again, her lower lip curling, yet there was an obvious hint of humour. "Not a single moment longer!"

Margaret lifted her own sewing, a new shift she was making for herself. Though she hadn't gained any height recently she had filled out, her breasts now stretching the material of the one she was wearing, so much so that the stitches were fit to burst.

She was glad that the Mistress made no complaint about Margaret sewing for herself during what was a sewing lesson for Rachel, so long as there an improvement to be seen in Rachel's standards.

It was an increasingly difficult challenge to keep Rachel motivated, the girl's general levels of energy now constantly at a low ebb. Since the end of January, Rachel had been plagued by chesty coughing spells which seemed impossible to shift, even when taking the tonics prescribed by Doctor Oliver. They tended to make

Rachel drowsy, and even when she was trying hard to stay alert, the girl was finding it so difficult.

Once Rachel began to ply her needle with the renewed thread, Margaret let her mind drift to the earlier question. Rachel's bedroom would need to be re-organised to add yet another bed frame to accommodate all three Duncan sisters in the one room.

The previous evening, Kate had mentioned that Victoria had been extremely sulky about the need to give up her room. Even though she had shared with Elspeth for years, it was always still 'Victoria's bedroom' and never her littlest sister's. According to Kate who heard Victoria's grumbles a lot more than Margaret did, it still rankled that as the eldest Duncan daughter Victoria always felt that she should have a room of her own. It was, of course, all Rachel's fault for being an invalid nuisance who'd been given the second biggest bedroom on the first floor.

Kate had entertained Jessie and herself, recalling that Victoria had protested that her male cousins could easily use the attic bedrooms, even knowing that those small draughty rooms were only used by older family members, or sometimes unrelated guests.

Margaret could never put her finger on what set Victoria off on one of her high-handed tirades, but she acknowledged there was definite justification for the girl to feel deeply unhappy. Victoria was acutely aware of being unable to partake in many of the exploits her school friends engaged in, now that she was twelve years old. Helen Duncan's need to swaddle Victoria from potential harm had grown to be beyond the obsessive during the last couple of years. Contrarily, the woman didn't feel the need to be in Victoria's company every hour of the day, but she did prevent the girl from leaving the house unless it was deemed absolutely necessary. Going to school only a short walk away, was an exemption, though Victoria was grilled if she was even the tiniest bit late in returning.

Though Margaret continued to tutor only Rachel, she had tried to intercede on Victoria's behalf a number of times before she gave up.

Elspeth, on the other hand, had not been fussed about decanting from her room at all.

To Margaret's surprise, and definite delight, Elspeth had grown into a likeable child after she started to attend school. It seemed that being out of the household environment, and especially out of her mother's cloying and unpredictable sphere even for a few hours a day, was good for the little girl.

Helen Duncan's health had become extremely fragile, her outbursts verging on hysterical. The word 'unhinged' came into Margaret's head often enough, but not one she'd ever dare say out loud.

In contrast, Mister Duncan maintained a strict daily routine and left his wife to her own devices.

During the first year of living in their house, Margaret had overheard too many arguments, too many attempts by the master of the house to dispel his wife's fears that she was to blame for Rachels' condition. As time went on, the arguments appeared to cease, and any interaction she witnessed now was of a polite near-silence. Not to the same degree of hostility as she'd witnessed between her own parents, but sufficiently strained for it to affect the household in general.

Though Mister Duncan now only spoke to his wife when he absolutely needed to, as far as Margaret could tell, his genial relationship had never changed with his children. However, Margaret regretted for Rachel's sake that his time at home was so limited, even at weekends. When her tutoring job had begun Mister Duncan was a daily visitor to the parlour, that small amount of time so looked forward to by her little charge. But since Mister Duncan's improved standing in the Edinburgh law profession, he was often far too late home to spend time with Rachel.

Mister Duncan also wasn't experiencing the daytime traumas of Helen's making. The many changes of medication that his wife had tried made little difference to her mood swings. Kate had shared how she was having to deal with getting rid of the numerous bottles the doctor delivered. Indeed, the woman veered from frantic activity – as in the present circumstances of planning meals and activities for overnight visitors and day guests – to spells of resting in her own room for much longer durations during the day.

Helen Duncan's daytime rests had been established as a feature of the management of Rachel's overnight care. To make it less disturbing for Mister Duncan, Helen had installed a permanent truckle bed for her use in Rachel's room.

Lately, Margaret couldn't say for sure if the Mistress ever shared a bed at all during the night in her husband's room. What she did know was that the Mistress returned to their shared bedroom at some point before Margaret was upstairs in the early morning ready to tutor Rachel, after Jessie had helped with the girl's personal care. To ensure that Jessie, or she herself, had access anytime to Rachel's bedroom if something was needed for Rachel, the Mistress always used Mister Duncan's bedroom for her daytime naps.

Margaret had overheard sufficient conversations to know that attempts by the Master to employ a nurse overnight were spurned by his wife as an unnecessary expense.

The imminent arrival of Mistress Duncan's sister and family from Inverness needed changes to what had become the normal sleeping arrangements. If all three of the Duncan daughters shared Rachel's room, then it meant Mistress Duncan would need to sleep all night in the bedroom with her husband. This might maintain a veneer of all being well between the couple but Margaret knew it definitely wasn't.

Reflecting for a moment on how her own parents had needed to sleep in the same bed in Milnathort, since there weren't any spare beds to do otherwise, she decided that marital relations were very complicated. Her parents had seemed to hate each other vehemently at times, yet circumstances had forced them to be in what she realised must have been very intimate circumstances.

It was an easy step to then think of what their bedroom was like in her uncle's house, though her mother had never mentioned it years ago when they'd visited Edinburgh. Margaret hoped her parents were more at peace with each other now, if only when using the same bed.

Almost three years had passed since their visit. And she still hadn't a clue about the baby her Aunt Jeannie had mentioned.

A smile broke free. Aunt Jeannie had recently written to say that her little boy was hale and hearty and was quite the little terror already.

"Is this better, Margaret?" Rachel held out her sewing for inspection.

"Has the extra bed frame been brought out of storage?" Margaret asked Kate later that night as they sat in the kitchen, each sipping a welcome cup of tea.

"Frames. And mattresses." Kate nodded before a huge sigh slipped free. "All sorted. Tom will help me move them up tomorrow, in plenty of time to get all of the beds freshly made up."

Jessie looked up from the stocking that she was mending, her wages not nearly enough to buy a new pair every time she wore a hole in one of the heels. "At least the Easter festival doesn't need all the fuss of decorating that Christmas entails."

Margaret set down her cup, not the delicate china that was used up in the parlour but the serviceable earthenware crockery that was for servant use. "There may be no decorating, but it's still lots of extra work for Mistress Abernethy to create a special Easter Sunday meal."

"Not to mention extra labour for Jessie and me as well!" Kate harrumphed justifiably.

Margaret was quick to mollify. "Of course, for you two as well. Your workload is never properly appreciated."

Jessie launched into one of her mimicking sessions. *'I do hope you appreciate this rise to your annual remuneration, Jessie. Not all kitchen maids are allowed to finish their schooling and earn the substantial amount Mister Duncan thinks you are worthy of.'*

The way Jessie could slide into the voice and mannerisms of Mistress Duncan was quite remarkable, and it never failed to send them all into fits of giggles.

Jessie grinned, back to her own voice. "Finish my schooling? And a wage that's substantial? That woman has definitely lost her grip on reality."

It was true that Jessie had been sent to school for a few months till Rachel's accident – for which Mister Duncan had paid the fees – but when she stopped giggling Margaret couldn't fail to recall a conversation from years before, one that she had inadvertently overheard. Though she sometimes mocked the situation, Jessie always seemed content with her position in the Duncan household. And in the light of that, Margaret had found it so difficult to raise a subject that she still had no verification of. During the years she had been tutoring in Albany Street, the Reverend Duncan of Milnathort had never visited his brother.

A general nodding of the heads presently sitting around the kitchen table showed their agreement that the treading on eggshells regarding Mistress Duncan's volatile moods was extremely wearing, and the shards of the Mistress' tongue had become even more devastating when they were fired at them.

"Remind me again of how many of the Forbes family are coming?" Jessie prompted.

Kate's sigh was profound. "Six of them. It will mean an extra bed frame in Rachel's room, to accommodate all three Duncan girls. We need one more in Victoria and Elspeth's, for the three youngest Forbes sons. The older boy will share a room with David, so that's another extra bed to be sorted out there."

"How many other children do they have?"

Kate's expression was comic, her lips twisted to one side. "I can barely remember their last visit, though I had just started to work here at that time. I know they have five sons, one who is quite a bit older than the others, but I've never heard of any daughters mentioned."

"Five sons!" Margaret totted up the extra places that would be needed at the Easter table for the Forbes family. "That's going to be a big squeeze at the dining table."

Jessie's next question was for Kate. "Have you heard if Robert will be home?"

Kate's shoulders rose, her expression one of mystification. "Who knows with Robert? He seems to be content to remain at university since he's not been home for months. If he does come, I'm guessing he'll be demoted to an attic room again, since his ground floor bedroom is being prepared for his uncle and aunt."

Talk of the attic made Margaret's breath hitch. She had avoided being up there since the previous Christmas.

Kate continued to update as she gathered up the cups and headed for the sink in the scullery. "I've been instructed to air out all three attic rooms, in case they are needed."

Jessie stabbed her needle into her stocking and did a couple of quick stitches to finish off. "I'm off to bed then. I'll be the butt of Mistress Abernethy's ire, since as you well know, she hates not to know exactly how many she's cooking for. She'll be sending me to the butchers with extra meat orders five times a day."

231

"Will that be such a big problem?" Margaret knew the butcher's shop was only a few streets away, and the errand wouldn't take so long out of Jessie's admittedly busy day.

Jessie almost leapt out of her chair. "You try telling the butcher that you must have the meat immediately, but he won't get the money for it till the end of the month!"

"All you need to do is give him one of your big enticing smiles and he'll forget all about money," Kate chuckled, having returned to the kitchen with a full kettle of water to set at the side of the range for the morning. "Besides, maybe that mystery admirer of yours will just happen to be out on Albany Street when you're off on an errand!"

Margaret watched Jessie's tongue poke out behind Kate's back, though it was done in mirth.

"How many nights will they all be staying here?" Margaret hated that she always seemed last to know these things.

"They'll arrive on Good Friday and stay over till Easter Monday. That's more than plenty of extra duties for all of us!" Jessie's exit held a flourishing, cheeky smile.

As Margaret made her way to their room in Jessie's wake, she agreed that they needed to bank up as much energy as possible to cope with what looked to be a busy long-weekend ahead. Routine for Rachel was going to be difficult, and probably impossible, to accomplish.

Lying in her own bed, not long after, Margaret sighed as she put down her book before she snuffed out the candle, unable to concentrate. She'd like to confess that she had completely banished Francis Douglas Scott's 'Christmas Gift' kisses to the ends of the earth, but she hadn't. It would take a few more kisses to know whether the feelings he had roused in her were what happened any time a young man she had a liking for made advances. However, the notion of gaining more experience battled with natural caution. But then again, due to her daily routine, she knew that her chances of being in the close company of any man who might want to kiss her were slim if not impossible.

When out and about in Edinburgh on her own, during the previous few months, she had been more actively aware of any young men who had passed by. Though, if any of them had shown a flicker of interest in their gaze, she hadn't felt any curiosity at all.

A smile sneaked out. One positive thing for sure was that she had managed to thoroughly dampen Bernard Jackson's ardour. It had taken time and rigid persistence, but the man's sneaky touches and over-blown compliments had eventually ceased after Bernard had declared that he had gained himself a fiancée. Margaret's thoughts veered towards pity for the poor woman that she couldn't see the leech that Bernard was, and despair that the fiancée could possibly consider Bernard good marriage material.

Margaret turned around to get even more comfortable, adjusting the pillow under her head and trying not to waken Jessie who seemed to be asleep already. Jessie, always her best friend, was still holding out on who her sweetheart was, Jessie claiming that the person she sometimes bumped into in the street was just an acquaintance. And that, Margaret knew, was a euphemism for a planned assignation. It was beginning to irritate that Jessie wasn't forthcoming and honest with her.

But then again, she still had something that was sort of a secret about Jessie that she'd never divulged either.

Her last thought before succumbing to sleep was that the process of becoming an adult was definitely making life more complicated.

"Oh, Margaret, I do love it when the house fills up for a celebration. Don't you?"

Rachel's thready whisper reached Margaret across the parlour where she was putting a book back into one of the glass-fronted bookcases.

She wasn't quite so enthused, but she plucked a smile from nowhere and sent it Rachel's way. "It certainly makes the day a much busier one, for certain, young lady."

Margaret walked over to the bell pull at the side of the hearth and gave it a gentle tug. The ringer down in the kitchen let them know that assistance was needed in the parlour, and given the situation of the imminent arrival of the guests, Jessie would know that Tom's services were needed to lift Rachel from her wheeled-chair and into her bed. She thought she was strong enough to do it herself, if Tom was elsewhere on coaching duties, but there was always a risk she would hurt Rachel. It was safer if one sturdier man did the lifting.

Jessie must have galloped her way upstairs, since she entered the parlour almost immediately after her typical brief knock, even though Mistress Duncan had gone for a lie down in her own bedroom along the corridor after her luncheon.

"Tom's gone off to collect some supplies for Mistress Abernethy, so it's my clumsy hands that will be helping Margaret get you into bed today, young lady," Jessie joked, speaking directly to Rachel, using the familiar term they both used for the invalid.

In minutes, Rachel was lying prostrate on her own bed.

"Are you looking forward to seeing your cousins again?" Jessie asked, mutely indicating that Margaret should help her to raise Rachel to a sitting position, so that she could undo the ties at the back of the dress before it could be slipped off.

"Again?" Rachel's quirky sense of humour slipped out. "I don't remember seeing them before. I was only a wee thing when they last visited."

"Ha!" Jessie joked, efficiently stripping Rachel of her underclothing. "And you're such a big thing now!"

A memory of Jessie saying something similar to her many years ago popped into Margaret's head, making her grin. Lost in her own memory, she accepted the damp underclothing Jessie passed across to her and dumped it into the laundry basket at the side of Rachel's bed before she turned back to her favourite two people in the whole world.

"You are quite the lucky girl, you know," Jessie cajoled as she made quick work of a clean-up before replacing the clean linens that were part of the mid-afternoon routine. "You have lots and lots of cousins, even if you don't see them very often. Whereas I don't have a single one to my name."

Striding to the far side of the bed Margaret watched Jessie select a clean dress from the wardrobe, and fresh underwear from the chest of drawers.

"But you have Margaret." Rachel's eyes glistened with mirth. "And she's worth a hundred of my cousins."

Margaret watched Jessie's face bending close to Rachel before she slipped an arm under the girl's shoulders, ready to lift her up again to don the clean clothes.

"Aye, I do, don't I." Jessie grinned. "So, are you saying little miss that I am also the lucky one?"

A stunned feeling jolted Margaret. A realisation that she'd tried to deny for so long slid down her spine as she helped bring Rachel to a sitting position, the faces of the other two so close. Though Rachel's face had none of Jessie's healthy roundness, their eye shapes and iris colours were similar, the fact made more prominent since Rachel's eyes now dominated her haunted pallor. Where Jessie's golden curls, framing the sides of her cap, indicated a healthy constitution, Rachel's lank hair was the opposite. The colour, however, was made up of the same hues.

Shame flooded Margaret. She had put aside that furious conversation between the Duncan parents held so many years ago. Even her own mother's observations, after a very brief meeting with Jessie and Rachel, indicated the similarities.

Surely the situation of ignorance couldn't stay that way? Had she been keeping the knowledge to herself because she hadn't wanted Jessie's status to change? Was Jessie truly oblivious? Or was it just that her best friend and almost-sister was unwilling to rock the boat by acknowledging it?

Margaret wondered if she really was so selfish? Was she becoming the kind of sneaky person that Peggy always railed against when they lived in Milnathort? People her mother disdainfully said were nasty meddlers?

She honestly didn't know.

Chapter Twenty Five

By late afternoon, the house had filled up with the Forbes family whom Margaret had been informed had not ventured down from Inverness to Albany Street since just after the birth of Elspeth, some six years previously. It was no wonder that Rachel couldn't remember any of them.

The parents congregated in the drawing room; Mister Duncan having kept his promise to return home early from his chambers.

Up in the parlour, Margaret played a mostly observant supervisory role, surprised at having been asked to remain in the room. All of the Duncan girls were in attendance, and after an initial reserve, the lively questioning forced the Forbes cousins to come out of their shells.

She almost bit her tongue out of sheer surprise when David's voice rose above the clamour. Though she had to acknowledge that David had in fact become much less shy in her presence during the past months.

"I vote we all play a game together!"

His tone was so decisive that a hush descended immediately, the animated younger ones in immediate agreement.

"Blind Man's Bluff" shouted Ruaridh, the youngest of the Forbes boys.

"We can't play that!" Elspeth's tone was so censorious that Margaret feared she'd have to soothe some feelings.

She was spared the need by Victoria's tactful explanation. "We would really need a bigger room to play that game properly, Ruaridh."

"I agree." David really was taking charge. "Who thinks we have enough room to play Pass the Slipper?"

A chorus of *'I do'* settled the matter.

Margaret sat down near the window with her embroidery, since concentrating on reading a book was impossible. She was not supposed to join in the play, but consoled herself it wasn't part of her job, though the impulse to have fun was hard to repress.

The choice of Pass the Slipper was a good one, since the circle was easily set around Rachel's wheeled chair in such a way that she could pass on the little book they'd decided to use instead of an actual slipper.

Kate's entry into the room a short time later almost went unnoticed. It took a small cough for her to gain attention such was the fun being had with the current card game of Old Maid. Margaret had moved to help Rachel play her hand. It wasn't that her charge didn't know how to play the game, it was just for the ease of presenting Rachel's pairs of cards onto the little table set down in the middle of their circle, David having reorganised the settees and chairs accordingly. David had also tactfully paired up with Ruaridh, with Brian and John managing their own hands of cards.

"Your dinner is being served soon."

A disappointed chorus followed.

"Never mind," Victoria appeased. "We can play another round some other time."

Margaret didn't have to remind any of the children that freshening themselves up was compulsory. All but Rachel skipped from the room, their animated buzz continuing along the corridor.

Rachel would be fed in the parlour, as was usual, though Margaret would get her own meal later. The Mistress had given the order for the duration of the

Forbes family visit, since Margaret tended to use her and Rachel's evening meal time as more of a social event where they discussed topics of the day. They were topics that she filched from the days-old newspapers which eventually wended their way up to the parlour. Things Margaret thought might be discussed with Rachel during the family 'duty-call' visits.

Helen Duncan had already informed Margaret, in no uncertain terms, that the woman had no intention of the cousins barging back in to the parlour to find Rachel still lingering over her food. Of course, Margaret knew that what bothered Helen Duncan most was the thought that visitors, even young family ones, would see the food that was being served to Rachel – which was much more akin to what a toddler would be eating.

Exiting the room, Margaret sped along the corridor and collected the basin and ewer from Rachel's room, just a quick handwashing being deemed sufficient. A full toileting would come before bedtime.

Closing the parlour door, to ensure some privacy after Kate delivered Rachel's food, Margaret got to work. Rachel's food intake was limited. Swallowing was now a hard-won process, so most of the girl's food was now mashed down to a suitable spooning texture.

"Can you try to eat just a little more?" she cajoled when Rachel declared she'd eaten her fill. "Your cousins are tiring you out, and a little bit more food will help you find the energy you need to keep up with them."

Rachel's wan face was quite heartbreaking.

"I am a bit tired but I'll try just a little more."

A few minutes later, Margaret was cheered to find her charge had eaten most of the nourishing potage. Sweeping the bowl across the table, she gave Rachel the pear flummery, which always seemed so much easier to swallow than main course food.

"Well done!" she praised when the small glass dish was emptied.

The door opened as she set the desert bowl alongside the larger one.

"I'll just set the drink down here, Margaret." Kate indicated a space.

"Thank you. Your timing is perfect, Kate. We'll soon be ready for it."

"I'll remove these now?" Kate waited for a nod to be sure, though her hands cradled the bowls.

"Shall we tell Cook that you enjoyed it, Rachel?" Margaret was always conscious of using every opportunity to be as normal as possible with the service provided from the basement.

Rachel summoned a tiny lift of her lips. "Yes, thank you."

Kate disappeared in an efficient flurry.

A swift wipe of her face had Rachel presentable again, the napkin tucked in place below her chin to catch any drips from the feeding cup.

"Mmm," Margaret grinned, "It smells like your favourite drink has been prepared, young miss!"

A very exhausted Rachel attempted a smile. "Cinnamon honey?"

Margaret's grin indicated agreement. "Indeed, it is!"

Rachel's warm milk was enhanced with a pinch of cinnamon and a spoonful of honey. She was never sure how Cook, or more likely Jessie, managed it but the milk was usually a perfect temperature for Rachel to drink when it arrived upstairs.

Rachel had had time for a short restorative nap before the room erupted into movement and noise once again, the children's meal over. Through the open door, Margaret could hear the dining room being readied for the adults to have their meal.

"Do you know to play Look Around?" David asked his cousins.

Margaret was intrigued. She wasn't familiar with it, but then the Forbes children didn't seem to know either.

"We play this down in the drawing room sometimes. I'll tell them how!" Elspeth was barely able to contain herself, and was claiming the limelight. She plucked up a small spinning top from a basket of toys that sat under one of the windows and held it up high. "You all need to go out of the room and wait in the corridor till I tell you to come in. While you're outside, I'm going to hide this spinning top somewhere around the room. When I'm ready, you'll all come back in and will look for it. But you mustn't tell anyone when you notice it! And you mustn't touch it."

Margaret was bemused, not really understanding the point of the game till David added what was needed.

"When you see the object," he said, "you must sit down. When there is only one person left looking around the room the game is over. You have to try not to be that last person."

It made better sense now to Margaret, but it wasn't a game that Rachel could participate in. However, when she looked at her Margaret found Rachel to be quite excited, though looking exhausted.

"You mustn't cheat, because I will know if you are!" Rachel chided playfully, the younger children the focus of her attention.

They were into the second round of the game when Jessie came in to the parlour. As soon as Jessie stopped near Rachel's side table to collect her special feeding cup, John's voice rose above the clamour.

"You look just like Rachel!"

A hush descended in the room. Margaret hardly dared breathe as all eyes focused on her best friend.

John was not to be silenced. "Are you my cousin, too?"

After a moment of tense silence, Victoria ploughed in. "No, John. You're mistaken. This is our kitchen maid, Jessie. She just happens to have the same colour of hair as Rachel."

241

John's intent stare and mulish tint to his expression suggested he was not at all satisfied with Victoria's response.

"But her eyes look the same, too."

Margaret watched the colour drain from David's face as he stared at Jessie before it came back in an immediate whoosh of red at his cheeks. What John had pointed out was clearly not something David had ever acknowledged before. Victoria, on the other hand, was brittle.

"Lots of people have the same shape and colour of eyes. It's just a coincidence, John. Jessie isn't related to us."

There was a momentary pause before Rachel began to babble through a huge grin, clearly delighted to be compared favourably to Jessie's loveliness. "Jessie is my best friend – after Margaret – and Jessie's definitely the prettiest girl in this room!"

Margaret turned her attention to Jessie, who looked down at Rachel before she swivelled around to stare at David and the other Duncan children. All were blonde and blue-eyed, though with subtle differences.

Jessie's cheeks flared with an embarrassment Margaret shared, before Jessie turned around and left the room, having forgotten the cup that she had come in for.

"Whose turn is it, now?" Victoria tried to steer them back to the game, but had to work hard to bring back the attention.

The Forbes boys were now giggling over the ridiculousness of the event, as was Elspeth, though John still looked belligerent. David appeared as if he was about to be sick.

Margaret looked at the time on the mantlepiece clock, wanting desperately to be in a position to speak to Jessie. It was past seven o'clock, far too early for Rachel to be taken to her bedroom for the night, but also well after the time for her own evening meal.

Kate's entry took decision-making out of her hands.

"The Mistress asks that Victoria and David supervise everyone while you go downstairs to eat, Margaret. And after that you're to take a half-hour break. Mistress says she'll be finished her desert soon and she and her sister will pop in."

"You need to eat, Margaret. You need plenty of energy, too." Rachel cheekily echoed her earlier words, seemingly unaware of the volcanic ripples that had disconcerted her older siblings.

Chapter Twenty-Six

Mistress Abernethy was in high dudgeon at the preparation table, and Jessie wasn't to be seen when Margaret entered the kitchen.

"Your plate is in the small oven!"

It clearly wasn't a time to enter into a conversation about why Mistress Abernethy was still around at that time of night, so Margaret whipped up a towel from the rack near the range and gingerly extracted her meal.

The cover plate was piping hot so she set it aside on the wooden board alongside her and delved into a stew which was thankfully not dried out.

"You'd think by now the Mistress would be able to tell me how many mouths I'm feeding this weekend. But no! I'm just to magic extra food at the drop of a hat."

It was easier to pretend that she had a mouthful rather than answer the wrong thing so Margaret made her expression sympathetic.

Mistress Abernethy added a final marzipan ball to the top of the sizeable Simnel cake she'd been making. Using her finger to count, the cook ensured she had the traditional eleven for the Apostles, as in twelve minus Judas. "I can't rustle up cakes like these in a blink, just in case the Mistress needs more. Though she may think I can."

"It looks delicious, Mistress Abernethy," Margaret tentatively ventured. "Is it for Sunday?"

"It is, if it's not eaten tomorrow filling guests I've not been told about, though it's unlikely you lot down here will get a taste." The cook's words got quieter as she entered the pantry with her creation. "See that nobody puts a finger on that, or I'll blame you, Margaret Law!"

Cook wiped her hands, whipped off her apron, hung it on the peg near the door, and was out to get her coat in a matter of seconds. Her irate voice drifted back into the kitchen. "Since I don't get paid for the extra time I've just put in, I might not be in early tomorrow!"

As the outside door slammed, Margaret grinned. "I'd like to see you do that, just the once!" She knew fine well that there was no chance the cook would not be back in her kitchen early the next morning.

It was a long-standing threat, but never carried out.

Cook didn't have a long walk home but why Mistress Duncan didn't employ a live-in cook was still strange.

Margaret finished her meal and, as instructed, took her time off. She half-expected to find Jessie in the scullery, but her friend was nowhere to be seen on the basement floor. It was just the way of things – when she really wanted to console Jessie, her almost-sister was nowhere around!

After a luxurious half-hour of being stretched out on her bed, reading the latest book she'd borrowed, Margaret went back up to the parlour to see what else the Mistress had devised for her.

Checking the table linens was usually Kate's job but Margaret did what she was bid to do. Kate or Jessie had already cleared the table of all the dishes used for dinner, so she checked the linen tablecloth. It definitely needed laundering, but thankfully the corner lace edges were still intact. The table napkins all needed to be washed but she groaned when she saw that some needed lace-edge repairs. How the delicate lace could get so snagged was mystifying, but in truth she realised it was probably because the children were using the same set of napkins. She scooped them all off the table and dumped them on the floor at the door.

It was just as well that the Mistress had a number of sets of table linens, because it would be impossible for Kate to wash, dry, starch and iron them overnight. Opening the long drawer on one of the sideboards, she selected a new matching set. It would never do to put out the wrong napkins! She could hear Jessie mimicking the Mistress. *'It would be so shaming to have mis-matched items on my table!'*

Margaret traipsed down to the laundry, ignoring the hilarity in the parlour as she turned for the stairs, the children obviously playing a noisy game. She popped the stained napkins into a basin to soak overnight then fetched the sewing kit and took the mending to the kitchen.

She could hear faint chatter coming from the drawing room upstairs, the adults conversing companionably, but otherwise the whole basement corridor was surprisingly silent.

"It's not often I give thanks to you, Peggy," she mumbled to herself. "But all those evenings of you forcing me to learn to do fine crochet edgework is now coming in useful!"

While thinking of whether Peggy might also be doing some kind of sewing that evening, it took her only a little while to complete her task. Popping the mended napkins into the basin to soak with the others, she determined to send Peggy another letter with a more direct plea for a reply. Hopefully, she'd get some useful information.

By the time she was properly in her bed sometime later, exhausted by the long day's ongoings, Jessie had still to appear in their room. It was unusual at that late hour, and quite concerning, but there had been occasions when the Mistress had needed Jessie's help with Rachel very late in the evening. Margaret had left them to it, glad that Rachel's personal care was someone else's duty, but how she could have missed Jessie getting such a summons that evening was very strange.

246

Determined not to fall asleep before Jessie returned, she began to think all manner of things, like what she might do to restart Rachel's lessons during the coming week, after the flurry of visitors. Vaguely hearing someone in the corridor was reassuring. Her last thought before she succumbed was that it must be Jessie in the kitchen.

Easter Saturday dawned bright and cheery, the nip in the air an expected one when Margaret eventually popped her head out of the basement door. Drawing in deep breaths of the air, as fresh as she was ever going to get in central Edinburgh, she readied herself for the day. The moment of peace and quiet was appreciated, although it wasn't exactly silent. She could hear distant clop-clopping of hooves on the cobble stones well along the lane. Closing her eyes, she concentrated on what else was to be heard. The cries of the circling gulls overhead were intermingled with a faint thumping that she knew was likely to be coming from the timber yard at the nearby Broughton Market.

The smells were predictable, though more acute because of the clear morning. The sooty reek from domestic and nearby foundry coal fires battled with the heavy blood and entrails stench from the market fleshers and fishmongers. The Duncan back yard would have directly overlooked the market had they bought a house only a few doors along Albany Street.

An unbidden smile broke free. Her employment in such a vibrant part of Edinburgh was so much better than what she might have been destined for had she remained in Milnathort. Turning back inside, she thanked her lucky stars she was employed in the Duncan house and prepared to get on with the new day.

"La! Look, Mistress Abernethy," Jessie quipped playfully flapping a towel in her direction although there was a brittle touch to her banter. "The sleeper eventually appears! While we've been slaving away for ages this slugabed has only just wakened up."

"Best eat quickly," Cook advised. "Kate is already setting up the children's breakfast in the dining room. They're not only a hungry lot but are early risers, unlike some around here."

Margaret took Jessie and Cook's joking with a pinch of salt. She wasn't actually any later than usual, her duties not officially starting till eight o'clock. Jessie, as kitchen skivvy – though rarely referred to as that any more – was expected to rise early to help Kate with riddling the ashes from the coal fires and re-setting them where necessary. Kate was always first up, and in action well-before six o'clock.

Breakfast for the children was a noisy affair along the corridor in the dining room, though it took a bit longer to get Rachel ready for the day than the rest of the children. Jessie normally did this with the Mistress, but this wasn't a normal situation. Margaret helped Jessie to cajole their sleepy charge into a clean frock after Rachel had eaten some porridge.

"You're going to have a wonderful day, young lady," Jessie teased, yet Margaret felt her friend's natural cheer was dimmed and was just an act to encourage Rachel to look forward to the day. "Margaret won't be able to inflict any of those dreaded handwriting or arithmetic lessons on you!"

Rachel's laugh was genuine, though a frail one that Margaret wished was more robust.

"That's true! She won't. We'll be too busy entertaining."

Margaret helped Jessie to get Rachel into her wheeled chair. "I predict we're going to have a very hectic though happy day ahead of us."

Jessie held the door open, her expression unusually serious. "And what you predict usually comes true, Margaret, doesn't it?"

What Jessie was referring to Margaret wasn't sure, but it seemed to be on a level not intended for Rachel to understand.

At the parlour door Jessie ruffled Rachel's hair, but not enough to muss up the careful hair brushing and plaiting that she'd just done. "I've got things to do downstairs but I foresee that you're going to have a great day with your cousins."

Margaret caught Jessie's bleak expression before her friend headed towards the stairs. Though they'd not been able to speak about the incident with John the previous evening, she sensed a disquiet in Jessie that hadn't been there before.

The parlour was soon filled with an excited hum on the return of the children, and the problem of what Jessie was feeling had to be temporarily shelved for a better time.

"You really must see the statue of Sir Walter Scott in his monument on Princes Street," David said, encouraging the interest of his young cousins.

Victoria wasn't quite so cheery. "Why would that appeal to them? They won't know who he is."

"I do know who he is!" Arthur was miffed. "I have read some of his novels already."

Margaret decided Victoria must have lost some sleep, for the girl's tone was more petulant than usual when she said, "It's just a monument."

David launched in to calm the atmosphere. "There's a Carrara marble statue of Sir Walter Scott and his dog, Maida, at the foot of the monument, and there's a great story about its journey to get there."

Victoria wasn't going to remain silent.

"I read that John Ruskin…"

Margaret watched Victoria's dramatic attempt to gain the full attention of the younger children.

"You won't know it, but my friend says Ruskin's a very great art critic."

The less than subtle pauses from Victoria made Margaret repress a grin.

Victoria rumbled on with, "Well. Ruskin wrote that the monument David is describing is just a vulgar Gothic steeple."

The expressions on the faces of the children around her seemed impressed, if more than a bit forced, though Margaret secretly guessed they had no idea what Victoria was talking about.

David, she was glad to see, remained unruffled by Victoria's rude interruptions. She watched him bend down to be more at eye-level with Ruaridh.

"There's a marvellous view from the top of the steeple, though you have to climb a lot of steps to get up to the viewing platform."

"How many steps?" It was clear to see that Brian was much more interested in David's information than Victoria's.

David's eyes glowed. "More than two hundred and eighty steps."

"Is his dog at the bottom because it couldn't climb up to the top?" Ruaridh asked.

Margaret watched most of the children grin at his naïve question.

David was so patient. "I'm not sure any dog could climb that number of steps up a very narrow and steep staircase, but Walter Scott's dog is at the bottom of the monument because it's part of the carving. You'll see it if we venture down to Princes Street."

Victoria's nose was in the air, but Margaret sensed the girl actually was interested in what her brother was saying. "Tell us, then. What's your great story about the statue?"

David proceeded to explain how a sculptor would take a huge block of stone and would gradually remove what he didn't want to create what he did want his viewers to eventually see.

"The first block of marble was dug out of a quarry at Carrara in Italy. That's where the best white marble for statues comes from."

"And?" Little Ruaridh was enthralled.

Margaret looked out of the window to hide her smiles. David was stretching out his story with great dramatic delivery.

"When they lifted the huge block of marble onto a ship to get it to Edinburgh, it was so heavy that…"

Rachel's animated tones interrupted. "I remember reading about this with Margaret."

David's stern looks shushed Rachel, who, in turn, began to giggle.

Three pairs of Forbes' eyes stared at David.

"It sank the ship!"

"Oh, my!" Brian said. "But there's a statue here, so how did they get the block out of the water?"

David playfully ruffled the boy's hair.

"It was a different huge block from the quarry that they shipped to Edinburgh, successfully the second time."

Rachel's excited voice piped up. "Do you remember, Margaret? The newspaper we read said that it took twenty horses to drag that piece of marble up to the sculptor's studio so that he could start work."

Margaret agreed. "And then it took Sir John Steell, the sculptor, six years to complete the carving."

"Steell?" Ruaridh chuckled merrily. "That's a funny name for someone who didn't work with metal but with a big bit of stone."

After a general chuckling session, Margaret was quite relaxed when they turned their attention to playing card games, guessing games, and then closer to luncheon time stories of what life was like for the Forbes children in Inverness.

The school that Brian and John attended was different from Margaret's experience at Milnathort, the main thing

251

being that only boys attended it. From the enthusiasm of the boys relating their Greek and Latin lessons, even though they were still young, she was both exhausted by their constant energy and jealous that she hadn't managed to have the chance to broaden her education in those languages.

"Did you know that Margaret and I have been learning French?" Rachel's intervention caused an immediate silence in the room.

Brian almost bounced off his chair. "I think that'll be much better than learning Greek! You can go to France but not Ancient Greece."

As though aware that what he'd just said was an impossibility for Rachel, he stuttered, "I mean you'll get more opportunities to speak to other people using your French."

"They're only learning some French," Victoria said, "because I'm the one who is having the tutor come to the house to teach me the language. Mother has given them permission to sit in on my lessons. But, of course, that means the lessons have to be up here in the parlour."

Victoria's dismissive tone and haughty stare immediately shut down the conversation.

Margaret kept her thoughts to herself. The Mistress could be shrewd and cunning enough when she wanted to be. Three people were learning at the cost for just one pupil. Nonetheless she was very glad that she was absorbing quite a bit of the French, by default, even if the tutoring was not directed her way. And what she learned, she shared with Rachel.

Kate announcing that their mid-day meal was about to be served in the dining room for the whole family, children and adults squeezing in together, was a relief from the tension that had sprung up.

When the parlour cleared, Margaret heaved a sigh of relief for Rachel who definitely needed a well-earned rest. Her dayroom wasn't usually so vibrant.

252

"You should come with us, Rachel," David declared an hour or so later. The other children had gone off to their allotted rooms to get their outdoor coats before venturing out for a walk. "The air will be fresh, but if you're well wrapped up you won't miss out on all of the fun."

Margaret appreciated David's tender care of his sister and looked down at her little charge who appeared eager, though also hesitant.

"How about a compromise? The others can go down to Princes Street first, as they have already planned, and we can meet them at Queen Street Gardens when they return?"

The excited nodding was worth it. Rachel had often bemoaned how long it took for them to get her ready for an excursion in her outside wheelchair. "Perhaps we could nominate a time to meet them, Margaret?"

"Excellent idea!" David enthused. "How about we meet you at four o'clock at the corner of Heriot Row and Howe Street?"

Margaret nodded her agreement.

David disappeared from the room but returned almost immediately. "I'll send a note along to my friend George who lives on Heriot Row. If he's not otherwise engaged this afternoon, I'll ask if he can meet us and gain us entry to his section of Queen Street Gardens with his pass-key."

"That would be wonderful if he's free, David!" Rachel said, beaming from ear to ear. "It's a very long time since I've been inside any of the garden areas."

Margaret was so pleased to see that Rachel's smile displayed her love for her brother.

Chapter Twenty-Seven

"Oh, it is so lovely to be outside, Margaret."

It was just after three-thirty, and they had reached the far end of Queen Street Gardens, Margaret having pushed the wheelchair past Abercrombie Place and along Heriot Row. It was actually the furthest they'd ever managed along that way, since the wooden wheels of the wheelchair tended to rattle along the uneven flagstones of the pavement. Margaret had been very conscious of how much that, in turn, rattled poor Rachel's thin frame. Entering any of the inviting private Queen Street Garden areas had never been possible for them, the access to the gardens being limited to occupiers of the Heriot Row properties which overlooked the green spaces.

"Oh, isn't that lady's dress beautiful, Margaret?"

"It is indeed and is the very height of fashion, as is the lace edged parasol she is delicately using."

"I don't suppose Mama would ever let me have a dress made from silk like that one over by the gate. It's such an unusual colour, too. I don't know what to call that shade."

She was heartened by Rachel's enthusiasm. "I've recently read something that mentioned it being named aqua."

"Aqua," Rachel rolled off the word. "It's a bit like the colour of the little bottles that Mama always has in the pocket of her dress."

Margaret preferred not to add anything to that observation. Helen Duncan was becoming less and less discreet about snatching little sips of her laudanum restorative, swallows which were well-past the category of 'now and then'.

Rachel was determined to make the best of the sunshine and was eager to meet up with her siblings and cousins. Margaret was always glad to escape the house and get any fresh air possible, but it was so much better when there was a purpose to their outing.

Easter Saturday was clearly such a day. Well-dressed ladies were accompanied by equally dapper gentlemen strolling along. There was a soldier, a Royal Scots Grey, easily recognised by his light grey-trousered uniform, hobbling along with a comely woman on his arm. Margaret winced. It seemed evident that this particular soldier had borne the brunt of some debilitating action, though from the adoring look on the woman's face there was a delight that his injuries were not too daunting. Many lives had already been lost out on the Crimean Peninsula.

"A very good afternoon to you, Miss Rachel."

The sudden statement took Margaret by surprise, since she'd been unaware of the approach from behind of David's friend.

George manoeuvred himself to the front of Rachel's wheelchair. "And a good day to you too, Miss Law."

Dipping into a brief curtsey, Margaret returned the young man's greeting.

"How nice to be Miss Law today," she laughed. "Is that to impress the passers-by?"

She had met George on many occasions when he had returned to the Duncan house with David after one of their extra classes. Though roughly the same age as David, he seemed so much more mature in appearance and sound. However, unlike David, whose legs had taken a recent spurt, George was only a shade taller than she was.

"It makes such a refreshing change to be meeting you outside, if I may say so, Rachel?" George's winning smile beamed down. "And who could not like such lovely weather after the gruelling winter we have lately experienced."

As during previous encounters, George always seemed an optimistic person. Attractive he definitely was, but his good looks didn't do anything to make Margaret's heart race, or bring a blush to her cheeks.

They spent the next few minutes discussing their respective family Easter plans. Margaret learned his folks didn't worship at the same church as the Duncan family. From what he mentioned, it sounded as though George would be spending a good chunk of his Easter Sunday at the Meeting House on Barony Street, in the hall which lay behind the Duncans' back yard.

"I don't know what you will do at the Glasite Meeting House, I'm afraid," Margaret replied, "but I expect the Duncan family to spend more than an hour at the Easter service tomorrow."

George's grin filled his slim face, his deep-set dark eyes twinkling with mirth. "Our services are likely to last a bit longer than that."

"How long might that be?" Rachel tentatively joined in the conversation.

"Oh, five hours is usual for any Sunday, so perhaps it will be even longer tomorrow." George hesitated at Rachel's horrified gasp but didn't seem perturbed about the duration of the worship. "My family used to attend the Bellevue Parish Church along at Bellevue Crescent…"

"That's the church Jessie goes to!" Margaret realised interrupting George was rude, but it was too late to take her words back.

George seemed a little disconcerted, a slight darkening of his cheeks before he ploughed on. "Yes, well. It's only very recently that my parents changed to worshipping at the hall on Barony Street, so I've not yet experienced a full Easter weekend of services. How long will depend on who our speakers are and which parts of the scripture are read." George's laugh rang out. "However, Psalms will be sung a-plenty, I can tell you that for certain, but I have no idea what else to expect."

Margaret was circumspect, since what she'd heard of the long Glasite Sunday worship was a bit derogatory. She wasn't going to mention that she'd heard the sect referred to as the 'Kail Kirk' and that the eating of an early afternoon meal consisting of – supposedly – only kale broke up the long hours spent in worship. It probably wasn't true that kale was the only thing they ate, but rumours abounded.

"George! I'm glad you managed to meet us." David's loud hailing ended the conversation as he towed the Forbes and Duncan brood towards them. "Can you gain us entry into the gardens? Just for a short while?"

George guffawed before producing a key from his pocket with a dramatic flourish. "I had a feeling you didn't just want my scintillating company!"

Margaret was delighted when David, and George in turn, volunteered to steer Rachel's wheelchair along what were thankfully quite smoothly paved paths inside the gardens. It gave her arms a little respite from the constant pressure of keeping the vehicle straight, and meant more enjoyment of the lovely green space, some early spring bulbs adding a splash of colour amongst the maturing bushes and trees.

Jessie happily took charge on their return to the Duncan house; Rachel having been lifted upstairs to her room by Tom before he stored her outside wheelchair in the coach house.

"Look at your rosy cheeks," Jessie cajoled as they manoeuvred her around for cleaning before a change of clothes was donned. "I'm sure that was a lovely outing for you."

"Oh, it was very fine, Jessie," Rachel's thready voice replied. "And George, David's friend, had a key to let us into the gardens. He whispered to me that I should tell you it really is a lovely place to have a daytime wander. I don't know why he mentioned it, but I've told you anyway."

Margaret looked at Jessie who had just stifled a gasp. She'd rarely seen her friend get flustered, but the blushes at her cheeks could have boiled a kettle.

"Can I just have a nap here for a while, on top of the covers, if there's time before dinner?"

Focusing on Rachel rather than her embarrassed friend, Margaret's practised gestures cleared aside the wash cloths. "I think that's just the ticket! I'll come right back after I tell the others of your plan."

Having updated the people in the parlour, she waited till Jessie came out from Rachel's bedroom with the dirty linen.

"Are you going to enlighten me about George's strange message?"

Jessie's nose rose in the air, but the blushes reappeared, less fiery but enough to give a delicate pinkish hue to flawless cheeks.

"There's nothing to tell. George likes to tease me if I answer the door when he comes to see David. But that's not important just now. I can tell Rachel enjoyed being outside but don't you think she's weaker than usual?"

Margaret nodded, wondering why Jessie was evading the issue of George's message. "I do, but I think we should just watch her carefully over the rest of the weekend before we ask Mistress Duncan if she thinks calling in Doctor Oliver is a good idea."

"Hellish Helen's in no fit state to make any decisions just now. She's in even more of a flurry than usual with all of these guests around, but we don't dare alarm her, or go behind her back and summon the doctor ourselves."

Jessie's whisper had been vehement and tinged with a critical edge Margaret hadn't heard her friend use before. Though in the light of what had happened the previous evening, she couldn't blame Jessie one bit for her attitude. Not a single bit.

Margaret was in the parlour with Rachel, the other children having their evening meal in the dining room, when there was a hubbub in the corridor.

The door burst open and two tall figures strode in, the first heading directly towards Rachel's chair.

"Forgive us barging in while you're eating, Rachel, but I didn't want to wait till after dinner before greeting you."

Margaret felt Robert's attention flicker from Rachel to her. Though only for a moment, it held an undercurrent of a question in it.

"You have rosy cheeks today. That's so lovely to see, sister." Robert's smile disappeared into Rachel's neck as he bent down to hug her.

For Margaret, there was an awareness of two immediate differences. Robert's customary hair ruffle was missing, and the hug lingered longer than usual.

After straightening up, Robert extended his arm out to the second new entrant to the room. "I don't imagine you'll remember him, Rachel, but this reprobate that I found walking towards our doorstep is Gavin, your oldest Forbes cousin."

Margaret sidled back from Rachel to allow Gavin space. She watched the young man formally lift Rachel's hand before he bent to kiss it lightly on the knuckles. A frisson of something ran down her spine, a reminder of a relatively recent past event. She had never met this man before, but he initiated the same sort of impact as Francis Douglas Scott had.

"I remember you from when you were toddling around the room, young lady, even if you don't remember me. You loved to bring me toys from a basket that sat under the window. For a while I was the centre of your whole universe!"

Listening to the thrilling cadences of his deep tones that rang with humour, Margaret watched Gavin's gaze drift to the window.

"Look at that!" Gavin's hoot spat out. "It's still there."

Margaret then watched Gavin's green-eyed gaze return to a bemused Rachel. "Are the same toys still in the basket?"

"I suppose so, if they haven't been broken by now." Rachel's amusement spilled over into frail chuckles.

It took a few more moments of conversation before Margaret heard Robert's words of introduction, so taken was she by the tousled, slightly-curly auburn hair of the man next to her charge.

"You might already have guessed that this is Margaret Law, Rachel's …tutor." Robert faltered when faced with finding a name for Margaret's position in the household since it was really well beyond a normal tutor.

"She is my companion!" Rachel finished his sentence with a little flourish. "I'm far too young for a proper lady's companion, but Margaret is my best friend in the whole world, along with Jessie."

Gavin looked confused and turned towards Robert. "Jessie?"

"Jessie is our kitchen maid." Robert's customary dismissive attitude jolted Margaret to pay proper attention.

Rachel huffed. "Jessie is much more than that!"

There was a bit of feather-ruffling going on so Margaret attempted to calm things down with a bit of jocularity. "Jessie helps me keep Rachel in line. Don't we, young miss!"

"Well, we'd best be off to find Jessie, or Kate. I haven't a clue where I'll be bunking up tonight, but I doubt it'll be in my own room." Robert's laughter echoed around.

Rachel's cheeky quip rolled free, even though it was almost a whisper. "Ha! You'll be up in the roof along with the creepy crawlies! You didn't let Mama know you were definitely coming home this weekend."

"Aargh!" Robert's expression was exaggerated, pretending to be mortified as he headed for the door. "Are you expected, Gavin?"

"Not really."

Margaret watched Gavin's face develop a dramatic squirm.

"My mother sent me a letter to say they were all coming here for Easter. But I didn't know till last night that I would definitely be allowed to take time off from my employment."

Rachel was in a playful mood, which was immensely cheering. "I think you'd both better find my mother and do a bit of grovelling!"

The two young men made mock soldier salutes.

"I've brought Aunt Helen a small gift from Glasgow. Do you think that will get me into her good books, Rachel?" Gavin was quite the charmer as he patted one of the pockets of his jacket.

Margaret thought Rachel was probably impressed by her older cousin. She certainly was.

Was she becoming obsessed by charming male visitors to the Duncan house? It was quite the giddy feeling. She decided she could very well get used to the renewed fluttery rushes it gave her insides.

Gavin Forbes wasn't as classically handsome as Francis, but there was something impossibly attractive about him that she hadn't quite worked out.

As the men left the room, Margaret caught Robert's whispers, "It'll be the attic rooms for us, but at least we'll be dining with the adults and not the tiddlers."

Chapter Twenty-Eight

"Margaret? Will the others be back soon?"

Rachel was fiddling with her needle in a desultory fashion rather than doing any sewing.

Margaret had expected a flurry of activity some time past, but the Duncan and Forbes contingents had not yet returned from the Easter Sunday church service. She was almost as impatient as Rachel, but there truly was only one particular member that she wanted to see again – and that definitely wasn't Robert.

The previous evening hadn't turned out as she had expected. The predictable part had been the re-entry to the parlour of the children after their evening meal, but Robert and Gavin had gone straight into dinner with their parents. It was Kate who had informed Margaret that Robert and Gavin had gone out after they had eaten, though Kate had no idea when they had returned since Robert had taken a key, and she had been instructed not to wait up.

Margaret had ruminated for the last couple of hours about where they had gone and, indeed, where they were now.

"I think they may be taking advantage of the beautiful morning," she eventually replied to Rachel's question, having peeped out of the parlour window, yet again, to see if the families were lingering in the street below.

Rachel still wasn't allowed to attend church services. The duration was deemed far too long for her, by her mother, even though her outdoor wheelchair had a comfortable seat, and in Margaret's opinion could be parked near the back pews without taking up too much room. The Mistress declared that Rachel couldn't take part properly during the liturgies, but Margaret knew the Mistress was ashamed to be seen in public with her invalid daughter. Margaret was still expected to continue as before – to choose a passage from the bible, read it together with Rachel, and then discuss it. On her once-a-month visit to church she had learned a few hymns, and she sang those with Rachel, even though they were nothing to do with the Easter festival they were currently celebrating.

After a brief knock, Jessie entered the parlour balancing two soup bowls on a wide tray that was crowded with plates of buttered bread, slices of ham and cheese, two filled cups and saucers and the appropriate cutlery. "Here you go! You must be starving, young lady."

Rachel's smiles indicated she hadn't noticed any tension in Jessie's expression, though Margaret did.

"I thought you were allowed to attend church today?" Margaret said.

"I certainly was, but I had to come straight home, unlike lots of wanderers who are making Mistress Abernethy very cross!" Jessie strode across the room to the table, where she placed the tray on an available space. Before setting out two places for the food, she slid the books and writing materials to the far end, well away from the eating area.

Margaret wheeled Rachel to the table, deftly removed the lap-tray and set it aside before she parked the chair under the edge opposite her own place setting. Since Rachel had become more able to feed herself, it was easier for Margaret to have her lunch at the same time as her charge, the indoor wheelchair making it possible for them to eat at their table. It had taken some self-discipline to train herself not to sit alongside the girl. Rachel's eating was sometimes a bit messy, but she had to be allowed to do what she could manage by herself.

"Oh, dear," Rachel's little grin belied her concern. "It's not just a usual Sunday cold collation that she's prepared?"

Jessie's open palm dramatically slapped against her chest. "On Easter Sunday? With guests in the house? Whatever will you think of next?"

Rachel looked so amused that she almost spat out the small mouthful she had just taken from her bowl. She swallowed it over and then added, "I imagine Cook will manage to keep it warm."

"Cook?" Jessie was scornful. "Me, you mean. Cook has gone home for a couple of hours to sort out her own family's Easter meal."

Jessie's spin around was so fast she was out of the door before Rachel could respond.

The young girl's mouth wobbled. "Mama expects Jessie to do far too much, doesn't she? For me, and for all of us. Jessie is a lot more to us than just a kitchen servant."

What words could be used to console without betraying the actual feelings that were circling around? Margaret couldn't see into Rachel's mind; however, it appeared that her young charge's statement was one of appreciation of the extent of Jessie's job. Or that Rachel was putting two and two together very well.

"Never fear." She encouraged Rachel to spoon up more of the soup, her smile as unforced as possible. "Jessie is dedicated to this family, no matter what she's asked to do."

Margaret's soup was long supped before Rachel was ready to tackle a small portion of bread.

"Would you like some of Mistress Abernethy's famed glazed ham that she's made for this special weekend, or a slice of cheese?" she cajoled, seeing that Rachel looked ready to refuse more food.

Rachel's sigh made Margaret's stomach curl. The girl really wasn't doing well with her meals at all, when it involved anything more than supping soup or spooning puddings.

"I'll try just a very small piece of the ham, so that you can send my compliments to Cook for me."

Margaret cut up some ham into small bites, and did the same with the bread before she placed Rachel's plate in front of her.

"There. Now eat it all up before the others come home. I'm sure it can't be too long now."

Tackling her own food, and drinking her now cold tea, she led the conversation so that all Rachel had to do was focus on clearing the tiny amount on her plate and finishing her cup of milk. Though she was always ready to act, she was delighted that Rachel rarely spilled the contents of her cup now, though it was a difficult task for the girl to accomplish the balance necessary.

The parlour was filled up almost immediately by an excited family which included Robert and Gavin.

"That was an excellent stroll." Gavin's cheerful tones immediately drew Margaret's attention as he continued. "I'm beginning to feel more familiar with the New Town streets."

Victoria was her usual snappy self. "Wait till you venture over to the Old Town. Apart from the High Street you can get lost so very easily."

Margaret was stunned when Rachel added, "Just be sure of your footing, Gavin, on the many very steep steps."

Gavin immediately came across to stand beside her charge. He lifted her awkward hand very gently. "Thank you, cousin. You are very, very brave to say that. I am proud of you and what you have endured."

After a momentary lull, because Rachel's infirmity was rarely ever remarked upon, the buzz again started, continuing a discussion of the many narrow and dark closes and the numerous flights of steep stairs to be found over in the Old Town.

When Kate called them to luncheon, the parlour emptied again as they flurried off across the landing.

Margaret's gaze followed only one person's exit, drawn as a moth to a flame.

Rachel touched her elbow. "It's so lovely to have a cousin like Gavin, isn't it? He's as kind as Jessie."

With her stomach in turmoil, caused by a different reason from earlier, Margaret steeled herself to appear normal. She restacked the tray with the almost-empty plates after Rachel had used the napkin to wipe her mouth and hands.

Pulling the wheelchair away from the table, she swivelled the lap-tray back into place and set Rachel closer to the window. Picking up a book about travel in Egypt, by a Scottish explorer that they had been delving into, she popped it open at the next lithographic plate and balanced it in front of her pupil.

"Why don't you examine the next few plates and engravings while I nip downstairs with the tray? Kate and Jessie have more than enough to do without traipsing back for it."

Rachel's tiny smile was accompanied by a happy nod. "Yes, Jessie won't need to come up right away to get me sorted for the afternoon. She can give Kate all the help needed to finish serving the family luncheon."

Margaret wiggled Rachel's plaits, the gesture that had come to display her love and high regard for her young charge. "I'll not be long."

Before leaving the parlour Margaret ensured the little handbell was on the side table next to Rachel's chair. Though small, it had a powerful ring and could be heard easily when the parlour door was left ajar.

On reaching the top of the stairs, Margaret was almost bowled over by Gavin who had bounded up them two steps at a time.

"My apologies!" Gavin's smile was genuine and devastating to Margaret's equilibrium. "I'm late to the table."

Seeing that her arms were occupied, she felt Gavin's finger-light touch at her elbows to steer her backwards a step or two, so that he could pass by. The gaze fixed on her lips was so intense she almost dropped the tray.

But, like a will o' the wisp, he was into the dining room before she could take another blink. Descending the stairs carefully, she willed her heated cheeks to cool down and her hands to stop rattling the tray. Questions flooded her head. Why was this effect only produced by the young men who visited the Duncan household? It never happened in the street, or at the Central Lending Library, or even during her church visits!

Was it just the close proximity in the house?

By the time Margaret reached the kitchen she had confused herself even more. Many young men had visited the Duncan household since she had arrived to tutor Rachel. She had briefly met friends of David, like George who was a regular visitor, and even old school friends of Robert. But apart from Francis, and now Gavin, none of the others had ever made her heart race, or make her body feel out of kilter.

Was this just fleeting desire? Another youthful fancy for a young man? Was the unsettling of her insides, a heating of her cheeks, and the palpitating heart rhythm something to savour or to suppress? Margaret had read enough novels to be fairly convinced this was what was going on. Though what to do about it was something different.

By the time she'd placed the tray in the scullery, Margaret had persuaded herself that she needed to avoid Gavin Forbes during his visit, just as she had tried with Francis Douglas Scott.

Thankfully, though in all honestly another huge disappointment, her resolve wasn't put to the test, since

Robert and Gavin joined their parents in the downstairs drawing room after their Easter Sunday lunch, and she didn't set eyes on them at all for the rest of the day.

The following morning, the Forbes family, including the parents, all entered the parlour after breaking their fast.

"It's been such a lovely visit, Rachel," Mistress Forbes gushed as she bent down to give Rachel a tiny peck on the cheek. "But we must leave now to head home. Even though we can journey to Aberdeen by train, we still have a very long coach ride after that."

A flurry of hugs, kisses and goodbyes followed, Margaret having stepped away from Rachel to give them space. Her thoughts were not ones that the Forbes family would want to hear. She absolutely hated the falsity of their effusive farewell. During their visit, Mister and Mistress Forbes had barely spoken to Rachel at all, having kept mainly to the downstairs drawing room with Mister and Mistress Duncan.

"You can all come to visit us sometime soon!" Ruaridh exclaimed. "Can't they, Mama?"

Margaret appreciated the Forbes boys' goodbyes which were definitely genuine, though Ruaridh's naïve enthusiasm lacked some tact.

"We'd love to visit the far north, Ruaridh." Victoria declared, easing the slight awkwardness, and actually sounding less tart than usual. "Will we still need our winter coats if we come to Inverness during the summer?"

She was delighted to see that Victoria's attempt to make jokes about the so-named Capital of the North, as opposed to the Capital in Edinburgh, kept the goodbyes from being too maudlin.

When the parlour quietened once more, Margaret joked, "Well young lady, I'm sure that is Easter well and truly over now. Shall we get back to some of those exciting handwriting lessons?"

"Are you serious, Margaret?" As she expected, her comment had caused Rachel to smile.

Her response was to lift up the book of lithographic plates on Egypt that they'd abandoned the previous afternoon, when parlour games for the younger members of the family had become the order of the day. "I suppose that we can defer penmanship for a bit longer. How about we fantasise over what it would be like to be in the heat of Egypt while on one of David Roberts' excursions?"

Though highly wistful, Rachel was so adept at adopting the persona of another person. Margaret thought her own imagination was good, but was heartened that Rachel's mind's eye could set a scene even better, especially as what she imagined sometimes could never be experienced herself. Margaret guessed that it was the budding artist in Rachel that gave the girl such vision.

"Can you feel the sand drifting over your toes, Margaret? It must be like the finest gossamer scarf barely touching your skin. Probably ticklish as well?"

"I've no idea what sand is like in Egypt, but I do remember what it was like on the shores of Loch Leven, not too far from where I used to live."

Margaret was lost in her description of the gritty sandy shingle that was always freezing cold, even on the sunniest day, when she and Jessie had paddled at the water's edge.

"Oh, you two must have had such fun together!" Rachel exclaimed.

"Who two?"

Margaret was taken aback to hear it was Gavin who was asking the question, he and Robert having re-entered the parlour.

"Margaret and Jessie grew up together, and had lots of exciting adventures when they were little children!"

It was delightful to hear Rachel's response so animated again.

"Did they now!"

269

Margaret felt uncomfortable under Gavin's admiring, though somewhat confused-looking expression.

"They both grew up in Milnathort," Robert interjected, "though not in the same house."

"Ah, I understand now." Gavin's gaze moved to Rachel. "I, too, am taking my leave of you, little cousin. If I make haste to the station at Haymarket, I should get a train to Glasgow quite soon."

Rachel accepted his light kiss, first to her hand and then to her forehead.

"You must keep working on those excellent lessons Margaret is teaching you. And when I next come back to visit, we can perhaps have that conversation in French that we mentioned!"

"Oh, yes. I shall," Rachel beamed, her mischievous personality coming to the fore. "*Au Revoir*!" Her grin faltered to be replaced by a squirmy facial expression. "I don't know how to say 'Goodbye my favourite cousin' in French."

Gavin chortled. "Then that should definitely be your first lesson!"

Margaret then felt herself Gavin's focus of attention, though his words were directed towards Rachel. "Don't let that French tutor lead you astray, cousin. Victoria tells me he is not much past twenty years old and is very, very handsome."

Margaret felt obliged to give more information, unable to keep her humour in check. "He is also married. He has two very young children and a wife who is from Dumbiedykes. She's a very lovely woman we sometimes meet when we visit the Central Lending Library."

Gavin tut-tutted and turned his full attention back to Rachel, his grins engaging. "That may be so, but I hear that he has a typical Gallic attitude to flirting with beautiful young ladies!"

Rachel was highly entertained when her brother, somewhat theatrically, dragged Gavin across the room declaring Gavin was the one who would miss the train, if he didn't stop his dalliance with the ladies!

Just as Robert yanked Gavin through the door, Gavin touched his fingertips to his lips and blew back a kiss in Margaret's direction. At least Margaret thought it was for her since his gaze was not on Rachel but was firmly on her. She told herself she wasn't in the least affected by him yet knew it was a downright lie.

Margaret breathed more easily once the two young men left the room.

"Oh, Margaret. Gavin is so nice. I like him very well, don't you?"

"Indeed, he's a lovely cousin. Not everyone can say that of their relatives."

A brief memory of her Milnathort second cousins came to mind, but nothing at all of her full cousins in Perth.

Her mother had still not responded directly to the last letter she sent. Her father's recent missive, from just before Easter, didn't mention her mother at all, nor her Uncle James, nor her cousins when she actually thought about it. William's latest news had only been about his attendance at his religious group on a Wednesday night and even that had been devoid of real information.

Chapter Twenty-Nine

May 1855

If Margaret thought that the house would settle down into a sense of normality after the Easter hullabaloo, then she was wrong. It was only a month later that Kate huffed into the kitchen, disturbing the evening lull that had settled upon Jessie and herself, a welcome cup of tea cradled in their hands.

"I swear that woman just wants to wear me down to death!" It was a dramatic statement from Kate, who generally took most things in her stride. "I can't wait to be married to Tom. I think we need to bring forward our wedding date, regardless of whether he thinks he has enough money to keep me in some style!"

That generated an awkward, sympathetic smirk on both Margaret's and Jessie's faces. Tom's earnings as coachman were not much better than Kate's, and the combination of both not sufficient to run beyond a very poor household.

It wasn't that Margaret or her best friend thought ill of the couple's ambitions, it was more of a gut reaction to a perennial problem that bedevilled most working-class people who were in service.

Jessie, ever the mediator, was first to probe as she fetched a clean cup to pour some tea for Kate. "What has that Hellish Helen done now?"

Kate flopped into a chair and accepted the drink. "One of the attic bedrooms is going to be permanently used for the foreseeable future, which means more work for me every single day, up and down those attic stairs."

She could see from Jessie's expression that none of this had been mentioned to her.

"Are the Duncans taking in a lodger?" Margaret asked.

Some of the houses in Albany Street had lodgers, usually single people of the lower professional class who needed simple and cheap accommodation on a more permanent basis. It just seemed to be so surprising for the Duncans to be letting out a room.

"Not a lodger," Kate said. "All I'm told is that Gavin Forbes is being transferred to the Edinburgh branch of the Commercial Bank, and he needs a room here till a decision is made on how permanent the Edinburgh posting might be."

Margaret stared at the low-banked coals in the kitchen range. "When is he arriving?"

"Why can't he use Robert's room?" Jessie asked.

The two questions coming at the same time made Kate's head dot between them.

"Robert will be home soon after his final examinations and will need his own room. You heard the Master recently saying that Robert is to leave university and be contracted to an Edinburgh law practice."

Jessie harrumphed. "Aye, I did. And we all know how displeased that will make the golden boy Robert."

Margaret couldn't deny that as she watched Kate's head swivel her way. Robert seemed to hate the idea of becoming an advocate like his father.

Kate took a few sips of tea before she continued with her update. "Gavin's expected to arrive soon, perhaps even later tomorrow. All I know is that I've to get the room prepared and the fire set in the grate tomorrow morning."

"Margaret? Why hasn't Gavin come yet?"

Rachel's unexpected, wistful, question was blurted out in the middle of an arithmetic lesson, Margaret teaching her charge the basics of counting change to five pounds.

She hadn't mentioned the potential arrival of the eldest Forbes cousin, so Rachel had clearly heard the news from another family member.

"I don't know."

Her response was cautiously given since Rachel was prone to becoming more poorly if her mood became despondent. Attempting to cheer up the invalid, her answer was jocular and her posture like Jessie's when riled. Her right fist placed in at her waist, she adopted the forward thrust of her upper body and inquiring facial expressions that Jessie would manufacture. Her frustrated tone of voice also aped her best friend.

"Nobody tells me anything!"

As intended, the statement made Rachel's weak laugh trill free.

"That's not nearly as dramatic as Jessie. You'll have to try harder than that at copying her."

"Ha!" Margaret responded. "*'Nobody can do Jessie, like Jessie can!'* You've told me that many a time."

They were still grinning at each other when the door to the parlour opened. Such an entry meant a family member, since the domestics always made a brief knock.

Margaret's smile froze.

"Well, that's a lovely way to find you, little cousin!" Gavin Forbes announced as he stepped across the Persian rug to greet Rachel with a whisper of a kiss to her forehead before he crouched down to give her shoulders a hug. "It's so encouraging to hear your chuckles. I can see that Miss Law continues to be a wonderful companion."

Margaret took a small step away from Rachel's wheelchair, Gavin's close proximity making her feel unaccustomedly giddy.

"What's this?" Gavin's gaze had encompassed the arithmetic on the wide slate on Rachel's lap tray. "You're finding adding up money laughable?"

"No, silly!" Rachel grinned.

"Just you try counting up money sums all day long, young lady. It definitely never makes me laugh."

The banter lasted a moment or two longer, which gave Margaret enough time to compose herself. She'd thought that any attraction to Gavin Forbes had been in her imagination, but seeing him again so soon, she realised just how wrong she had been.

She cleared her throat to make sure she could speak without showing any signs of her discomfiture. "Rachel is doing very well with her money addition. We have recently progressed to adding a number of items before giving change from a five pound note."

Rachel groaned, giving Gavin the benefit of one of her disgruntled lip-curled expressions. "It takes me ages to do the addition bit and then there's the subtraction to get the final answer."

Gavin tweaked Rachel's blonde braids. "Money makes the world go round, little cousin, and everyone should know how to handle what they have in their pocket, or their purse."

Rachel's grin had subsided to a weak twitch. "Are you staying with us because you've been given a new bank job?"

"In a manner of speaking." Gavin's answer was vague.

Margaret slid the slate pen from Rachel's fingers and reached forward to lift the slate. "Excuse me, Rachel. I'll leave you two to talk for a moment. We can finish this later." Turning her attention to Gavin, she asked, "Would you like me to organise a cup of tea for you? Or is that already in hand?"

The full force of his green-flecked eyes fell upon her as he straightened up from his crouch of greeting.

"No, don't stop your lesson for me. I'm expected back downstairs in the drawing room in a few minutes. Aunt Helen has already asked Kate to provide. I just came up to let Rachel know I've arrived."

Margaret found she could breathe again when he turned back towards Rachel.

"It seems you were plaguing your mother earlier today, little cousin, about my arrival."

"I've just been so excited about seeing you again." Rachel's excuse was met with another pat to her fingertips.

"And I, you, Rachel. And would you believe, it's very good to see Miss Law again, too."

"Gavin!" Rachel's giggles were faint. "You know we always call her Margaret."

Margaret felt the blushes rise when Gavin responded, his grin infectious.

"I'm not sure if I have yet had permission for that liberty."

"But you're family, Gavin. And we all call her Margaret." Rachel said.

Gavin's guffaw and searching raised-eyebrow gaze had Margaret intrigued before his next words came her way. "I'm quite happy to not be blood-related to your tutor, Rachel."

It was clear that Rachel was tiring, since her response was literal. "Don't you like Margaret?"

Gavin's reply was a definite one. "I like your tutor very much."

"That's good." Rachel's sigh and small smile of approval had Margaret bending down to tweak the girl's braids.

Gavin's next words were brisk, as though the topic of conversation had strayed too much.

"After a quick cup of tea with your mother I have to go along to the bank for the remainder of the afternoon. But I'll be back for dinner with your parents, and then I'll try to see you for a little while before you retire for the night?"

Margaret felt Gavin's gaze land her way, as though needing confirmation of when a normal bedtime was for Rachel.

"Before a quarter to eight would be best," she answered.

Rachel was retiring earlier and earlier, her energy levels all but sucked away by eight of the evening. However, the chances of him having finished his dinner by that time were slim. David now dined with his parents after turning sixteen, and they rarely began their meal before seven o'clock. Victoria's nose was, of course, huffily put out of joint, since she still had to take her evening meal with Elspeth as a first sitting.

"If I hurry, I'll manage to have a half hour in the Central Lending Library before it shuts," Margaret declared, the day after Gavin's arrival. "We've romped through our selection of books this week."

Thursday had become a fairly usual day for them to exchange books, which generally meant new material for them both to look at over the coming weekend, or for Rachel on her own if Margaret wasn't on duty. Though going late in the day to the library, wasn't so usual.

"Are you sure you want to venture out just now, Margaret?" Rachel was gazing out at the pitter-pattering rain on the window panes from her recumbent position on the daybed as she spoke, her recurring cough and listlessness having become a more annoying feature since Easter.

Margaret gave Rachel's arm a light encouraging pat. "By the time you've had a light nap, I'll be back."

"I am sleepy." Rachel's thready answer was followed by the drooping of her eyelids.

Jessie had just helped get Rachel out of her wheelchair and onto the daybed before disappearing downstairs.

After waiting for a few moments, to be sure Rachel was asleep, Margaret pulled the parlour door to an almost-close. The canvas bag containing the books she was returning to the library in her grip, she skipped down the stairs and lifted her cloak and bonnet from the peg near the basement door. Dragging the garment over her shoulders, she popped her head inside the kitchen.

"Rachel is asleep. I'm popping out to change our library books but I'll not be long, Jessie."

As happened too many times of late, Jessie nodded her acceptance of something but without her customary sunshine smile. A talk about her best friend's worries was long overdue, yet Margaret just hadn't found the right opportunity to discuss the subject properly. Something had been bothering Jessie, but although Margaret had tried to talk to her, worm it out of her, Jessie just wouldn't share her burdens.

The walk to the library was brisk, the rain not too heavy, but it took all her might to keep her feet steady since the typical Edinburgh winds were a-blowing fiercely. Till she'd come to Edinburgh, she'd not appreciated that some places were a lot more windy than others.

When first tutoring Rachel, she'd tended to use some of what was meant be her own afternoon break time for a long-browsing of the library collections. However, since the appearance of Rachel's outdoor wheelchair, they often went together, though never when it was raining.

Margaret paced the streets even more swiftly on her return. So intent was she on getting out of the now pelting rain that she collided with someone on her arrival at the gate that led down to the basement.

"Oh, I'm sorry!" she cried, lifting her head to see above the cap of her bonnet that she'd pulled down as low as possible.

Strong fingers gripped her shoulders to steady her, the voice that answered tinged with laughter. "That's quite all right. It would take a much heavier person than you, Miss Law, to literally knock me over."

Margaret stared up. Though Gavin at just over six feet wasn't really all that much taller, she was fascinated by the raindrops that dripped from the brim of his hat to land on his black-clad chest, and was momentarily robbed of words to properly reply. The palm grip at her shoulders transformed into more of a caress as his intense regard of her continued.

Her heart hitched. Gavin's fingertips and thumbs rose up to wipe away raindrops from her nose and cheeks, his feather-light touches not whimsical at all.

"Come." Gavin urged her towards the short staircase that led up to the front door. "We should get inside out of this waterfall."

Emerging from her mesmerised haze, and removing her gaze from his enticing green eyes, she shrugged off the light grip that had slid back down to her shoulders. "Yes, we must. But I go this way."

Without any further words Margaret opened the squeaking gate and descended on very shaky legs to the basement. Only when she was at the bottom of the flight of ten steps did she look up to see if Gavin Forbes was still outside. The sight of him taking the steps two-at-a-time to reach the main door meant he had hesitated for a few moments.

It was no real consolation, but she hoped that her actions showed him the differences in their station. The doors told their own tales.

Opening the basement door, she gave her canvas bag a shake before she set it down inside. Then she did much the same to her cloak and bonnet after she entered. Her mind and insides, however, were less easy to shake free of silly fancies.

Whatever Gavin Forbes' touch and searing eye contact did to her, she knew she must ignore it. Removing the books, she undid the oilcloth wrap that had protected them and hung both cloth and bag on the hooks under the shelf near the door.

Not finding Jessie in the kitchen, Margaret hitched up her long skirts with one hand and took the stairs two-at-a-time, unsure if she was trying to catch Gavin on his way up to his attic bedroom, or attempting to avoid him coming from the drawing room after greeting his aunt. On approach to the open parlour door, she could hear Jessie's hearty laughter.

"You do look like me, Jessie!" Rachel's tone was almost serious.

Jessie's reply was in humorous vein. "I think that should be that you look like me since I am considerably older than you are, you young scamp."

"Well, I would much rather have you as my sister than grumpy Victoria."

Margaret could see that the two had been engaged in one of Rachel's favourite Happy Families card games, since Jessie was slapping down a pair on Rachel's wheelchair tray.

Margaret made a noisy entrance, pretending not to have heard any of their conversation.

"Your nap couldn't have lasted very long, Rachel," she said. "Though you seem well-enough rested."

Rachel sent a weary, though cheeky, gaze her way. "You always worry too much, Margaret. I'm perfectly fine."

Margaret caught Jessie's glance as her friend rose from the seat. There was something behind it, an unspoken concern, yet something beyond it that Margaret couldn't decipher.

"Tom helped me get her back into her wheelchair, but since the dreaded carrots are awaiting me down in the scullery, I'll get back to my other entertaining duties," Jessie said as she stepped towards the door. "You can finish playing my hand now that you're back. Call me if you need me, Margaret, and don't let that scamp cheat!"

One backward glance made Margaret feel even more worried. There was definitely an anxiety about Jessie that wasn't normal even though she was still being jovial with Rachel.

"So, what was behind your concern up in the parlour earlier today?"

Margaret broached the subject that had been bothering her all evening. They were already in their respective beds and preparing for sleep.

Jessie's huge, huffed sigh was profound before she turned her face to the wall. "I know you heard Rachel talking about her similarity to me but I refuse, I absolutely refuse, to speak about that. Not now and probably not ever!"

Margaret paused before responding, no longer willing to maintain the silence on the subject. "It's a spectre that is going to haunt us, Jessie. And I do mean us. You're my best friend and always have been, but what life has thrown your way just isn't fair!"

Jessie's furious rustling as she turned back to Margaret was disturbing, as was the bitter look she sent her.

"We are not talking about me and my situation – in this house and in this family – not when Rachel is coughing up blood almost every time that I move her."

Margaret felt Jessie's hostile stare down to her very bones.

"Are you so rigid in your tutoring duties that you don't see that poor Rachel is barely able to function? So insensitive?" Jessie was so vehement.

Margaret knew that this talk was well overdue.

"Yes, of course I've noticed that she's declining more and more each day. And, yes, I have seen the blood spots on her handkerchief. For a good while now." Her own anger surfaced. "Do you think I haven't asked the Mistress to summon a doctor to check her?"

Jessie sat up and stared at her as though doubting her for probably the first time ever. Margaret refused to feel guilty and rumbled on.

"I told the Mistress just yesterday that Rachel seemed more poorly this week, that she's back to barely being able to eat, and that she's choking more frequently, like she did years ago when I first came here." She couldn't keep her own distress from showing. "And what did the impervious Hellish Helen say?"

Jessie for once didn't even attempt to mimic Helen's voice, the reason was far too serious. "That Rachel was never going to be well, so bothering the doctor wasn't on the cards?"

Margaret removed her legs from under her blankets and swung her feet around so that she could face Jessie directly, realising the position was also an attempt to calm her body from its furious agitation. "Actually, no. She coolly told me that a visit from a doctor could wait. There was no point in asking a doctor to come, at great expense, till her own medication ran out, which she expected to be quite soon."

Jessie looked fit to burst. "Helen Duncan is almost drowning the house with her hoard of medication. Kate is despairing about the number of empty little bottles she has found secreted all over the place."

Margaret slid over towards Jessie's bed and linked their hands, like they used to do years before but hadn't done recently. "I don't think going to the Mistress about Rachel will do any good. She's too much in a fug all day long about her own miseries."

Jessie's fingers clenched her own. "Mister Duncan? Should we approach him?"

Margaret nodded. "Yes. Even though it could mean the end of both of our employments."

Jessie's expression was bleak before she deliberately unlinked their fingers, turned away and curled herself into a ball. "Well, that might be sooner than you think."

"What do you mean? What aren't you telling me, Jessie? I know something has been bothering you for a good while now." When no reply was forthcoming, she persisted. "You're my best friend, and my almost-sister. If you can't talk to me, who can you share your burdens with?"

"Go to sleep, Margaret. I just can't talk about it."

The resignation in Jessie's tones made Margaret inwardly weep.

It turned into a long night of little sleep, and her worries weren't only for Rachel.

Chapter Thirty

The first week of Gavin Forbes' stay at Albany Street went past quickly. Margaret had largely managed to stick to her resolve of regarding him as nothing more than Rachel's kind cousin, though most of the time that approach was extremely difficult. Keeping away from temptation was at the forefront of her mind, her recent failed talk with Jessie intruding on her thoughts every single day.

Since the recently built Commercial Bank building on George Street was only a short walk away, Gavin had been arriving home a lot earlier than Mister Duncan. That meant Gavin spent a good while with Rachel, often more than David, Victoria and Elspeth did when they returned from their different schools.

During those first days, Margaret used Gavin's time with Rachel as an escape, adopting a well-recognised situation that she was not always needed in the parlour if a family member spent time with Rachel.

Robert, on the other hand, tended to be in late from his new employment near the Kirk of St. Giles on the High Street, where many offices of the law profession were situated. That he worked a very long day was a bone of contention he bemoaned often enough. She had overheard conversations between Robert and Gavin, the former annoyed that he couldn't explore more of the entertainment Edinburgh could provide for young men of a weekday evening, there being many public houses within a short walk.

"And where are you off to in such a hurry, Miss Law?"

Gavin's remark came one late afternoon, on finding her descending to the ground floor, his body blocking her steps and bringing her into direct eye-contact with him.

Annoyed with herself at her inability to control the heat rising into her cheeks, Margaret mumbled, "I'm just popping down to get Rachel some fresh water to drink. She's unusually acquired a thirst today."

"And are you also thirsty, Margaret?"

She bit down on a gasp. It was the first time she had ever heard Gavin use her first name.

"I find that I am thirsty all the time, Margaret. But not for water." His words were a low rumble.

Margaret felt the slide of Gavin's palms, first on her forearms and then up towards her shoulders.

His head moved forward and his lips met hers, tentatively at first, but that didn't last long after his arms bracketed her shoulders and drew her into a more encompassing embrace. Unable to resist, she opened up to him, their kisses seeking more of each other. It was only when the empty water jug she was holding almost slipped from her fingers that she drifted back to reality.

Pulling back from Gavin, she gestured with the jug, and used it to give a slight push to his chest. "I need to get water for Rachel."

Though Gavin relinquished his hold on her, and stepped aside, his gaze lingered on her lips. She felt his regard keenly before she turned and went down the basement stairs.

Late June 1855

And so, it began.

Margaret was once again in thrall to a young man. Gavin snatched every available opportunity to get to know her better. On arrival home from the bank each day, he made sure to pop in to the parlour where he lingered longer than any other family member, somehow persuading Margaret to remain in the room and not scurry away. Ostensibly, he was visiting Rachel though Margaret felt much of Gavin's attention was focused on her. He asked her direct questions, sometimes about her upbringing in Milnathort, and at others about her life in Edinburgh. However, Margaret acknowledged that he never focused on her to the exclusion of Rachel, far from it because he seemed to genuinely care for his little cousin. When Rachel needed time to answer him, he related many stories about growing up in Inverness and told silly anecdotes about his siblings. He effortlessly entertained both Rachel and herself.

At first, Margaret was concerned that Gavin's visits were impinging on Rachel's late afternoon tutoring sessions but, in truth, the little girl's lack of stamina meant more breaks across the whole day were necessary. She had initially had a worry that Helen Duncan would complain that she wasn't teaching enough to earn her wages, but that concern faded quite soon into Gavin's stay. Helen Duncan's visits to Rachel became less frequent, seemingly quite content to leave the daily visits to others.

One night, after dining with the Duncan parents, Gavin contrived to be at the parlour door when Margaret's day was over and Rachel was tucked up in bed.

The tug of Gavin's hand drawing her into the parlour after she left Rachel's bedroom was quite startling. However, the fingertip at his lips and the grin behind it meant Margaret's resistance was momentary.

Barely behind the closed parlour door, Gavin pulled her into an embrace she found herself more than happy to be in. The touches of his lips to her own were so natural that they banished any guilt for them being in a clandestine situation.

Similar interludes happened, though not every evening. They were necessarily brief, since it was highly likely that someone would be nearby – Kate or Jessie clearing the dining room, or David or Victoria entering their own bedrooms. Each rushed moment was an exciting, illicit promise for the next one.

Gavin's kisses, and increasingly more intimate touches, became a daily craving.

The summer progressed. The Duncan siblings continued to pop in to the parlour to greet Rachel as a daily duty-visit. However, they rarely spent very long with her, their renditions of what they had been up to that day tending to be brief, especially Victoria's.

Margaret found her own feelings were increasingly ruffled when Victoria was in attendance up in the parlour. The oldest Duncan daughter was becoming very much a clone of her mother, in that she had little to say that actually engaged Rachel. Margaret found herself increasingly treated as the servant being talked down to by the employer.

She understood some of Victoria's resentments, appreciating that the girl was still champing at the bit to be treated as an adult but it wasn't yet on her parents' plan. All the same, Victoria taking out her resentment on Margaret was so unfair.

David didn't purposely avoid Rachel, like Victoria did, but he was occupied most of the day. Since officially leaving school at the beginning of the summer, he now attended special lectures and events that were held in public buildings, like the art galleries that Margaret still had no experience of. Which university David would enrol at was being hotly debated. Mister Duncan favoured Cambridge to study classics. David had indicated he wanted to study medicine and Edinburgh was regarded as a good institution for that – possibly even the best in the United Kingdom.

An occasional amusement, for Rachel, was when David came to the parlour with his best friend George in tow. George was a stalwart in bolstering up David's choice of university since he was definitely heading to Edinburgh University to study Natural Philosophy. George had entertained Rachel plenty of times in telling her about a little project he'd been working on, a recreation of some form of engineering that he had read about being exhibited at the Great Exhibition in London. George loved tinkering and making things.

"You can hold it, Rachel, but although I've filed down the cast iron, there might still be some sharp bits I've missed," George warned as he set one of his creations onto Rachel's lap-tray.

"Do you like making these little models because your father is a builder?" Rachel had asked after George had described how his unfinished model of a merry-go-round worked.

George almost laughed his head off. "My father would love an answer to that, Rachel."

Margaret watched him show Rachel how to turn the little handle that moved the wheel plates that sat above and below the little horses.

"I'll bring it back when I've got the metal painted, but I brought it today so that you can see how well it turns around at this stage."

It was an impressive little model. Margaret complimented his expertise and told him how she'd love to see it when completed.

"Actually, my father did teach me how to do the welding to join the strips together, Rachel, so maybe it's a family thing after all!"

Margaret was surprised when George suddenly excused himself after looking at the clock. He carefully lifted his model from Rachel's lap-tray and popped it back into the sack he'd used to carry it.

"I have to go now. I'll see you tomorrow, David."

"Well!" David grinned at his little sister. "I wonder where he's off to in such a hurry. He won't be getting his dinner for a while yet, so he must be meeting someone."

Rachel's cheeky grin cheered up her pale features. "Maybe he's got a lady friend he doesn't want to miss."

David ruffled her hair. "I do think that might be the case, little sister, but he's keeping the lady's name close to his chest."

Margaret couldn't resist, her own laughter breaking free. "Well, indeed. That makes two people I know who seem to have a secret sweetheart."

"Do tell, Margaret. Who else are you talking about?"

Margaret kept her smiling lips sealed, her head shaking from side to side. "Oh, not my secret to divulge, David."

The following day it was Elspeth who broke the routine of tutoring, when she all but galloped into the parlour.

"Look at my dress, Rachel. Isn't it lovely? Mama had it made because my reading is getting so much better."

Rachel slid her chin to the side for the little cheek-peck that had become part of Elspeth's daily greeting.

"Actually," Rachel in turn attempted to ruffle her sister's hair. "Mama told me earlier today that it's because your reading and writing are both improving so much."

Elspeth preened.

Rachel continued, "And the fact that you are growing out of clothes so quickly was another good reason to have such a pretty new frock made for you!"

Elspeth's daily visits were looked forward to by Rachel, since the littlest Duncan sister continued to have a sunny nature, regardless of the fact that Helen Duncan monopolised most of her youngest child's time down in the drawing room. Margaret also looked forward to Elspeth's visits, but found them bitter-sweet. The older Elspeth got the more she resembled Rachel, or what Rachel should have looked like if she didn't have the less-than-healthy spots of colour on her otherwise wan white cheeks. It also meant they both were looking more and more like Jessie. Though Elspeth's hair was very straight compared to both Rachel and Jessie, the colour was darkening to Jessie's streaked-golden-blonde. The eye shape, and the iris of all three of them, were a remarkably similar azure blue.

Gavin proved to be very thoughtful and found many ways to give Rachel his attention – not regularly enough to make her eagerly await a daily offering, but sufficient to make it still be a surprise. A bunch of wild flowers might be presented. A small bag of soft sweets from the speciality sweet shop that had recently opened in Edinburgh was occasionally popped on Rachel's wheelchair tray. Gestures which were delightfully accepted. But although the gifts were much appreciated as the summer grew into the autumn, it was Gavin's time that Rachel valued the most.

Habits were easy to acquire, though some made more impact than others.

"How has the day been for you, Rachel? Has Miss Law been too strict with you?"

It broke Margaret's heart to see the tired smile on Rachel's face when her pupil answered.

"Never. Margaret is the most patient of people, the most lovely person, but I think you already know that, Gavin."

The teasing was always entertaining with Gavin, but the exchange of smouldering looks was becoming too hard to ignore. If the emotion-driven eye-contact with him had been all that had developed it wouldn't have been so disconcerting. Gavin seemed to have an uncanny second-sight for when she was likely to be moving around the house even late at night. Those exchanges in otherwise empty corridors became more than just accidental collisions.

Making it clear on one particular occasion, that she was remaining to mark a piece of story writing Rachel had just completed, Margaret took a seat at the big table and left it to Gavin to entertain his little cousin.

Some twenty minutes later Gavin declared, "Thank you for showing me your drawings, Rachel. You have to be the most skilled artist in the whole family."

"You haven't shown me any of yours, so how can I know yours aren't better than mine." Rachel giggled, then fell into a fit of coughing that wracked her little frame.

Margaret stepped forward to wipe the girl's mouth when the coughing fit had eventually subsided. Her usual routine of late was to check whether there were any visible blood spots, but she didn't like to do it so blatantly in front of Gavin.

"I would never lie to you, little cousin. Telling lies of any sort is such a waste of everybody's time." Gavin's laughter rang out towards Margaret as she accepted the drawings to store in the big cloth-covered art file that she had created. Since he was not facing Rachel, she also interpreted his look of concern.

The file was stored in the nearby cupboard, then she returned to her pupil. "You look as if a short nap before dinner might be in order. What do you think?"

"Yes." Rachel acquiesced too easily. "But I'm comfortable in my chair. I don't need to lie on my daybed."

She ruffled Rachel's braids. "You mean you don't trust Gavin and me to get you out of the chair without dropping you?"

Rachel's eyes drooped. "I trust you both more than anyone else in this house, except Jessie. I love her just like I love you two…"

Rachel's eyes were already closed.

Gavin padded across to the door, one finger beckoning Margaret to do the same.

Outside in the landing, she pulled the door almost shut.

"I'm worried about my cousin's health, Margaret. She's getting weaker every day I come home, and that cough is really troublesome."

"Do you think I haven't noticed her decline?" Margaret couldn't help the defensive tone.

Gavin took her hand and squeezed it reassuringly. "I know exactly how concerned you are, but my aunt and uncle are another matter. Does my aunt spend any time with Rachel, these days?"

She knew her expression would be damning, but she was past worrying. "Not really. Both Jessie and I have spoken to Mister Duncan about our concerns but so far we've had no visits from Doctor Oliver, none since his last check-up, which was ages ago."

Gavin looked utterly appalled. "I thought he visited once a week. My aunt told me that when I was here at Easter."

"He used to do that, but Mistress Duncan decided he didn't need to come so often as he was no longer giving Rachel the manipulation exercises that benefitted her arm use. The Mistress told me only yesterday that it would be an unnecessary expense for Doctor Oliver to visit Rachel, since her own medication is now being dispensed by a different doctor."

Gavin's snort of disdain made her feel very awkward. "Ah, yes. Even for the short time I have been living here, I have seen how my aunt depends on the laudanum medication for her nerves."

The slight shake to his head and the pursing of his lips she took as an indication that he was feeling he had overstepped the bounds with someone who wasn't family.

He let go of her hand. "I'll let you get back inside."

She turned to go back into the room, but was halted by another terse question from Gavin.

"Who ensures Rachel doesn't choke on the bloody phlegm she's coughing up at night? If she's hacking up the amount I see happening during the day, then it has to be as irritating at night, too. I know it isn't your duty to do overnight nursing, but who does it?"

Margaret inhaled a sharp breath and hesitated. Gavin might be very enticing, and already as close to her heart as any young man had ever been, but he was family.

Gavin looked even more aghast. "Please don't tell me that my aunt sees to Rachel overnight?"

She could barely nod.

The immediate brief hug, being held so close to Gavin's chest that she could barely breathe, she took as a signal of his alarm more than any romantic gesture. He then released her to frame her face with his palms.

"This has to be dealt with."

She managed another nod before the tiniest kiss pressed to her lips, one of reassurance.

But that didn't last. The next and the next again kisses were deep and drugging. She didn't want them to ever stop as his palms slid down her back, caressing and soothing, pressing her into him. In turn, her hands sneaked around to bring him as close as possible.

It was Gavin who eventually broke free. Again, he framed her cheeks. "You know I want to keep on kissing you, but as I said before, something must be done."

Gavin leapt for the stairs as if a whole swarm of bees was after him, leaving her feeling utterly thrilled, but also thoroughly guilty for thinking of only her own needs and wants and not Rachel.

The incident on the landing with Gavin seemed as though she'd imagined it, because for days afterwards nothing changed regarding Rachel.

Nevertheless, something cataclysmic had shifted between the two of them. The change was so abrupt it left Margaret reeling.

Gavin continued to visit Rachel when he came home. He was still as endearing and jovial with his little cousin, though he only stayed for a very short time claiming he had brought home work to do up in his attic room. Margaret thought this very unlikely. Or it was something he had promised to do for Robert. Manufactured excuses.

Margaret shared no smouldering glances with Gavin over the top of Rachel's wheelchair. He avoided eye contact with her and during any inadvertent occurrences he drew his gaze swiftly away from her, a tension in both his eyes and shoulders that she felt deeply in herself, but couldn't understand any cause for it. There were no smiles or touches deliberately made to Margaret's hands, or arms or shoulders. And there were definitely no stolen kisses of any kind.

Like a will o' the wisp Gavin was in and out of the parlour, emotionally stiff-upper-lipped once his back was turned from Rachel's sight.

Gavin made no attempt to talk to Margaret privately. There were no accidental – or on purpose – encounters in the corridor, or on the stairs. It was the opposite of the previous weeks in that he managed to be elsewhere when she was moving around the house.

Margaret took it to heart that she'd been too forward in allowing his kisses and caresses. Pretending that his hurtful distancing from her didn't matter was a lie, because she was hurt to her core by his changed attitude.

For around one week, Helen Duncan popped into the parlour to speak to Rachel at least once a day, but the duration of the visit was always short-lived. The woman was increasingly twitchy and sometimes unaware of what she was doing. Margaret thought it was as though some prompt in Hellish Helen's mind made the woman climb the stairs, but by the time Helen entered the parlour the woman had forgotten why she was there.

The Mistress was prone to telling Rachel to buck up and shake off the constant colds that were keeping her daughter in her chair. Margaret also got a tongue lashing for being too lenient about Rachel's laziness. There was occasionally a steely determination to Helen's gaze when Margaret was the focus of the woman's ire, yet sometimes Helen's tirades of how Margaret should improve what was going on in the parlour made no sense at all.

Margaret's emotions were so mixed up that she cared not a whit that she loathed her Mistress as much as the woman appeared to despise her.

The worst new development was that it was as though Helen had completely erased the reason that Rachel was an invalid from her mind.

The high colour that blossomed across Helen Duncan's otherwise ghostly-white cheeks when she was in an outburst Margaret guessed wasn't due to increasing temper. The cause seemed to be as unhealthy a one as was being experienced by her poor little daughter. Margaret found she could drum up no sympathy at all for Helen Duncan.

She was also increasingly feeling a resentful dislike for charming young men who toyed with her affection.

The interludes with Helen Duncan tended to make Rachel gloomy for a while after her visits. Margaret found she had to work harder to lighten the little girl's mood, because the poor little thing was melancholy, weak, and constantly lethargic.

Gavin's mesmerising spell followed by a complete lack of attention was making more than one person feel neglected.

Chapter Thirty-One

July 1855

It was more than a week later when the parlour door opened without ceremony and Doctor Oliver strode in. Margaret could see a tension around the man's mouth and anger flaring across his eyes that wasn't usually there before he walked across to Rachel, whose chair sat near the window. By the time he reached her, his greeting was amiable.

"It's been far too long since I saw my star patient, young lady!" He wasted no time in taking Rachel's pulse and in placing the back of his hand to her forehead. "What's this you're doing for Miss Law?" He indicated the piece of paper on her lap-tray. "Writing a letter to an admirer?"

The pinkish colour at Rachel's cheeks blossomed even more than was now customary. "Yes, it's a letter. But to an imaginary friend."

It was so encouraging at first to hear Rachel's tinkling laugh though not when she fell into a paroxysm of coughing. Margaret stood at the ready with a handkerchief.

"Dear, dear! That's a bit of a rattle."

Doctor Oliver seemed to make light of it as he bent down to remove an instrument from the copious bag that he always carried during his visits. If Margaret hadn't seen him use it before, she could be forgiven for thinking he was about to play a tune on it.

After waiting till the coughing had almost stopped, the doctor slid the wider end of the trumpet-shaped instrument to Rachel's chest and listened at the other end.

"Mmm." He lifted his ear off the end and and looked at his patient. "Can you try to give me another of those coughs, little lady?"

Rachel's head nodded. Margaret wasn't surprised to hear what came next.

"I'll try, but the best ones take me by surprise."

"I'm sure they do," the doctor replied before getting himself back into listening position to wait for another cough, which Rachel produced with no difficulty.

Margaret helped to prop Rachel up when her restraints were unfastened, so that the doctor could use the listening tube at her back.

A few more questions were asked of Rachel while the doctor put away his instrument. Then, after a kindly leave-taking of Rachel, Margaret watched him turn towards her.

"Can you show me the pillows on Rachel's bed, please?"

Thinking it was an unexpected question, Margaret followed him out of the room.

Once out in the corridor Doctor Oliver pointed to the dining room. She tiptoed after him into the nearby room, realising his conversation wasn't to be overheard by Rachel.

"It was only today that I was personally summoned by Mister Duncan. I feel I know the answer, but have you sometimes asked for me to make a visit to Rachel these last few weeks.

Margaret decided it was far too important to prevaricate. "Yes. I've asked Mistress Duncan to request visits from you for months now. She wasn't inclined to humour me." Margaret decided to clarify even more. "I've also spoken to Mister Duncan on a few occasions, though you did not appear after that, either."

297

Doctor Oliver nodded. "Mistress Duncan and I had a disagreement and she decided to consult another doctor some months ago. I believe you will know why, though that isn't what's important right now. What is crucial is the deterioration in Rachel's condition." The doctor seemed to hesitate only a fraction. "Mister Duncan, apparently, asked his wife to summon me after speaking with yourself and Jessie, but she failed to do so. Or chose not to do so. Whatever the truth of that circumstance, her husband is only now aware of this rock."

Margaret couldn't prevent the tears from welling up. She could barely answer. "Rachel's very frail, and so tired of the persistent coughing. And there's the blood as well."

"You've mentioned that to her mother?"

"I have, but she doesn't seem interested in making things easier for Rachel."

"Does Rachel have these coughing fits during the night, keeping her from sleeping?"

The tears welled up again. "I don't know. It's her mother who looks after her overnight."

Doctor Oliver's expression was tight, showing little outward emotion, but the blaze at his eyes told of his alarm.

A curt, extremely serious nod came her way before the doctor headed towards the stairs.

Just one day after the conversation with Doctor Oliver the household was in an uproar. Margaret could hear Helen Duncan screaming like a banshee out in the corridor.

"I must have access to my own room. David can move up to the attic floor. Go and get Tom to help move David's things."

The woman was so loud that Margaret feared it would waken Rachel from her third nap of the afternoon. She debated whether going out to help would actually be useful given her employer's anger.

298

"Can we, please, leave the removal of David's things till he comes home from his class? Then he can choose which room he would like."

When Margaret realised it was Jessie who was bearing the brunt of Hellish Helen's ire, she hesitated no longer and opened the door.

"David does not need to choose." Helen was so infuriated spit that was leaking from edges of her lips. "The rooms are exactly the same."

That was a lie if ever Margaret had heard one. The two unoccupied attic rooms might be roughly the same size, but one of them faced out to the backyard and had an even tinier window than the two which faced out the front to Albany Street.

Helen Duncan pushed open the door of the master bedroom. "There's absolutely no need to bring anyone into this house to look after Rachel at night."

Margaret then watched the demented creature whirl around. "If someone else needs to be in Rachel's room overnight you can do it! You're a Duncan bastard, after all is said and done, so why not you?"

Unfortunately, the woman was so unsteady the poke she directed at Jessie's chest jabbed at Jessie's throat instead. Margaret jumped forward to pull Helen Duncan away, Jessie standing transfixed as though made of stone.

"Mama?" Rachel's weak voice reached the corridor. "Why are you shouting?"

Steering Helen straight into the master bedroom, Margaret forced the woman to lie down on the bed. No niceties were conducted, but they were not needed since Helen Duncan was suddenly dead to the world. Not actually dead, though.

Margaret had experienced this sudden loss of consciousness once before, when she'd briefly visited the drawing room to ask her employer a question. She knew it wasn't just an alcohol stupor, but one brought on by a combination of both alcohol and laudanum.

Dashing back out to the corridor, she caught the tail end of Jessie stepping into the parlour to comfort Rachel.

"It's nothing to be alarmed about," Jessie consoled Rachel. "Your mother isn't happy about your father employing a nurse for you overnight. I've just met her, and her name is Mistress Brand. She's a lovely lady who is downstairs just now having a cup of tea with Cook. She came to meet you but was told you were having a little nap."

What little blood Rachel had seemed to leak from her cheeks. "She's not going to replace Margaret?"

Jessie took hold of Rachel's hands to allay the visible rising panic. "Oh, good heavens, no! Mistress Brand will just be with you overnight when you're sleeping, instead of your mother."

Margaret absorbed the incredible news. It seemed that Doctor Oliver had worked quickly, when properly appraised of the dire situation. She dropped down to Rachel's eye-level, mirroring Jessie on the other side. "Your mother needs more rest."

Rachel's little head nodded. "Mama doesn't hear me coughing anyway. She snores quite loudly and sometimes wakens me up. Perhaps Mistress Brand won't snore?"

Rachel's naïve question made her smile, Jessie too.

Jessie's response was vehement, though. "Mistress Brand will be awake all night, young lady. Any snoring she does will be in her own house when she goes home during the day."

Rubbing her throat where there was a visible red mark blossoming, Jessie excused herself to get back to the kitchen.

It wasn't till later that evening, after various bouts of door-slamming and shouting by different family members, that Margaret got the full story. By then Jessie was pacing the kitchen floor.

"I've never seen Mister Duncan so irate. He has absolutely forbidden David from moving up to the attic floor, and declared that if Helen needs a bed that's not the bed he will be in, then she can move up there herself." Jessie grimaced. "You can imagine that was not received well by Hellish Helen!"

Margaret picked up two cups and filled them from the teapot that still held some warm tea. Handing one to Jessie, she urged her friend to sit down.

"David wasn't a happy lad, either," Jessie said.

Jessie's smile was thin, her exhale huge. "It was just as well that Helen slept off her rage for the time that she did. Neither Kate nor I had attempted to move anything from David's room. It was just a pity that David's return coincided with her waking up."

"I heard them out in the corridor. Gavin, too. He was in the parlour with us when she started to bawl at David."

"I know. I went up there with David, after Kate and I warned him of what had occurred." Jessie nodded. "As soon as she started on David, Gavin came out into the corridor to intervene."

Margaret watched Jessie's lips wobbling; her friend's expression just short of bursting into tears.

"Gavin's so good at being a go-between," Jessie said between sniffs.

Margaret felt the shift in Jessie before her best friend even muttered her next words.

"He's the right sort of cousin for me to have, Margaret."

Margaret swallowed over and over, and tried to banish the surprise from her face. Jessie's expression pleaded.

"There! I've said it!" Then the tears began a trek down Jessie's cheeks. "It would have been nice, though, if that screaming banshee had mentioned me being a Duncan bastard in a less awful way."

Margaret darted around the table and drew Jessie into the tightest hug possible without crushing her bones.

"She's the worst bitch I've ever encountered, Jessie."

A terrible thought descended, one which might have been better suited to one of her father's religious fanatic cronies.

"Maybe what's happening to Helen Duncan right now is the punishment that woman needs."

Jessie nodded against her shoulder. "Yes, but Mister Duncan is culpable, too."

After minutes of heart-breaking sobs wracking her frame, Jessie eventually stirred herself and pulled out of Margaret's arms, wiping the flood from her cheeks. Her words were so determined.

"If Rachel wasn't so poorly, I would walk out of that basement door right now and never come back!"

And right that moment Margaret felt exactly the same. Jessie's confidence in Gavin being a worthwhile person wasn't shared in the least by Margaret. She had built a little wall around herself and kept her feelings tight inside. As far as Margaret knew, nobody in the house had known of the budding relationship between Gavin and herself, save perhaps Rachel. She was thankful of that and yet still so confused by his mercurial behaviour.

Did the arrival of Mistress Brand make any difference? Margaret asked herself that question over and over as one day was followed by the next.

Mistress Brand was indeed a huge reassurance. Rachel was being properly seen to overnight, the widow being used to nursing jobs and efficient in all she did. She even stayed longer than she needed to in the morning, unpaid time as it were, chatting to Margaret and Jessie as they all got Rachel ready for the day. What the nurse was unable to do was to halt the gradual deterioration in Rachel's lungs. That was beyond the bounds of expert nursing care.

Margaret avoided Helen Duncan when she could, she and Jessie ensuring that Elspeth spent more time up in the

302

parlour. They contrived simple excuses. Rachel needed her sister for a particular game, or to share a book, or some such reason. It was actually not often a confrontation because when not in a laudanum filled-rage Helen was withdrawing into herself. Her responses were limited to mumbles or an automatic accord, often when blind agreement was not a correct response. Staring at the wall was commonplace.

"Does the Master ever come home for dinner?" Margaret asked one night as she finished off the last stitch of the mending that she'd been doing at the kitchen table. "I've not seen him for days."

"Oh, yes. He eats with them all up in the dining room, though Helen sometimes refuses to eat at all, and won't leave the drawing room," Kate said as she twiddled her cup in a nervous fashion. "But the Master's taken to going out again around ten o'clock."

Jessie gently removed the cup and patted Kate's hands to halt the agitation. Margaret felt they were all on edge all the time since the arrival of Mistress Brand, though it was in no way the woman's fault. Only a week had passed, yet it felt like months.

"Where does he go?" Jessie asked.

Kate shook her head. "No idea, but he's not there when I rake out the ashes in the master bedroom around six o'clock in the morning. Helen's alone, sprawled all over the bed."

Margaret shared mute looks with the others.

Kate's gaze first went to Jessie, then her.

"Though he does come home sometime after that. I've seen him going straight up to his bedroom. I deal with the laundry, so I know he changes his clothes before he's in the dining room for his breakfast."

Jessie nodded. "Then he's back out to go to his chambers."

Margaret had little to add, except that Mister Duncan now stepped into Rachel's bedroom to give her a good morning kiss before he left for work. That was a development since Mistress Brand had arrived.

She wasn't sure if what Mister Duncan was doing overnight popped into Jessie and Kate's heads as much as it did into hers during the next few days, but she couldn't shake it free.

It was inevitable that it would be discussed when both she and Jessie were in their beds late one night.

"He's just not the type to have a woman friend. Is he, Margaret?" Jessie sounded so unsure.

Margaret couldn't give credence to that solution either, but if not that, where was he sleeping?

"I doubt he's sleeping much at all," Margaret answered. "I think he looks quite haggard, don't you?"

Jessie agreed. "I've noticed that, too."

Margaret knew that Jessie hadn't forgiven the Duncans for being complicit in her situation, but the mainly good regard Jessie had always had for Stewart Duncan stubbornly remained.

For a few more moments, they discussed if there was a way that they could find out where he was going, but Margaret fell asleep before any good ideas occurred to her.

Chapter Thirty-Two

August 1855

The wind was howling like a banshee as Margaret made her way along George Street towards St. Andrew Square the next day. Clutching her hat with one hand, and her bulging cloth bag with the other, she battled to keep her balance. Hardly noticing the buildings that she was passing, her eyes downcast, she became aware of someone calling out from behind. It was only when the call came a second time, she realised it was her name being shouted. She turned around.

"Let me help you with that bag!" Gavin's expression was concerned, the wind almost whipping his words away as he skipped down the last step of the short flight that led into the building he'd just vacated. It was ages since she had seen him while on her own.

Looking up, she realised she was outside his workplace, the impressive building which housed The Commercial Bank.

"What a day!" she said, wondering why he was even speaking to her.

Gavin's arm steadied her when she almost toppled after a particularly strong gust, then he drew her towards him. She tried to extract her bag from her arm, but found the handles had twisted around her forearm so much it was an impossible task.

"Come up with me." Gavin urged her up the flight of steps, not to the main double doors but to another door alongside. "We'll get it untangled indoors, out of the wind."

He held the door open and allowed her to enter first. "Stretch out your arm, if you can."

Gavin's instruction pulled her from her daze.

"Thank you. It's such a nuisance when this happens." Margaret maintained a polite exchange.

His attitude was so different from his recent indifference, and she didn't know why it was so. It confused her but she also felt starved of his congenial company that had thrilled her so much.

The dark wood-panelled corridor led through to a bright space up ahead which looked so tempting.

While he unwound the cloth handles, his conversation was a treat to a starving soul. "The exterior is impressive but that interior even more so, don't you think?"

Margaret gulped. "I can't see it properly, but it looks truly remarkable."

Gavin popped the bag down on the floor and set to righting her bonnet. "I'm afraid I'm not allowed to take you all the way into the foyer. Unless you have a full load of money in that bag! And, in case you think that's where I work all day, you need to think again. My desk is in a tiny office up high in the building." His words tingled at her ear; his face so close she could see the bristles at his cheeks. "It'll be years, even decades, before I expect to be working at the customer desks down here on the ground floor."

"Thank you. I can feel my arm again." She gave it a bit of a shake, then retied the bow under her neck. "And for that little glimpse into another world."

Taking her by the elbow he pulled her along a couple of steps towards the foyer. "Peek in quickly so they don't notice, or they'll take you for an intruder bent on robbing the premises."

Gavin's joke made the hairs on her neck bristle. What a dreadful concept!

306

There was a wonderful mosaic floor underfoot, and a huge cathedral-like dome way up in the roof. The light filtering down through the beautiful stained glass was slightly diminished by the outside grey cloud-cover, but there were plenty of ornate gas lamps dotted around to give warm illumination to all of the glossy desk surfaces on the ground floor. Above that an upper balcony led off to numerous offices. Shining wood and gilt adornments robbed her of her breath.

Gavin's palms at her shoulders drew her back from the scene that she had taken too long to snatch a glimpse of. He turned her round towards the door they had used to enter, assuring her that nobody was going to complain. At least he hoped they weren't.

"Are you going straight home, now, or have you other errands to do?" Gavin picked up her bag from the corridor floor.

"Straight home." Again, she was gripped by his changed mood. "I actually had a bit more free time today, which is unusual. Mistress Duncan dismissed me for an hour since she decided to stay longer with Rachel."

"Really?" Gavin sounded as surprised as she'd been herself, though she also sensed an element of disquiet.

She couldn't be as circumspect as she probably should, given her position in the household. "It was no hardship for her. Rachel was having an afternoon nap when Mistress Duncan came up to the parlour. Elspeth and Victoria were due home from school and would be there to keep Rachel company." After a slight pause she said, "Jessie was alerted."

Gavin held open the door. "So, you decided to make an escape?"

"Rachel needed some more silver and grey silks for her special embroidery sampler, and I took the opportunity to buy some material to make new dresses for myself and Jessie. It was a good enough reason for me to leave the house, in the Mistress's opinion."

"Do you make Jessie's clothing?"

She clucked at his surprise. "No, I don't. We help each other to measure and cut. And when we've sewn the dress, the hemming is so much easier with someone else helping."

"When do you find time to do it? You're too occupied during the day with Rachel." He held the outside door open.

"It takes us weeks, but we encourage each other to get tasks finished." Margaret secured her bonnet ribbon.

"Breathe deeply before we skip down the stairs. Then we'll make a run for it."

With Gavin steering her by the elbow, and him having taken over the rotating cloth bag, it took them no time at all to reach Albany Street.

Conversation had been almost impossible; not much more than short questions and even more brief answers, the wind whipping their words away. When she felt the first rain spatters, their pace increased even more.

At the house Gavin made no hesitation. He nipped down the basement steps with Margaret in tow. Once the basement door was open and they were inside, he handed over her bag.

"You could have given it to me up there," she said, setting the bag down on the floor, while attempting to be matter-of-fact. "And gone in the front door."

"I could have, but I know you'd not have come with me."

Gavin's eyes searched her own, his expression changing from a silent plea to a furious frustration.

Margaret's breath snagged in her throat when Gavin grabbed her into his arms as though he couldn't help himself.

"Margaret. Forgive me? I'm so very sorry I've been so…"

Since he didn't seem to know how to finish, she blurted out, "Why have you?"

308

He shook his head. Regret and embarrassment were what Margaret sensed he was feeling, according to his torn expression. But there was more.

"That day at the top of the stairs – after our kisses that I've never forgotten in any way – I went down to find my uncle." One of his hands slid away from her elbow and pushed back a rain-sprinkled lock of his hair that had fallen on to his forehead. "Of course, it was too early for him to be home but my aunt was in the drawing room." His expression changed to one of extreme anger and yet was also racked-full of rueful pain.

She was sure the deep gaze that seared her couldn't be fake.

His palm returned to her back to hold her tight.

"Aunt Helen was furious when I said that Rachel was being neglected and needed a visit from the doctor. She was like a virago, yelling at me to mind my own business and all sorts of other stuff."

Margaret stared at him, and believed every word.

"Suffice to say she also warned me that if I progressed my interest in you, then she'd not be allowing me to stay in Albany Street."

Margaret struggled to free herself, unable to credit that he was so mercenary.

His fervent gaze drew back her attention, if not her body.

"I could handle finding other lodgings easily enough but the other things she threatened? Those I couldn't ignore. She is far too volatile and unstable, Margaret."

His unspoken plea for forgiveness was what tipped the balance of Margaret's thinking.

"Did she threaten to do something awful to Jessie?" she whispered.

He nodded. "Yes. Though not just to Jessie. I had to keep my distance from you."

"Did she threaten to get rid of me?" Margaret voiced it though knew what his answer would be.

"She did. With no salary due and no reference." Gavin's eyes pleaded again. "I couldn't let that happen when I was out at work."

The words were out before Margaret had properly thought them through. "What's different today?"

"I can't hold back any longer." Gavin's groan was tortured. "I can't help myself from wanting you."

His fingers crept round to unfasten her bonnet, which he set upon the nearest peg. And then he kissed her, a lingering one since the corridor remained empty except for them. Another followed the first, and then more, each new one probing and re-learning more of each other.

Gavin's fingers deftly undid the tape at her neck, freeing her cloak which drifted away from her shoulders, again to be hung up without him even looking.

Drawing her back in close to him, she felt his warm palms slide a tortuous pathway from her shoulders, all the way down to mould her buttocks. The kisses deepened and deepened till she was almost dizzy from lack of breath. She found she couldn't get near enough even though it was only clothes that separated them.

When she became aware that Gavin was aroused, the heat at her face and chest that had been generated by their fiery kisses only got hotter.

She couldn't prevent the gasp that escaped when he set her slightly away from him and stared at her, his palms sliding down from her shoulders to cover her aching breasts. His thumbs kneaded the undersides of them, the rest of his open palms tentatively squeezing as though he was waiting for something. Perhaps her reaction to his boldness?

Excited beyond measure at the feelings he was invoking, she inhaled deeply, unable to peel her gaze away.

"You are so beautiful, Margaret." As he spoke Margaret was held in fascination. His warm green eyes took on a different hue, little flecks of his irises emitting a visible emotion of their own. "You have no idea how much I've missed you and about what I really want to be doing to you just now."

Without thought, since she was beyond that, Margaret brought her palms up to cover Gavin's, holding his hands in place.

The only thing that stopped what might have developed next between them was the sound of someone clumping their way down the stairs, muttering to themselves.

By the time Kate had rounded the stairs and was into the passage, Margaret had dragged Gavin into her bedroom, a finger at her lips.

The comical slant of his expression was as warming as his kisses had been. "This is a dangerous place to bring me to if you want me to avoid being seen or heard," he whispered, his lips back onto hers.

After a moment of sheer luxury Margaret extricated herself and put him from her, one of the most difficult decisions she reckoned she'd ever had to make. Drawing a deep breath, and hating herself if truth be told, she faced him.

"Gavin, no. This can't happen. That's not why I brought you in here."

"Ah! You wound me, Margaret."

His wry expression and the gesture of his open palms being raised up to his shoulders made her giggle, because the stretching only made his arousal all the more prominent.

"Err…" Margaret had no personal experience of knowing how a man got himself out of arousal in such circumstances, but had had enough conversations with Kate to know he might need a little bit of time. "I'll keep Kate occupied in the kitchen while you make your way upstairs."

"You'll need to give me at least five minutes, then." he said, adjusting his stance, a grimace of a smile matching some eye-rolling. "Your effect on me isn't going to disappear in just one moment."

Embarrassment flooded her. Kate had also mentioned that some men might get very annoyed if thwarted during an attempt to make love, though she had assured them that her Tom wasn't at all like that.

When Gavin's slightly laboured smile changed to an expression that was more sombre, she knew he wasn't really angry with her.

"Before you go, there's something else I wanted to talk to you about but didn't get the chance earlier. There's no other way to say this save to blatantly come right out with it."

Margaret was alarmed but also absorbed. From his now concerned expression, she just knew it was nothing to do with any development of their relationship.

"Have you noticed my uncle is looking exceedingly exhausted this last week, or so?"

"Actually, I have. Jessie, too."

After such a romantic interlude, Margaret gulped at his sudden change of mood. She found she was stumbling over her words. "Kate is concerned that he's…" She'd no idea how to continue.

"That he's going back out late in the evening?"

Margaret nodded, rivetted to his expression.

"And he's only returning in the morning, to change his clothes?"

Another bob of the head was the best she could manage. Her eyes beseeched. "Kate only shared that with us because we're all concerned about him."

She felt the tears rising, which Gavin obviously noticed since his arms encircled her again. However, it was a light embrace with less of the heat from before.

"It's not your fault. None of you are being nosey."

It was Gavin's turn to look uneasy. "I know this won't go any further than you three, but Robert has told me that Uncle Stewart is sleeping in his chambers."

Margaret felt her mouth gape. "The poor man! No wonder he's exhausted. I didn't think his office was big enough to have a bed in it."

"It isn't. Robert says he's fashioned himself something like a *Duchesse Brisée.*"

Margaret was startled by the French words. Only one of which she recognised.

Gavin was quick to reassure, a smirk lightening the moment. "A *Duchesse Brisée* resembles a couch but is made up of two very comfortable armchairs with a sizeable stool set in between, to allow someone to stretch out. Unfortunately, my uncle's office is so small he's setting two wooden chairs together with a footstool in between."

Margaret whiffed out her concern. "That's no good at all."

Gavin's lips descended another time.

Margaret felt this time his kiss was driven by tenderness, rather than raw passion.

"I think my Uncle Stewart has major decisions to make about Aunt Helen. Robert thinks so, too. You're all aware of how unhinged she is. My uncle has been devastated for a long time about what he must do."

Silent tears slid down Margaret's cheeks.

Gavin's fingertips wiped them away, his voice a whisper.

"Stay here till you compose yourself."

Margaret felt another peck at her forehead as though he couldn't stop kissing her. "I'll slip out and go up via the basement stairs."

Chapter Thirty-Three

September 1855

The following week Doctor Oliver visited the parlour once again.

"How are you feeling today, young lady?"

Rachel managed a small smile for him, though her eyes lacked sparkle. "Sleepy. Margaret fusses more than ever."

Doctor Oliver's laugh was a hearty one as he set the back of his hand to her forehead. "You know by now that Margaret is following all of my instructions very, very well."

That hint of cheek that was Rachel's very own slid free, in spite of the effort it took for her to respond.

"Mistress Brand, too. She's nice when I cough a lot… in bed."

"Doing a good job, is she?" the doctor asked as he listened to Rachel's chest.

Though Rachel couldn't see it since he was bent down towards her chest, Margaret felt the doctor's full focus on her. His head didn't move and his facial expression remained unchanged, but Margaret sensed his eyes were alerting her to some change he couldn't voice at that present moment.

When Doctor Oliver stood up again, he popped his listening instrument in his case. He felt around Rachel's throat and neck area and then Margaret saw him set light touches down towards her stomach.

"Are you happier eating soup or bread and cheese?"

Margaret watched Rachel's eyes widen and an almost-smile appear. It was such a funny question but her answer was quick to come. "Soup."

"Mmm. I thought so. Your tummy is quite tight, so I think for the next few days Margaret should ask Cook to just give you soup for every meal. And maybe some warm milk would be nice, too."

Doctor Oliver picked up his bag.

"Does the cough elixir make you feel nice and warm inside, Rachel?"

"Hmm, it's good." Rachel's eye lids flickered.

The doctor set his hand gently on her shoulder. "I'll have some more delivered. So… before you fall asleep on me, I will take my leave." He gave Rachel his usual curt bow. "If I'm lucky, I might meet Jessie on my way out. She pops along to the kitchen to get me one of Cook's lovely shortbread biscuits."

His parting words made Rachel giggle, a very tiny one, but lovely to hear.

Margaret was sure that the doctor's words were intentional and designed to get the desired reaction.

"Leave one for me!" Rachel managed before succumbing to another coughing fit.

Margaret was glad that Rachel was unaware that if Doctor Oliver mentioned Jessie, it was now a signal that he would be leaving further instructions for Rachel's care. Guidelines that he didn't want the poor little thing to hear.

For various reasons, Margaret didn't see Jessie till late in the evening.

The kitchen table was the place of confidences, and had been for quite a long time. Margaret sat down beside Jessie, with Kate sitting opposite them. Kate filled a cup from the teapot and slid it across to her.

Margaret turned towards Jessie. "Did Doctor Oliver leave more instructions?"

"Yes," Jessie confirmed, her eyes brimming with tears. "He says if Rachel feels too tired to get up in the mornings that we should use our own judgement, but not force her. The overall weakness will progress quickly now, and we should make her comfortable wherever she prefers to be."

Margaret couldn't prevent the shivers at her spine.

"Oh, that's going to be so hard for both of you." Kate was almost weeping too.

The lump at Margaret's throat was so big she could hardly swallow. "Did he say that she'll be…" Her voice broke and the tears began to fall. "…in pain?"

Jessie's head shook, her expression more and more distressed. "No. Apart from when she coughs, that is. He just said she'll want to sleep a lot more, now. That we should only give her liquid food and care for her as we always have been doing."

"He mentioned to me that he'd send along a different cough tonic tomorrow."

Jessie nodded, her lips wobbling. "It will contain more of whatever he's giving her to take any pain away."

"Oh, my goodness," Kate gasped, her own tears dripping. "I understand that he's telling you these things because you're the ones looking after her, as well as Mistress Brand, but it's that heartless, selfish bitch upstairs who should be getting this information."

"Hellish Helen isn't fit for anything these days!" Jessie's fist thumping the table jolted Margaret so much the cup she'd just raised to her lips spilled over, the tea dripping down and off her chin. Jessie got up from the table and began to pace around the kitchen. "Did either of you know that Doctor Oliver popped up to see Rachel while he was visiting, though he was actually summoned here to examine Hellish Helen!"

Jessie was now so angry Margaret could feel the tension radiating in rivulets from her. "I was coming out of the drawing room, having just tidied up the mess that

316

Helen had left strewn around her tea table before she went up to her room for her afternoon nap."

Kate looked mollified. "Oh, I'm sorry about that. I intended to check the room after I came back from dropping off the bedding at the laundress' house along the road."

Jessie patted Kate's shoulder as she passed her by. "I'm not complaining about that, Kate. I was just about to say that I was struggling with a tray filled with broken crockery and ornaments from her frenzy when the front door opened and both the Master and Doctor Oliver walked in."

"In the afternoon?" Kate's surprise wasn't about the doctor entering but more about their employer being home.

Jessie stopped pacing and sat back down. "Doctor Oliver is so astute. He took one look at the mess on the tray and asked if such *'accidents'*, as he delicately put it, were rare. Naturally, I said they were happening more frequently. Almost every day."

Margaret patted Jessie's hand, so glad that Jessie didn't mince her words.

Jessie's mouth tweaked up at one side. "Doctor Oliver continued to stare at me but the Master remained silent. I couldn't resist. I just said that I was thankful that I wasn't in the way of any of the weapons when they were fired. Though I couldn't say for anyone else, for sure."

Margaret jostled Jessie's shoulder. "Did the Master say anything to you?"

Jessie's head shook. "Not then. When I confirmed Helen was upstairs that's where they went."

"Did you see them after that?" Kate asked.

Jessie nodded. "They came down to the scullery and asked me to sit at this very table with them. Just where you are now."

Margaret was agog with curiosity though also concern, and Kate seemed to be as well.

"They asked me if I was willing to sign a statement about some of the things Helen has been doing these last few years."

Margaret gripped Jessie's fingers and found her friend's hand so cold to the touch. "Did you sign it?"

There was shake of Jessie's head, then her attention went first to Kate and then to herself.

"They have to write it up first. But Doctor Oliver also said that he'd be asking you, Kate, and anticipated that you'd sign as well. I told them that I was certain you would."

There was dead silence in the kitchen while they absorbed the importance of the news, the hush eventually broken by a wail from Jessie. "Helen Duncan can rot in any hell they put her in, but what's important is what Doctor Oliver also said about our little girl, who is currently up there with Mistress Brand."

"Dear God," Kate said, reaching her hands across the table so they could all link their fingers together.

Jessie gulped and sniffed her next words. "He says to tell you that he can do nothing more for the lung disease. It has progressed too far for recovery, but it has also weakened her heart beyond repair now and she'll just get more and more feeble."

Margaret felt Jessie slump against her shoulder. She released her fingers to curl her arms around her almost-sister, comfort for both of them.

Across the table Kate's exhale of breath was deep. "Is he saying it might not be long now?"

None of them could voice the inevitable words.

Jessie nodded through huge gulping sobs; her eyes bleak. "I'm telling you two now. After Rachel dies, I will not stay in this house a moment longer after the funeral than I need to."

Erupting from Margaret's arms, Jessie rushed out into the corridor. Before Margaret was even at the kitchen door, Jessie had banged the outside door shut.

Margaret felt Kate clutch at her elbow. "Let her run, Margaret. She's grabbed her shawl and will return when she's composed herself."

Kate propelled her back to the table and pushed her into a seat.

"You don't need to say it, Margaret. I know that Jessie is sometimes out quite late at night, after you're asleep."

Margaret gasped. "How do you know that?"

Kate's look was conspiratorial but not abashed.

"Tom and I are circumspect, but that doesn't mean we're oblivious to everything around us. Sometimes I've been down at his coach-house late at night and have noticed Jessie sneaking out through the archway into the lane. You're a heavy sleeper, I know, but haven't you noticed anything?"

Margaret nodded. "Of course I have."

Jessie was quiet as a mouse, but Margaret hadn't prodded her about her night-time wanderings. It was no use. Her stubborn friend had kept her admirer's name a secret, in the same way that she didn't share her assignations with Gavin.

Kate's expression consoled. "Whoever she's with, I think you can be sure Jessie's safe with him."

Margaret felt a deepening of Kate's gaze, a hint of a smile appearing to lighten the low-spirited atmosphere.

"Jessie might not want to say who he is, but I'm fairly sure he doesn't live all that far away. Tom's been ensuring her safety, you know, though she doesn't have a clue about that."

Margaret gaped at Kate. Such shocking revelations in one night! "Tom's been following Jessie?"

Kate patted her hand. "Sufficient to know it's just the one young man she's seeing, and that she doesn't need to go along any dangerous streets to reach him."

"Has Tom told you who he is?"

Kate's shook her head. "I've not managed to worm that out yet. But he hasn't denied my suspicions."

While Margaret sat trying to absorb it all, Kate cleared the used cups and took them into the scullery. On her return she was brisk.

"Go to bed, Margaret. Jessie will be safe. Get some sleep."

"Sleep?" she said. "I'm not sure that's likely."

"Who knows what tomorrow will bring? For sure there are going to be differences in this house that will take all of our resilience to cope with."

Kate's parting words filled Margaret with dread.

Chapter Thirty-Four

Margaret felt that everyone was circumspect in the Albany Street house as the days unfolded into the following week. She continued to be extremely concerned about Rachel's deteriorating condition. On two days out of the previous seven, she and Jessie had decided to follow the doctor's advice and leave Rachel in her bed all day, but the decision had major ramifications.

On the first occasion, Margaret was sitting on a chair beside the bed, reading to poor Rachel who was struggling to stay awake, even though it was not much after nine o'clock in the morning. She'd helped Jessie with the usual morning hygiene ritual. Rachel had had some very thin gruel-like porridge that she'd supped out of a cup and was now in a clean nightgown rather than a day dress. Jessie had gone down to do her kitchen duties a few minutes earlier.

When the door suddenly burst open, it startled them both.

"What are you still doing in your bed, you lazy girl!" Helen Duncan was unsteady but absolutely livid. "I insist that you get up right now and stop this pathetic wilting around like a dead flower."

Margaret watched the violent madwoman turn towards her, so angry that spittle was drooling out of Helen's mouth.

"And you? What are you thinking? I will not be paying your wages for sitting around like this! My household budget does not extend to such idleness. I pay you good money to tutor, money I need for my own expenses. I do not pay you to encourage sloth!"

Margaret was aghast. How could the woman be so cruel? Creating such a spectacle in front of her dying daughter.

Steeling herself not to shout back, Margaret chose her words very carefully, repeating in her head that Helen probably knew nothing of Doctor Oliver's instructions. Or if she had been told, the woman had likely chosen to forget.

"If she feels better soon, then Jessie and I will get her ready to go into the parlour."

"See that you do!"

Without actually speaking at all to Rachel, Helen Duncan stormed back out of the room.

"Mama's very angry." Rachel's voice was so despondent.

Margaret watched Rachel struggle to reach out her arm from where it lay on the bedcover. Keeping an incredibly tight rein on her own anger, she grasped the seeking fingers lightly, and soothed her pupil who was so much more than just that.

Another couple of days passed where Margaret spent all day dreading a visit from Helen in the parlour, but it never happened, and she didn't set eyes on the woman at all during those days. Both Jessie and Kate had signed the documents the Master had brought home, but Margaret never had the request made of her. She decided that was fair since she spent a minimal amount of time in Helen's presence compared to Jessie and Kate.

On the third afternoon, she was in the parlour with Rachel who was attempting a little bit of reading out loud when Jessie came into the room. She came straight across to the wheelchair, knelt down to be at eye-level with Rachel, and made an unexpected suggestion.

"It's a really lovely day outside, little lady. Nice and warm with no wind to speak of. What do you say to us bundling you up like a little parcel and taking you outside for a breath of fresh air?"

Margaret gulped, not sure if Rachel was up to the fuss of being moved from one wheelchair to the next. Catching Jessie's eye, she realised there was a lot more to the suggestion than was being said. Whatever was behind Jessie's reasoning was vital, not a whim.

"I think that's a wonderful idea, Jessie," Margaret said. "It's been quite a while since the weather has been good enough for a walk."

It was heartbreaking to see just the tiniest spark of enthusiasm that brightened Rachel's eyes, the best she could summon up, before she said, "I'd like that."

Tom was at the parlour door almost immediately to carry the girl downstairs.

"There," Jessie said, having tucked in the bundle of blankets around Rachel, more than usual since they hadn't spent time putting on a cloak and bonnet. "Just wait a minute for me, please, Margaret. I'm going to get our shawls and come a little of the way with you. I've an errand to run."

That was quite unusual though Margaret didn't question it. "We'll meet you out at the front, on Albany Street?"

"Good idea," Jessie said. "That'll give me time to ask Kate if it's only the wood polish that she needs."

Margaret idly chatted to Rachel as she propelled the wheelchair down the path to the coach house and out to the lane at the back, before bending round towards Albany Street. The last bit was quite steep, so Margaret stopped talking till she regained her breath after pushing the wheelchair up the incline and onto the street.

By the time they reached the Duncan front door Jessie was waiting for them.

Margaret had barely pushed Rachel a few more yards before the wheelchair occupant was asleep. Even the small disturbance from one chair to another had exhausted the patient, for that is what she definitely was now.

Jessie handed over Margaret's shawl and kept her voice very low, speaking close to Margaret's ear.

"We needed to get her out of the house. Kate told me that Doctor Oliver and that other specialist doctor, the one who visited last Monday, are coming back around now with other reinforcements."

Margaret stared at Jessie, suppressing both her horror and elation. "Reinforcements as in strong-armed helpers?"

Jessie nodded. "Helen Duncan is being removed this afternoon to a special hospital facility."

"Oh, goodness!" Margaret was shocked but knew it had been long in coming.

"The Master was anticipating that Helen wouldn't go quietly from their bedroom, so he wanted Rachel elsewhere for a while. It's just as well the weather is in our favour this afternoon."

After a few minutes of silence from all three of them, Margaret looked to Jessie. "Was the errand a little white lie?"

Jessie's grin was forced. "I couldn't bear to see that lunatic being carted out. I might have strangled her in the corridor before they even managed to get her downstairs."

Rachel was still asleep when they returned almost an hour later.

"You go in the basement stairs, Margaret, and see what's going on. I'll take Rachel around to Tom's and wait for news."

Margaret wasn't sure if it shouldn't be the other way around, though she complied. At the kitchen door, she peeked in. Kate was at the table her head in her hands and she was sobbing her eyes out.

"Oh, Kate!" Margaret bent down and hugged the housemaid's shoulders. "Was it so awful?"

Kate raised her head, nodded, and gulped down her tears. "You've never heard the likes of the wailing when they all but dragged her down the stairs. Mister Duncan didn't quite make it out of the front door behind them all. He was sick on the doorstep. If Robert hadn't been next to him, I swear he would have swooned and fallen down the steps. He was so torn up by the whole affair."

Margaret squeezed Kate's shoulder. "Is it safe to bring Rachel back inside?"

Kate jumped up, furiously wiping away her tears and back to her organised self. "I'll help you and Jessie. Tom's away, driving the carriage to take the Master and Robert to the Edinburgh Royal Asylum. We don't have much time to get Rachel settled before the others come home from school."

Margaret felt Kate clutch at her hands.

"Jessie and I have been asked not to tell them anything till the Master returns, but how we do that I don't know!"

"When they come home, tell them Rachel's asleep and the first floor needs to have peace and quiet. They'll hopefully think that includes Helen in her own bedroom. I'm sure they'll all quite happily keep to the drawing room."

Kate nodded. "That's not been too unusual, of late. The Mistress isn't always out of her room by the time they arrive home these days, and when that happens, I can tell you they are very happy to entertain themselves! They've had to contend with Helen's volatile moods for a long time."

Margaret couldn't seem to keep away from the parlour windows after they got Rachel safely back upstairs again. The fresh air and long sleep seemed to have been good for Rachel, so they decided to settle her in the wheelchair. She felt able to do a little of the sketch she had started the previous week of an imaginary landscape. In between surreptitious glances out of the windows, Margaret paced around the wheelchair giving advice and congratulating

Rachel for getting the shading done so beautifully even though only a few new strokes had been added.

When she saw the Duncan carriage stop at the front door, she heaved a sigh. It wasn't exactly relief, though. Somehow or other, Rachel would need to be told about her mother's absence.

She'd no idea what was going on down in the drawing room but no loud noises filtered up to the parlour. Whatever the Master was telling them, it was being received without any of Helen's caterwauling.

It was getting close to Rachel's dinner time when Mister Duncan entered the room. His face was ashen when he bent down to speak to the little shell in the wheelchair.

"I've some news, my dearest daughter."

Rachel's drained eyes stared at him.

"You know that your mother has not been well for some time." Mister Duncan halted, but didn't wait for any response. "I've come to tell you that she has gone to a special hospital this afternoon where we hope she will get the help she needs to make her feel better. You might not see her for some time."

Margaret could not have been more proud of anyone when Rachel's whisper came.

"That's good, Father. I hope they can fix her."

What Rachel murmured wasn't anything like what Margaret wanted to say. It was astounding how Rachel could be so magnanimous and compassionate.

Margaret watched her employer's gentle hug of Rachel and the kiss he bestowed on her forehead. "You are the best daughter a father could have, Rachel. I'm sorry if I haven't said that in a long while."

"Margaret?" Mister Duncan got back to his feet. "May I have word with you when Jessie comes up with Rachel's dinner?"

It wasn't long before Margaret approached Mister Duncan who was alone down in the drawing room,

Elspeth and Victoria currently having their dinner in the dining room.

She was surprised when Mister Duncan asked her to take a seat alongside him. His grey pallor was still evident, but the tweak at this lip was wry. "I fear that standing up right now is not what would be good for me."

Margaret sat down and waited for him to continue. The look he bestowed on her was a strange one.

"For a very long time I have not been properly appreciating the work that you've been doing in this house, similarly Kate and Jessie. You have all pulled together much less like servants and somewhat more akin to family."

Before Margaret could say a single word, he raised his palm. "Before you say anything, you are not, and never have been just a servant, Margaret. Unfortunately, I cannot say that for Jessie, who has been seriously maligned by both myself and my wife during all the years Jessie has been with us, but I will personally take this lack of appreciation up with Jessie."

Margaret didn't know what to do except nod and allow the man to continue.

"I should have had my wife examined and committed to a medical facility long before now, and for that I must bear a huge blame. Absenting myself from this house for so much of every day for years now was sheer cowardice, and seriously misplaced pride, but I cannot bring that time back. All I can hope for now is that the household can settle down to some semblance of peace and calm, but also be a place for my children to gain some enjoyment from being together."

The breath Margaret had been holding during the long speech hissed out. She still had no idea what to say. It was all true, but not her place to agree to his deductions.

"Robert and I have just had a long talk with David, Victoria, and Elspeth. I realise, now, just how much the older ones have been shielding Elspeth from my wife's unpredictability. They all have scars that will take time to heal. But my main concern now is that Elspeth, still being so young, will need a bit more than the others to get her through the coming weeks, even months." Mister Duncan stopped and visibly shuddered. "The prognosis is that it will take a very long time for my wife to improve, and she will not return to this house before that happens."

In the slight lull, during which the Master seemed to need to take stock of his thoughts, Margaret tentatively took up the conversation.

"Will it help if Elspeth comes directly up to the parlour to be with Rachel and myself, after she returns home from school?"

The look she received was full of gratitude but also bleak. "For how long that solution will last, you have my thanks. You won't need to give her any tuition, but the company would be an excellent idea."

Margaret watched her employer then slump forward, his palms rising up to cradle his bent head. His voice was cracked.

"I'm not oblivious to how weak Rachel is, and though I don't want to accept Doctor Oliver's diagnosis of her decline, it's one more thing we are all going to have to contend with."

The silent tears that tracked a path down his cheeks were heartbreaking to watch, though he brushed them away quickly.

"Please resume your duties with my heartfelt thanks for your dedication."

Margaret stood up to leave.

"Ask Jessie to come here, please. She and I need to talk about the unfair treatment she has been receiving from my wife."

Margaret shut the door behind her and let the held-back tears fall. Most were devastated ones, though she had to admit some were of hope. Hope that Jessie would cope with the conversation that was about to occur.

Unusually, Gavin was late home from the bank though it didn't take him long to find out the situation. He spent the ten minutes he had before dinner with Rachel, attempting to make light of the extra re-counting he had had to do of particular ledgers that he was responsible for.

Margaret watched him ruffle Rachel's braids affectionately, glad that the little girl seemed to be more spirited after eating all of her soup.

"You never ever want to have columns of money that cover pages and pages for just one entry!"

Rachel's little quirk was endearing. "I bet I could count it faster than you!"

Gavin slapped one palm to his chest, pretending to be astonished. "What's this? You think so?"

His little cousin drew a nice breath before she continued. "Definitely. Margaret has drilled money sums it into me."

They were all laughing when Kate called him through for his meal.

On reaching the door Margaret watched him beckon her with a curled finger.

"I'll just nip down with your feeding cup, Rachel, so that it's clean for later."

Knowing that the little bell was to hand if Rachel needed it, she followed Gavin out.

He wasted no time before he drew her into his arms and kissed her thoroughly.

She was delighted but highly embarrassed. "Gavin," she gasped. "Someone might come out." She indicated the nearby dining room from where some sombre voices could be heard.

"I want to talk to you after Rachel is in bed."

Margaret stared at his back as he entered the dining room, her mind whirling. How they could manage that was yet to be worked out. But she wasn't averse to more of his comforting kisses after such an awful day.

Or even some very rousing ones. The flare at her cheeks was instant. Down in the kitchen she told Jessie her red cheeks must be because she had run down the stairs and was eager to get back up to Rachel.

Chapter Thirty-Five

November 1855

Margaret was surprised when she did some counting. Not of money sums but of the number of weeks since Helen Duncan had been carted away to the asylum. It was seven weeks already, the one recently passed having been the most difficult.

The Duncan household had settled down up to a point, but major ructions were still afoot. Jessie hadn't divulged exactly what the conversation with the Master had entailed, but she had told him that she was going to look for a new post. Though no move would happen while Rachel was alive!

It wasn't a subject that cropped up with the Master, but Margaret knew she too would have to begin to consider her future. It was something presently too hard to contemplate, but was going to become a necessity.

A main result of Helen being removed was that the drawing room became less used and the parlour a greater focus of attention. Both Elspeth and Victoria spent more time after school with Rachel, but it took a bit of adjusting to.

True to her word, Margaret kept seven-year-old Elspeth occupied, though the youngest Duncan daughter was a very bright little girl who had learned well to amuse herself with solitary games.

Mister Duncan had indicated that he believed Victoria would take her mother's removal in her stride, but that wasn't the case. Without Helen's tenacious hold on Victoria's out-of-school time, the girl was falling foul of both Robert and her father for not coming home promptly. Even in such a short time Victoria was asserting her authority but in a rebellious fashion. Being only two years older than Victoria, Margaret couldn't modify Victoria's mutiny but she did try to give advice where it would be accepted. Kate was Victoria's confidante whereas Jessie was still unfairly resented with a vengeance.

Margaret pulled her cloak from her peg, wrapped it around herself and stepped out of the basement door. She didn't have to step far before she felt herself in the clutches of someone who was becoming far too familiar.

Gavin pinned her to the wall and made the first kiss last a very long time. The November night was dark and bitterly cold, and any outside time would be determined by how long they could be out before her nose froze.

"Oh, God, Margaret," Gavin gasped, "I missed you all day today."

His fingers sneaked up inside her cloak to burrow at her waist.

"How I wish we didn't have to snatch furtive moments outside like this," he said.

It was her wish, too, but she couldn't see a way around their situation. She gasped when his warm fingers slipped up to caress her breasts, his lips claiming another searching kiss. She had long since allowed him such liberties, but as yet Gavin had not got to a point where she would have to prevent a consummation of their relationship. She was frustrated that her mother's warnings from so many years before kept surfacing at such moments of intimacy, and was well aware that Gavin's control was only hanging on by a thread.

Without breaking the kiss, Gavin's open palms slid downwards, past her waist and onto her buttocks. The bumping against his aroused front was very deliberate, and not new either, but when she felt one of his hands bunching up the front of her dress and petticoats, she made a weak protest. What she termed liberties had been taken there as well, Gavin's deft fingers leaving her trembling and fulfilled, though only through a clothing layer. Kate's advice had been more than helpful with that, but she and Gavin had yet to take what Margaret deemed final and irrevocable steps.

They were currently on the brink, again, but not only did she feel a huge cold draught that slightly dampened her ardour, it was a senseless move that she just couldn't take. Although she desperately, desperately wanted to. She had no idea how she managed to summon up the necessary restraint but she did.

"No, Gavin, we can't. We can't." She pushed him away, thankful that he was sufficiently controlled to comply, though he tried to hold on to her as long as she allowed.

"I'm sorry," she gasped, the tears she couldn't prevent overflowing to drip down her chin. "We can't do this any longer. I need to go. We have to stop meeting here at night. It's too risky, and I'm the one who'll likely pay the price."

"I'm sorry." Gavin strode a few paces away from her in the moonlit darkness, shoving his wayward hair back from his forehead. "I know. It's a hellish situation to be in. I just want you so much."

After tense moments, he returned to her. "Maybe you could come up to my room? And we could perhaps just…"

"No, Gavin. That definitely won't work." Margaret stepped away from him. They had discussed that setting before but Margaret found even the suggestion ludicrous. A room with a bed in it was definitely to be avoided.

Margaret grasped her cloak around her. It absolutely was hellish. She wanted him to take their relationship to the next stages, was naturally curious about what she was missing, but her cautious instinct was huge. It would be a step much too far for her, too risky, if they weren't married.

Yet, she also recognised that she was far too young to enter into such a life commitment. And there was an increasing niggle that perhaps the current infatuation with Gavin wasn't the everlasting kind. She wanted his sexual overtures, yet wasn't entirely sure what actual love was.

At the very worst moments, Peggy's dire warnings about being wary of false love rang too loudly in her head.

"Gavin. I'm sorry. I just know I... we'd... regret such a step." She was now pleading. Convincing herself as much as attempting to sway him. "We can't do something that brings consequences that we might hate for the rest of our lives."

Gavin's silence wasn't reassuring. She knew he was frustrated, both physically and emotionally, and just barely holding on to his control. She didn't think he was angry but she was unable to accurately gauge all of his feelings.

She took in a huge breath and ploughed on "Not so long ago, you told Rachel that there was never any point in lying to someone else. I can't lie to you now. I do want to know what it's like for you to make love to me properly, but at the same time I'm just not ready to give myself to you. I've only recently turned sixteen, and I know my life is soon to have huge challenges and changes."

Margaret was sure she was in lust with Gavin but had a feeling that an enduring love was something different. Something that she wasn't quite feeling. Gavin lusted after her, she definitely knew that, but a vow of love wasn't something he'd ever brought up.

Only night sounds were all around her. Gavin's hush was deafening.

"I'm so sorry it has to be this way," she sniffed, using the back of her hand to wipe tears off her chin. "I have to go back inside. Jessie will already be in bed."

Gavin nodded, just the once, his expression tortured before he turned towards the lane, to go back the way he had come via the front door.

She'd only taken one step towards the basement door when she felt him grasp her arm.

"Margaret? Can you try to understand that, no matter how much I might want to right this minute, I can't make any lasting commitments to any woman until my position is more secure at the bank?"

Margaret's smile was full of regret. She'd already learned that bank employees like Gavin were almost hidebound by regulations, and that they tended to wait till they were closer to the age of thirty before they married. That was years and years away!

Gently detaching herself, she opened the basement door. "I know, Gavin. I understand, I do. I really enjoy being with you, and I'm honest enough to tell you that I like what you do to me, but going further is just something I can't do. We've been so close to..." Margaret felt her heart breaking. "...succumbing too many times."

In a wash of tears, Margaret grasped the dunny door, opened it, and stumbled inside.

Though Gavin often sent her frustrated, beseeching looks during the next days and weeks, she was glad he didn't encourage her to continue with their clandestine relationship. It took strict discipline, and a desperate ache at her chest that refused to subside, for Margaret to accept the situation for what it really was. Gavin made no declaration of unending love. Neither did he ask her to wait years for marriage to him.

She acknowledged that such a wait would have been unrealistic for her given that her future was so uncertain and knew it was even more unrealistic for Gavin. On a visit to Rachel, he whispered that his current bank employment in Edinburgh was not going to become a permanent post. He had been told to expect a secondment to yet another branch, in a different city. For how long, and where, he didn't yet know.

Rising up the ranks in the banking system was a slow process and movement around the branches was not unusual for those earmarked to become senior staff – eventually.

The fault was half hers that they had gone as far as they had, yet she was increasingly annoyed and frustrated that Gavin hadn't done more to convince her that a lasting relationship between them could work.

Margaret eventually, and very unfairly, decided his feelings were shallow. She made herself believe that all he had wanted was a dalliance with her, and that he was far too immature for her needs when he declared he was to immediately begin work at a new bank branch in Stirling.

In some ways, it was fortuitous that Rachel's deterioration meant the poor little girl had needed all of Margaret's daytime attention during those weeks, sufficient for her to put aside her continued longings and regrets to focus solely on her pupil.

When in bed before sleep eventually claimed her, it was another matter for Margaret. Jessie still stayed like a shut clam about the name of the young man she continued to meet, but Jessie at least told Margaret that the love Jessie felt for her sweetheart was definitely of an enduring kind. For both of them.

Margaret was torn between sheer jealousy and delight that Jessie and her suitor were making long-term future plans.

By mid-November, Rachel didn't ever get out of her bed again. Bedridden had taken on a truly different meaning.

"I'm going to speak to the Master on my way out," Mistress Brand whispered. She was preparing to go home after being with Rachel overnight.

Jessie finished tucking in the covers of Rachel's bed, the girl already back to sleep again after the morning cleaning ritual. "Is there a problem we don't know about?"

Mistress Brand nodded. "Yes, but it's not Rachel."

Margaret looked at Jessie, who seemed just as perplexed as she was.

"It's Victoria," Mistress Brand continued. "She's not sleeping properly, and I hear her sobbing her heart out. She doesn't ever waken Elspeth, but the girl is suffering terribly."

Jessie went over and put her hand on the nurse's arm. "What do you think the Master can do about it?"

Mistress Brand's look was kindly. "I have no idea really. But I'm sure he thinks all of what's happening in this house isn't affecting her, but that isn't true."

"What about if you wait another day or two before talking to the Master? We'll mention it to Kate. She's the one that Victoria goes to for reassurance. Maybe Kate could find a way to ask the Master to allow Victoria some freedom, perhaps to attend events with friends, ones she was never allowed to go to before?"

Mistress Brand nodded. "I just felt something needed to be done, but I trust your judgement, Jessie. I hate to see anyone wounded like Victoria is."

A few days later Margaret heard Victoria dash into her own bedroom, the girl having just returned from the school for young ladies that she'd been attending since the previous August.

It seemed only seconds later that Victoria erupted into Rachel's room and immediately halted noticing that Rachel was asleep. Margaret watched Victoria's finger beckoning her.

Following the girl out into the corridor she could see the excited flush on Victoria's cheeks.

"Papa has allowed me to attend the twilight lecture at the Institute."

Margaret grinned for two reasons. One was witnessing Victoria's elation. And the second was that she was being taken into the girl's confidence.

"Kate has to accompany me to the front door where I'll meet my friends, but that's fine."

Margaret absorbed that piece of information. She wasn't sure if Mister Duncan didn't quite trust his daughter, or he was giving her the façade of having a lady's maid.

Margaret lightly tapped Victoria's bent elbow. A gesture to show solidarity but not enough to disturb the distance Victoria always placed herself in regarding Margaret's position in the household.

"You'd best get yourself ready then. Maybe ask for a light snack to keep you going since it sounds as though you'll maybe miss your dinner?"

The girl surprised her by returning the briefest embrace, a mere brush of palms to Margaret's shoulders.

"It'll be worth being hungry!"

Margaret was amused, and interested. "What is it going to be about?"

"I don't care!" Victoria trilled on the turn back towards her room. "I'm being allowed to go!"

Though nothing was said overtly, Margaret felt they were all more acutely aware of looking after one another during the following weeks.

It was great news that Kate only had to report back the first time to Mister Duncan, because Victoria was allowed more freedom to see friends on the next two Saturdays.

As each day slid into the beginning of December it got more and more heartbreaking to watch Rachel's very gradual descent into nothingness. Doctor Oliver had advised that Rachel might linger on for a few more weeks, though no doctor could ever be sure. They were counselled that responses from Rachel would now be limited.

"I'm really not doing anything overnight, you know. The Master is paying me for doing nothing," Mistress Brand declared. "One or other of you two could easily sit with Rachel overnight."

Mister Duncan wouldn't hear of dispensing with the nurse's overnight services, his main concern being that Jessie was busy all day long and Margaret also had enough to keep her busy.

Though no more teaching happened, she kept Rachel company, reading to the little girl when she was responsive enough to listen and sometimes even when Rachel was almost unconscious.

According to a new agreement with the Master, Margaret supervised work that Elspeth brought home from school. She made sure that the youngest Duncan daughter always had something to occupy her in the parlour, but more often than not the little girl would make a valiant attempt to entertain Rachel by chattering the time of day, or she practised her reading out loud to both of them. Elspeth was proving to be an amazingly resilient little girl. She was sensitive to what was happening to her sister, but displayed a maturity that reminded Margaret of how Jessie had been at the same age. The tender yet practical attitude Elspeth bestowed on Rachel made Margaret quite sure the littlest Duncan daughter was going to be a good mother, or a very fine nurse.

One late morning, Jessie entered Rachel's bedroom and sat down next to Margaret. There were always two chairs at the bedside, now.

"Should we rouse her to give her some water?" Jessie whispered.

Margaret wasn't sure. "She's been deeply asleep for quite a while."

Rachel's incessant coughing had ceased some days previously and she was now mostly in slumber.

Jessie patted Rachel's hand, a loving gesture that brought no visible response, not even a twitch of a finger.

Margaret looked more closely at Rachel whose little chest now didn't seem to be moving at all. Not even the faintest of rises that she'd noted happening just a minute before Jessie had come in. Lifting her gaze to Rachel's face the girl's eyes flickered open, just a tiny bit, then they closed again.

"Love…you…cousin. Margaret…too." The faintest huff of breath slipped past Rachel's lips, then nothing more.

Margaret felt Jessie's painful clutch of her hand. She turned to her best friend whom she loved most in the world.

"Is she…?" Margaret couldn't finish her sentence.

In turn, each bent low to listen at the poor little girl's tiny frame. The tears that flowed soaked the fine cotton lawn of Rachel's nightdress, but there was no sound coming from Rachel's chest.

Margaret clutched Jessie, hugging as tight as tight could be. "What do we do now?" she bawled into Jessie's neck.

She really did know what to do, but it was such a momentous next step.

After a few moments, Margaret felt Jessie put her a little bit away from her, breaking the tight grip.

"I'll stay here with Rachel…my lovely little cousin…" Jessie's voice came in fits and starts. "I'll…give her face a little wash." There was a pause while Jessie wiped her nose with the back of her hand, her tears dripping freely. "You go down and ask Kate to fetch both the Master and Doctor Oliver."

Margaret grabbed Jessie's hand again before she left the room. Staring into her best friend's eyes, Margaret had never been more sure of anything in her life.

"She waited for you, Jessie."

Jessie's head dipped, and she nodded, her reply a whispered echo of Rachel's words. "Cousin. I didn't imagine her saying that?"

Margaret was the one to give the comfort hug this time.

"Her words, Jessie."

It seemed the longest set of stairs that Margaret had ever descended. How she didn't break her neck was a miracle because she didn't see a single one of them.

Chapter Thirty-Six

December 1855

The funeral came round far too quickly, yet not swiftly enough. It was only a few days after Doctor Oliver had officially certified the death that the house filled with various adult family members, those who could come at short notice, and other people whom Mister Duncan called real friends, stalwarts whom Helen hadn't driven away during her last years at Albany Street.

Cook was busy. Kate was busy. Jessie was busy. All of them preparing for a small wake.

Margaret's main task since Rachel's last breath had been to assist Victoria with contacting those invited to attend the funeral, since the eldest Duncan daughter was in effect standing in for her mother who was not in any fit state to deal with anything to do with the burial.

Along with Jessie and Kate down in the kitchen, Margaret had pored over the recent newspapers to find advertisements for traditional mourning clothes for Victoria. Two days before the funeral, Kate and Jessie had gone off to one of the places advertised with Victoria in tow, leaving Margaret to look after a very upset little Elspeth. At the outfitters, Jessie had also bought swathes of black ribbon to trim Elspeth's white dresses, a suitable way for the youngest Duncan daughter to indicate that she was also in mourning. Thankfully, Mister Duncan ensured the males had suitable attire because Margaret felt that would have been beyond her abilities.

It was a great relief that she hadn't needed to make too many alterations to the new dresses that Victoria would wear for months to come.

Elspeth was rarely far from Margaret's side, the little girl like a lost wraith.

It seemed so ironic that the little coffin containing her well-loved pupil sat across two tables in the drawing room, in the room Rachel hadn't inhabited since before her accident.

With tears clouding her vision Margaret stood well back near the window, holding Elspeth tight to her side as prayers were said for the final journey that Rachel was now embarking on. And then Margaret kept Elspeth huddled against her skirts when the coffin was sombrely carried through the doorway and out to the horse-drawn funeral carriage that stood waiting outside.

During the short time it took to place the coffin just so, Margaret felt Victoria lead her little sister away from her clutches and up the stairs, something that had been prearranged.

None of the females in the house were meant to be accompanying Rachel on that last long walk through familiar Edinburgh streets to the Western Cemetery near Dean Water, but Margaret was slammed with an inexplicable urge to follow after the male-dominated funeral procession.

When she descended the front steps, the first time she had ever done so, the procession had already moved off, ponderously and reverently, all the men of the house pacing behind, including Gavin who had managed to come from Stirling.

Hesitating to gain some composure, it came as no surprise to find her hand grasped by Jessie who propelled her into motion.

Keeping well behind, she clutched Jessie and arm in arm they followed the bier all along Heriot Row and down towards Randolph Crescent. She was silent in memories of her time with her little pupil. On the last part through Dean Village, there was no escape from the flood that dripped off Margaret's chin. Jessie was in like straits, yet both were determined to see it through. Neither had seen a proper burial before, though Jessie had stood beside her granny near the graveyard gates after Ruth's death.

It wasn't curiosity but rather a compulsion that compelled Margaret to be there right at the end. The little girl who lay ahead of her, whose short life had been so momentous, had touched Margaret's heart so deeply.

They say that it never rains but it pours and so it was with the distressing events. On the evening of Rachel's funeral Mister Duncan came to the parlour where Margaret was sorting out materials she had been using to tutor. The big table held neat piles of work, the largest space of it being taken up by the wide folder she had created for Rachel's drawings and paintings. Needlework – unfinished and completed – sat to one side. A pile of books was set ready to return to the Central Lending Library.

Her employer looked at the piles and visibly blanched. He opened the art folder and studied some of the drawings that lay near the top.

"She did have a budding talent, didn't she?"

The man was almost in tears. Margaret kept her response brief, not wishing to make him more distressed. "She did indeed, sir."

Mister Duncan raised the back of his hand to wipe his forehead. "I have no desire for this conversation, Miss Law, but I regret it must be had."

Indicating the centrally-placed armchairs he asked Margaret to sit down, and took a seat himself as though it was a necessity or his legs would fail him.

"You did sterling work with my daughter, unquestionably so, but I'm afraid we must now all look to the future."

Margaret waited patiently, dreading, yet aware of, what he had to do.

"You will be paid till the year's end, but there is no rush for you to leave the house before then. I will, of course, give you a glowingly true testimonial which will hopefully help you in your search for new employment. To my regret, I know of no-one who needs similar services to what you've been providing for us. Otherwise, I would recommend you directly and immediately."

What was there to say? Margaret knew her job was at an end. "Thank you, sir. Your reference will be much appreciated."

"I have no right to ask you, but do you have anything in mind?"

"No, sir." She decided to be entirely truthful. "I'm afraid I couldn't think ahead when Rachel was so poorly. I couldn't contemplate my future before now."

Margaret was in bed first that night, though not by much. She had already told Kate and Jessie of her conversation with the Master while they had their usual chat in the kitchen, impressed with herself that she had managed not to burst into tears. As expected, Kate had been supportive and sympathetic. Jessie, too, yet with a tension about her that Margaret couldn't explain.

"Are you still awake?" Jessie asked.

There was a hesitancy to Jessie's tone that Margaret didn't feel comfortable with.

Jessie carried on. "The Master didn't only talk to you, tonight."

The words made Margaret sit up again, though the candle was already out. It was so dark she couldn't even see Jessie's face.

"Go on," she urged.

"I went to him in the drawing room before he even came up to find you. The others were still up in the dining room, toying with the food they couldn't swallow, so it was a good opportunity."

"Oh." Mister Duncan hadn't said a single word about Jessie.

"I gave him notice that I was leaving tomorrow."

"What? Tomorrow?" Margaret fumbled for the candle holder. "I'll be right back."

Feeling her way back into the kitchen, Margaret grabbed a taper from the mantlepiece and lit the candle using the low-burning coals in the kitchen range.

She guarded the flame as she rushed back to the room before she set the candlestick down between the two beds.

Jessie looked more determined than upset, now sitting propped up against the wall. "I told you I was leaving after Rachel died!"

Margaret sat down on her best friend's bed and grasped her fingers. "You did. But why didn't you mention it when we were chatting to Kate?"

She felt Jessie squeeze her hands. "I wanted to tell you first."

"Oh, Jessie." Margaret squirmed forward and hugged Jessie tightly. "Did the Master tell you to leave tomorrow?"

"No, of course, not." Jessie sniffed. "He was shocked. He told me I couldn't just walk out of the door."

Margaret patted Jessie's back like a little baby but stayed silent.

"I told him there was no longer a reason for me to stay, and I would not expect any payment from him for this month, since I wasn't fulfilling my contract."

"Oh, Good Heavens!" Margaret released Jessie and sat back to see her expression. "What did he say?"

"He paced around the drawing room then stopped right in front of me. He grasped me by the shoulders, not hurtfully, but as though it was the only way he could continue the conversation. He looked me straight in the eye. That's something he hasn't really ever done before."

Margaret could only stare.

Jessie huffed out a very deep breath, her gaze drifting to the side wall. "We then had a long-overdue talk about my origins. You know – the one we should have had when I first came here."

Margaret felt she was walking on glass shards. "He confessed to keeping your identity a secret?"

"In a manner of speaking." Jessie flashed her a tiny smile, just a hint of Jessie humour in it. "It seems the reason we have not had a visit from the Reverend Duncan of Milnathort in years is because the Master told his brother he was never welcome again unless I was acknowledged."

Margaret put two and two together.

"That disgusting weasel wasn't up to claiming you, so he's now estranged."

"Yes. Well, the Reverend's worse than that. It seems he told Stewart Duncan a very long time ago that my granny was going to make my situation very public. So public that it would ruin his reputation in Milnathort, but that he had no money to bribe my granny with. Or the mothers of at least two other bastards in Milnathort who would be queuing up."

"Oh, heavens above!" Margaret had a feeling she knew what was coming. "Was it Stewart Duncan…?"

Jessie finished her sentence. "Though my granny was never told, it was the Master who paid my granny's rent and who paid for the schooling I got in Milnathort."

"That snivelling scum probably told your granny it was him who was paying."

Jessie grabbed her hand. "I think you know who I'd be believing." Huge gulping sighs escaped.

Before Margaret could think of anything to say, Jessie carried on.

"The Master told me he has no idea how he could ever redress my situation. Making me suddenly into a proper family member is too far a step for the rest of the family, which – by the way – I heartily agree with."

Margaret was still obsessed with the fact that Jessie might leave in the morning. "So, he will now let you leave, having cleared his conscience?"

"He's offered to pay me till the end of December, and like you he will give me a reference."

"Oh, Jessie." Margaret was shocked. She didn't know what else should happen, but somehow it wasn't this. "Please don't leave tomorrow. Maybe we could both leave together?"

Jessie drew her into another hug, she now the one on the receiving end of the compassion. "I'm sorry, Margaret. I have something I must do, and I'm not waiting any longer. Now we have to try to sleep – I'm going to have a very big day ahead of me tomorrow."

Jessie's little push before she whiffed out the candle sent Margaret scurrying across to her own bed. Snuggling under the covers since she was now frozen, she had a last question.

"Does your secret sweetheart know about your plans?"

She knew Jessie was smiling even though she couldn't see her.

"He does."

She heard Jessie wriggle into a more comfortable position.

"By the way, Margaret, we are unofficially engaged. Even though it may be years till we can get married."

"Will you ever tell me who he is?"

Jessie's chuckle lightened what had been a very tense evening. "You saw him this afternoon. He joined the line of mourners when the bier passed his house."

Margaret's thoughts were scattered at first but then clarity fell like a hammer on an anvil, the concept ringing in her head. "George? Is it David's friend George?"

"Go to sleep, Margaret. You know now that whatever I do next, he will always have my back."

Chapter Thirty-Seven

She should never have fallen asleep! Margaret woke up after a very fitful night, followed by a lull into a deep sleep, to find Jessie's bed already empty. Searching around the room she took note that Jessie's two dresses, those that hung under her uniform dress overnight, had gone. The only things left on the peg were the uniform dress, her white cap, and her apron.

Sitting up so quickly that she was almost dizzy, Margaret propelled herself to her feet. All the rest of Jessie's things were gone. Her tooth stick and hairbrush were no longer on the washstand. Scrabbling down onto her knees she looked beneath Jessie's bed. The bag that Jessie had made not long since out of a tattered canvas bread sack was nowhere to be seen.

The room seemed so empty, even though her own belongings were still where they always were.

Gulping tears began to fall and just wouldn't stop. She sat down on her bed, her chest heaving. The door opened but she didn't even hear it.

"Oh, Margaret!" Kate rushed to her side to comfort her. After a few back-pats and soothing rubs, Kate gave her a great big cuddle. "It's what she wanted to do. She had lots of things to work out."

Margaret turned to Kate who seemed to be fighting tears, only keeping herself strong since someone had to.

"Jessie told me last night. I tried to persuade her to wait till I was leaving, and we could go together, but she's gone." Margaret clutched at Kate's fingers. "My best friend in this whole world has left me!" The wailing was unpreventable.

"She has left the house, but you'll see her again," Kate soothed. "Maybe even soon, and before the end of the year."

Margaret raised her eyes. "How can you possibly know that?"

Kate chuckled, lightening the sombre mood Margaret felt shroud her. "I spoke to her before she left."

"Did she say where she's going?"

Kate's head shook. "No, but she knows, and that's good enough for me. She's not going to wander idly around. I have an inkling of her destination, but I could be wrong."

Margaret roused herself, wiped her face free of tears and stared at Kate. "Do you think she's gone to Milnathort to confront Reverend Duncan?"

Kate's nod showed her agreement. "She'll be fine. Jessie knows what she's about, and won't get herself into any trouble."

"Do you think she's gone alone?" She was tentative about naming Jessie's sweetheart.

Kate smiled, then rose from the bed. "Do you mean has George gone with her?"

Margaret felt her mouth gape.

"I don't think so," Kate said. "This is one demon Jessie has to sort out by herself, if I know Jessie. And we do, don't we?"

This time it was Margaret who nodded.

"Come on now," Kate urged. "It's still very early. Get yourself sorted out for the day, because you have to find yourself a new job, and I have to help the Master find a new kitchen maid!"

Finding a new maid turned out to be surprisingly easy. By the time Margaret had washed herself, dressed, and was stepping into the kitchen, she caught the tail end of a conversation between Cook and Kate.

"Yes, I can hardly believe it either, but my Betty is now twelve, going on thirteen." Mistress Abernethy reached for the dough that had been proving and plopped it onto the newly-floured wooden table. Her hands busy, she continued, "Betty's been picking up work here and there, on a day by day basis, since she left school last May. She would do well working here, since I've already taught her about how a kitchen works! She's adaptable and a hard worker."

Kate grinned. "It all sounds too convenient, but I'll see if the Master is willing to give her a go."

Margaret watched as Cook stopped kneading, her hands still wrapped around the ball of dough that was enough for two full loaves. "She'll only want a day job, though. She'll still bide with us at home overnight."

"Things are looking up, Margaret." Kate collected the ash bucket and hearth cleaning materials from the cupboard and smiled her way. "I'll see if the Master will talk to me about Betty, after his breakfast."

Cook restarted her dough thumping. "Get yourself a cup of tea and something to eat, Margaret. Then, if you don't mind, you could help Kate take up the breakfast things? By then she'll be finished raking out the hearths and will have the fires set."

A short while later, Margaret was still staring at her empty cup. She had absolutely no idea what to do with herself.

Cook was brisk, not allowing her to wallow. "You go and put those used things in the scullery then pop up with that breakfast tray."

Margaret's first thought was that the used preparation dishes that sat in the scullery would have been washed by now if Jessie was in the house. Helping out would be no hardship but she also knew she had to spend some time looking at the recent newspapers that sat in a pile awaiting some other use, like forming paper spills for lighting the fires.

It was later that morning before she felt she'd done enough to help Kate. So many questions had occurred to her while doing some of what would have been Jessie's chores that required application though not much real thought.

She had never truly appreciated how much work Jessie, and Kate, accomplished in a day.

It made her realise how easy her tutoring job had actually been in so very many ways.

Who was going to employ her now?

Females of sixteen years would have lots of working experience. How could she match up to that?

Should she avoid the parlour since there was no longer a tutoring excuse to be in there, and keep to her bedroom when she looked at the newspaper pages to see if anything in the Classified Adverts gave her any idea of how to find a suitable job?

Mister Duncan had always favoured the newspaper entitled *The Scotsman*. It sometimes had tiny columns where people put themselves forward, giving their experience and availability to take up a new post, but putting an advert in such a newspaper must cost a lot of money. It had been sometime earlier that year of 1855 that *The Scotsman* had gone from more of a weekly edition to a daily one so, perhaps more opportunities were a good thing for finding a job? Of course, the copy that was popped up to the parlour for her to find things of interest to share with Rachel had always been a couple of days out of date having gone first to the drawing room.

Having had a look at the most recent *Scotsman* copy, Margaret realised she needed a different type of newspaper which advertised the kind of employment she might be suitable for. But who could she ask?

For the next four days she continued to help Kate where possible since Betty wasn't available to come for a trial, Betty having already entered into an agreement with a different household for that current week.

Tom had asked some friends, who suggested a particular evening edition newssheet, and Margaret managed to buy the most recent copy. It had plenty of jobs advertised, but none that seemed to fit her experience.

Which was the whole problem. Her experience fit no particular category.

"Have you found information on how to become a fully accredited teacher?" Kate asked, again at the kitchen table on the fourth night but with an empty space where Jessie should be.

A best friend who had not yet made any contact at all.

Margaret sighed into her cooling cup of tea. "Yes. But fully-qualified female teachers are still rare across Scotland. And they've all done the required years of service as a pupil-teacher. By my age of sixteen, like trainee male teachers, they've already sat practical inspections in their classroom environments and also completed paper examinations."

Kate sympathised greatly. "What about applying to a private school for young ladies, like the one Victoria attends?"

Margaret had certainly considered it, and had even looked up some details, though again most wanted experience of teaching multiple pupils, and she didn't have that.

"Won't the Master's recommendation help?"

Margaret patted Kate's fingers. "I do hope so. I've sent off to an establishment in Musselburgh and to three in and around Edinburgh."

"What about Victoria's school?"

She shook her head. "They don't need anyone just now."

"Don't despair, Margaret. Something will turn up."

Kate was so encouraging, considering the changes that were happening in the household.

Chapter Thirty-Eight

The following morning, Margaret was startled when Kate rushed up to the parlour where she was fetching the batch of books to return to the Central Lending Library. She had intended to return them days before, but other priorities had stolen her time.

Almost out of breath with excitement, Kate pushed a piece of paper into her hands. "It's a telegram. For you, Margaret."

With great trepidation she unfolded the missive.

"Oh," she cried. Kate steadied her elbow when she almost overbalanced. "It's not from Jessie and it's not about work. It's from my Uncle James. He says my mother is extremely poorly, and I shouldn't hesitate to visit her."

She felt Kate steer her to sit down on a chair.

"Has your uncle ever sent any letters to you?"

She shook her head. "No. It's only my father who writes to me. Or occasionally my Auntie Jeannie."

An alarming thought occurred to her, but Kate was in first with the words.

"Why would your uncle write about this and not your father?"

Within a half-hour Margaret dropped her bag near the entrance to the front door and set down her letter on the silver tray that held any correspondence for Mister Duncan's return from his chambers.

It was only the second time she had ever left by the front door, but she was in a hurry when she clipped down the steps. She clutched the bag containing a change of clothing, her hairbrush, the tiny purse which held her savings, all held tight to her chest knowing that the sooner she reached the railway station, the sooner she'd catch the first train out of Edinburgh.

Recalling the day that her parents had come to the Scottish Capital city, she sped along the streets. The trains for Glasgow were quite frequent, but she'd no idea of how many trains would leave the junction on the line that went northwards to Perth.

She'd no real idea of how long it had taken since leaving Albany Street but she was soon battling through the dense billowy fug created by the steam engine to find the correct carriage for those who, like her, had paid the cheapest fare.

The stinking smoke permeated everything inside the carriage as she made her way to an empty space on one of the long benches, praying that she was on the correct train though knowing that there was no question about this first part of the journey.

By the time she reached the junction where she needed to disembark, she felt she'd learned quite a bit about the jostling and rocking that carriage wheels could make along the iron rails. Apart from hugging Jessie or Kate, or kissing Gavin, she'd never been so close to anybody in her whole life.

So many people had been crammed into the carriage that she'd been squashed, shoulder to shoulder, between two ladies – one whose thin bones poked into her right side; and another stout lady who almost swallowed her left side and pressed her into the uncomfortable wooden struts at the back of the bench.

The excitement heightened though when she got more comfortable on the journey northwards. The carriage was still busy though not so crammed.

"You look like you're the cat who licked the cream, young lady!" the woman seated next to her declared with a friendly smile. "Would this be your first train journey by any chance?"

Margaret clutched her bag to her chest and grinned back. "It is. Well, technically my second, since this is my connecting train from Edinburgh."

The woman nodded. "You have that buzzing excitement about you. Lots of people are like that at first, but you get used to the train very quickly."

The conversation continued in a friendly manner though not too personal.

"Well, no-one will meet me when I arrive at Perth but I believe my uncle's house is only a short walk from the station."

She gave the woman the address she'd committed to memory.

"I know that street. It isn't far," the woman said. "I'll point you in the correct direction when we arrive."

The woman proved very knowledgeable and was able to tell her about places they whizzed past along the journey.

The tummy-flutters that had begun with the sheer excitement of being on a train changed to being ones of apprehension when she remembered the purpose of her journey, though that reason was too private to share with the stranger seated next to her.

The door opened quite quickly after she tapped her knuckles on the front door of her uncle's house.

A girl of about ten years of age stood and stared at her, though said nothing.

"My name is Margaret Law." She kept her tone soft because the girl looked quite skittish. "I'm your cousin from Milnathort."

Big fat tears leaked from the girl's eyes and the wails came. "Why did you not come before?"

Leaving her standing on the doorstep, the girl fled down the corridor.

Margaret only hesitated for a tiny moment. She stepped inside and closed the door behind her. Having set her bag near it, she took a few paces in the direction the girl had fled in.

"Margaret?"

A man emerged from the door at the end. He resembled an older version of her father. It had to be the uncle that she'd no memory of.

"I'm so sorry, Margaret. I should have sent word earlier, but till yesterday your mother didn't want you to know."

Her uncle looked haggard. "Come." He indicated the stairs. "She's up here."

Margaret removed her shawl on the way up and folded it across her arm. "What's wrong with her?"

While waiting for his answer, she decided her father must be by her mother's bedside. But when she reached the opened bedroom door it was an even younger girl who sat at the bedside, staring at the figure lying on the bed. The little girl's right hand clutched Peggy's left hand where it lay on top of the blankets. Using her left hand, the girl pressed a large handkerchief to her nose. The reason was clear: there was an unhealthy stench in the room, a mixture of dried blood and other putrid causes, that was wafting all around.

Her uncle took her elbow, holding her back from entering. His voice was a broken whisper at her ear. "Peggy gave birth to a baby boy five days ago, but she has succumbed to childbed fever."

Margaret was aghast. There were many reasons for dying, plenty of diseases that Peggy could have succumbed to, but an imminent death from childbed fever seemed so unexpected.

She turned to look at Uncle James' face. Tears clouded his vision. His expression was bleak, but the agony on it told her that her mother meant a whole lot more to him than just being his sister-in-law.

357

"I was just seeing the midwife out of the back door when you arrived. She's left now that the fever has abated a bit, but she'll return in a few hours."

The relative that she didn't know wiped his palm across his face before he turned away from her and gazed back towards the stairs, his pursed lips working furiously to contain his feelings.

"She doesn't think Peggy can pull through. The poison is spreading all through her insides."

Margaret stared ahead at the still figure on the bed, pale and already almost lifeless. It looked like her mother, and yet not. She had questions to ask but the first one wouldn't form.

Her uncle held her back when she started to move towards the bed. "It was a very difficult birth. She lost a lot of blood over the first two days, and then the fever started."

"The baby? Where is the baby?" Some women could give birth to babies who survived the difficulties though the mothers didn't.

The tears began to leak from the edges of James' eyes, his valiant attempts to blink them away futile, his mouth squirming up. "He only survived a few hours."

In the depths of her uncle's misery, she suddenly remembered what should have been immediately obvious to her. "Where's my father?"

James held himself back from her. His expression immediately changed to one of contemptuous disdain. "Your father left my employment and hasn't lived here for more than a year. Why on earth would I have called him to her death-bed?"

Margaret was stunned. She tried desperately to remember how many letters William had sent her since the New Year greeting heralding the year 1855. He had sent her a couple of very short missives after that, but he'd never mentioned leaving James house.

"He never told me."

Whether her uncle believed her didn't seem important right that moment.

"But Peggy wanted you to let me know now?" Margaret asked.

"Yes, but give me a moment before I tell you." James said.

James urged Margaret forward towards the girl at the bedside.

On reaching his daughter, he patted her shoulder. "Well done, Eilidh. You go down to the kitchen, now, and ask Lizzie to make some tea for Margaret."

The little girl was out of the door before Margaret blinked. After she dropped her cloak on the floor, she sat down on the vacated chair and took her mother's cold hand in her own.

She watched James go around the bed to take Peggy's other hand, which he patted gently before he took it up to his mouth to bestow a loving kiss on papery-thin fingers.. His bleak eyes faced her across the bedding, troubled and so, so despondent.

"There's a lot you haven't been told about, Margaret, but I think you can now guess as to what's been happening. You're old enough to know that relationships and partnerships come in many forms."

James focused on Peggy while he continued.

Margaret gently squeezed her mother's cool palm, but there was no reaction from the woman who seemed in a very deep sleep. Only the tiniest visible movement from her breathing raised the woollen blanket that loosely covered her.

James' tone beseeched. He was talking to her mother and yet Margaret knew the conversation was also to tell her all the things she didn't know.

"Peggy, can you hear me? I fell in love with you the moment you came to stay in this house. I knew it was impossible back then, you being my brother's wife, but our love for each other was too strong, wasn't it?"

Margaret watched Uncle James' focus change direction towards her.

"They were only days here in my house when I realised how badly my immature brother was treating Peggy."

He alternated his focus between her mother and her, still explaining.

"Never physically. William's hurt was indifference."

Margaret didn't have to be told about this aspect of her parents' marriage.

"He should have resisted. Their marriage was a disaster, except perhaps for it resulting in you being born. Performing his marital duty was like serving a prison sentence for William."

She gulped. Though, in some way, she really did know all of this.

"And that is the greatest tragedy for me." James' gaze steadied on her. "You have to believe that your mother became the way she was when you were growing up because my brother's total lack of interest in her as a sensuous woman killed off any tenderness that she had in her. She initially thought that a son was what William wanted, so birthing a daughter was a great regret. She felt a failure. And then William's continued rejection repressed all compassion."

Margaret felt the ripples of shock run through her. To know it was something, but to hear it spoken of, so bitterly and callously, was something else.

"I knew of their coldness to each other but could never make it change," she said.

James' smile was rueful. "A child cannot change adults who don't want to be changed."

She watched James bend forward to tenderly kiss her mother's cheek. "Though you have no idea of it, your mother is one of the most loving women I've ever met. She is so sensual and has been the most wonderful lover. Don't get me wrong, Margaret," James broke off to stare at her. "I loved my wife, the woman who was the mother of my children, but not in the same sexual all-encompassing way that I adore this woman lying here between us."

Margaret couldn't help the torrent that dripped down her cheeks. Her words tripped out.

"I felt she had something to tell me when she came to Edinburgh. She seemed a lot happier in herself, which was confusing because I didn't see any shift in my parents' relationship. They were still two people who knew each other but not in any overt or intimate way."

She used the back of her free hand to wipe at her cheeks and eyes, the better to see her uncle's expression. "I wrote lots of letters to her but she never replied."

James nodded. "I tried to get her to write to you. But she was too proud, too embarrassed, but mostly too fearful that it might change what she had with me – though I couldn't imagine how telling you would change things."

The revelations were incredible. "All through my growing years she drummed into me that respectability was paramount. Maybe she felt she had lost that."

James' smile was full of very sad love. "Peggy may have felt she lost some, but together we gained so much more."

A strident call from downstairs had her uncle rising from the chair. "Since you're here, I can go and see what's going on. We've had someone at the bedside all the time during the last long days, for Peggy, when she wakens."

Margaret took a look at her mother's pallid features while James slipped out of the doorway. Familiar and yet changed. Was that because the recent revelations made her see not her mother as she used to do, but a woman who had been neglected so badly by her father, and then an entirely changed one because of being in a reciprocated loving relationship?

She wanted desperately to talk to her mother, yet didn't know what to say to the shell that lay in front of her. Eventually she began to speak.

"You might not be able to hear me, but after what Uncle James has told me, I'm very pleased that you've had happy times with him in this house. I always knew you were desperately unhappy, without properly knowing why."

The tiniest stir at Margaret's palm caused her breath to hitch. "Can you hear me, Mother? It's Margaret. I'm here."

For endless moments she talked and talked. She told her mother that things had changed in Edinburgh and that Jessie had gone off to probably confront her father. A lump appeared in her throat so large it almost choked her when she began to talk about Rachel and how much she loved her tutoring job. This was definitely not the moment to tell her mother of Rachel's recent death or of Helen's removal to the asylum, but she burbled about the others in the Duncan family, trying to keep it light-hearted.

It didn't happen immediately, but Margaret became certain that the woman on the bed beside her was stirring, although Peggy hadn't yet said anything, or even opened her eyes.

When James came back into the room with a cup of tea balanced precariously on a tray, Margaret was wiping her mother's face with a cloth that she'd dipped into the basin of water that was set near the bed.

"Is she wakening?" James sounded so full of hope. The rattling of the cup on the saucer indicated his agitation as he set it down on the table.

Lizzie followed her father in, carrying a plate with bread, sliced cheese, and a piece of Madeira cake. "We thought you'll be hungry after such a long journey."

She nodded first to Lizzie then popped the cloth back into the basin.

"I am, thank you." She smiled to her cousin as she reached for the plate. Then she turned to James. "I think she may be."

"Peggy?" James pleaded, bending down to her at the other side of the bed, bestowing soft kisses to her cheek. "I'm here with Margaret. Can you hear us?"

Lizzie gasped when she noticed the small flickering movement of Peggy's fingers then flutters at her eyelids.

Margaret's emotions were suddenly overflowing. She had expected to see her mother sometime soon, due to her change of circumstances, but not under such stress.

She sank down onto the chair finding her trembling legs wouldn't support her. Like before, she sneaked her palm under her mother's fingers.

"Mother. I'm here to see you."

In gradual increments, Peggy opened her eyes. At first, they alighted on James, the small smile coming to her face one of pure love. Then without turning too much, Peggy's gaze swivelled towards Margaret. Her words were harsh whispers, as though her throat was parched.

James didn't remove his gaze from Peggy, but quietly asked his daughter to fetch some fresh water, a spoon, and a cup. Lizzie whirled out of the door leaving a draught in her wake.

"Margaret." Peggy was exhausted but determined to speak. "Forgive me?"

"I've nothing to forgive you for." She hoped she sounded as sincere as she intended.

"You do." Peggy's eyes flickered as though the effort of speaking was too great. "I should have given you all the love I have for James."

Margaret watched silent tears leak from Peggy's eyelids. James bent his forehead close to his dying lover.

Margaret couldn't see, but was sure his own tears were bathing Peggy's cheek.

"I didn't…" Peggy's voice broke. "…know love till I came here."

Margaret fought the huge emotions that were drowning her. She thought she should hate her father for the situation Peggy now faced, yet she knew it wasn't all his fault.

"Please forgive me, Margaret," her mother repeated. "For God surely won't."

Her mother wasn't dying because she had borne her husband a child. The child was from her uncle's seed. A Law, for certain, yet not the legal one. Margaret felt fenced in, compressed with confusing feelings.

Yet the love resonating between James and her mother was palpable, so how could it be wrong?

"Of course I forgive you." She bent down and kissed her mother's cold cheek.

James exchanged a few more words of love with Peggy and she seemed to rally for a little while, especially after she had been given sips of the water brought by Lizzie.

But it wasn't to be. Margaret holding one hand and James the other, Peggy gradually slipped away while looking lovingly at the man who was not her husband.

Two funerals in such a short time had Margaret reeling.

During the days between laying out her mother and the funeral, she got to know her uncle and cousins a lot better. Many surprises were wonderful to learn, but there were a few which initially seemed startling, but actually weren't so much. Peggy had been pregnant with James' child when she had visited Edinburgh that long-ago day with her father, but she had miscarried not long after. Her father had known but had chosen to ignore it. James' house was large enough that William had claimed an attic room of his own immediately after moving in.

James' assessment of his younger brother was that William was incapable of forming an emotional and sexual attachment with any woman, but he reckoned it was the same with men.

Her uncle's way of putting it was, "Some men are born loners and will die loners."

Peggy's burial three days later was a very quiet one. Her baby was in the coffin beside her, and the ceremony at the graveside wasn't only comprised of male mourners. Margaret had pleaded to be there, and James had defied convention, just like he had defied convention by loving her mother out of wedlock.

William had not been informed. James had no idea where his brother was, or even if he was still alive, because when he had quit his employment and James' house, William had left no forwarding address.

"William has written to me this year," she had said, "But you must have received my replies."

Her uncle nodded. "Your mother put them along with the stack of letters from you. You'll find them in that box in the corner. She kept them all."

Margaret realised that Peggy must have loved her, in her own strange way.

Chapter Thirty-Nine

Margaret had immediate choices to make.

Uncle James had been quite clear that although he really didn't know her, he would not leave her in want of somewhere to stay, or without employment.

The thought of taking her mother's place as his housekeeper and carer of his children sent chills running down her spine.

His suggestion of employing her in some capacity as a seamstress held more sway, but that would entail her either living in her uncle's house, or finding temporary lodgings in Perth. The sewing, she realised, might be what she would have to fall back on, but living in Perth didn't appeal.

"I'll write and let you know how I get on," she promised, accepting the hug from her uncle at Perth General Station. Looking directly into the eyes of the uncle she had got to know better in the few short days she'd been with his family, she was absolutely sincere. "Thank you for giving my mother a few happy years."

There was no need to embellish her words; the subject had already been well-covered.

"Off you go then, lass. And good luck be with you." Uncle James' parting words were as important as his support. "Should I trace either of my brothers, I'll let you know. Finding Edward might be quicker, since the tailoring trade in Scotland is a tight community. Someone has to know his whereabouts."

***

It was a very strange feeling to be standing at the gate down to the basement in Albany Street later that day. Her second train had been delayed, meaning her arrival in Edinburgh was after darkness had fallen. She stared at the wrought ironwork in front of her, a memory invading of her first arrival to this house.

The little prayer she sent to no-one in particular as she descended the stairs reflected her mood. She wasn't expecting Jessie to open the door and welcome her, but she wished it to be so.

Her knuckles were ready to rap on the door when she realised that she didn't need to. She was still technically employed by Mister Duncan for another seven days.

The fluttering at her stomach wasn't welcome. The strangeness of the whole situation was almost overwhelming, but she had to get herself in hand and move forward with her life.

"Margaret!" Kate cried, drawing her into an immediate hug. "Oh, it's lovely to see you back." Setting her back from the embrace, Margaret sensed that Kate was aware of her insecurities. "Come on. A cup of tea will set things right!"

It wouldn't, but she appreciated the gesture.

What she'd experienced in Perth was difficult to put into words, but Kate was discreet.

"Oh, my!" Kate's genuine sympathy oozed after hearing the distressing update, her conspiratorial smile encouraging. "Now you must try to focus on your future. And …I have news of Jessie! And…some news of my own."

Margaret's stomach flipped again.

"I'll tell you my news first, since it'll be quicker."

Kate looked so pleased Margaret knew it could only be good.

"The Master has given us permission to live in the coach house."

It was difficult not to gape. "Together?"

Kate giggled and squeezed her fingers from across the table. "We're going to be married next month. Tom was due for a wage increase, and so am I. The Master has made them very generous ones, considering all of the work we've done for him."

"That is such good news for you both." Margaret was absolutely delighted. "And for him, too, since you'll still be here."

Kate nodded. "The workload will be lighter since…"

She didn't need to finish. There were two fewer occupants at present, and really four if Jessie and herself were counted.

"There's a letter for you in your room, but I'm sure the basics are similar to the one Jessie sent to me. Go and read yours. We'll catch up later tonight, but for now I have to get the dining room prepared."

"I'll read it, then come and help you."

Margaret's feelings were irrepressible when she read the two-page missive. Jessie had indeed gone to Milnathort to confront her father, the Reverend Duncan.

'You of all people can imagine my anger when I found out that he'd had to leave Milnathort with his tail between his legs. He'd been philandering one time too many in the area.'

Margaret found herself holding her breath as she read on.

'He was sent to a church on the outskirts of Dundee.'

Jessie's next comments made her grin.

'I think they must have decided that his errant ways would be less obvious in a big-town community than in a village where everybody knows everyone else's business.

I decided to seek him out and that was an enlightening revelation. It seems a demotion doesn't come with the same cosy conditions that he had in Milnathort. He is not actually the main minister of the Tay Square Church but a secondary one who officiates at some services, though not all. There is a mission attached to the church which

368

seeks to cater for the poor of the area which includes a Seamen's Mission. That's not surprising since the church is not far from Dundee Harbour and fairly close to the Railway Station.'

Margaret read on, sure that Kate hadn't got all of the detail that she had.

"Oh, Good Lord!" Her exclamation went unheard since she was alone. "She went to Dundee to find him."

Jessie's story continued. Mister Stewart Duncan had given her money that night before she left, money she'd not wanted to accept but when he'd seen she was determined to find his brother he had deemed it appropriate for her to accept it. She said in her letter it had been a goodly sum but she'd been using it wisely.

'Leslie Duncan wouldn't believe me! Can you credit that, Margaret? He claimed he'd no recollection of putting me on that brewer's dray in Milnathort. I was absolutely nothing to do with him and not even details of his brother's household in Edinburgh would make him confess. Or acknowledge me.'

As Margaret read the end of the letter, she felt her own fury rising. There were no words strong enough for the disgusting man.

'I walked away from him with my head high feeling I had accomplished my task. The result wasn't too different from my expectations. I mostly wanted to commit his countenance to my memory so that I can dredge it up and rail at him during any weak moments in my future.'

"Oh, Jessie!" Margaret was so very proud of the sister of her heart.

The last part of the letter vindicated why Jessie had been feeling that way. She went on to say that she didn't think the years had been kind to the Reverend Duncan. She mentioned that there was the vaguest resemblance to Mister Duncan of Albany Street, in the fair hair and blue eyes that she'd inherited, but said that the Reverend's hair was dull and lifeless, and that he was thin almost to the point of being skeletal. His face was gaunt and those blue eyes so dulled they were almost haunted.

"Oh, serves him right!" Margaret cried to the empty room.

'I think he might have some awful disease, or is so poor that he's not been eating properly for some time. I walked away feeling no remorse for his present condition.'

Margaret sighed, her lips wobbling just the tiniest bit. Being horrible was just not in Jessie's nature: the very last sentence being typical of it.

'I truly pity that poor wife of his. He and I never discussed her but the woman who indicated to me where I'd find him mentioned that she was a poor kindly soul who'd never harmed a fly.'

Jessie finished the letter with an address. She'd found cheap lodgings that she could afford, though the room wasn't up to much. She was waiting to find out if she would be taken on at a large house on the west side of Dundee, having used her reference from Mister Duncan.

Kate confirmed Jessie had also given her the address in case any letters arrived at Albany Street for her. Though, to Margaret's knowledge, the only person who'd ever written to Jessie was herself.

The weather was bitterly cold close to the end of December, which matched the mood of the inhabitants of the Duncan house. On Christmas Eve Mister Duncan sent David, Victoria, and Elspeth off to his wife's sister who lived in Musselburgh, not feeling it appropriate to have any celebrations in the Duncan house since they were in mourning.

"No, the Master won't be alone, Margaret," Kate had said days before. "Robert will be with him. And Gavin, if he can manage time off work to come to Edinburgh for a day or two."

On Christmas Day, Cook had tried to cheer up the staff by producing the same meal as was being served up in the dining room. Tom had even been invited to join them, which seemed like a huge concession on Mistress Abernethy's part.

"A roast is a roast," she'd declared. "I ordered my usual weight for a special event and we can't have any of it going to waste. Doesn't taste the same if cold!"

Cook had also said something similar about the dessert she'd concocted. "Yes, it is the same as those upstairs are having. If anybody deserves a treat, then you all do!"

Margaret was taken aback when she went up with Kate late in the evening to clear the dining room. Gavin stopped her on the stairs, her arms laden with table linens for laundering.

"I've been trying to speak to you, Margaret," he said.

She looked at him, keenly, assessing his mood. She wondered if he had imbibed too much of the special wines that Mister Duncan had insisted on being served. It quite amazed her to realise that she hadn't really thought much about him at all. She waited for him to speak. Which he eventually did, after a thorough appraisal of her features.

"You really are quite beautiful, you know." One of his teasing grins appeared, but was tinged with a regret that managed to be whimsical. "I do love you. We could have been very good together, if you'd just given me a chance."

Nothing could prevent Margaret's reply. "I think so too."

She watched the hope blossom across his expression.

"But…" she said. "I'm the one who would bear the consequences. Hindsight comes too late, Gavin, and I'm definitely not prepared for that to become an issue. I really do like you." She stopped and rephrased her words. "I really did like you. But please do remember in future that it tends to be the one of inferior station whose life can be the most irreparably damaged."

She shrugged past him and continued down the stairs, her insides quivering over what she'd just stated. The words were true, but she could so easily have given in to sheer desire.

Margaret made sure to speak to David very early on Hogmanay, the morning of her eventual departure from the Duncan house on Albany Street.

"I don't want to put you in an awkward position, David, but can you tell me if George knows of Jessie's whereabouts?"

"Oh, yes, don't worry about that. He definitely knows." David sounded very sure. "George wanted to accompany Jessie when she left to go to Milnathort but she wouldn't have it."

Margaret was surprised when he took hold of her fingers and gently held them. She'd not been aware she was wringing them in her agitation.

"George is the most steadfast person I have ever known. He told me he had made an agreement with Jessie, that although they are far too young to contemplate marriage, he insists they will be wed sometime in the future. That is after he finishes university and has the means to support a wife."

Margaret felt happy tears well up. "Yes, she told me this before she left the house."

David squeezed her fingers. "There was a time when I thought that I might be in love with Jessie because there was a bond with her that I couldn't explain. I was devastated when I learned she was my cousin, but then it made everything clear."

He grinned, slipped his fingers free then patted Margaret's shoulder. "She'll do very well with George. He's totally smitten and he'll move heaven and hell, maybe even invent something new, to maintain contact with Jessie. Fear not. He's only a train ride away, and that's not such a great distance these days."

Margaret stood in the drawing room a short while later. Her bag was packed with all of her belongings and it sat waiting for her at the basement door.

"You were not only a very good tutor to Rachel, but an excellent companion," Mister Duncan said before he handed over a folded piece of paper and a sum of money. "I do hope this endorsement will gain you good employment."

Margaret thanked him, though wasn't so confident about the job she might find. Nothing likely had turned up so far.

She glanced at the amount in her hand. "This is much more than my agreed salary, sir."

"Yes, it is, but you deserve the extra. Hopefully, it will go towards your living costs in the near future while you secure a new position."

The Master, as Jessie always referred to him, brought out a little tied parcel from his pocket.

"Can you please give this to Jessie, and say it's from me?"

The smile was easy to form. Margaret couldn't help but make her answer. "If this is more money, she might well send it back to you."

"I think she might want to keep this. There is money in there, but it belonged to Rachel." Mister Duncan pushed the package into Margaret's hand. "And something else that belonged to Rachel, for Jessie to keep as a memento."

Margaret watched him reach behind to a side-table where he lifted another package. "And these are for you to keep, Miss Law. I hope you'll enjoy looking at my daughter's sketches in the future, and similarly her embroidery sewing, the one she named her special Silver Sampler. She was so proud of the design that you allowed her to create by herself."

Margaret couldn't stop the grin. "She was, indeed, very proud of it but it took blood sweat and tears to get

373

her to do the sewing. The designing of it was a pleasure for her but…the actual stitching was something else!"

Her farewell of Kate down in the basement produced even more tears than that of her employer. It was a very soggy-faced Margaret who clicked the railing gate closed up at Albany Street level. It took purposeful strides for her to walk away in the direction of the railway station.

The traumatic Hogmanay – New Year's Eve – was not yet over, though the year of 1855 was definitely on the turn. Less than three hours later, Margaret was standing at the door of the lodging house where Jessie was staying.

"I'm here to see my friend Jessie Morison. My name is Margaret Law."

The woman who'd opened the door was brisk. "Aye. Jessie said you'd be arriving today, and told me you need lodgings." The woman stepped to the side. "In ye come, lass. I'll take ye upstairs to Jessie."

Margaret inhaled a very deep breath. It felt yet another momentous moment in her life. When she had arrived in Edinburgh years before she had no idea how long she would be there. It was the same now.

Dundee beckoned in her future, but for how long?

Read on for a tiny excerpt from Book 2 *Tailored Truths*

Author's Note

Writing about the Mid-Victorian period in **Novice Threads** has been a delightful diversion from my *Celtic Fervour Series* set in Late First Century Roman Britain. However, it isn't my first experience of dipping into the Victorian or Edwardian eras since two of my contemporary mysteries have ancestral elements set during those times.

Since I began to do personal Ancestry research some years ago, I've had a notion to write a series of three novels which begin in 1840s Victorian Scotland and end around the mid-1920s. If you delve around sufficiently in your family background, I believe you will find fabulous fodder for writing saga-type fiction, as I have. *The Silver Sampler Series* includes some themes and situations which have been adapted from information uncovered during my ancestry research.

To the many Margarets…

The main character of the three books of my *Silver Sampler Series* is named Margaret. It's a first name which has been handed down on my maternal side of the family for centuries. I'm therefore delighted to also devote this first novel of the series to all of the Margarets who pepper my family tree.

Acknowledgements

I'd like to give hearty thanks to all of the people who have helped me during the writing process of this novel, to those not specifically named below.

Laurence Patterson has produced a perfect Cover Design for **Novice Threads** which I adore, and hope you do, too. I'd like to also thank Laurence for producing the little *Silver Sampler Series* logo which I can use in the other books of the series, and for promotional purposes.

I give a huge thank you to my fellow authors at *Ocelot Press* – Sue Barnard; Vanessa Couchman; Miriam Drori; Cathie Dunn; Liza Perrat and Jen Wilson for their continued general support, and for assisting with very much valued Beta reader comments and editing. They are all stars!

I'd like to pay tribute to the lovely authors in my Scottish Chapter of the Romantic Novelists' Association who are a fantastic moral support. Our regular Zoom sessions are fun and challenge me to get on and write! Their general writing support is also highly valued. Thank you everyone!

Lastly, I'd like to thank Phyllis Hannah, the great-granddaughter of my grandmother's sister! Phyllis is a wonderful ancestry sleuth and any interaction between us regarding our shared ancestry is hectic, fun, and profitable. Thank you, Phyllis, for helping find details of our shared black sheep!

About the Author

When not researching or engaged in various writing and marketing tasks, Nancy's a fair-weather gardener who lives in the 'castle' country of Aberdeenshire, Scotland. Thousands of years of history are on the doorstep which she often escapes to.

Nancy signs and sells paperback versions of her novels at various local venues, relishing the meetings with new readers and with regular return customers. She gives author presentations to various groups about her novels and Roman Scotland. Current work is *The Silver Sampler Series*.

Present society memberships include: Historical Novel Society; Romantic Novelists' Association; Scottish

Association of Writers, Federation of Writers Scotland, and Alliance of Independent Authors.
Website: http://www.nancyjardine.com
Facebook: https://facebook.com/NancyJardinewrites
Blog: https://nancyjardine.blogspot.com/
Twitter: @nansjar

Nominations

Nancy's work has achieved award status in various places: Scottish Association of Writers; IndieBRAG Medallion; The People's Book Prize; Discovered Diamonds; Coffee Pot Books.

Endorsement

"A gripping story that beings Victorian Scotland to life." Sue Barnard, bestselling author of The Ghostly Father.

Other Novels by Nancy Jardine

Celtic Fervour Series
Prequel – Before Beltane
Book 1 – The Beltane Choice
Book 2 – After Whorl Bran Reborn
Book 3 – After Whorl Donning Double Cloaks
Book 4 – Agricola's Bane
Book 5 – Beathan The Brigante

Time Travel Historical Adventure
The Taexali Game

Contemporary Mystery Thriller
Topaz Eyes

Contemporary Romantic Comedy Mystery
Monogamy Twist
Take Me Now

Ocelot Press

Ocelot Press

Thank you for reading this Ocelot Press book. If you enjoyed it, we'd greatly appreciate it if you could take a moment to write a short review on the website where you bought the book e.g. Amazon, and/or on Goodreads, You can email the author and/ or recommend the book to a friend. Sharing your thoughts helps other readers to choose good books, and authors to keep writing.

You might like to try books by other Ocelot Press authors. We cover a range of genres, with a focus on historical fiction (including historical mystery and paranormal), romance and fantasy. To find out more, please don't hesitate to connect with us on:

Website: https://ocelotpress.wordpress.com
Email: ocelotpress@gmail.com
Twitter: @OcelotPress
Facebook: htpps://www.facebook.com/OcelotPress/
Have a look at our range on Amazon.

Dear Reader

Thank you for reading *Novice Threads*. I very much hope you enjoyed meeting young Margaret Law and will continue to immerse yourself in her life as she matures in the next books of *The Silver Sampler Series* – she experiences far more excitement, and also trauma, than many women of her generation!

Happy Reading!

Best Regards,
Nancy Jardine

Excerpt from Book 2 Tailored Truths

"Oh, Margaret!" Jessie cried. "It's so good to see you again."

Margaret found herself encircled in the kind of huge hug that her best friend Jessie was famous for. It was the voice of the landlady that broke their connection.

"Jessie tells me you'll also be looking for lodgings, Miss Law?" said Mistress Webster.

Margaret detached herself and faced the chubby woman who was probably not much more than five feet high.

"Yes, I do need to rent a room," she answered a bit hesitantly because she was unsure of how much to divulge. She really had no idea how long she might need to stay in Dundee, but that maybe wasn't what a landlady would be wanting to know.

Mistress Webster's expression displayed sympathy and yet Margaret also sensed a hint of shrewdness.

"I've no spare rooms to let but Jessie and I had a wee talk earlier today." Margaret watched the landlady turn to Jessie.

Jessie was beaming. "My bed, as you can see, is far too narrow to share but Mistress Webster says she can bring in another truckle bed."

"That's if you don't mind sharing with Miss Morison."

Margaret almost felt the landlady rubbing her hands in glee at the thought of more rent money coming in.

"I've agreed to the extra payment for next month, Margaret, for bringing in another bed." Jessie's tone was so businesslike Margaret had to suppress a grin. And suppress another one when she watched Jessie's blatant stare at the landlady.

"I'll just get on with arranging for that bed to be brought up as soon as my nephew returns from the mill."

Mistress Webster bustled her way back down the stairs.

Margaret felt Jessie yank her inside the room which wasn't much bigger than the one they had shared in the Duncan house in Edinburgh.

Jessie waited till the door was closed before she put her finger to her lips to indicate a moment of silence was needed. From the grins on Jessie's face, Margaret surmised that Mistress Webster wasn't averse to creeping back up to listen at the keyhole.

Jessie removed her bag from her grasp and plonked it down on the floor at the foot of the bed. "Hang up your cloak on that peg that I've cleared for you."

Margaret laughed on seeing the crowded peg next to the only other empty one. She popped her thankfully dry cloak on it since the day had been pleasant enough. "I'm guessing your landlady isn't expecting her tenants to have many spare clothes."

"Not likely!" Jessie guffawed. "I've not seen all the tenants who live in this house, but there's barely a spare penny to rub between those I have seen."

***